MW01138317

Humanity Abides

Book Three

The Search For Home

A Post - Apocalyptic Novel

By C. A. Bird

Special Thanks to:

Christine Temple - Editor
David A. Bird - Illustrator
Lori A. Bird – Contributor

www.carolannbird.com

Acknowledgments

I would like to thank the people who have bought the books in my Humanity Abides Series and who have followed me and my career on Facebook.

Thanks, as well, to my friends and family who have supported me, and given me the time to pursue my dream of writing.

Books by C.A. Bird

Humanity Abides - Book One - *Shelter*

Humanity Abides - Book Two - *Emergence*

Humanity Abides - Book Three - *The Search For Home*

www.carolannbird.com

1

Deadly radiation swept across the face of the earth, concealed in clouds of dust and fog. Swirling around obstacles and funneling down canyons, it penetrated yielding bodies and tissues, destroying DNA, the very foundation of life. It came down in torrential rains, settling on the land and poisoning plant life, rivers, lakes and oceans. After months had passed following the Great War that had ravaged the planet, the radiation had finally decayed enough to allow healing to begin.

The attack came just before dawn.

Mark was cozy warm, curled around Lori's back, when the gunfire erupted off to the side of their wagon. He and Lori both came awake with a start, flinging the wool blankets to the side.

"Not again," she moaned, as they grabbed the guns that were never out of reach and quickly crawled to the rear of the wagon. After the first night out of Eagle Nest, they had learned to sleep in their clothes.

"Ashley and Kevin, keep your heads down and stay in the wagon!" Mark yelled, as he checked the space behind the tailgate and then vaulted over it. Hitting the ground, he rolled under the wagon, hearing Lori grunt as she hit the ground right behind him. They had positioned a board, from the front wheel to the rear wheel, giving them minimal cover. It wouldn't stop a bullet, but might slow it down a little depending on the caliber. Mark poked his rifle barrel over the board and fired at the muzzle flash off across the plain.

By now there was return fire from the other two wagons.

"Son-of-a-bitch!" The cry came from the wagon to the south of the camp and Mark recognized Willy's voice, the younger of the Yancey brothers.

"How the hell did they get past the perimeter?" Mark yelled at Lori.

"Beats me. I hope the guys are all right," she replied, shooting at a shadow as it flitted from bush to bush, moving closer to the circled wagons.

A bullet smashed through the side of the wagon just above Mark's head and he quickly calculated where it hit in relation to the kids. Getting off three more shots in quick succession he put a small, brass horn to his lips and blew hard, the signal to hold fire so the rear guard could approach the attackers without fear of being hit. Lori crawled to the back of the wagon and Mark felt it shift as she went over the tailgate to check on her children.

More muzzle flashes, like flashbulbs in the distance, and then surprised yells came from the darkness as the attackers found themselves surrounded. The shots ceased suddenly when Einstein's voice called out, "Throw down your weapons! Get on the ground." Mark saw a mounted phantom draw a bead on a shadowy figure, and the flash from an AR-15. A grunt came from the shadow, as he threw his weapon to the ground and reached for the sky.

The inhabitants of the camp stayed behind cover until a half-dozen, scrawny men, their hands in the air, were herded into the space between the wagons by three men on horseback. Some of the captives looked angry and some defiant. All were scared.

"That's all of 'em, Mark. They were dug in under a big pile of rocks off to the east, just inside the perimeter. We almost camped on top of 'em," Jimbo said. He sat astride a horse rather than his usual mount, an old Indian motorcycle.

Mark crawled out from under the wagon, brushing the dirt off his jeans.

They shoved the prisoners to the center of the space and had them sit by the campfire.

"Get on the ground," Einstein told them. "In a circle. Backs together." He nodded at Mark and then he and the other two guards turned and rode back into the brush, ghostly figures swallowed by the early morning fog. The sky was beginning to lighten in the east and the chill penetrated the light clothing Mark and the others were wearing. Terry Holcomb, his nineteen year old son Cody, and Sheri Summerland stood guard over the prisoners while the others returned to the wagons to put on warmer clothing.

Mark climbed into the wagon, and immediately noticed the hole in the side was only a few feet from where the children had hidden. His anger flared and he resolved they would find a way to make the wagons more impenetrable.

"Are they gone Daddy?" Ashley asked Mark. "Can we get up now?"

Mark smiled, vividly remembering the first time she had called him Daddy. It was after he had awakened in pain from the fight with the mutated creature that had haunted him since the day the Remnant had been forced from the bomb shelter. She had stood beside his bed, tears in her eyes, "Daddy, are you okay?" As terrible as he'd felt, his spirits rose as he realized how badly he wanted Lori's children to accept him as their dad.

"We captured them, Ash. They can't hurt us now."

Kevin rubbed sleep from his eyes. "Mommy, why do people keep shooting at us? Did we do something wrong?" He slipped his jacket on and pulled a knit cap down around his ears as he crawled from his sleeping bag.

Lori reached over and pulled Kevin into an embrace. At six years old he was having trouble understanding why others kept trying to hurt them.

"They're just hungry, Kevin. They didn't get to live in a shelter like we did, and didn't have supplies to build a nice town like ours."

The sound of a baby crying and of pots and pans banging together got them all moving, as they prepared for another day of travel. Paul "Skillet" Masters had the fire started and the coffee brewing when Mark made his way back over to the prisoners. The sun slid above the horizon and crept into the clouds, backlighting them in fiery colors.

One of the six was no more than a boy, maybe twelve or thirteen. The others were all adults, with two of them appearing to be elderly. They were dressed warmly in hunting coats and gloves. The boy wore a knit cap. Since the nuclear war, even though food had become increasingly hard to find, clothing and other supplies were plentiful, as a result of the small numbers of people who'd survived. Gaunt and pale, their clothes hung loosely, and their faces were filthy. Twigs and brush were stuck in their matted, greasy hair, as though they had been rolling on the ground.

One of the younger men who appeared around thirty, was hunched over as if in pain, and was looking up at Mark with a sideways glance.

"What are you going to do with us?"

"We're gonna shoot your sorry asses." Danny Fielder said angrily.

"Shut up, Danny. Mark's gonna decide what we do." Jimbo squinted over at Danny with a menacing look.

Mark scratched his chin. "We don't know yet. We'll decide after breakfast."

"Think we could get some of that breakfast?"

"Of course."

The man looked surprised. "We haven't eaten for two days. Game's gettin' real scarce."

"Are you hurt?"

"Took one of your bullets across my ribs. It'll be all right."

Aaron Brown, a surgical resident before the Great War, came over and ran his fingers inside the man's coat. Wincing, the man pulled away. "I said it'll be okay."

"It's just a graze. Should heal without treatment." Aaron accepted two plates from Skillet and headed toward the wagon where his wife Chris and their three month old baby were getting ready for the day's trip.

Walking out on to the plains, east of the wagons, Mark sipped from his cup of coffee and gazed out toward the sun. It had broken through the clouds and was burning off the remainder of the fog. The land was uneven and there were piles of large rocks where the attackers had hidden until dawn, hoping to catch the occupants of the wagon train off guard as they slept. The aggressors and the people they had attacked were all normal people in very abnormal times and Mark's group was still learning to defend themselves. They had made mistakes that could get them all killed. Tonight, they would thoroughly search the area inside the perimeter where the sentries patrolled.

Squinting into the sun, he could just see I-25, an empty, straight ribbon of concrete crossing north and south in the far distance, and the smaller Highway 64 much closer to their position. They were paralleling the highway, where the ground was easier going for the mules and horses. The Holcomb family, driving their Jeep, and Sheri Summerland riding on her bicycle, used the highway. Sheri's bike wasn't made for off road travel and she had quickly given up trying to stay with the wagons soon after they'd left Cimarron. Jimbo could ride the old motorcycle anywhere, on any surface.

The guards weren't visible, but Mark knew they were out there surrounding and defending the camp. Since leaving Cimarron they had been attacked twice, the first time just shots out of the dark, and tonight, a full-on assault. Yesterday morning they'd met a man and woman who'd approached peacefully. They were unarmed, and helpless, and had been allowed to join them.

Once again, Mark wondered if they were doing the right thing. Twenty-one months had passed, since the Great War had obliterated civilization in the middle of summer. Over two hundred people had made their way to a bomb shelter in the

9

Sangre De Cristo Mountains of New Mexico, alerted about the coming war by handheld devices that notified them to immediately leave for the shelter... that attack by China was imminent.

For eight months they'd lived a life of relative ease, while those outside the shelter had barely survived the bombs, the deadly radiation and their first winter without electricity. Two types of radiation had been released by the bombs; alpha, beta and gamma radiation from the hydrogen bombs, and a previously unknown radiation, caused by "Red Mercury," a substance the Chinese had placed in neutron bombs. Large cities with important military installations had been destroyed by the hydrogen bombs. Other cities, hit by the neutron bombs, were spared physical damage but all life was completely annihilated. While ionizing radiation from hydrogen bombs can last months and even many years, the neutron radiation only lasted for a few days or weeks, and covered a much smaller area than the thermonuclear bombs. It sterilized the areas affected and left whole cities and regions intact.

It also had an unanticipated effect... it created unimaginable creatures. Certain groups of men, evil men, had been transformed into huge, reptilian monsters. They had grown in stature, and their nails and teeth had lengthened into fangs and claws. Their skin appeared putrefied and they had lost all ability to feel human emotions or to think as reasoning beings. They were driven only by the need to survive.

And one had been driven by revenge.

When the creature had first seen Mark Teller during the last few days in the shelter, it had transferred all its hatred of authority, of human beings in general, to Mark, who represented the privileged class of people that Arby Clarke had always despised. These creatures, and a series of devastating earthquakes, destroyed much of the shelter and drove them out into a protected valley behind the mountain in which the shelter had been constructed.

Right before winter, in a final deciding battle with the creature, and aided by his friends, Mark had prevailed. He still had a slight hearing loss from the report of the gun fired into the face of the creature just inches from his ear.

Will Hargraves, the billionaire defense contractor who had built the shelter, had also provided tools and supplies in an arena-sized, storage building, allowing them to get started on construction of a town and cabins, and to grow crops and learn skills they would need to survive in the new world they now lived in. They were barely prepared before the second winter hit, and without enough cabins, they had doubled up and spent their first winter outside the shelter just trying to stay warm.

Will had died in their final hurried flight to escape the destruction of the shelter, his head crushed by a rock fall. He had been like a father to Mark, and even after a year, Mark still missed him.

Others had joined them. Einstein, as his followers called him, and a small number of the residents of Cimarron, New Mexico, had survived the war by sheltering in basements. Clay Hargraves, Will's son, who had gone rogue after being banished from the shelter for attempting to rape one of the other residents, enlisted their aid. Along with forty people from Red River, and an equal number from Eagle Nest, they tried to conquer the inhabitants of the little valley. In the 'Battle of Platte Rock,' Clay Hargraves and his gang were killed, partly due to Einstein and the Red River folks hanging back and not participating in the fight.

Will's daughter Chris was a member of this small group that had left the safety of the valley, and the home they had made for themselves, to make this crazy trip to California, trying to find out about the aftermath of the war and who else may have survived. Many of the members of this party had originally come from the West Coast and were anxious to discover if their homeland still existed, and whether they could live there.

Except Matthew. Matthew Pennington was local, from Santa Fe and Albuquerque. He had come along with the group, still trying to discover where he wanted to live and what he wanted to do.

After a breakfast of biscuits and gravy, dehydrated potatoes and coffee, the group began to break camp. The boards that provided cover under the wagons were slipped inside. Carlos and Chang had slept under the chuck wagon, and rolling up their sleeping bags, stowed them inside, while two small dome tents were taken down and packed.

Chang Lee, a Korean engineer and his best friend, Carlos Zamora, a computer programmer, had come from Silicon Valley. They flew to the shelter together, barely making it to Albuquerque before the airport shut down with the news of the incoming, Chinese missiles. Recently widowed, Chang had to be convinced by Carlos that it was worth the effort to get to the shelter. They pitched in to help Skillet get his equipment ready.

Three teams of horses and mules were harnessed to the wagons. The outlying guards rode into camp for breakfast and were replaced by three others who headed out on foot to allow the horses to rest.

Their wagons were made of wood, the outer rims of the spoked, wooden wheels lined with metal. Covered with water-proof canvas, stretched over iron ribs that fit into metal brackets on the sides, they looked like the Conestoga wagons of the old west. Mark, Lori and the children used one of the wagons, Chris and Aaron another and the third was Skillet's chuck wagon. All three wagons were crammed full of supplies: grains, dehydrated foods, barrels of water, ammo and other supplies, barely leaving enough room for the occupants to sleep.

When they were ready to move out, most of the group met in front of the prisoners. The men sullenly looked up at their captors, waiting to hear their fate.

Mark stood in front of the man that had addressed him earlier. "You people attacked us, so we can't let you join. How the hell did you think you could overpower us?"

"We didn't know there was so many of you. We just wanted to scare you to surrender. You gonna kill us?"

"No. That would make us just like you. See Bob and Eydie over there?" He pointed to a couple on the edge of the crowd. "They joined us yesterday. Came up to us waving a white shirt and asked if they could join. Civilized like. But you would have killed us for our food and possessions. We'd never be able to trust you."

"We have families living in that cluster of houses you passed yesterday. We're out of food and gettin' low on ammo. Not much game around. What did you expect us to do?"

"I expect people to band together to survive!" Mark raised his voice, frowning at the man. "If we fight each other for the limited resources, we'll all die."

"What about our guns?"

"We'll just hang onto them."

One of the elderly men said, "Can you at least take the boy? He's only twelve."

"No! Grandpa. I won't go." The boy jumped to his feet and moved to the old man, throwing his arms around his neck.

"He doesn't want to go. Look, I understand that you folks are desperate. That doesn't allow you to hurt others. We came from Willsburg, a new town just north of Eagle Nest. Took us three days to get here. There's a growing colony in Eagle Nest, Willsburg and Angel Fire. Get your families and hike on up there. We've only made fifteen miles a day so you should be able to get there in four or five days, maybe six."

"What if they won't help us?"

"If you've got any more guns, and you go up there with bullets flying, they sure as hell won't help you. But if you arrive with a white flag and offer to work, they'll welcome you with open arms. They need families that will help rebuild. They have schools and a doctor. If you wait until you're completely out of supplies you'll never make it."

He waved toward the south. "Now, you've had a good breakfast. Get the hell out of here, and if you follow us, we'll kill you." The men climbed to their feet and left, checking over their shoulders as if they expected treachery.

When the attackers had crossed over a small rise, blocking them from view, the wagon train moved out. Mark and horses didn't get along too well, so today he rode on the seat of the front wagon, holding the reins of the mule team.

Mike called out, "Hey Skillet, why don't you let one of us drive your rig? Wouldn't hurt you to walk a bit today."

"Screw that. These mustangs are barely trained. If you don't handle 'em just right they'll bolt. You wanna eat on this trip?"

"Shit, Skillet. Me and my brother trained those cusses real good. They won't bolt," Sam Yancey said, as he pulled the third wagon up alongside Skillet's. Chris was nestled behind him, toward the front of the wagon with Karen sleeping in her arms. Greg Whitehorse, who'd had guard duty that night, slept in the back.

Greg, a geologist and University professor had come with the explorers to try and find out what had happened to his home in Arizona, and if any of his people, the Navajo, had survived

The group had four other horses. Matthew Pennington's magnificent Appaloosa stallion and his mare Tulip, usually ridden by Einstein, were tied to the back of the chuck wagon, the two men sleeping in the back after their night on guard duty. The Yancey's gelding, Jasper, was ridden by Aaron, and Willy Yancey rode their mare. Willy hung back and watched their rear for any sign of pursuit. Mike, Chang and Carlos, all in their late thirties, were on foot, walking easily beside the wagons. They rotated riding the horses and driving Chris's wagon, enabling them to make better time.

"It's not fair he won't let anyone else drive his wagon," Danny complained to Jimbo.

"Shut up, Danny."

The previous day the travelers had come upon Eydie and Bob. They were in bad shape, having survived for over a year with four other people in the small town of Maxwell. Their food had run out and they didn't know anything about gardening... even if they'd had seeds. The others had all died during the winter, and Bob and Eydie were just waiting to die of starvation when they saw the wagon train coming along the road.

They thought they were hallucinating.

Bob had taken off his shirt and was waving it at the wagons, when riders slipped up behind them and covered them with rifles. A long discussion ensued and the wagon folks, convinced the couple were decent people, agreed to let them come along. After cleaning up, eating Skillet's excellent dinner, and getting a good night's rest, they had recovered somewhat, but not enough to walk. They rode in the wagon with Chris and the baby. Both joined in when Chris began to sing at the top of her lungs.

"Head em up, move em out, Rawhide!"

2

Two weeks after the Great War:

The rains continued to fall, washing radioactive particles to the ground all around the world. The pattern of fallout was inconsistent, some areas receiving massive amounts of radiation and others receiving almost none. Weather patterns were unusual with prevailing winds blowing from completely different directions than before the war. Dust clouds and rain clouds were blown from southern New Mexico around the Sangre de Cristo Mountains to the four corners region and then northeast, directly across Durango. The clouds were trapped by the mountains surrounding the beautiful town. Although distant from the hydrogen bombs, Durango received a sterilizing dose of radiation. Other towns in the four corners region were spared. Farmington, only fifty miles south of Durango, received very little radiation. As bad as it was, within a few months the radioactive clouds had passed on and the radiation had begun to dissipate.

Hiroshima and Nagasaki had been directly hit with atomic bombs during World War II, but within a short period of time had begun to recover. The effects of the radiation were felt many years later in the form of various types of cancers, but the cities *had rebuilt and before the Great War were thriving, modern metropolises.*

Present day:

An anemic, morning light flooded the warehouse, penetrating dirty window panes running along the top of the walls. A large rat raced into the corner as Jon pushed a stack of cardboard boxes tightly against the right hand wall. Another stack was already against the wall on the left and the only opening was filled by his thin figure.

"He's a cornered rat," he whispered, and chuckled. "He really is a cornered rat."

The only way out was between Jon's legs. The rat darted to the right, and then juked left, and as it made a mad dash toward freedom, the man smashed down with his boot, trapping it to the floor. The rodent squealed loudly, and twisting, tried to bite the foot holding it down. Jon reached toward it with his hunting knife and deftly sliced off its head. Blood splashed over his boot and the filthy floor. Grabbing the tail, Jon held the rat up to allow the blood to drain from its body. This was the third time he had managed to catch a rat in this warehouse using the trap in the far, back corner.

As famished as he was, he stuck the rat into a large satchel he had slung over his shoulder and quickly slipped to the roll-up door at the rear of the warehouse. Stacks of boxes and shelves full of auto parts filled the space behind him. He paused to ensure no one lurked in the semi-darkness. Lying down on the floor, he lifted the door a few inches… waiting and listening, peeking out to the alley behind the building. Satisfied it was clear, he raised it another foot and rolled under the door. Leaping to his feet, he crouched down and ran along the back wall to the end of the alley, and made his way east, past Ft. Lewis College, down a street to where the pavement ended and a dirt road continued into the hills.

A gnarled pinyon pine marked the spot where he had set up one of his snares and his heart leaped when he saw it had a squirrel trapped within. The animal still struggled feebly but Jon made quick work of putting it out of its misery and added the carcass to the satchel. He wiped the knife on the grass that was just beginning to turn green in the early spring, and stuck the weapon in the sheath hooked to his belt.

Carefully checking his surroundings, he came down out of the hills and made his way to 3rd Street, then jogged several blocks to a residential street north of the downtown area where he slid past a house into the backyard. Slipping over a low, wooden fence into the next lot he paused and stared at a faded, plastic play set that sat in the corner of the yard, a reminder of the happier days before the war. It was half hidden by weeds.

Jon crossed the street and slid down a bank to the swiftly moving Las Animas River, swollen with the water from the spring snow melt. Slipping the strap of his plastic, one-gallon water container off his shoulder, he took it to the water's edge and filled it up. Even at eight pounds, he carried it easily. As skinny as he was, he had become stronger over the months since the war.

Twenty one months ago… when the power went out.

Durango had been spared the blast effects of the bombs, but clouds of radiation-saturated dust and rain had blown across the town, killing most of the residents, damning them to an agonizing death. Skeletons littered the streets of the picturesque town and were found in most of the houses. Jon tried to stay on the outskirts of town as much as possible to keep away from these wretched remains.

He ducked through a hole he had created months ago in a chain link fence and snuck through more backyards to a modest wood frame house at the end of the block. Glancing over his shoulder, he moved a rock, and grabbing a key, unlocked a door that led into the dim interior of a small garage. Jon almost sobbed as he went through his house to a door where he descended into the unfinished basement. He was almost knocked off his feet as an emaciated woman threw herself into his arms.

"Oh Jonathan, where have you been? You've never been gone this long." Her speech was slurred, the result of being hearing impaired since the age of seven, when a severe ear infection had stolen her hearing. She felt, rather than heard, his footsteps on the stairs.

He signed to her, "I'm so sorry, Mary. The food's nearly gone and they watch me like a hawk to make sure I don't run. It's okay, I'm here now." They clung together for a minute, and then, gently disengaging her, he moved to the corner of the room. Tears ran down his face as he saw the twins, Jason and Josh, lying on a mattress, their bellies swollen and dull eyes staring up with the barest of recognition. Josh had healing sores on his arms which Jon thought might be a good sign, indicating that his immune system still functioned. He sat down beside them and pulled them into his lap, holding them as though he could will energy into their tiny bodies. They were just over two when the war came, and now at almost four, they hadn't grown much and showed typical signs of starvation.

"Here." He handed her a plastic bag full of cans. "I went back through all the restaurants and stores along Main Street again."

"Is this all there was?"

"Yeah," he signed. "I've already been through every building many times. Before the war, everyone depended on 'just in time delivery' to supply their needs. They didn't keep much inventory."

"I know. Me and the boys have gone through all the nearer homes and we haven't found anything in days."

"Mary, please, you need to stay home. If anyone sees you, you have no idea what will happen to you and the boys. These guys are hungry and I can't catch enough game. If they suspected I was feeding you, they would kill you."

"But I can't bear to see Josh and Jason starving!"

He tilted her chin up and looked directly in her eyes. He signed quickly, "I will never let you starve."

During the war, Mary and Jon had put covers over the windows and stayed in the basement for weeks trying to wait out the radiation, but even with severe rationing, their food and water had run out and he had to risk going into town for supplies. They used the water in the water heater, and the faucets had actually worked for two weeks after the bombs. After that Jon went to the river and filled plastic milk cartons with water he prayed wasn't contaminated. He always ran as fast as he could, to minimize his exposure to the radiation, and upon returning, left his clothes in the garage... until he ran out of clothes. He hoped by then, three months after the war, the radiation has lessened to a safe level.

He never got sick.

Gathering up the clothes, he'd thrown them in a dumpster well away from the house. He took more clothing from his neighbor's homes and from the stores in town. They lived just east of the river and only a mile north of the historic downtown area.

Fort Lewis College lay on the east side of town and Jon had spent hours scouring the campus for signs of life. He had found none, just hundreds of rotting corpses. The cafeterias and bookstore had been trashed. He figured much of the food had been eaten before the students had died from radiation poisoning or before the survivors had killed each other over the little that remained. He found evidence of violent death amongst the bodies... bashed in heads and broken bones. Jon scavenged what he could find and had never gone back to the campus.

During the first winter, he was able to find food in the supermarkets and smaller grocery stores in town, but just like at the college, many of the shelves were empty. Finding sleeping bags and wool blankets in the sporting goods store, they managed to stay warm. Mary and the boys had lived in the basement for months and as spring and summer had come, they spent time in the backyard, never venturing far from home. She and Jon took turns fetching water from the river. She gathered plants and determined if they were edible by chewing them up and spitting them out to see if she got sick. Then she swallowed a small bite and waited a full day before deciding which could be safely eaten. One plant caused a burning sensation when she put it in her mouth and twice she vomited after swallowing a plant. Over time she had a few that they could eat without symptoms. She didn't know how much nutrition they provided but at least it was food in their bellies.

Most of the stores were empty after the first winter but Jon had built up a supply of canned goods. He trekked three miles south to Walmart and Home Depot where he found seeds and gardening tools. They'd had a small garden in the summer. Mary tried to save seeds from their vegetables but they didn't realize the hybrid plants could not produce seeds and wouldn't grow in subsequent years. Eventually he'd had to enter homes and apartments, gagging on the smell, but finding cans of food that hadn't been consumed before the occupants died.

He had to go further and further from home as he tried to keep his family fed. In the beginning he hunted with a rifle, a .22 caliber he'd found in a sporting goods store, but there was very little game. He knew that if they were going to survive he had to find other people or figure out a way to leave town.

As Jon foraged, he had seen few signs of life. He was becoming desperate to find other people they could join up with and he began to actively search for fellow survivors. In his zeal, he became careless.

In September, just over a year since the war, he was crossing the street to the Durango and Silverton Narrow Gauge Railway Station when he was shocked to see three men sitting on a bench in front of the station. One of the men had long legs stuck out in front. He looked like he was well over six feet tall. One man was small, and Jon was amused to see that he wore a stained, rumpled suit, complete with a bow tie. The third man looked Asian. The Asian man was clean shaven but the other two had long, unkempt hair and heavy beards.

21

He didn't see the liquor bottles and handguns until he was too close to retreat. He waved tentatively and they waved back and smiled, but when he got close enough they grabbed him, threw him to the ground and kicked him in the ribs until he could barely breathe.

"Who the fuck are you?" the tall man asked.

"I'm Jon," he wheezed. "I just came into town from Pagosa Springs." He had realized the danger too late and lied to keep the whereabouts of his family secret.

"Well, you came to the wrong town," the man wearing the suit told him. He picked up his gun. "Let's kill him, Vance."

"No, Ben's gonna want to see him." The large man jerked Jon up by his hair and he gasped as pain shot through his chest.

They shoved him ahead of them, laughing at his discomfort, to the Parker Hotel located at the north end of the railway station. They went up the back steps, through double doors and past the registration desk. There were three men and two women sitting in beautiful, Victorian chairs around a table.

One of the men came to his feet. "What you got there?" he asked.

"Hey, Ben. This guy just walked right up to us over at the railroad. Says he came from Pagosa Springs."

Ben walked over to Jon. He was about Jon's height, just under six feet, with long brown hair, a scraggly beard and mustache, and large, hazel eyes. He shook back his hair as he walked around Jon, eyeing him up and down.

"Who are you? How have you managed to stay alive all this time?"

"Jon... I'm Jon. I'm a hunter," he lied. "I catch game with snares and traps."

"Yeah, where's Pagosa Springs? Are there people there?"

"Ah... It's east of here. About sixty miles. I hiked it. Nobody's left. That's why I came here."

"Well, we just came down from Telluride and we're having some trouble finding game. Jessica, what do you think?"

"We might just keep you alive if you can make yourself useful," one of the women told him. She looked tall, with wavy brown hair and dark eyes, and even without makeup had flawless skin. Sitting in one of the gorgeous, Victorian chairs, her legs crossed, she sounded like she was used to commanding. "We definitely need someone who can hunt."

Jon was bent over, holding his ribs. "I can help, but I'm hurt. Can I rest?"

"Fuck that," Ben said. "Here's the deal. You can stay here at the hotel. The rooms are great and the beds are super comfortable. We'll feed you. Now get out and scour this town for stuff we can eat. Stu is going with you. If you try to leave town, we'll kill you. Slowly."

He waved Jon away in dismissal and pointed at the big man that had beaten him. "Make sure he doesn't bolt. Switch off with Kim and Shane until we know we can trust him."

Since then, almost eight months, he had continued to scavenge what food he could find in town, and set traps in the forest. After a couple of weeks they let him hunt alone and he was finally able to get back to Mary and the kids. He split the food and game between Ben's group and his family, knowing full well that if they caught him skimming food, they would kill him. And if they found Mary and the boys he knew what would happen... they would kill his twins and Mary would become their plaything. Before the war these people had been civilized businessmen and businesswomen, but hunger and cold and helplessness had turned them into animals.

Jon felt trapped, with no way to get his family out of town. He knew Stu and maybe Vance would kill his family without hesitation. He was forced to do their bidding until he could find a way out.

The second winter was bad and Mary and the boys lost a huge amount of weight. He hunted continuously and was sure he had found every last can of food in the town. The group was so desperate that even some of the other men had been sent out scrounging. But Jon was the one who brought food back every day. He wouldn't return until he had. Ben didn't allow him any weapons so he used his traps and snares, not daring to use his rifle for fear they might hear his gunshots. As long as he produced, they would allow him his freedom.

Mary had the propane, backpacking stove lit and put the pot full of water on the stove. Jon had brought boxes full of propane cylinders from the hardware and sporting goods stores. He thought again about them trying to escape but he didn't know where they could go or how they would get there.

Taking the squirrel upstairs and out into the yard, he butchered it and buried the entrails in the yard adjacent to their own. He cut up the squirrel meat into small chunks and added them to the pot along with some greens and a couple of roots he pulled out of his satchel.

The boys had fallen asleep, and as the soup simmered Jon and Mary lay in each other's arms on the thin mattress that served as her bed. They had sparsely furnished the basement not wanting it to look lived in if anyone searched the house. He stroked her dry, thinning hair.

Sitting up on the thin mattress, he faced her and signed, "It's going to be alright, Mary. Winter's over and I've noticed there's more game out there. Rabbits are everywhere but I'm having trouble getting them in my traps. I wish I'd been a hunter before all this went down. The mortgage business didn't exactly prepare me with survival skills."

"No, but you've kept us alive and I know we're going to be all right." She checked the soup and said, "Wake up the boys, the meat's done."

He shook them awake and carried them to the corner of the room where they always ate their meals. Mary kept that area scrupulously clean, trying to prevent sickness. She fed the boys slowly, hoping they could keep the nourishment down. Even as little as they ate, they had started to have digestive problems. Mary gave them each a multi-vitamin. It was one thing they had an abundance of.

"When can you come back?"

"Don't know. You might need to go out for water… so you can grow these." He pulled out some seed packets from his pack. "Ta da." He grinned at her and she grabbed the packets to see what he had.

"Carrots and beans! Oh Jonathan where did you find them?"

"They were in a garage. Even though we didn't use very many seeds last summer I can't find any in the stores. I think someone else found them all and they're either very good at hiding, or they've left town. Be really careful. You can't grow them where the garden was last year. It's too exposed. Put them between the side yard and the fence."

Jon hadn't eaten any of the soup. He would try and get his share of the meal that Ben's group would have that night.

"I need to get back." He poured the remainder of the soup into a plastic container. Mary would have to make it last for a couple more meals before it went bad. He hugged the little ones and was glad to see they had perked up after the meager meal. Josh tugged at Jon's scraggly, blond beard and laughed.

"Yeah," Jon said. "I'm a real Grizzly."

He went to the wall and removed a board between two studs. Mary handed him the plastic bag and he added the cans to the small pile hidden in the recess.

"Jon, don't take any chances of getting caught with food. I couldn't bear it if you never came back."

"I'm always careful, and as for the corporate bigwigs… they're idiots. Baby, I really need to go. I'll be back tomorrow if I can make it." He signed goodbye to her and the boys.

The sun was west of overhead and he only had a few hours left in the day to catch more game to make up for the squirrel he had used to feed his family. Running into the hills he checked his trap line and found he had caught another squirrel and a rabbit. He gathered more roots and greens and by the time he approached the hotel it was almost dark. He hoped the others had found some food. Ben always saw to it that he got a few bites

25

since he needed Jon alive, but if the food he brought was all there was he was likely to go hungry… again.

3

Chris gazed with wonder at the little chocolate bundle in her arms. Karen was asleep, her belly full of warm milk. With light brown skin, the beginnings of dark, wavy hair and full lips, she had characteristics of both her parents.

Before this baby, Chris had been secure and tough, a scientist… but now she was scared to death. When Mark had suggested they go back to California to try and discover what was going on in the outside world, the old Chris had jumped at the chance, but now she was beginning to realize the dangers outside their protected valley. Before the war she and Dr. Tanner's team of scientists had traveled the world, looking for the perfect environment to farm the oceans. Chris had a Ph.D. in Marine Biology with a specialization in sustainable food production, and was a professor at The University of California at San Diego. Life was exhilarating and full of promise.

Then came the war, and she, along with over two hundred others, had traveled to the Sangre De Cristo Mountains of New Mexico to ride out the worst of it in a bomb shelter built by her billionaire father. She was excited about helping the Remnant survive and prosper, even after they were expelled from the shelter by terrifying mutants and earthquakes. They'd built a town and planted crops, and she was a major part of that. She'd lost her father in an accident, and her brother Clay, who had been banished from the shelter for attempting to rape another resident, was killed at "The Battle of Platte Rock" when he and over a hundred others had tried to attack the colonists for their provisions... and for revenge.

But now she was a mother. She and Aaron had fallen in love and married, as had several other couples that had been thrown together in the new world. Her best friend Mark, who had been raised by her father, had met and married Lori. But although Chris was scared, she still had her sense of adventure and realized they couldn't remain in the valley without knowing what was happening on the outside.

Chris laid the baby in the box she used as a bassinet and covered her against the cool of the evening. Climbing down from the wagon, she walked over to the campfire they built each evening, using it for cooking, and to gather around for companionship and conversation when the chores were finished. Mark and Lori stood with hands around hot cups of coffee and several others had joined them by the fire.

"This isn't exactly turning out the way I expected," she said, as she joined the others at the fire. Aaron came over, put his arm around her and pecked her on the cheek.

"No? What did you expect?" he asked.

"Well, I didn't expect to be attacked almost every day. And, is it just me, or are we making really slow time?"

"We're definitely taking it slow but I think we need to be careful," Mark told her. "This morning could have been real bad if there had been more of those guys. We spent almost an hour tonight making sure our camp was safe."

"Yeah, and we don't know how often we'll find water," Skillet said through his greying beard and mustache. "So it was good we stopped at the reservoir by Maxwell yesterday, and refilled our barrels."

Mark took a swig of his coffee. "I'm sure after we check out Raton that we'll make better time heading west. What do you think Terry?"

"I heard that the wagon trains in the old west traveled fifteen to twenty miles a day. I don't think we're doing so bad. How fast did you expect us to go, Chris?"

"Back in the day, at around eighty miles an hour, I could have made the trip in a couple of days."

"Hell," Mark said, "I could fly it in a few hours. In a slow plane."

They all laughed and stood a few minutes recalling the days before the war.

"What do you think we'll find in California?" Chris asked.

"I think we'll find a radioactive wasteland, if you ask me," Skillet said.

Mark nodded his head. "Most of the cities along the coast had military targets so you may be right. But I have to know. And we need to see if there are any signs the Chinese are following up the attack."

"At this rate we won't get to California before winter," Chris said.

"It's California. Does it matter?" Terry asked her.

"Sure as hell be a lot warmer than our friends in Willsburg." Jimbo chuckled, as he tossed a limb from a Juniper tree onto the fire. It flared up and sent embers into the air as they all watched them float into the night sky, mesmerized by the tiny, twinkling fires.

Mark broke the spell. "It's about twelve hundred miles to the coast. Take us anywhere from two to three months to get there. It'll be mid-summer. We need to stop and rest a day every now and then. And it depends on being able to find food. And whether we get attacked again or run into bad weather."

"It's spring. Other than our afternoon downpours, how bad can it get?"

"Oh no, Terry. You did not just say that," Lori told him. "That's always a bad omen."

"How far to Raton?" Jimbo asked him.

Terry and his family had come from Raton after sheltering in place for the first winter. They were "preppers" and had planned ahead with provisions to get them through the worst of the war's aftermath. They left town after having to defend themselves against hungry survivors, and after seeing one of the mutated creatures in their neighborhood. Mark sometimes thought Terry resented the easy time they'd had in the shelter. Terry's family had suffered horribly. His son Cody had been shot and almost died, his right arm forever weakened. Terry and Izzy's eldest daughter Marci had been raped by Clay Hargraves' gang when she and Terry were captured while trying to pass through Eagle Nest.

"We're only a few miles away. We'll drive up there in the morning. God knows what we'll find."

Izzy, chimed in, "It will really be good to be home. I wonder if our house is okay."

"Do you think you'll stay?" Chris asked her. "What if there's no one there?"

"I don't know. Surely some people survived. But with Marci living in Willsburg we may go back, or maybe she and Tucker can move up here. We could start another town. Set up trade."

"You need a minimum number of residents to have a viable population," Mark said. "I guess it'd be okay if there's enough people. You need to be able to plant crops. You'll have seeds, of course. We have boxes of them."

Skillet and several of the others moved off to their tents. Skillet was always the first up in the morning to get breakfast ready. Mark and Lori, Chris and Aaron and Terry stood staring into the fire.

"Tomorrow, we'll drive up the freeway and check it out, but we won't go into town until you all get there. Maybe Matthew can ride up and see what it's like away from the freeway. He's real good at scouting."

"We need to have someone else take the night shift tomorrow night for sentry duty then. He and Einstein always get stuck with graveyard duty," Chris said.

"They like it. They're both loners," Mark said. "Let's get some sleep."

***

"What do you suppose that is?" Terry turned to Izzy and pointed up the freeway to where they could see a line of some kind across the road. Izzy, the binoculars up to her eyes, had reached over and put her hand on his shoulder and told him to pull over. They were parked on the right shoulder gazing north. The mid-day sun cast almost no shadows, making it more difficult to see.

"It looks like a barrier. I can see a guy standing on top of a wagon. Oh shit!" she exclaimed. "Take a look. He has binoculars too, and he's looking right at us."

Terry took them from her and scanned left and right along the barrier. "You're right. They've put a barrier across the freeway. There's a chain link fence stretching into the plain on either side of the road for at least a quarter mile. I see some kind of a trailer with the guy on it. But there are others, and they all look armed."

"That's not the kind of reception I was hoping for," she told him. "Can you see if it's anyone we know?"

"Naw. They're too far away."

Cody, riding in the back seat and acting as rear guard, said, "Here comes Sheri."

Sheri rode up to the Jeep on her bike. "What's wrong?"

"Looks like they have the freeway shut down." Terry handed her the glasses.

"Hmm. They know we're here. We better get back to camp and let the others know."

Terry swung the Jeep around and they headed back to the intersection of Highway 64 and the I-25. Pulling to a stop, he saw riders to the northwest and waited for Matthew Pennington and Willy Yancey to join them.

"So what's up?" Willy asked, as he reined in Jasper.

Terry jerked a thumb back the way they'd come. "There are armed men up ahead and they saw us. They barricaded the freeway. I think we need to leave the camp where it is and beef up security."

"Did you see any working vehicles?" Matthew asked in his soft voice, with just a hint of a British accent. He and Willy both wore cowboy hats and long sleeved white shirts but with the spring weather warming up neither man wore a jacket. Willy had on cowboy boots but Matthew wore beige, work boots. He had always hated cowboy boots, even when working on his grandfather's cattle ranch south of Taos, New Mexico. Both men were in their twenties, Matthew twenty-six and Willy twenty-two, but Willy looked much younger than Matthew. His wild, blonde hair stuck out from under his hat while Matthew's long, black hair, tied in back with a leather thong, hung halfway down his back.

"No, they had some kind of trailer shoved up against the fence, and I spotted what looked like small shipping containers. They could have moved all that by hand or dollies."

"If they don't have cars or trucks they probably won't follow us. But we can't chance it. Let's get back to camp and have the wagons stay put."

"I'll tell 'em." Sheri swung her bike around and took off. She had been an Olympic cyclist before the war, and standing on the pedals, shot off toward the south.

Willy grinned, "That gal can really fly."

"Hey Willy, don't forget you have a fiancé back in Willsburg," Izzy reminded him.

"Hell, I don't mean nothin' by it. She's just the fastest thing on wheels."

Matthew gestured to Willy and they kicked the horses into a canter, riding west into the brush. Gunning the engine of the Jeep, they headed after Sheri who had already disappeared over a rise in the freeway ahead.

As they drove, Izzy looked around at the vast emptiness. It was eerie, driving along I-25 without a sign of another car and no evidence of humans or animals anywhere to be seen. No contrails in the sky. No sounds of civilization. Two dust devils played tag in the distance until they disappeared behind a line of barren hills. The grasslands were still winter brown but there was a touch of green as spring overcame winter.

She felt a great sense of loneliness in the vast, empty high plains.

But Terry and Cody were with her, helping to relieve the feeling. Her two younger daughters, Missy and Kris, had stayed behind with the wagons and her eldest daughter Marci, who was newly married, had stayed home with Tucker in Willsburg. They had all spent the last year with the survivors from the bomb shelter, and had made good friends, but Izzy wanted to know what had happened to her home and the friends she had known in Raton. Some, she was painfully aware, had died from the radiation, but there were others she had known for years, and she needed to know what had happened to them. She hoped they would find out tomorrow, one way or the other.

As they sped south on Highway 64 they spotted the wagon train about five miles south of the barricaded freeway. The Jeep passed Sheri and arrived a few minutes ahead of her. Their four-wheeler left the road and jounced across the plain toward their companions. Sheri had to dismount and push the bike the final two hundred yards through the brush and soft earth. As she arrived she heard Terry finishing up his story of the barricade at Raton.

"Maybe we should skip Raton and just head west," Dr. Whitehorse suggested. "We don't need any trouble."

Terry and Izzy both protested at once. Izzy said, "It's our home. We raised our family there and had friends and neighbors. We need to find out who's blocking the road. It could be people we know. Terry was in the Better Business Bureau and knew a lot of the town leaders. You folks don't have to go with us but we have to know."

Jimbo patted her shoulder. "Don't worry, Izzy. We're gonna find out."

"Yeah," Mark told her. "We need to know too. If there's a large population that's self-sufficient, maybe they can trade with The New Mexico Colony. The more people that've survived, the better everyone's chances are."

They decided to camp there for another night. If the town didn't have any working vehicles the five mile buffer should provide safety. Only a few days out of Eagle Nest, they still welcomed the afternoon off, free from travel. Especially the kids, who talked Sam and Willy into playing a killer game of touch football. Jesse, Danny, Sheri and Carlos formed a team to play against them and the game wore on until dinner.

The kids won the game with high fives all around.

"That was nice of you to let Ash and Kevin win," Lori told Sheri, who was red-faced and filthy.

"They beat us fair and square," Sheri said with a wink. "I hope Skillet has some hot water for a sponge bath."

They doubled the nighttime guard. Matthew and Einstein had stayed up during the day so they could sleep at night rather than pull their normal sentry duty.

That night, standing in front of the fire, Mark told Matthew, "We need you and Einstein to sneak up on their flanks, to make sure they aren't pulling any funny business." He gestured toward the town. "Do you think you guys can go out before daylight?"

The two men nodded. "We'll make sure they don't send out anyone to try and take Terry from behind. They saw Terry's Jeep. They're going to want it pretty bad." Einstein threw the last of his coffee into the fire. "I'm going to hit the sack. What do you think Matthew? 0400?"

Matthew, never one for much conversation, nodded and walked over to the horses. He scratched Chief on the poll and patted his neck while Chief nuzzled against Matthew's chest and shoulder. "Ready for some action tomorrow, my friend?" The horses were tethered to the line and Matthew's belongings were stacked up a few yards away, covered by a tarp against the possibility of rain. Pulling out his bedroll and a wool blanket, he stretched out on the ground, wrapped the blanket around him and fell instantly asleep.

4

Las Vegas, Nevada stood shimmering in the heat, surrounded by the desolation of the Mojave Desert. "The Entertainment Capital of the World," hadn't been spared in the Great War, the once famous casinos along the glamorous Strip falling, as the blast wave from the thermonuclear device had swept down from the Nevada test site, traveling at tremendous speed. The distance had been great enough, however, to mitigate much of the damage from the one bomb that had hit the area. For some reason Nellis Air Force Base hadn't been targeted.

Smaller structures had survived and hardy men and women came up out of the basements and found provisions to get them through the next eighteen months. Aided by moderate weather, many thousands had been spared... until the second die off.

Vegas was a large city, with almost two million people in the metropolitan area. In the beginning, even food was plentiful. But Sin City was cut off from civilization in all directions, and there was one thing they needed desperately, but didn't have... water.

Incorporated in 1911, Vegas remained fairly small until Hoover Dam was completed in 1935, forming Lake Mead, the largest reservoir in the United States. When full, the lake was 112 miles long, had 759 miles of shoreline and was 532 feet deep. Fed by the Colorado River, it hadn't been filled to capacity since 1983 due to increasing drought conditions

Even though most of the major hotels used water from their own aquifers, ninety percent of Las Vegas' water supply came from Lake Mead. It was transported through 30 miles of pipeline from the two intake pipes or *straws*. The pumping stations required electricity, and they had stopped working when the bombs created electro-magnetic pulses that knocked out the power. Prior to the war the lake was as much as 80 feet below its normal level and would soon have been below the level of one of the intake pipes. A monumental engineering feat had been underway to build a third intake at the bottom of the lake. It was a race to finish it before the first intake would be lost when the lake reached 1050 feet above sea level. The war stopped that effort.

Without water from Lake Mead there would be no Las Vegas.

Gravity fed systems continued to supply water from water towers for a few weeks after the war, since the population was so decimated, but people began to panic when water stopped coming out of the taps. Fortunately, hundreds of stores had bottled water which lasted well over a year. It seemed like an inexhaustible supply and the survivors didn't bother to conserve. A year after the Great War, the summer was hotter than usual and the supply of bottled water diminished. When they started drinking water from swimming pools, much of it contaminated, hundreds died.

The population had fractured into numerous factions, with one of the groups hanging out in the smaller, local casinos downtown. A large community to the west, around Summerlin, died off as the water disappeared, as did several groups in the newer areas around Green Valley. Over two thousand people living in Henderson, realizing the water wouldn't last, stuffed their belongings in backpacks and trekked along Highway 564 over thirty miles to Las Vegas Bay on Lake Mead. There they had built mud huts and planted crops the first summer. But they had started late and cold weather prevented them from growing enough to sustain them all.

Going into the second summer they were becoming more self-sufficient but their lack of knowledge, and the learning curve, had cost them more than half their population.

To the east of I-15, in a seedier part of town, the motorcycle gang, Satan's Horde, had taken up residence in a commercial area, attempting to repair scores of motorcycles they had previously owned, or they had found in dealerships and garages all over town.

"We've got another one running, Chase." Bing strolled through the open door and plopped down in a chair, its Naugahyde cover ripped, exposing the stuffing within. "It's a Honda, but it's 900 cc so it's got a little power." He was dressed in Jeans and a denim shirt with a red bandanna holding back his straw colored hair that fell to his shoulders. His coarse, three day-old stubble was shot through with gray.

Chase sat staring at Bing, never blinking or acknowledging that the man had spoken. He was six-feet, four-inches tall and had shaggy, brown hair with curly locks that hung in front of his eyes. The whites of his eyes were visible all around the pupils, and madness lurked behind his staring countenance. Although his clothes were dirty, his hands were creamy white, his nails perfectly manicured. He washed them at least once an hour and had a huge supply of anti-bacterial hand rub to armor him against the ever present danger of the germs that hid everywhere, waiting for an opportunity to infect and kill him.

"That makes fifty-two working bikes and two trucks. We need another twenty or so and we can split. The guys are bringing in more every day and we've found parts in five more shops. Three new guys showed up today to join us." Bing was becoming uncomfortable under the scrutiny, squirming and looking around the room. It was the waiting room of a Quick Lube, containing a few chairs and a useless T.V.

"How long?" The voice was like sandpaper against a rusty pipe.

"I don't know, maybe a week or two."

Several motorcycles: Harleys, Hondas, Suzukis, Ducatis and Yamahas, were torn apart in the bays of the lube shop, waiting for one of the men to replace their electronic parts.

"Who are the new guys?"

"Came from North Vegas. They all have bikes."

"Get them out looking for parts and water. And put 'em through initiation."

"Sure Chase. Well, I'll ah, just get out there and give em' a hand." Bing rose and slipped through the door, throwing a backward glance at the leader of Satan's Horde. As he left, with Chase's eyes following him, a tiny smile ticked up the corner of Chase's mouth. As crazy as he was, he kept a firm control over the Horde.

The men were scared to death of him.

Bing went to the far side of the shop and squatted down beside a mechanic in greasy coveralls. "New guys need to prove themselves. Chase wants them out getting supplies but they need to bring us some new, young tail."

"It's getting harder to do with the Westsiders dying off and the Henderson group leaving town. What happens if they can't find anyone?" Cutter asked.

"He'll probably kill 'em. They have nice bikes, two BMW 1000s and a Honda CBR 1000. We'll give 'em to Nutts, Johnny and Rod."

"Yeah, well remember, if they find anyone, it's my turn after Chase finishes with her."

"You might have to fight off Clancy. He wants a piece of every chick we bring in."

"When are we gonna blow this place?" He rubbed his greasy hand across his forehead and through his jet black, short-cropped hair, leaving a black streak.

"Couple of weeks I'd say. Water's running out and we need to find a place to hold up before all our supplies are gone. Chase thinks the world is ours for the taking. If everyone else that's left is like the pansies in Vegas, he's right. There must be plenty of cities left that didn't get bombed and we can just move in and take over. Cities with rivers."

"I used to live in Indianapolis. We could be fucking kings."

"Yeah, well let me know when you get another one running. We can't take over our kingly duties 'til we get the fuck out of this desert hellhole."

For the first year they had spent all of their time partying and drinking. There was enough booze in Vegas to last for a decade but no one thought about the water. It seemed with so few survivors that the food and water would last forever, but after the first hot summer it became obvious that water was going to be the problem. They looted every store and casino in the downtown area, and using one of the old pickup trucks one of the men had repaired, they brought thousands of bottles of water back to the shop. The horde had one hundred and seven men, and a half-dozen women, and other people were showing up every day wanting to join the gang. Most were looking for protection, realizing there was safety in numbers and wanting to be on the side of might.

Chase walked into the back office to get a bottle of water and saw that there were only two or three hundred bottles left. "We fucking need to blow this town," he said in his raspy voice. Caused by a throat infection when he was six years old, he had endured teasing his entire life when the kids had called him Andy, for Andy Devine the old cowboy star that was a regular on Roy Rogers. He was in a constant battle to ensure he would never be infected again.

Bing went next door to the auto repair shop where the three new guys were waiting. "Chase says you're in if you can pass our initiation."

Carswell, skinny and mean looking, with wild, bushy eyebrows and deep-set eyes, looked suspicious, and glancing over at his brother Keenon, said, "Yeah? What do we need to do?"

"Kidnap a girl from one of the colonies, maybe out by Green Valley. Should be far enough away they can't trace her back to us if they don't have vehicles. And gotta be younger than sixteen."

"Fuck, man. That might be really hard to do. Most of them have died off or moved out. How about we just kill someone?"

"You want in, that's your job. Take it or leave it. We're leaving town in a couple weeks, before it starts getting too hot. We're going east to find a town to take over. You can come with us or stay here and die of thirst."

Keenon snickered, "Won't die of thirst. We'll just drink booze until we die."

"Shut up, Asshole. I'm not staying in this town. There's bad shit gonna happen when there's no water," Carswell said. "Why don't we go west? It's closer."

"Chase says L.A.'s probably been wiped off the map. And all the other cities, too. Radiation or something. So what's it gonna be?"

"We'll get your girl."

"Make sure you don't mess with her. Chase wants her pure."

Carswell hit his electric starter and the others stood on their kick starters. The bikes roared to life and they accelerated out through the parking lot and disappeared up the street heading for Green Valley.

5

It was after midnight. The angry young man threw his shoulder against the door. "Tell me where my children are. Where's my wife? We haven't done anything wrong!" He slid to the floor and sobbed, "Why are you keeping me here?" Jumping back to his feet, he pounded on the door with renewed energy. "Where are my children?" he screamed.

"Shut up, Roger. You better shut up or we're screwed," the other prisoner in his room said through clenched teeth. "You've only been here one day so you don't know the ropes, but if they hear you, they will beat us both, or give us extra duty. So shut your mouth." The other, larger man swung his feet over the edge of his cot and moved over toward Roger. He grabbed him by the arm and pulled him back to the center of the room.

"Get back in your bed and get some sleep. We have a lot of work to do tomorrow." He shoved Roger down on his cot. "Just stay there."

Roger started to get up but, glancing at the huge, black man decided against it. Roger was five-eleven and lean, with muscle built up by physical labor, but his roommate was way bigger. "But why are we here? I didn't do anything wrong. Me and my wife and kids were living on our farm, taking care of ourselves. We were doing great. Why did they bring me here?"

"Shh, keep your voice down. It doesn't matter to them whether you were thriving or starving, they're rounding up people for work parties. To hear them tell, nobody's doing okay. They say everybody needs their help or nobody will survive."

"Well, it's not true. In Marshall, we were doing great on our own. All the neighbors had gotten together and were helping each other out. One of the guys had a working tractor and he went around and plowed everybody's fields. Bartered his work for produce and eggs. We all had something we were good at and we traded labor. Then these jack-booted guys came rolling into town in a couple of trucks, dressed in fatigues, with full riot gear and carrying military rifles. Said they were going to help us... but we didn't need any help."

"Yeah, that's kind of what happened in my town as well. A bunch of armed guys resisted and were shot down in the street."

The big, dark-skinned man lay back on his cot and put his hands behind his head. "They're rounding people up and throwing them into these camps. They're putting all the men on work details, repairing roads, and building stuff and making the women do household chores."

"That sucks."

"I agree. So, what did you do before the war?"

"My wife and I owned a flower shop in Marshall. We lived on a ten acre farm that's been in my wife's family for generations. Had a couple mules and some other domestic animals, but they took them all. They separated us and threw us in the back of trucks. After they took my animals, they raided the root cellar and the basement. Everything we'd stocked up is gone. Their commander said an executive order allowed them to confiscate people's food for the good of the majority, whatever the hell that means. How about you? What did you do?"

"I was a high school principal, in Danville, Virginia. Not really used to all this physical labor. I'll bet I've lost 50 pounds."

He sat up on the edge of his cot. "Believe me, they don't give a shit about you. They're rounding up anybody that can work for them. We just need to keep quiet and do our work, and who knows, maybe we'll get out of here someday."

"Really? How soon?"

"Not for a while. I've spent the last two months with a group of guys working on the train tracks leading into Charleston. They have an old steam engine from a railroad museum. It's running between here and Parkersburg up north. One of the guards said they're restoring the whole West Virginia area to establish government control."

"We're in West Virginia? I couldn't see outside the truck so I had no idea where they were taking me. I live in North Carolina."

"Not anymore, you don't. They brought my whole work crew down from Parkersburg for a new job. We'll find out what it is tomorrow. Or today, now that it's so late. Now shut up and go to sleep or we'll be exhausted tomorrow."

Roger lay back on his cot. "What will happen to my family?"

"Your kids will be educated, or indoctrinated, whatever you want to call it. Your wife will work with the other women, cooking, laundry, that kind of thing. Just keep your mouth shut and do your own work. Otherwise it will go hard with you."

***

Only a few hours later, the slamming of doors and the bellowing of the guards woke Roger and his large roommate, Ashe. Six-foot, three-inches tall, and dark as mahogany, he looked like he could break Roger in half.

"Damn," Ashe muttered, half asleep, "you kept us awake half the night."

A guard dressed in military fatigues, going door-to-door and unlocking them, stopped in front of theirs and turned the key in the lock. He shoved it open and leaned around it.

"You guys should be ready. If you don't have your boots on in fifteen seconds, you'll get a taste of the baton. So get your asses moving." He tugged on the door and, as it swung shut, he continued down the hallway to the next room.

"Come on Roger. He wasn't kidding. If we don't fall out real quick, you'll get a taste of that baton and I can tell you from experience it hurts like hell."

The two men quickly slipped on their boots and hustled out into the hallway. They joined others similarly dressed in denim overalls and filed out the door into a large, open, grassy area. Roger saw the men lining up like a military platoon and fell in line with Ashe to his left. There were three groups of men, each having about fifty individuals. Across the field on the other side of the street he could see another group of three formations. Surrounding each formation were at least four soldiers with assault rifles.

The rifles were held ready to fire.

He heard a cadence, and a platoon of soldiers marched down the street between his platoon and the ones across the street. The marching soldiers were followed by a truck carrying a 50mm full-auto machine gun in the bed. Roger recognized it from one of his old favorite TV shows.

"You stragglers get into line or we'll make you sorry," said one of the soldiers behind the formation.

"Hey Ashe," Roger whispered out of the corner of his mouth, "who the hell are these guys?"

He felt something hard across his hamstrings and yelled out as he fell to the ground. The pain was excruciating. Writhing on the ground and rubbing the back of his legs, he looked over his shoulder and saw a uniformed soldier standing behind him with a wicked looking baton.

"What the hell, man. What did you hit me for?" He tried to get to his feet and the man hit him again. Due to the angle, the blow fell on the side of his thigh and he slumped back to the ground.

"You don't talk when you're in formation, bucko. So open your mouth again and you'll get this baton across your face. You got that?" The man, whose name on his uniform was Mitchum, stood slapping the baton into his left hand. Mitchum was career military, and enjoyed the fact that he was no longer constrained by the old rules of military discipline. His current superiors only cared that he got the job done. He had steel grey eyes and a military buzz cut.

"Hey, Captain Mitchum. Lay off him, man. He just got here. He doesn't know the rules." Ashe turned toward the soldier but carefully stayed in his spot.

"Well, this is the way he's gonna learn real fucking fast. And if you know what's good for you, you'll keep your mouth shut, too." But he didn't get any closer to the big man.

They faced front as someone addressed their platoon. "All right men, listen up. I'm Major Cartwright and this is Colonel Faricy and his aide Lieutenant Marrs." The speaker, dressed in fatigues, with the insignia of a major, stood on a wooden box at the front of the formation. He wore a camo baseball cap. Standing beside him were two other men, one a full bird colonel with a chest full of ribbons, and a lieutenant.

"Some of you have been working on other projects and some of you are new, but we have a job that you'll all be working on for quite some time. As soon as y'all eat breakfast you're gonna march on over to the campus of the West Virginia State University. It's on the other side of the Kenawha River. You'll be staying in one of the dormitories over there while you work on this new job. Colonel Faricy is in charge of the entire project and we need to bring it in on schedule. You should all be very proud to be part of it." He paused and looked over at the Colonel.

"You will be building the new White House for the President of the United States of America."

***

"Sir, we're picking up a message from some ham operator in Georgia. He's telling people there are government troops in the area, and they're rounding up people and putting them in FEMA camps. He's calling on citizens to resist." The sergeant stood at attention, straight as a rod.

Jeremy Rissman sat in a deep, leather chair that had belonged to the president of the college. The government had taken over the campus as their headquarters after exiting the bunker they had sheltered in during the war.

He came to his feet and pounded his fists on the desk. "He must be silenced! We have enough people resisting our attempts to bring order to the country without these insurrectionists fomenting dissention. General Ladner, see if you can contact Colonel Reisling to find the man and bring him in. If he fights us, he'll need to be taken down."

"Yes, Mr. President. But we don't have a very large presence in Georgia. We don't want the troops to be at risk. Once the Carolina Campaign is finished, we can send a large contingent further south and wipe out all the dissenters."

"Send the 1st Southern Elite Company down there, now! Nobody's going to mess with them. How is the campaign in North Carolina going?"

General Ladner shrugged his massive shoulders. "Of course, we're hampered by a lack of equipment but we've cleared several small mountain towns in the western part of the state. The troops are moving mostly on foot. We have plenty of rifles and ammo but could use more trucks."

Rissman looked over at the handsome, rugged man sitting on the couch. "How many more trucks do we have, Jordan?"

The former Secretary of the Interior scratched his chin. "We have all the vehicles from the National Guard Armory. The state's Disaster Preparedness Department was pretty smart. They had electronic parts for the trucks and personnel carriers protected by Faraday cages. That way they didn't have to try and protect the vehicles themselves. It's too bad so many of the government personnel were lost, as we only found the repository where the parts were located a couple of months ago. We've repaired another dozen troop carriers and a half a dozen jeeps."

"Can we get those down to Carolina?"

"We're sending a convoy tomorrow. We're keeping a few here to augment our border security."

"It's imperative we continue to push south and move the workers into our camps. I can't believe these people would rather eke out a meager existence in the mountains than join us in rebuilding the country and taking care of everyone." He ran his fingers through his hair. It had gone from a steel gray prior to the war to almost white.

There was a knock on the door and an aide stepped inside the room.

"Mr. President, the Congress has gathered in the auditorium. They're waiting for you, sir."

"Let them wait. Jordan, get that equipment fixed ASAP. Have we made any headway toward getting working planes or helicopters?"

"We have a few aircraft mechanics working on it. We haven't been able to locate the parts for the planes. I'm sure they must have squirreled them away like they did the truck parts, but we've been unable to find them. We have men checking every warehouse in the city."

"Find the plans for the city buildings. They may have underground bunkers or basements."

Rissman walked toward the door. "Follow me gentlemen, let's see what the Congress wants."

They exited the Administration Building and crossed to the Student Center where the auditorium was located. There were a score of men and seven women standing down by the podium and several more sitting in the first row of seats.

Rissman put on his most diplomatic smile, as he moved down the aisle toward the surviving members of the Congress of the United States. The Chinese had attacked during a Congressional recess and most of the almost five hundred members of the House of Representatives were in their home districts around the country. Only two of the persons in the auditorium were representatives, the rest being senators and a member of the President's cabinet. West Virginia was far enough from ground zero at Washington, D.C. to build bunkers that could withstand the barrage of thermonuclear bombs.

There were three separate shelters, that the President, the Congress, cabinet members and military personnel had evacuated to. Hardwired communication between them, that didn't rely on radio, enabled them to keep in touch during the war and for the year they remained in the bunkers. Their instruments indicated that it took that long for the radiation to lessen to a level that was safe, due to the tremendous numbers of bombs that had obliterated the entire East Coast. Areas west and south of Washington had been spared due to the mountain ranges and prevailing winds.

When they noticed the President approaching, the group quieted. He walked into their midst, shaking hands and greeting them individually by name as if he were campaigning.

"Gentlemen, ladies. To what do I owe the pleasure of your company?"

"Cut the crap, Rissman," Henry Simms told him. "What the hell is going on in Carolina? We've heard reports of free people being rounded up and brought here against their will."

Rissman's face darkened. "Senator Simms, don't take that tone with me. You are speaking to the President of the United States. I insist you show me respect." He waved toward the seats. "Shall we be seated and discuss this rationally?"

They shuffled around and took seats. General Ladner grabbed a chair from the side of the room so the President could face the Congress.

"To answer your question, Henry, yes… we are rounding up citizens and bringing them here to protect and care for them. In many cases they're very happy to come. They are fed, clothed and housed. Most of them were close to starvation. Do you have a problem with that?"

One of the women, Representative Claire Burnham, said, "I don't have any problem with that, Mr. President. We've known for years that many people would be unprepared to survive even an economic collapse, not to mention a nuclear war. That's the reason we prepared the camps in advance. I think Henry's concern is for the people that prepared for these tragedies and do not want to come to West Virginia." She looked over at Simms and found him staring at her through his thick, horn-rimmed glasses, nodding vigorously.

"Ms. Burnham, why do you think Executive Order 12919 and the others were passed? They make all emergency food and supplies, communications, livestock and weapons, the property of the government. Those supplies can be used to provide equally for all the people. In times of emergency, and I think we can all agree this qualifies, it is legal to confiscate those items, and to have men and women rounded up to work for the government to rebuild the country's infrastructure." He turned, stared at her and stressed, "Again, we have every legal right to confiscate stocked foods, animals, guns, etc. in order to save everyone's lives, not just a few." He stood up and paced before them as if giving a lecture to school children.

"This war was terrible. But we have a chance to start over, to take care of everyone equally. No more poor people... or income inequality. We will disarm the citizenry so we don't have these dissidents destroying the good things we're trying to accomplish. The United States will rise again as a great nation, with all her people being taken care of."

The senators exchanged glances. Representative Burnham said, "Yes, Mr. President. But we've heard that people are being kidnapped from their homes. We still have a constitution, sir. What about freedom?"

"Freedom is overrated. Is it better to have freedom, and starve, or work with others to rebuild our great nation? They get three meals a day, which is more than they had on their own."

Rissman waved his hand at General Ladner. "Using Executive order 13603, I've had to declare Martial Law. In order to save the country we need to bring everyone into the fold. At some time in the future we may allow people to return to their homes. But until..."

"Mr. President," several of the Congressmen said at the same moment. Chad Garrett, the senior senator from Texas spoke over the others, "With all due respect, sir, that's what every dictator has said since the beginning of time. This isn't right. It seems more like a police state."

At the sound of rounds being chambered, he and the others looked up at the entry to the auditorium. Soldiers entered the room and moved down the aisles, their rifles covering the senators. "What's going on here?" Garrett said, with eyes wide.

"There are two choices, ladies and gentlemen. You will continue in your roles as advisors to the President and help me save this country, or you can join the work crews outside. What's it going to be?"

6

Once the dust had finally settled after the war, the nighttime skies were spectacular. It was mid-May, and at four o'clock in the morning Vega gleamed overhead in the constellation Lyra and the Milky Way blazed across the void. The chill was greatest at that time of the morning and Matthew wore a sheepskin-lined jacket and gloves over his normal attire. He told Skillet the night before it wouldn't be necessary for him to get up and fix coffee but as Matthew walked to the smoldering campfire, a steaming cup was thrust into his hands.

"Thank you," he said in hushed tones, his breath visible in the morning air. "Seen Einstein?"

"He's out talking to Mike on the eastside. Want something to eat?"

"No, I'll eat some jerky. I need to head out." He patted Skillet on the back in silent thanks and went back to the already saddled Appaloosa. Swinging into the saddle he rode east to where Einstein waited for him.

"Hey Matthew, you ready?"

Matthew nodded at Mike, 180 pounds of lean muscle, with hazel eyes and thinning, brown hair, and answered Einstein's question, "Yes. I'll cover the west flank, you go east. I'm going to leave Chief a mile out and go the rest of the way on foot. If you see anyone trying to sneak up on our guys, don't engage them. Just ride back and warn Terry they're coming. Agreed?"

"Yeah, I'm not anxious to fight. You too?"

"Agreed."

He stuck his empty cup into a saddlebag and the men rode out, Einstein disappearing behind some rocks as he rode east. By dawn Matthew was riding into the outskirts of Raton. He dismounted, leaving the reins hanging; the signal to the horse to remain where he was. They were in the bottom of an arroyo where Chief was invisible to anyone who chanced to look their way from the freeway.

Matthew pulled a sniper rifle from the scabbard, a beautiful weapon he'd found in Taos when he spent the previous summer there, trying to decide whether he would join with the shelter people. He had searched a gorgeous hacienda, perched on a knoll overlooking the town, and found a large cache of collector's weapons. The rifle was a Heckler and Koch PSG1. Considering the import ban on this type of rifle, and a cost of $15,000, he guessed the rifle had been purchased illegally.

Slinging the rifle across his back, and carrying a small backpack, he moved forward on foot, gliding noiselessly from bushes to rock piles, and crawling carefully over small rises. The pack contained NATO 7.62mm x 51mm ammo for the rifle and a 50 round box of .45 caliber for his pistol. He had an ample supply of jerky and a liter of water. When he could see the end of the chain link fence jutting out into the desert he settled down to wait behind a small pile of rocks.

He had sent Einstein to the east knowing that when the sun rose it would be difficult to see on this side of town. He was looking almost directly into the sun when he swept the plain ahead of him with his binoculars. As the sun moved higher, and visibility increased, he saw several armed men behind the fence on his side of the freeway about 200 yards away. They seemed relaxed.

He set the bipod of the sniper rifle on the rock in front of him and covered the black hair on his head with a desert camo scarf. The rifle's original telescopic scope had been replaced with a Hensoldt ZF6x42PSG1. He scanned the men along the fence through the lighted reticle. Although Matthew had often practiced marksmanship at his grandfather's ranch while growing up as a boy he had never before used such a precision rifle. He knew that much of that precision was wasted since few people maintained any kind of efficiency without continued practice. Still, even if he achieved 1 to 3 minutes of angle he knew he would be more accurate with the sniper rifle than with his AR-15.

Matthew heard the Jeep in the distance.

***

Leaving the Jeep a quarter of a mile from the fence, Terry moved along the median toward the barrier across Interstate 25 just south of Raton. There were cracks in the concrete and weeds strained through into the light of day. The median was overgrown with brush and he tried to stay hidden so he could see how many were at the fence before breaking cover. Izzy and Cody were hidden behind the Jeep with long-range rifles, but they stayed down, so as not to be seen as aggressors by the men at the barrier. Terry couldn't see Matthew or Einstein but he knew they were protecting his flank. When approximately fifty yards from the barrier, he left the median, his hands in the air, and stopped in the middle of the fast lane of the freeway.

"Hello. Hello, I just want to talk," he yelled as he continued to wave his arms, hoping they would realize his intentions were friendly. He saw movement behind the barrier and after a few minutes a large gate in the chain link opened and three men walked through. Unlike him, all three men were armed with hunting rifles. Sweat broke out on his forehead and he suddenly wanted to run, but he held his ground, realizing he would be shot in the back before he had made five yards.

"You need to get the hell out of here!" one of the men yelled. "We're not taking in any strangers."

"Hey man, I just want to talk for a minute, okay?" Terry took a step forward and saw several men behind the fence raise their rifles and point them directly at him. "Whoa, I'm not armed. I just want to talk."

"What part of, *get the hell out of here,* don't you understand?"

"I'm Terry Holcomb. I live in Raton. I have a house and a business there. I just want to talk. I'm not just some stranger and I think I can help you guys." He waited anxiously as he saw the three men conversing. He let out the breath he'd been holding when one of them raised his hand and beckoned to Terry. More scared than ever, He walked forward, trying to appear nonchalant.

***

A half second can mean the difference between peace and war. Matthew was watching the men behind the fence and when Terry began to approach the barrier one of the men raised his rifle, pointing it directly at him. Matthew tensed. He looked through the scope, at 42x magnification the man appeared to be just in front of him, close enough to see the man's finger was on the trigger. Matthew's own finger was on the trigger of the Koch and Heckler. He took a deep breath, let it out and froze as his trigger finger began to squeeze. A half second before he completed the shot, the stranger in front of him raised his rifle and took a step back on the trailer. Matthew released the trigger and put his finger outside the trigger guard along the receiver of the weapon. Usually fairly calm, Matthew felt the adrenaline racing through his blood and shuddered to think he had almost taken a life unnecessarily. He watched as Terry and the three men passed through the gate in the chain-link fence. Backing away from the rock, he turned and sat in the sand, pulling the scarf off the top of his head and sitting quietly to allow his heart rate to slow down. He gulped in several deep breaths, and regaining control, again took up his position.

Over fifteen minutes had passed, when the gate reopened and Terry walked through to wave at the Jeep, beckoning Izzy and Cody forward. He also gave a subtle signal that told Einstein and Matthew that all was well and they could stand down. Matthew waited, as the Jeep approached the gate and stopped 10 yards in front of the barrier. The gate was swung wide open and three men pushed the trailer aside to provide an opening for Izzy to drive through. Once the Jeep had passed beyond the fence, Matthew pulled the sniper rifle off the rock and closed down the bipod. He gathered his belongings, slung the rifle onto his back, and retraced his path to the Arroyo where Chief awaited, having never moved.

"You're a damn good horse, Chief," he said to him, rubbing Chief's favorite spot between his ears. Stowing his gear he mounted the Appaloosa and headed back to camp.

***

The Holcombs and John Perry rode back to town in the Jeep, John raving the whole way about how great it was to be flying down the freeway at 70 mph.

"This is a real nice Jeep you guys have. We have two cars and a pickup and they're all pure shit. The only ones we could get running are at least 40 years old and we try not to use 'em unless it's an emergency. How did you guys get this running?"

"I stored it in a grounded metal garage. It acted like a Faraday cage and kept the EMP energy from affecting the Jeep." The wind whipped through their hair and John had a big grin on his face, splitting it from ear to ear.

He had to yell to be heard above the wind. "Get off on Clayton Road, go left to 2nd Street and make a right. You remember the Sheriff's Office, right? It's over on 3rd Street."

"Yeah, we called it the mausoleum."

John laughed. "That pretty well describes it." In a few minutes, after following John's directions, they pulled up in front of a five-story, concrete building. The yard was overgrown with tall grass and bushes and several cars in front of the building sat on flat tires, two with the doors thrown open. One of the windows on the first floor had been broken and was covered by a sheet of plywood.

They passed through the front door and entered a lobby with a service counter, and a door on either side. It looked like someone had taken a sledgehammer to the key-card security modules beside each door. The door on the left stood open and they entered a room filled with old, utilitarian desks.

A man and a woman sat at two of the desks. Appearing about 45 years old, the man had black hair and a black mustache drooping down on both sides. The woman was plump with round, pink cheeks and curly brown hair. They both had cups of coffee on their desks.

Surprised, the man stood up and grabbed a rifle from a rack behind his desk.

"Whoa, hold up there William," John said. "This is Terry Holcomb, his wife Izzy and their son Cody. Terry owned the big construction company out on the east side of town. They were doing the Highway 24 bypass, remember?"

"Oh yeah, I remember. Hi." He nodded at Izzy and Cody.

John motioned them to some chairs in a waiting area where they all took seats, Terry propping his feet up on the railing separating the area from the desks.

"This is Guillermo Fernandez and Rosa Collins.

"You can call me William," the man said.

"Coffee?" Rosa held up the pot.

"Yes, thanks. In Willsburg, they have to grow it in the greenhouse, and it's always in short supply."

"So," John said, "we all take turns hanging out at the Sheriff's station. Rosa makes a schedule for everyone and this is where anybody can go if they need to contact the others. It's kind of a central meeting place. Where have you guys been?" John asked.

"We had to leave town for a while. We were here when the bombs fell and we sheltered in our basement until it was safe to come up. Prior to the war, people called us 'preppers.' We had a year's worth of food and other supplies to get us through the worst part of the radiation. The problem was, that once people were able to start moving around they wanted what we had."

"We ran into the same problem," Rosa told them. "There are shelters around town stocked with supplies, mostly for unlikely events like blizzards or other disasters. A lot of people were saved by staying in those shelters for several months after the war. But there were others that tried to stay in their homes or came to the shelters too late and we couldn't let them in. Those few months through the winter were hell. We ran out of supplies and people died, but over 500 made it through to spring. When we started trying to come out of the shelters we were attacked and had to fight back against our own neighbors. To this day, we have no idea how they survived the aftermath of the war."

"We had to turn away some of our best friends," Izzy said, remembering how they had turned away Max and Lily. "We gave them food and supplies but they had already been exposed for too long and they were dying. We couldn't do any more for them." Tears sprung to her eyes and Rosa went into a glassed in office, formerly the Sheriff's Office, and brought her some tissue and a bottle of water.

"I'm very sorry, Izzy. I think we all have similar tales to tell. It was a very difficult time but things are getting better. Our supplies are limited, and we're having trouble growing food, but some ranchers have a small herd of cattle that somehow managed to survive the war and the first winter. They were able to shelter and feed them through the second winter and their numbers have actually grown, so we're confident we will always have beef. The ranchers make us trade things for the meat."

"Most of us don't think that's right," Guillermo told them. "They're lucky the cattle survived the war and I think they should share the meat with us."

John said, "We decided on a policy to turn away strangers since our supplies are low and we can't seem to grow very many crops. We have a barrier across the freeway at Raton Pass. We've had to turn away several groups from Trinidad to the north in

Colorado. They say the town has descended into anarchy and no one is safe."

Terry slowly sipped the hot coffee, savoring the taste and the aroma as the steam curled around his face. "That sucks. In Eagle Nest and Willsburg the townspeople set up an area for bartering. It seems to be fair. It's a little different though, because they're trading stuff they made themselves or meat from game they hunted."

"Another little problem we ran into," Terry continued, "was a creature we saw across the street from our house. We've seen several more since then and everybody thinks they were once men who were changed by the radiation into god-awful monsters."

"Yeah, we saw them too!" William exclaimed, his Hispanic accent stronger in his excitement. "They were vicious. We had to shoot them down like dogs, three of them. We think they were killing people and even eating them, since several of our people disappeared and we found partially consumed bodies."

"We haven't seen any for months," John said, "so we're pretty sure we got them all. Thank God. So you went to Eagle Nest when you left Raton?"

"Yeah. We had some trouble there, but we ran into a group of people that had spent the war, and the first winter, in an underground bomb shelter and they helped us. We're with a group of them now and would like you all to meet them. They're good people and won't cause you any trouble. They're on their way to California to try to find out what's happened since the war, and to see if anything's left on the coast. Izzy and I would like to stay here. It's our home. Right, Iz?"

She realized that she wanted nothing else. She was home. "Yes, we really want to stay. Three of our children are with us and our oldest daughter, who just got married, is still living in Willsburg. We can visit them and hopefully she and Tucker will move here."

William shifted in his chair. "I don't know about that. We'll have to call a meeting and see if the others wanna let you stay."

"What do you mean, 'let us stay'? This is our home and we have as much right to be here as you do," Terry bristled. His feet slammed to the floor.

"Look, we can help you," Izzy told him, putting her hand on Terry's arm, trying to calm his infamous temper. "We have heirloom seeds that will grow from year-to-year and we can teach you how to save the seeds. We have the Jeep and survival skills. I really think you should reconsider your policy of not allowing strangers to enter Raton. Willsburg, Eagle Nest and Angel Fire have all banded together to form the New Mexico colony. They help each other out, they trade with each other and they're stronger for it. It's the choice of your community, of course, but we will all be better off if we work together."

John looked at William and Rosa. "It just might be time to do that. Let's start by inviting your friends for lunch."

7

Game was definitely more abundant this year than last. Jon was discovering more each day in his traps. He even spotted a small herd of deer in the hills and he could see the polka dot hides of two or three fawns. He'd been worried that the radiation had sterilized the wild animals, so the fawns were a welcome sight. If they would allow him weapons he could have brought down the buck he saw at the top of the hill. Even after eight months they still didn't trust him not to run.

Although they didn't allow him weapons, he could hear the reports of rifles in the distance and knew that some of the other men were out hunting. At the time the bombs fell, this group of men and women had been on a corporate retreat in Telluride. They were completely unskilled in anything useful, like survival techniques, and proved to be incapable of procuring their own food. John was thankful for that, as it meant that they still needed him. He was worried however, that one of them would get lucky and bring down one of the does or fawn. Their continued survival depended on the animals being able to reproduce.

He filled his water containers from a tiny creek and moved from trap to trap adding the small game to the satchel he carried. Lingering by the creek, he cleaned the game before heading home. Although he couldn't be sure, he was concerned that some of the men were becoming suspicious of him. Jamison had asked him only yesterday why he was always gone all day to bring back such a small amount of game. He began to vary the route to ensure no one followed him home. When he arrived at the old wooden house on the east side of town he went around to the side yard. He grinned when he saw the rows of turned soil where Mary was carefully planting her seeds, while the boys played in the corner, digging holes with plastic trowels.

Little Josh, spotting him first, let out a squeal and ran to him. Jon knelt just in time to receive the little boy into his arms. Josh was followed quickly by Jason and Mary.

"Shh, be quiet boys." He held his finger over his lips. "We don't want the bad guys to hear us. Go back and dig your holes while I talk to Mommy, okay?" He hugged Mary and led her to the corner of the house where they sat on the ground, their backs against the wall. Opening the blood-stained satchel, he handed her a plastic bag filled with the carcasses of two rabbits.

He signed to her, "Mary, I think we need to get out of here. I've noticed some of the guys watching me more closely and Ben said he didn't think I was catching as much game as he thought I could."

"But Jon, where can we go? How would we get there?"

"I'm going to try and find a car. They can't all be broken. I tried a few when we first came up out of the basement but none of them worked, so I quit trying. I read somewhere that an EMP would fry the electronics in the car, but I also heard that if the EMP was inconsistent that some, especially if they were in a metal building or garage, would escape damage. Maybe they just have a dead battery. Anyway I have to try because I think they're on to me."

"Do you think we're in any danger?"

"I don't think so yet, but if they follow me and I don't detect them, they might find you. I just want to get ready, in case. I just don't understand it. These guys were all civilized, corporate employees. I heard from one of the other men that Ben was a really nice guy. As soon as the world changed, so did he. The power's gone to his head and he acts like a petty gangster. I don't know what it's like anywhere else, but I think we need to get out of here and find out."

He reached in his pocket and handed her a small, round, cellophane-wrapped cheese. "I've already started to look for a car and I found this in a small refrigerator in one of the garages. I don't know if it's any good. Be sure to check it out before you guys eat it." He stood up and pulled her to her feet, kissing her. He hugged the boys, spun on his heel and hurried away as he always did, unable to prolong the parting.

***

Matthew and Einstein sat astride their horses, with Jimbo on his motorcycle, and Jesse, Carlos and Chang standing beside them, as they all watched the last of their friends disappear through the open gate in the chain-link fence. These men were skeptical of the invitation they received from the townspeople, but most of the rest of their party had eagerly accepted. Greg and Mike were on guard duty.

"I still don't like it," Carlos said. "We don't know if we can trust these guys." Carlos was in his forties, and a small wiry man with a head full of thick, black hair. Deep lines emanating from his brown eyes made him look like he was always smiling.

"Maybe not, but Terry seemed to think it was okay. I'm glad they decided to leave the wagons back where we're camped," Einstein said.

"Yeah, that would've been too big a temptation," Jimbo told them. "I'll see you guys back there." He stood on the kick starter of the old Indian motorbike and it roared to life. Jimbo swung it around and shot off toward the wagon train. Matthew looked over at Einstein and nodded. Einstein reined his horse around and started toward the freeway while Matthew rode toward the western portion of Raton. Riding onto a small rise, he glanced back to see Einstein crossing the freeway to take up a position at the other end of the chain link fence. The other men walked back a hundred yards to where they'd left the horses and mules, and mounting up, followed Jimbo toward the West and their camp.

***

As they passed through the gate and it closed behind them, Mark had a sudden sense of anxiety. Lori rode behind him on Jasper and he could feel the tenseness in her body as she too was concerned about the reception they would receive. Sitting on the freeway fifty yards ahead was the Jeep, with Terry, Izzy, Cody and the girls. They seemed at ease and this lifted Mark's spirits. Chris and Aaron had remained at the wagon train to care for the children, as no one was willing to take a chance with their kids.

The Yancey boys were mounted, Bob riding behind Sam, and Sheri was riding her bike. Danny and Skillet were on foot, so when they reached the Jeep they jumped onto the running boards, hanging on to the roof. Eydie Scoffield was riding double with Willy Yancey. They had decided to minimize the number of horses they would take into Raton in case some of the townspeople decided to rustle them. Although Terry had vouched for these people, they didn't want to take any chances.

"Hi folks," Terry greeted them, "it's three or four miles to town center. They're putting together a barbecue for us and they're anxious to hear about our experiences. Hey Eydie, I think if we scrunched together you can fit in the Jeep." She gratefully climbed down from Willy's horse and they made room for her in the Jeep. Wanting to stay together they proceeded at a comfortable pace for the horses.

They arrived at the Sheriff's station where they found close to a hundred people waiting for them. Again, Mark felt his gut clench as they were completely outnumbered if anything went wrong, but he soon found he didn't have anything to worry about. Even though these people had a closed community they were friendly enough when they realized Mark and his group were no danger to them. Willy Yancey stayed with the horses and kept an eye on Sheri's bike while the others entered the building. They found that a large first floor room had been cleared of desks, filing cabinets and chairs and had been set up with tables loaded with food. There were meat and potatoes, but Mark noticed there wasn't much produce. With the season being early, Mark knew Izzy would have plenty of produce to barter in a couple of months.

When they entered the room, Izzy squealed with delight and hurried forward to hug three women she recognized from before the war. The four of them drew to one side of the room to catch up with mutual tales of survival and hardship.

As they ate, John and the others quizzed them about the conditions on the outside, hungry for news from beyond their borders. "The whole reason we're heading for California is to get that information," Mark told them. "We came from Eagle Nest which is kind of central between Red River, Angel Fire, Cimarron and Willsburg. We really haven't seen anyplace else. So I'm afraid I don't have an awful lot to report to you."

"What about the radiation?" John asked him. "You folks are living closer to Albuquerque and Los Alamos. The radiation must be stronger down that way."

"We have instruments that can detect it. We know it's safe down to Angel Fire. One of our guys took a Geiger counter down the highway and he started getting upticks about 20 miles south of there so he hightailed it back. We sent someone up to Taos and that seemed clean as well, so we have some people talking about moving up there since it had a much larger population with a lot of stores and a lot of supplies."

"Do you think you could take your Geiger counter up to the Raton Pass? We're kind of worried about the possibility of radiation coming down from the Colorado Springs area. They had a lot of military bases and Cheyenne Mountain, which would've been targets."

"What do you think, Terry? Can you take me and Lori up to the pass?"

Guillermo was rubbing his drooping mustache first left than right. "Now wait just a minute. I hope you have your own gas 'cause you can't be using any of ours. You can't just come in here and start using up our supplies."

"I told you before, this town is my home, too." Terry jumped to his feet.

"Well you abandoned it, so you don't have any rights here anymore!"

"We didn't abandon it. We've been on vacation asshole… at the French Riviera. You can't just claim someone's property because they've been gone awhile."

Mark took Terry's arm and John got between the two men, angrily pushing William back.

"You know what, William, they're doing us a favor. A lot of us have been worried about radiation. Even if we have to give them some gas it's worth it. Your own son spends a lot of time in that pass." He waved off others that had approached at the sound of the argument. "Let's just enjoy lunch and listen to Mark's story."

"Yeah Mark, I'll take you up there. It's okay, John, I have my own gas. We'll be fine." Of the ninety people or so that had greeted them initially about fifty had entered the building to participate in the barbecue. Mark noticed that everyone but the guests had paid for their meal with silver coin or small jewels about the size you would find in a ring. He realized that most of the townspeople had perished in the war and that many of them had diamond rings or jewelry with other gems. *So this is the new currency*, he thought.

After Mark had told the story of the shelter and the 'Battle of Platte Rock' they all sat with empty paper plates in front of them and cups of hot coffee on the table. Most of the others had left to walk back to their homes.

"Izzy and I are pretty anxious to go out to our house and see what kind of condition it's in. If you've all finished lunch, you want to come out with us?"

"We're going to need to send a guard with you," Guillermo said. "We're not ready to trust you yet, and as long as your friends are in town, we'll just send a couple guys along to keep an eye on you. We can't take a chance on any of our supplies going missing." They had insisted that Mark's group come into town unarmed and they had complied. Now they found themselves under armed guard as they left the building and headed for Terry's house.

"We live out west by the golf course," Terry said. "It's only a couple of miles. You guys with the guns, I guess you'll have to walk." He looked over at Mark and grinned and Mark knew exactly what he was thinking as Terry gunned the Jeep. The horses took off behind him with Sheri standing on her pedals, having no trouble keeping up with the horses. The armed guards were left in the dust.

Izzy was nervous. She hadn't seen her home in almost a year and she wasn't sure how she would feel about it. But when they rounded the corner and the house came into view she knew everything was going to be just fine.

"Wow," Cody yelled, "it looks just the same. Well, except for all the weeds." Terry coasted the Jeep to the curb in front of the house and they all got out and went up the walk. They'd left in a hurry but had locked the front door out of habit. Terry moved a small brick out of place on the front of the house, and retrieving a key, opened the front door.

"Terry," Mark said, "I think we'll all wait out while you guys go in. You can call us when you're ready."

"Thanks Mark. I think we'd like a few minutes alone." Terry and his family entered the house, walking through the entryway into the living room. Izzy had thought the house might be trashed but other than a layer of dust was just as they had left it. Without speaking, Cody went to his own room and Missy and Kris to the room they shared.

"Hey," Missy said, "I guess I can have Marci's room." She hurried down the hallway to the room her older sister had occupied.

As soon as Izzy walked into the master bedroom she burst into tears. Terry enfolded her in his arms and held her for several minutes. "It seems as if we never left and the last year has been a dream. But once we walk outside this house we know what reality is," he whispered to her. "But everything's gonna be okay now."

"I know. It'll take some getting used to since the world is definitely different than it was before, but I feel like we can start our life over here and have a sense of normalcy. I'm okay now." She backed away and wiped the tears off her cheeks. "I'm going out back to check my garden area and see what it will take to get it going again." The sadness over, they were now excited about getting back to their life.

"I'm gonna check my garage. I have a lot of tools and supplies out there that we couldn't take with us and I hope nobody has had a chance to steal them. The remaining population of Raton is pretty small so they probably haven't had a chance to raid every house and take anything they could find. And I have a few surprises. Hopefully nobody found out about my underground gas tank." They walked back out into the living room and found Cody standing in the center of the room holding his Xbox.

"I don't suppose this thing is ever going to work again," he said, the corner of his mouth quirked up in a wry grin.

"No son, I don't think it ever will. But we still have the family games in the basement and decks of cards. We're gonna be fine."

Terry went out and brought the others into the house. It seemed strange to them to be in a normal pre-war home. In Willsburg they had all lived in log cabins they'd built to get ready for the last winter. Mark, Skillet, and the Yancey boys went with Terry out to the garage. It didn't look like anyone had been there or stolen anything.

"Wait until you see this," Terry said, and he led them to a metal storage garage in the back. "This is where I kept my Jeep. It's a metal building and it's grounded so it conducted the EMP energy away from it." He led them to the rear of the building where he showed them a false wall that partitioned off a space six feet by the width of the garage. A door behind a shelf unit led into the space. It was crammed full of supplies: dehydrated food, nonelectric tools and other survival supplies.

"And over here I have a pump that I can use to get the gas out of my underground tank. The gas is stabilized so it should last five years or so. If we don't do too much driving the gas should last us until it goes bad. I realize my good Raton neighbors are going to be jealous, but they're jealous of the farmers and ranchers and haven't tried to kill them or steal from them. Funny how those who didn't prepare think that those who did should share their possessions with them."

"Yeah," Mark said, "human nature, I guess."

"Well, let's head up to the pass and see what kind of radiation reading we get." Terry led them back to the house where they found the women sitting around the dining room table as if the calamity of the war had never happened. Mark could hear the voices of the Holcomb kids coming from the basement.

"Were heading up to the pass, anybody want to go with us?" Terry asked.

Izzy looked at the faces of the other women and shook her head. "No, we're good. It feels so good to be home in a normal house."

"Izzy showed us your little cache in the back of the hall closet. Nice little hidden space you have there." Lori held up an AR-15 with a thirty round magazine.

"Me, Jimbo and Willy will stay here with the girls. You got any more of those weapons?"

"Yeah, Sam," Terry told him. "There are several more rifles, a few handguns, and boxes of ammo. You guys should be fine while we're gone. Me, Mark and Skillet will head on up and get the radiation readings and be back in a couple of hours."

The three men went out and climbed in the Jeep and Terry swung around heading back toward town. A couple blocks away they passed their guards still heading toward Terry's house. The men waved their arms trying to flag down the Jeep, and as it sped beyond them Terry laughed as one of the men kicked a pile of rocks, sending them flying. "He seems a tad upset."

"What are they doing, Terry?"

Terry looked in the rearview mirror. "They're turning around and heading back toward town. I don't think we have to worry about them bothering the girls or the guys."

It took them twenty minutes to get up to Raton Pass, once they hit the freeway. There was another chain link fence across the highway on the south side of the pass. Guards were posted, just like on the other side of town. An old, battered pickup truck was parked alongside the highway approximately fifty yards back from the barrier. Apparently they used this truck to transport the guards back and forth to town. The men had been briefed that Terry and the others would be coming.

One of the men walked toward them, a smaller, younger version of Guillermo, with shoulder-length, dark hair and a black, drooping mustache. But he had a large, welcoming grin on his face as he shook hands with the three men.

"I'm real happy to see you gentlemen. I'm Cullen. I think you met my old man in town. William? We've been kinda worried about pulling guard duty in this pass, not knowing if there's radiation coming down from Colorado Springs."

Mark looked beyond the barrier where he saw several groups of people sitting in front of tents. "It's been our experience that the radiation stays put. After the first few months when radioactive particles were carried by wind and rain it all seems to have settled down. The ground in areas where the H-bombs hit is probably radioactive but we haven't been in any of those areas to find out." He looked back at the people beyond the barrier. "Who are all those people?"

"They come from Trinidad, at the northern end of the pass. They tell us horror stories of what's going on down there. I guess a lot of people survived the initial radiation but the food's running out and there are rival gangs that kill anyone who won't join them. Most of these folks have families. I don't really agree with my dad about not letting them in town. But he has most of the townspeople on his side."

"You mean you just leave them out there?"

"After a while some of them go back down the mountain to Trinidad. But it seems like more of them just keep coming and their numbers are growing. None of them have any weapons so we don't think they're going to try and get in to Raton. I think the gangs have all the guns in town. They know the townspeople will kill them if they try to get by the barrier but they keep sending people to talk to us every day. They never give up."

"Would you? They have families and they're hungry. Can I go talk to them?"

"Sure, I don't see no harm."

"Terry, I'm gonna go talk to those people. Let me know when you have an accurate reading." Mark walked to the chain link fence and one of the guards opened the gate. He raised his hands in the air and took a few steps through the gate.

"Hey, you out there," he yelled. "Do you have a leader? I just want to talk to you guys."

The tent people had been sitting around on the ground or reclining in their tents. They all stood and a small group of four men approached Mark. Two were Hispanic, one black and one white man. Like most of the postwar males they had long hair and beards. The black man's hair had grown so long it poofed out in a huge Afro. He had attempted to style it into dreadlocks and the result was truly frightening.

"What's going on, man? You gonna let us in?" The black man asked him.

"No, I'm sorry. Me and my friends came from the South and are just visiting Raton. They let us in because one of my friends lived here but we'll be leaving tomorrow. I just wanted to tell you that there's a community about sixty-five miles south of here in Eagle Nest and the surrounding areas. They would welcome you. They're family-friendly and have schools and a Doctor."

"That's pretty far away. How do you expect us to get there?" one of the Hispanic men asked him.

"It looks like you guys have a few supplies, tents. You have any backpacks? You made it here from Trinidad."

"We got a few things. But we've got women and kids. That's a long way for them to walk. And they won't let us through on the highway. It makes it even longer if we have to go around through the mountains to get back down to the highway on the other side of Raton."

"How many of you are there?"

"We got six families with 11 kids. The youngest is only two."

"My friend has a Jeep. Maybe I can talk the townspeople into letting you pass through Raton. If my friend can give the youngest kids a ride to Eagle Nest the rest of you should be able to make it in less than two weeks."

"Man, there's no way my wife would let you take our kids."

"I understand, but you're going to die if you stay here. I don't even know if I can talk them into it but I'll try. I'll be back." He backed away for several steps and then turned and strode quickly back to the barrier where Cullen opened the gate to allow him through.

"What's it look like, Terry?"

"The Geiger counter indicates a very low level of radiation. Nothing to worry about. I didn't even turn on the scintillation counter because I don't want to waste the batteries. They're good to go. So what's the deal with the people over there?"

Mark took Terry's arm, led him to the side and spoke softly. "Do you think there's any way you could take a Jeep load of kids down to Eagle Nest? The rest of them could make the trip on foot. We just need your fellow townspeople to give them safe passage. You think they would do it?"

"They're probably pretty pissed off that we left their guards behind," he chuckled, "but I can't see why not. We've only been gone seven days but Izzy would love it if I can talk Tucker and Marcy into coming back with me. It would be worth the gas."

Terry turned to Cullen. "Here's the deal. We want to take the small children, pass through Raton and transport them to Eagle Nest, and we want the residents of Raton to let the adults and older children pass safely through to the South. You have weapons, they don't. You just need to let the guys at the South barrier know their coming and let us through. Nobody else in town will even know we're zipping down the highway."

"Oh man, my dad's gonna be ticked, but I really don't see it can hurt anything." He chewed his lip for few seconds. "Let's do it." He went over to another of the guards who seemed reluctant to let them through, but clearly, Cullen was their leader and Mark heard the other man agree.

"Okay, let me go see if they're game." He returned to the group of men.

"I'm Mark. Who are you guys?"

"I'm DeShawn," the black man told him. "This is Sanchez, he's Leo and the white dude over there is Palmer." Mark explained the situation and waited while they went to confer with the rest of the tent people. He could see a group of adults arguing and one of the women burst into tears, but he saw her nodding her head. Mark fidgeted, and looked around at the mountains and the pine forests, hoping these people would make the right decision. After ten minutes DeShawn returned.

"They're not happy about it but they'll do it. We're desperate, man. That's the only reason we would even consider this, but somehow I feel like you can be trusted."

"You won't be sorry. There are good people in Eagle Nest and Willsburg. You can contribute there and be happy. Bring the kids."

Mark went back to the open gate and waited until DeShawn, the two Hispanic men and a woman came through the gate carrying two toddlers and leading four others by the hand.

"This here's Carissa," DeShawn told Mark.

"They can't go unless I go with them," said the small black woman. "Me and the other mothers can't let them go with you alone. Please."

Mark looked over at Terry and Terry shrugged. "I guess we can all jam in together." Terry walked over to Cullen. "You don't have anything to worry about. The radiation level is very low.

I'm going to take these people to my house, then I'll come back for you. You can go with me to the south gate and tell them to let us through. Then I'll…"

"No need man. I have a radio. We try not to use it but I'll just radio ahead." He walked over to the old pickup and Mark saw him speaking into a handheld radio. Cullen nodded at them and they all piled into the Jeep. Terry drove and Mark rode shotgun with a four-year-old girl on his lap. Skillet sat behind Terry with a 2-year-old sitting on each knee and the woman Carissa, sat with her three-year-old on her lap. Another child sat on the seat between Carissa and Skillet and the oldest child, Beth, road behind the back seat.

Before they drove off Mark looked over and saw the tent people waving at them. He could only imagine the fear they felt with their children being carried off by total strangers. But he knew they felt it was their only hope and one of their own was a long to keep them safe.

DeShawn and the others would stay another night in the pass and pack up and start their journey in the morning. Cullen assured Mark and Terry that there would be no problem allowing safe passage for the tent people.

"I don't always agree with my dad. Now that we know there's a place for these people to go, maybe we can let others through."

In another half hour they had arrived back at Terry's house, Izzy and the others surprised to see a Jeep full of children pull up.

Lori shook her head. "I can't leave you guys alone for a second."

"There was nothing else we could do," Mark explained, "we just couldn't leave them camped out on the freeway with no food and nowhere to go." Lori came over and gave him a hug.

"That's why I love you," she whispered.

They brought everyone into the house, broke out some dehydrated food and fed Carissa and the children.

"It's only 3 o'clock," Terry said. "Me and Carissa will drive the kids down to Eagle Nest. I'm going to drive up to

Willsburg and see if Tucker and Marcy are ready to come back with me. Either way, I'll spend the night and be back in the morning." He walked over and put his hands on Izzy's shoulders. "I know you'd like to go with me Izzy but there just isn't enough room in the Jeep."

"I know honey, we'll be fine. We're home."

Terry took a rifle and stashed it between the front seats of the Jeep. Beth rode in front with Terry, and Carissa sat in back with the other children. They all waved as the Jeep pulled away from the curb. Izzy had tears in her eyes and Lori put her arm across her shoulders.

"Don't worry Izzy, they'll be down there in an hour and a half. It's funny, sixty-five miles is nothing in a Jeep and it took us seven days to get here with our wagon train."

8

Being more careful than ever, Jon checked every corner and peeked over every fence to ensure he wasn't being followed. Once he entered the forest he picked up speed and rechecked all of his traps. "Uh oh. I'm going to be in trouble," he murmured. He still had the carcasses of a squirrel and a rabbit and he prayed it would be enough as all of the traps were empty. Spending another hour collecting roots and plants, he didn't get back to the Parker Hotel until almost dark.

As Jon entered the hotel, he could tell immediately that Ben was pissed off.

"Where the hell have you been?" He threw an empty beer can into the corner. "I sent some guys out looking for you and they couldn't find you anywhere. We've decided to get out of this town and you're the only one from around here. If we stay, we'll all starve to death. What other towns are in this area?"

Jon's mind was racing. He was near panic. "Ah, I don't know Ben. There's Cortez, about forty-five miles west of here, and Farmington and Bloomfield about fifty miles south, on Highway 550. Farmington's the largest town in the area. I couldn't tell you if they're any better off than we are. You know, there's a lot more game now that winter is over. I swear, I'll bring back more."

Ben squinted over at Jon. "Why do you care? You aren't even from here. You said you came from Pagosa Springs at about the same time we arrived in Durango, so it shouldn't matter to you whether we leave here are not. You got something going on we don't know about?"

"No Ben. It doesn't matter to me. It just seems strange to leave now when the hunting is getting better. That's all."

"Well we want out of this town. I've been thinking about getting back to Denver but we have to take it one step at a time. You're coming with us, 'cause we need you to keep food on the table."

Jon looked around at the dozen or so people in the room. He stammered, "I... I kind of thought I could maybe go home. You know, back to Pagosa Springs. I'm not sure why I left in the first place. I was looking for a place with better hunting."

Ben glanced over at Vance and they both laughed. "You're not going anywhere, boy. You're coming with us and you're going to keep us fed or there will be hell to pay. There isn't any other reason you want to go to Pagosa, is there?"

Jon looked at the floor and shook his head.

"We're gonna leave in a couple of weeks, as soon as we figure out where we're going. Be ready."

Jon lifted the strap of the satchel over his head and headed back to the kitchen. Putting the two carcasses on the sink, he nodded at Jessica and Paul. Jessica had been the vice president of Jensen and Kroft Manufacturing and Paul was her staff assistant. Now they were just two people trying to survive in a very different world than what they were used to.

"Is that all you found?" she asked him. "It's not going to stretch very far. Did you already eat?"

"No, that's all that was in the traps."

She flashed him a brilliant smile and tucked her wavy, long hair behind her ear. "Well, I hope Ben will let you eat."

Jon raced up the two flights of stairs to his room and fished in the back of the closet for his flashlight. Hoping the batteries hadn't gone dead he turned it on, relieved when it emitted a steady beam of light. He put it in the front pocket of his satchel. Not daring to leave until after dinner he went back downstairs and took his usual spot at the end of the table in the dining room where they all ate. He took a miniscule spoonful of the stew.

"I gotta tell you Jon, I'm getting sick of rabbit and squirrel. Those traps of yours don't ever catch anything different?" Ben waved a fork at him.

"I could bring down a deer if you let me have a rifle," he told him. "I saw some on the ridge behind the college today."

"Oh yeah? Well, that ain't going to happen so don't ever ask again. Take Vance and Paul with you tomorrow and show them where the deer are. Maybe one of them can bring home the bacon... or the venison." He laughed at his own joke.

After dinner, Jon went back to his room. He rummaged in the closet for the little metal box that held his working Timex. It was his sports watch, and had been in the box when the EMP hit, apparently providing some shielding... because it still worked. He kept it hidden, since he knew Ben would take it from him if he saw it. Stretching out on the bed, he tried to take a quick nap. He'd been clearly told, when they first captured him, that he wasn't welcome in their group, so he wasn't worried they would miss him. Setting the alarm on his Timex for midnight, he tossed and turned for an hour, finally falling into a troubled sleep.

Awakened by the soft beeping, Jon quickly sat up and pushed the button to silence it. Grabbing the satchel, he tiptoed to the door and carefully, quietly unlocked it. He had never gone out at night and didn't even know if they set a guard. He turned right and went to the back staircase being as quiet as possible, listening for any sounds of pursuit. As he opened the door it made a small squeak, and he paused, waiting a full minute before proceeding. When he didn't hear any sounds out of the darkness he slipped through the opening and pulled the door closed. Descending rapidly, he pushed through the emergency door at the rear of the hotel and exited into the alleyway.

He went past the railway station and across the bridge to the neighborhoods on the west side of town. The moon was full and he left the flashlight off until he needed it after entering the houses.

It was a long night.

He searched two entire neighborhoods. First, he would enter a house looking for the keys to a car. He found them more often than he thought he would since they were usually somewhere near the front door, on an entryway table, hanging on a key holder in the entryway or on a kitchen counter. He found a few in the bedroom on the dresser. By now any bodies left in the houses had deteriorated. Although hair and flesh still clung to the bones, there was very little odor. As he searched through the homes, he had an eerie feeling he was being watched by those silent beings.

The night was a bust. In hours of searching not one of the cars started up. He realized the batteries were all dead and there was no way for him to know whether or not the electronics had been destroyed. He would need to try a different approach. Time was running out, but tomorrow he would search an auto parts store for a battery and hide it away for another attempt tomorrow night.

Bitterly disappointed, he snuck back to his room in the old hotel, catching two more hours of sleep before he was back up to begin a new day of hunting.

***

They'd played Scrabble and Yahtzee until well after midnight. Izzy spent the first night at home alone, while the kids slept in their own beds and the others crashed on couches in the living room and basement.

She had lain in bed staring up at the ceiling, thinking she would wake up in the morning and send the kids off to school. She and Terry would go off to their old jobs and life would go on as if the war had never happened. Then she ran through all that had transpired since the war, trying to get her head back into the present. The months in the basement and the horrible incident when they turned their best friends away.

She re-lived the flight from Raton, when they tried to get to the mountains to establish a retreat for survival. Terry and Marcie's capture and she and Cody rescuing them. She relived killing a man, and Cody being critically wounded. Meeting with the shelter people and getting their lives back to a semblance of normal. She finally fell into a restless sleep.

When Mark and Lori awoke the next morning they smelled bacon frying, mixed with the smell of fresh coffee. They dragged themselves out of bed even though they'd only slept six hours. Upstairs they found Skillet hard at work.

"Umm, that dehydrated bacon smells just like the real thing," Lori said. As she tried to snatch a piece, Skillet slapped her hand and she laughed and jumped away.

"It's nice to cook on a propane stove instead of a campfire."

"Yeah, but you make really good meals on that campfire," Mark said, as he gratefully accepted a cup of coffee. Soon others were drifting in, drawn by the irresistible smell of the bacon. Cody and the Holcomb girls took their plates to the breakfast nook and the adults sat at the dining room table. Just as they finished their breakfast they heard the sound of an engine and Izzy jumped up and ran to the front door.

Throwing open the door she gave Terry a big, bear hug. "Honey, you're back earlier than I expected." She looked beyond his shoulder to the front yard. "No Marci?"

"No, but they're fine. I told them what happened and they both agreed to think about moving home." They went into the house and Skillet slapped a plate down in front of Terry.

"So how did it go?" Lori asked him.

"Instead of Eagle Nest, I took them up to Willsburg. Thought they should be checked out by Dr. Jim. They put them up in your cabin, but Dr. Jim said once the rest of their families get there, they'll find places for them to stay." He looked over at Mark. "When are you guys leaving?"

"I guess right after we all finish breakfast."

They all jumped when there was a loud knock at the door. Terry pulled his Glock 19 and approached the door, while three of the others followed behind, rifles pointed at the forward.

"Who's there? Identify yourselves."

"Hey Terry, it's John. Can I come in?"

Terry pulled open the door and John's eyes widened at the sight of the armament.

"Shit, Terry, are you expecting a home invasion?"

"Sorry, John, but we're pretty security conscious. Come on in. You alone?"

"Yep, just me."

He nodded at the others and Terry led the way into the living room.

"Want some breakfast?" Skillet asked.

"Ah, thanks." Skillet already had the plate of food and a fork and handed them to John with a cup of coffee.

"Look, I just wanted you to know that almost everyone in town is glad you're here. I, for one, know you have a lot to bring to the community." He was shoveling eggs into his mouth.

"Do we need to worry about William?"

"No. He's all talk. Cullen told him about you letting the folks from Trinidad travel down the highway. He was pretty upset and he has some guys escorting them through town this morning. I'm going to ask for a vote to allow any others to pass through on their way to Eagle Nest."

"I'm glad to hear it," Mark said. "They really need more people. There's so much work to be done."

John had cleaned his plate and stood to go. "I'll just hoof it back to town. Izzy, did you say you had some seeds? We didn't know what we were doing and planted all the ones we could find in the first summer. Very few of them produced seeds, so we're short on vegetables."

She went to the kitchen and returned with a can the size of a pound of coffee. "There are enough seeds here for about an acre of plants. I'll be putting in my first crop in a day or two. Even between the two of us there probably won't be enough for everyone. I'll be bartering for meat from the ranchers. Let me know when you have your crop in and I'll teach you to save the seeds for next year."

"Thanks. You guys are great. See ya later." He waved as he left the house and started up the street toward town.

Terry grinned. "It's nice to have an ally."

When the group returned to their coffee in the dining room Bob said to Terry, "Ahh… me and Eydie were wondering if we could stay here. We could pick a house in the neighborhood and could help with the garden and security. We'll be in good shape pretty soon. I was a handyman and know some trades."

Terry grinned at him. "I don't see why not. It would be worth it to see the look on old Guillermo's face."

"That would be wonderful," Izzy said. "It won't seem so isolated with you guys close by."

Reluctant to leave the Holcombs and Bob and Eydie behind, they all wasted time with small talk, eventually running out of things to say.

Saying goodbye was hard. Mark stuck out his hand and shook Terry's. "Terry, I can't thank you enough for everything you guys did for us. I'm glad you found your home and I wish you the very best. Terry pulled him into an embrace patting him on the back.

"You guys did as much for us as we did for you. If you're ever back this way look us up." The Yancey boys had spent the night in the backyard with the horses. They rode around the corner of the house leading the other two mounts. Skillet climbed up behind Sam. Mark and Lori sat on Jasper waving at the kids looking out at them through their bedroom windows.

Sheri and Danny would *ride and tie*, a method of travel where one person would ride ahead on the bike, leave it in the road and start running. The other person would run until they got the bike, climb aboard and ride past the runner for another mile or two, leave the bike and start running. A very effective way for two people and one bike or horse to travel, as neither of the runners would become overly tired.

When they reached the barrier the guards threw open the gate, and they left Raton, New Mexico, and the Holcombs, behind.

9

The dark shadow ascended from the depths of the ocean, gliding through the waters off the coast of California. The massive form crossed the continental shelf break and moved into shallower water. But this was no shark or whale. At 576 feet in length, almost as long as two football fields, with a 42 foot beam, and towering three stories from the bottom of the hull to the deck above, the *U.S.S. Louisiana* was all that was left of the United States, pre-war submarine fleet. She had survived by diving to 800 feet while the nuclear rain of death fell upon the world, and cruising along the West Coast for three months before surfacing. An *Ohio* Class SSBN, or nuclear ballistic missile submarine, this boat could run underwater indefinitely if not for the need of her human crew for food and supplies. She had only been a week into her seventy day mission out of Bangor, Washington when the Chinese had launched their attack.

China, with a much smaller nuclear arsenal than Russia or the United States, hit both countries simultaneously, knowing they would retaliate not only against them, but would destroy one another in the process. The plan worked to perfection, not only causing the U.S. and Russia to attack each other, but to launch missiles against most of the rest of the civilized world.

All of the other countries with nuclear capability had unleashed their arsenals as soon as the U.S., Russia and China had started lobbing theirs. Israel hit several Mid-Eastern Countries, as France and the U.K. bombed Russia, the Mideast, and the southern countries of the old Soviet Union. India and Pakistan bombed each other. North Korea attempted to hit South Korea, but their bombs failed to detonate... and China obliterated Japan.

South America and Sub-Saharan Africa actually escaped the initial blasts of hydrogen bombs but over the next few months the radiation soaked atmosphere cleansed the land of billions of human and animal life forms. Those that survived were unprepared to carry on. Only in the Andes, parts of Asia and other areas where indigenous populations were capable of subsistence farming and had lived for millennia without power, did groups of people endure.

The seven blade screw slowed its rotation.

"Bring us to periscope depth, Carter," the Captain told the Chief Petty Officer.

"Level off at 75 feet," Carter said. "All stop."

The XO examined the sea, as he moved the periscope through a 360 degree rotation, finally coming to rest on the oil platform lying 100 yards to port. "All clear, Captain. Periscope down," he drawled in his Mississippi accent. The XO, a Lieutenant Commander, was a stocky man, with his thick, red hair trimmed in a flat top. After finishing Officer Training School, he had risen swiftly through the ranks and had just received his first assignment as an executive officer when the war broke out. Before joining the Navy, the only body of water he had ever seen was the wide, muddy Mississippi River, but he had taken to the water... to the ocean, like a porpoise.

Kyle Crane, the Communications Officer approached Captain Dombrowski. "Captain, the boat's on its way."

"Let's get going then. How long ago was the transmission?"

"About an hour, sir. It was very clear for a few words before the static resumed. Radioman Santana is trying to get it back."

He turned to the XO. "You have the conn, Mr. Finney."

Captain Richard Dombrowski, Commanding Officer of the Gold crew of the *Louisiana*, climbed the ladder to the deck of the boat. As his head rose above the edge of the hatch he felt the wind for the first time in over two months and he drank in the salty spray. He loved the ocean, and when underwater he missed it, even though he and his crew were in the embrace of the sea.

The submarine crew, standing at attention, saluted as Capt. Dombrowski raised his lanky body through the hatch onto the deck.

"At ease," he said, as he returned the salute. Dombrowski walked down the deck and turned to the west, to the unlimited expanse of ocean that stretched over the horizon to the country that had started the war, and then turned back around to the oil rig they had made their base. He could see the California coastline beyond the rig, with poisonous strips of land to the north and south of their position. According to their instruments, only a narrow ribbon from Point Arguello inland across Vandenberg Air Force Base and the city of Lompoc, was safe from radiation. This corridor of safety allowed them to replenish their food and supplies from the military facility.

He raised his ball cap and ran his fingers through his thinning hair. Reseating the cap, and hands behind his back, he addressed his men.

"Gentlemen," he called out loudly to the men stretched down the deck, "you are the best the Navy has to offer. Every single one of you is a volunteer from the regular Navy. You went through exhausting training, including physical and mental training. You went through tough psychological testing to ensure you could stand the stress and live in the confined environment of a nuclear submarine." He walked down the deck looking each man in the eye as he passed him. "You earned those dolphins on your lapels, and I am proud of each and every one of you." Reaching the end of the line of men, he turned and started back down the line.

"The *Louisiana* has distinguished herself in both peacetime missions and in war. She was the last United States nuclear submarine to come out of Groton, Connecticut and she has earned recognition for both her crews, the Gold and the Blue. But now gentlemen, the Blue crew is gone and our home base at Bangor has been destroyed by the enemy. We are quite possibly the last member of the United States nuclear triad. All of the missiles in the ground based nuclear arsenal were launched immediately following the detection of incoming ICBMs from Russia and China. This of course was necessary to ensure those missiles were fired before the silos were destroyed by enemy action. The second part of the triad, our fleet of missile carrying bombers, the B-52s and stealth bombers took the war to the enemy. In peacetime, of course, these planes ran simulated missions, with mid-air refueling, and returned to base. During wartime, with no refueling, and no place to return to, these planes and their brave crews were probably lost."

The captain looked beyond his men and saw the boat sliding across the calm sea toward the submarine. "We have no way of knowing if any of the other thirteen boats in the nuclear submarine fleet survived but we haven't had any contact with any of them. After launching their full complement of submarine-based ballistic missiles I suspect most of them put off their crews and the boats were abandoned." Dombrowski took a deep breath of the salty ocean air.

"We've continued to patrol the Pacific Coast to ensure the safety of the nation. After each seventy day mission we've returned to this platform to replenish our supplies and to try and contact the legally established government of this country. I'm sorry to say that each time we've returned to Vandenberg we've lost crew members who have gone ashore and not returned. Of the original one hundred and forty crew members and fifteen officers we have one hundred and three sailors and twelve officers. You men have had an opportunity to leave, but have stuck with me, and for that I thank you. Your dedication to duty is commendable. At some point in the future, when we determine there is no further danger to the United States, we may decommission this boat and everyone will have an opportunity to try and make their way home."

"We've had trouble establishing communications with anyone since the war. But recently the ionosphere seems to be settling down and we have been getting squawks from what appears to be the East Coast. In the last transmission we were able to make out enough words to be able to tell it was a focused message meant specifically for us. And gentlemen, we think the message is from the President of the United States." He paused to let that sink in. "It's possible that we are about to find out if we have a mission."

The Captain looked over at the Chief Petty Officer and nodded. "Atten...hut!" he shouted and the line of sailors snapped to attention.

"Chief, maintain our standard eighteen hour rotation but give one third of the men twenty four hours off the boat at a time."

"As you were men," The Captain said, and the men fell out to return to their duties. The twenty foot skiff pulled alongside the sub and sailors on the deck of the vessel extended a gangway to the sub's deck. This boat would ferry the Captain to the gigantic oil rig 100 yards to port. Platform Harvest stood over the wellhead at a depth of 675 feet and stood seven miles from the mainland. It was one of twenty three platforms in federal waters that pumped oil from the Tranquillon Ridge oil fields.

The men held the gangway steady as the captain crossed over to the deck of the boat. The gangway was withdrawn and the boat slowly moved away for twenty yards and then accelerated toward the enormous oil rig.

Dombrowski moved forward along the edge of the boat, past the small cabin to the front, where he held on to the railing and felt the spray kick up as the bow sliced through the water. They had stopped the sub a hundred yards from the platform to ensure they didn't collide with it if the seas became rougher, and to make sure they maintained a safe distance from the flexible piping that stretched from the wellhead to the platform. They had chosen Platform Harvest as their base of operations, at seven miles offshore, rather than Platform Irene, which stood just off Point Arguello. Although closer to shore, Irene had extended wellheads with underwater paraphernalia that could create a problem for the *Louisiana*. There was no way for the sub to approach the mainland, as this part of the Pacific was known as the *Graveyard of the Pacific,* due to underwater seamounts, rocks and the wrecks of over fifty unfortunate vessels that had crushed their hulls against those underwater obstacles.

The boat cut power and drifted under the floating city to a small dock. Dombrowski and several sailors climbed the stairs to a number of offices, including a small bunk room the captain used when in port. He walked behind the desk and examined a large map pinned to the wall. It showed the location of the oil rigs and the boundaries of the underwater oil fields with the mainland covering the right hand side of the map. Beyond point Arguello, running north along the coast was the 99,000 acres of Vandenberg Air Force Base.

Three months after the war, when they first surfaced, they cruised up and down the coast trying to find an intact port they could make their base. Radiation detectors indicated that their home port of Bangor had been hit, as well as San Diego. Unable to find any land based ports they eventually docked at Platform Harvest. After repairing the two boats they found moored at the oil rig they went to shore, discovering a small contingent of Air Force personnel maintaining the base.

Colonel Benjamin Packer was in charge and was very relieved to see the crew of the submarine approaching the dock. Aside from a couple of hundred civilians in Lompoc they had wondered if they were the only people left in the world. Since that time the sub crew had gone ashore on several occasions and found the Air Force personnel more than willing to assist them in gathering supplies for transport to the sub.

"Captain Dombrowski, the Air Force communications staff, and our technicians we left here in February, have completed the new antenna and it's now operational. Sir, whenever you're ready they will make another attempt to contact the government."

"Mr. Holder, have the mess prepare lunch and ask the ship's officers that are on the platform to join me. We will make the attempt at communication this afternoon."

"Yes sir."

Four of the ship's officers met with Dombrowski for their first meal off the sub in over two months.

"Gentlemen it's been a long 21 months, not knowing if we still had a country or a government. Hopefully today we will get some direction."

"Yes sir," Crane said, "but it still may take us quite a while to make contact. The messages have been clearer lately but we still haven't been able to keep up the link for any length of time." The short, thin, communications officer sounded worried.

"True, Mr. Crane, but I am prepared to stay here until that link is established."

"Captain, the men are wondering how long we'll continue to man this boat. I guess once we're able to contact the government, we'll have a better idea?" Weapons Officer Holder asked him.

"Mr. Holder, I'm sure that if the President and the government are still in place in the east, they have some weapons, but they're probably small arms. I'd be willing to bet we have the only nuclear armament left on the planet. I could be wrong, of course, and hope we don't have to find out. It's naïve to think the government would allow us to decommission this boat at this time. What are you thinking? That there's another submarine crew out there that can do what we do?"

"No sir. But we... I mean the crew and officers of this submarine can't be expected to serve aboard this submarine forever. Do you think they might change our base back to the East Coast? Maybe back to King's Bay or Norfolk? Maybe they could train another Blue crew."

The captain laughed. "Do you remember the training you received, how intensive it was? Those facilities are gone, as are the instructors. And I'm sure Groton, Norfolk and Kings Bay were all primary targets. If the government still exists on the East Coast, and they have any kind of military left, they will have to guard our eastern shores. What they really need, is for us and Vandenberg to protect the West Coast from invasion."

He put his napkin on the table and picked up his ball cap. "Come on gentlemen, let's get up to the radio shack."

They climbed up to the fifth story of the oil rig. Dombrowski could see the empty helicopter pad rising above the top floor in the corner of the massive structure. They crowded into the radio room, crammed with mostly inoperable electronic equipment. Before the war, this structure was completely self-sustaining. It had its own generators, desalinization plant and crews quarters with kitchens, dining facilities and recreation areas.

Once they'd made Platform Harvest their base, the Air Force and Navy personnel had managed to repair the generators and some of the radio equipment. The two boats they had found moored to the dock had been fixed the first time the sub had anchored here. The electricity would last as long as the fuel in the reserve tanks lasted.

"Santana, please fire it up and let's see if there's anybody out there to talk to." They waited patiently while the equipment warmed up and Santana fiddled with dials and switches. Almost immediately they heard bursts of static and, in the background the sound of faint voices. The signal faded in and out and the voices strung together into unrecognizable words. Santana continued to refine the signal when suddenly a loud blast of static occurred and then subsided. A single voice came through, loud and clear.

"This is Charleston. Hello? Vandenberg, this is Charleston. Do you read?"

"Charleston, this is Vandenberg. So happy to hear you. This is radioman Santana and I have Captain Dombrowski of the *U.S.S. Louisiana* and Colonel Packer, Commander of

Vandenberg Air Force Base. Can you tell us your status? Is this a government agency?"

"Yes. We are located in Charleston, West Virginia, the capital of the United States of America. President Rissman... " Another burst of static emitted from the speaker and the signal went dead.

"Dammit! Oh, sorry sir. I've lost the signal."

"Keep trying to get it back Santana."

The radioman continued to play with his dials, trying to reestablish the signal. "I'm not having any luck, sir." Just as he finished that statement the radio came back to life.

"Yeehaw, I've got them back, sir. Charleston, Santana here. Captain Dombrowski would like to speak with President Rissman. Can we set up a meeting?"

"This is Charleston. The president has a standing order that if we contact anyone to give him 30 minutes to get here. That would be 1700 hours Eastern."

"Understood Charleston. We will be standing by."

The Captain turned and shook Colonel Packer's hand. "This is what we've been waiting for." The men all shook hands and patted each other on the back. "Santana, will we have any problem getting the signal back at 1400 hours, our time?"

"I sure hope not, sir. I would hate to keep the President waiting."

At precisely 1400 hours Santana received the signal from Charleston. The static was worse but a voice could clearly be heard through it. "Dombrowski... Richard? This is President Rissman. We've been trying to contact military personnel throughout the country for months and you and Colonel Packer are the only people we've been able to get a hold of." The voice faded out as the static became louder. Santana had sweat pouring down his face, soaking his uniform shirt.

"Take your time, Santana. Just get me my signal back."

"... status. Dombrowski, did you hear me?"

"No, I'm sorry Mister President, we didn't catch your last statement."

They heard the president's voice, barely audible, in the background, "Dammit Mister Miller, get them back."

"I have them, sir."

"Dombrowski, what is your status?"

"Mister President, the *Louisiana* is operational. I made the decision during the war not to fire our complement of missiles. I felt that enough firepower was being used to disable or destroy our enemies, so I made the decision to hold our nuclear armament in reserve in case it was needed later."

"You mean... are you telling me you still have your missiles?" Rissman sounded surprised and excited.

"Yes, Mister President. We have been patrolling the Pacific Coast of the United States to ensure there wasn't a follow-up attack. So far there's been no sign of enemy action."

"Well, we've heard some chatter in the past couple of weeks in Chinese. From what I've been told, as the ionosphere settles down it's actually easier to get signals bounced around the earth than it is from closer up. My advisors feel that there may be an imminent threat from China. Our worry all along was that they started this war in the hopes of coming over here later and mopping up."

"Do you have orders for me Mister President?"

"I certainly do Captain Dombrowski. I need you to deploy to China immediately. See if you can determine if they are launching an attack toward the United States. Communications are very poor and I don't know if you will be able to report back what you find but I am giving you full discretion to launch an attack if you feel the Chinese are being aggressive and moving toward our country. There will be no launch codes, no authentication. Do you understand what I'm asking you Captain Dombrowski?"

"Yes sir. We've just arrived at Vandenberg and are resupplying as we speak. We will deploy as soon as we're ready. As communications improve, we will try and stay in touch with Colonel Packer at Vandenberg. It may be easier for him to relay our communications to you."

"Yes, yes. Try and stay in touch as much as possible. Get underway as soon as you can. We're counting on you, Captain Dombrowski."

"Thank you, sir. Vandenberg out."

"Wow," Packer said, "those bastards just never give up. I'm fairly relieved here, sir, that you kept your missiles."

"Yeah, I wasn't so sure it was the right decision at the time."

The next few days were a flurry of activity as Packer's troops assisted in gathering and transporting supplies to the boat that would deliver them to the sub. Shore leaves were cut short which produced some minor grumbling, but the men were actually relieved to have a purpose again. Four days after talking to the President, the *Louisiana* was prepped and ready to begin its mission.

"I have the conn, Mister Finney. Chief Petty Officer, let's get underway."

"Engine room, all ahead one quarter, bring us about to bearing 270."

This was a time Richard Dombrowski loved, the sub underway, and about to descend into the depths of the cold Pacific.

"Dive, dive," sang the Chief Petty Officer. "Take us to level 150." The sub crossed the shelf break where the ocean bottom dropped off hundreds and then eventually thousands of feet.

Dombrowski turned to Carter and grinned "Take us to level 500. We have no GPS, so just point us toward China and try not to run into the Hawaiian Islands."

10

The Horde left Vegas and traveled south toward the small town of Boulder City. Seventy-six motorcycles, four pickup trucks and a van roared through Railroad pass on Highway 93. The beds of the pickup trucks were crammed with supplies and bottles of water.

The men loved speed, but the pace set by Chase was too great even for them. Bing watched him pull away at well over a hundred miles per hour. They found him waiting for them twenty minutes later where the highway turned into Boulder City's main street. He stood in the center of the highway, his arms crossed, and scowled as they pulled to a stop in front of him.

"Fucking pussies," he growled, as he stood rubbing alcohol gel on his hands. "There's a service station over there on the left. Everybody top off their tanks. I want you to go through this town with a fine tooth comb. Break down doors and bring me all the food and water you can find."

They went through Boulder City like a plague of locusts. Splitting up into groups of three or four men, several groups rode down the main street of town, stopping and entering every store along the way. Others rode up and down residential streets checking every house for food and water. There were only a few residents stupid enough to be seen.

Nutts and Johnny rode their new motorcycles, taken from the men who had failed their initiation, and were shocked to see a man and woman walking toward them down Adams Street. They were probably in their 30s but looked much older. Pale and thin, they had dark circles under their eyes and their clothes hung on their frames like garbage bags.

"Hello. Can you take us with you?" the man begged. "We're out of food. Please, we can't stay here any longer."

As the couple came within ten feet of them, Nutts pulled out his .45 caliber revolver and shot the man twice in the chest. The woman screamed. She turned and tried to run back down the street, but appeared to have an injured leg and could only limp away slowly. Johnny turned to Nutts and grinned. "You want to chase her down bro, or should I?"

"Wish I had a lariat. I used to do calf roping and it would be fun to take her that way. But you go ahead."

The woman was darting for a gap between two of the buildings but Johnny easily cut off her retreat. As he rode by he reached out and slammed his fist into the side of her head. She collapsed like a felled tree. Whooping loudly, he slung the backend of the chopper in a 360° circle, sending clouds of dirt into the air. Nutts rode up, left the bike a few feet from the fallen, unconscious woman and quickly unfastened her pants, as Johnny grabbed the pant legs around her ankles and slid her jeans off.

"Hell man," Johnny said, "I wish she was awake so she could fight us."

"I don't care about that. I'll take her any way I can get her." The two men spent the next hour making up for not having had a woman for many months. She regained consciousness after five minutes to find herself the playmate of two insatiable animals. When they finished with her, Nutts shot her through the head.

In other parts of town the bikers encountered a few other residents with the same result. They killed the men and raped the women. But just as everywhere else, they found no food and only a few bottles of water. The few residents that had survived had stripped the town clean.

Chase pulled into the parking lot of a motel, with a few of the bikes, the ones carrying the women, following him into the lot. He gestured at Carmella and she followed him to the door of one of the rooms. He tried the knob and found the room locked. Backing away a few feet he raised his leg and aimed a vicious kick at the door just below the lock. With a loud crack the door flew open, smashing into the wall behind it. Grinning down at the woman, he reached out, took her arm and pushed her into the room.

In only a few minutes he was back, buckling his belt as he walked out into the parking area. "Bring the furniture from the motel office and from some of the rooms. Bring the bedding too," Chase ordered.

"This sucks, we're almost out of food and it's over eighty miles to Kingman," Bing complained to Don and Jimmy, as they hauled the furniture and bedding from the motel rooms and threw it all in the middle of the parking lot. Rod broke into the motel office and came out holding dozens of keys.

"Good thing they don't use those electronic keys. Damn things needed a computer to code them to the rooms." He handed out the keys and some of the men led their women into rooms at the far end of the motel.

"There aren't enough rooms in this one for all of us," Chase called out to the riders, check out that other motel across the street."

Happy to get away from him, a dozen cyclists gunned their motorcycles out of the parking lot one hundred yards up the highway and into the parking lot of a second motel.

As the gang members started returning empty-handed, Chase's mood darkened. He turned to Bing. "We'll stay here tonight and head for Kingman in the morning. Get me a bottle of whiskey out of the pickup truck."

Nutts and Johnny rode into the parking lot, and pulled up in front of where Chase was sitting in a motel room chair, a half-empty bottle of whiskey in his hand. He had his boots propped up on the railing, a cigarette held between two fingers of his gloved hand. Chase blew a smoke ring. "You losers find anything?"

Johnny walked back to his saddlebags and withdrew two bottles of water. "Yeah, Chase. We found a house with a couple cases of water. Couldn't bring them all but we can get them on the way out of town." He walked over and handed Chase a bottle of water. "Had a little trouble with a couple of residents. We had to kill 'em."

Chase opened the bottle of water and drank the entire contents in one long swig. "Get back there and bring the water now, before someone else gets it."

"Sure, Chase. Anything you say, man." Climbing back in their saddles they roared off down the street. When they were 50 yards down the street Johnny looked over at Nutts and rolled his eyes.

The last of the riders had returned with similar tales of murdering hapless survivors. It was clear this gang was never going to leave anyone behind alive.

Bing and Cutter sat in chairs brought from a motel room out onto the walkway. They each had a bottle of water and a cigarette. "Do you think all the towns will be like this one? Cutter whined. "We'll starve or die from thirst if they are."

"Just the small towns. If there aren't any people there should be more supplies. And big cities should have a ton of shit."

"There aren't any big towns until we get farther east. Except for Phoenix and Tucson. What about them?"

"Chase says we have to go farther east. Out of this whole southwest desert area. Where there's a lot of rivers and lakes. And hunting." He wore a bright pink bandanna today.

Smelling something burning, Bing glanced over his shoulder toward Chase, who was lighting a big bonfire, stoked with piles of bedding and furniture from the motel. Chase walked over to the street, and placing his gloved hands on a road sign, began rocking it back and forth. There was a loud crack, and throwing the stop sign onto his shoulder, he carried it back and chucked it onto the fire, looking over at Bing and Cutter with a grimace that served as his smile.

"Bing," he yelled, "go get some of the other guys and bring me the bodies of those idiots the men killed this morning."

"Bodies? Seriously, Chase?"

Chase just glared at Bing, then tilted his head.

"Sure, Chase. We'll get 'em."

Wide eyed, Bing started down the rows of rooms, banging on the doors and waiting for the occupants to come out.

"Chase wants you guys to bring the bodies of the people the guys killed this morning," he told the first man to answer the door. He lowered his voice to a whisper, "I think he's gonna eat 'em."

"That's bullshit, man. You go get 'em, I'm busy." He looked over his shoulder and grinned at the woman in his bed."

"You want me to tell Chase you're not gonna do what he said?"

"Ah, fuck man, I'll go. Just shut your trap. I'll be back, baby," he said to the woman.

Bing was right. When they brought the three bodies, Chase butchered them himself, slicing them into steaks and other cuts of meat. In another five minutes he'd chopped down a small tree by the motel swimming pool, using the small branches as skewers and throwing the larger branches onto the fire.

He threw the entrails into the pool.

"Ain't nothing like a barbecue, huh boys?"

11

A dark sky lowered over the wagon train as it moved west. Mark and Lori, sitting on the seat of the wagon, were engaged in conversation, their voices low due to the somber mood set by the weather. Ashley and Kevin were fighting in the back of the wagon. They were just over a week out of Raton. Saying goodbye to Izzy and Terry had been difficult and had created a void in their little party.

Terry had given them directions to the west, following New Mexico Highway 555 through the Sangre De Cristo Mountains. Skillet and the Yancey boys didn't like having to drive the horses on the asphalt road for too great a distance, but the topography was mountainous, making them have to stay on the road paralleling the Canadian River. They were relieved when the road became dirt after about 40 miles. Asphalt roads were much softer than concrete but still harder on the horse's hooves than the ground. The road provided the best route through the mountains, taking advantage of passes along the way.

Like Mark and Lori, Jesse Cameron had been a runner in his former life. He was the only one of the men that tried to keep his hair short. Since no one knew how to cut hair properly, his brown, curly hair was uneven and stuck out from his head. He tried and failed to grow a decent beard, ending up with patches of fuzz on his cheeks. His friend Danny Fielder, who was a year younger, and six inches taller, was growing a full thick beard, and teased him unmercifully.

Jesse hated horses, and became bored when riding in a wagon, so every day he ran up ahead of the wagon train, trying to keep up with Sheri. Then he would run back for lunch.

Sheri flew down the dirt road, dodging the bushes and weeds that had sprouted up through the ground, arriving at the same time as Jesse.

"You know you're never going to catch me, right?" she laughed, as she skidded to a stop.

"I'll never catch you on foot, but if I had a bicycle I think I could keep up with you. With all the rain, the bicycles in Eagle Nest were rusted hunks of junk. Dan tried to buy us a couple of bikes in Raton but they told him our money was no good."

"I know. I tried to buy some new clothes and they told me they were holding on to all the supplies they had, because they didn't think they would ever have any more. One of the women told me they couldn't eat gold and silver."

"But they use gold and silver, and even jewels, for currency."

She leaned her bike against the wagon. "They're just using it as a method of exchange to buy things amongst themselves. They're scared to death to let outsiders have any of their supplies. I think they're making a big mistake by not learning how to make things themselves. What are they going to do after the supplies run out? Especially if they don't set up trade with others towns."

"I don't know. Now that Terry and Izzy are there, maybe they can teach them to do things for themselves," he said, "and maybe Willsburg can lend them books and software. They must have generators and working computers. At least for a few years until things break or they run out of gas. By then they'll be a lot more self-sufficient."

Jesse had his foot on the top of the wagon wheel leaning forward and stretching out his hamstrings. "I heard Mark say that when we get out of these mountains we would pass through a couple of small towns. I'm hoping for a bike shop. Then I won't have any trouble keeping up with you." He switched legs and continued to stretch.

"Well… you can sure try."

***

In two more days they were almost through the Sangre de Cristos. They had seen no towns, nor any people, but had passed an occasional ranch and a small cemetery. As often as possible they tried to drive the wagons alongside the road, if the ground was flat enough. They had left the Canadian River behind and, according to their map of New Mexico, were now close to the end of New Mexico Highway 196. Another, smaller river now paralleled the road. They had filled all the water barrels at Costilla Reservoir but, except for the game brought in by Matthew and Einstein every day, their food stores were getting low. Terry had told them to take the 516 that crossed into Colorado to take advantage of the best pass through the Rockies.

"Wow, take a look at that view," Lori said, as they came around a bend and looked out west over an expansive valley. The road led down out of the mountains to the plains before crossing another mountain range in the far distance. "Do you think we can get out of the mountains before the rain starts?"

Mark shook his head. "I don't think so. It looks like there's still a few more miles before the road begins to descend into the valley, and I don't think the rain is going to hold off much longer."

Matthew and Einstein ranged ahead, continuing to scout, missing having the Jeep to check out the miles ahead. The terrain became more uneven, and they were forced to move the wagons onto the road itself for the next thirty minutes. Sheri usually rode ahead on her bicycle, but today she stayed with the wagon train, something about the clouds making her want the comfort of her friends. It was midafternoon when Mark felt the first raindrops, as the fog settled down around their shoulders like a wet blanket. Mark blew the battered, brass horn, signaling for the sentries to return to camp.

Riders materialized out of the thickening fog. Chang rode up from behind, Mike came in from the right and Danny came from the left as they could all feel the oncoming storm. The acrid smell of ozone was in the air.

"Hey Mark, this looks like it's gonna be bad," Sam called out. The rain started to fall harder, the wind kicked up, and suddenly the flash of a giant lightning strike was seen off to the right, followed by a low rumble of thunder.

"Yeah, we need to get undercover, fast," Mark yelled back. Mark's wagon was in the lead and, as he pulled the reins to left, the horses headed down a short slope into a flat area filled with brush.

"Circle up," he called out. The other two wagons came down the slope and circled to the left into their usual triangular shape.

"Chang, Danny and Mike. You guys finish up your guard duty and as soon as the next shift finishes their dinner I'll send them out to relieve you and you can come eat. Sorry about the rain."

The camp became a flurry of activity. Willy and Sheri drove stakes into the ground and strung a rope between them. They unsaddled the horses and tied them off to the rope, leaving enough slack for them to graze. Quickly covering all the gear with a large plastic tarp, they piled rocks at the corners to secure it against the brisk wind. Skillet and Jimbo unharnessed the team that pulled the Chuck wagon, while Mark and Lori unharnessed their own. Chris and Aaron took care of theirs and everyone else started pitching their tents, as the rain became a downpour. As soon as the wagons had stopped, Ashley and Kevin, tired of being cooped up all day, bailed out the back of their wagon and began playing in the mud.

"Jesse, Greg, Willy and Carlos," Skillet called out, "can you guys rig the shelter for my fire?" They pulled four long stakes approximately seven feet long out of the Chuck wagon, and standing on a box, drove them deep into the ground in a square pattern in the center space between the wagons. They strung up a large cover between the poles and tied off guy ropes to stabilize it.

"Yo, Skillet. It's all ready for you to start your fire, you old coot," Jesse told the grizzled cook.

"I'm not old. I'm only fifty-four. I just look old, but I'm still prettier than you."

Skillet walked around collecting rocks to ring the fire, oblivious to the rain. Once he had the ring formed he went to his wagon and fetched dry firewood stacked alongside one wall. Throwing a small plastic tarp over the arm full of logs, he ran back to the fire ring and inside of three minutes had a roaring campfire going.

"Ashley, Kevin," Lori yelled out, "get in here, out of that rain."

"Aw, mom, we're tired of that old wagon," Kevin whined, "can't we play just a little longer?"

"Certainly not. It's starting to get cold. Come on."

Between the Chuck wagon and Chris and Aaron's wagon, Mike and Greg set up their dome-like, nylon tent, staking it to the ground and placing basketball-sized rocks on each of the tent stakes. Carlos and Chang had pitched theirs next to it. The wind had become a gale and from inside his tent Mark heard Sam and Willy's voices shrill on the wind, diminishing as they chased their tent across the plains. Mark stuck his head out of the wagon just in time to see them disappear in the fog, returning five minutes later with no tent.

"Son of a bitch! Why'd you let it go?" Sam shouted.

"You stupid slacker. You're the one that let it go." Willy reached out and shoved Sam. He tripped over a bush, falling into a rivulet now flowing along one side of the camp. Both Yancey boys started laughing. "Way to go, Willy. Now where we gonna sleep?"

"Under the wagon I guess. We'll hang a tarp down the sides. It'll be okay, bro. You shouldn't have let go of the tent."

"Screw you! You're such a dick."

Mark shook his head and pulled it back into the wagon. "Those boys just never quit."

"No, but they keep things interesting. Come on kids, get out of those wet clothes."

She helped Kevin change into warm jeans and a long sleeved shirt. Ashley put the wet ones against the tailgate, out of the way. The wagon lit up from the flash of another lightning strike and the thunder crashed a few seconds behind. The canvas cover of the wagon magnified the hammering sound of the rain. They all huddled together, seeking comfort from the storm, and Lori shivered, remembering another maelstrom in what seemed like another life.

"Mark, what does this storm remind you of?"

He looked over at her, and saw her eyes wide with fear. "Lori, it's okay. That storm was worse and you were hurt."

"As bad as it was, I wasn't scared. I was injured and cold but you were there, and I felt safe."

He moved over toward her, putting his arms around her as the kids nestled in their laps. Before the war he had never felt as warm, comfortable and safe as he did at that moment.

Willy and Sam, already drenched to the bone, helped Skillet get dinner ready. They couldn't get any wetter so they made several trips back and forth from the Chuck wagon to the campfire. A large kettle sat slightly off kilter on a rock, a stew of venison and vegetables just beginning to simmer, and giving off a heavenly aroma. Skillet stirred it with a long wooden spoon. As quickly as it had come, the wind died away and the tarp over their heads quit flapping.

"Hey, you guys. Look what I found." Willy came through the rain and ducked under the tarp holding up a can of something in his right hand. Water ran off his battered cowboy hat creating a tiny waterfall before his eyes

"Okay, I'll bite. What is it?" Sam said, as he tried to grab it out of Willy's hand.

"Get off me, man. It's a can of frosting. Cake frosting. It was buried in the bottom of a box of other cans. We're going to have dessert tonight."

"Yeah? What are you gonna put it on?"

"Hell, we'll just eat it right out of the can. You got a spoon?"

"Come and get it!" Skillet yelled at the top of his lungs. Sixteen hungry people, all but the baby, most with plastic tarps held over their heads, hustled to the campfire and grabbed plastic plates and tableware off the small wooden table under the edge of the area protected by the tarp. Skillet ladled the stew onto everyone's plate and Greg sliced a loaf of bread for everyone to share. They huddled around the campfire, bumping into one another in the confined space and tripping over the children. By the time they'd finished their meal, the lightning and thunder had stopped, and the rain had settled into a steady whisper. Skillet and the Yancey boys gathered the dishes and took them to the Chuck wagon.

Matthew, Einstein and Greg headed out to relieve the guards. A few moments later the wet, hungry men came into camp and dug into the pot to finish off the remainder of the stew. The others huddled around the fire.

"Hey everybody, don't leave yet," Willy yelled. "We've got dessert." He held up the can of chocolate frosting, and a spoon. The sun had set and the last of the twilight was settling into the West as brilliant points of light illuminated the western sky. They moved the small table into the center of the space under the tarp which had settled down, no longer snapping in the wind.

Willy removed the plastic lid and yanked on the pull-tab to open the can of frosting. He sunk the spoon into the frosting and, eyes wide, scooped up the sugary, delectable treat, deliberately and slowly licking it off the spoon.

"Oh my God, that is so good."

"Can I have some? Can I?" Kevin wormed his way to the table and held out his hand for the frosting. Using his finger, he scooped out his portion and stuck it in his mouth. The can was passed around from person-to-person, everyone laughing and enjoying this reminder of life before the war.

Matthew watched everyone pass around the frosting can. There was no moon and the night was now completely dark. He was around fifty yards from the campsite and the campfire illuminated the area in a warm glow. Matthew thought he could've been observing a scene from the 1870s, except for the motorcycle parked alongside a wagon, several plastic items, including the tarp that provided shelter by the campfire, and a couple of nylon, backpacking tents set up in the meadow between two of the wagons.

Chief swung his head to the left, his ears pricked forward, as he nodded his head up and down to alert Matthew to another's presence. A shadow materialized out of the night and Einstein rode up to Matthew's position. Einstein was wearing a poncho to keep off the rain and was uncharacteristically wearing Willy's cowboy hat. His long hair fell out from under the hat to his shoulders. The rain had dwindled to a drizzle.

"Hey, Matthew," he greeted him. They heard the group down at the campfire start to sing and Matthew recognized *We Are the Champions,* by Queen. "What are they doing down there?"

"I heard Willy say they had dessert and they're passing around some kind of a can. Go on down there if you'd like something sweet."

"Naw, I need to watch my waistline."

The two men, ten years apart in age, sat astride their horses in companionable silence. They had both lost their families, Einstein losing his wife and two children in a motor vehicle accident before the war, and Matthew losing his beautiful, pregnant wife when a hydrogen bomb had obliterated Albuquerque, New Mexico.

Derek Thorson, or Einstein as the people he lived with in Cimarron had called him, had been a rich, real estate developer in

Albuquerque. He survived because he was in a state prison for killing the man that had run over his family.

Matthew was a Ph.D. geologist, just out of graduate school, working at his new job with the New Mexico Bureau of Mines. He'd been at his grandfather's ranch just South of Taos, when he saw the mushroom cloud over Albuquerque… and he knew she was gone. He lost his parents in the same blast, and his grandfather as well, who died of a heart attack when he saw the blossoming nuclear explosion.

Einstein reined Jasper to the left. "I'll see ya, I'm gonna go check on Greg."

Matthew smiled at the scene of his friends enjoying the evening as they were now singing *Bohemian Rhapsody*, but he'd been thinking more of his family lately and felt a deep loneliness even as he watched their camaraderie. He yearned to allow himself to become closer to these people, but the pain he had experienced in losing his entire family still haunted him.

It had been almost two years since the war, but when he thought of his wife, she still seemed so real to him, like he could pick up a phone and she would answer. Knowing it was him calling, she always said, "Hi baby," instead of, "hello." He recalled conversations they'd had about their future. She'd teased him about his choices of names for their son or daughter, and they talked about how Matthew would teach the child how to ride and work at the ranch.

He remembered making love with her, lost in their intimacy.

He whispered her name, *Sophie*.

12

Although the day was pleasant, the men were sweating from the exertion of digging the foundation for the White House. The setting was in a beautiful meadow, at least twenty acres, at the eastern edge of the college grounds. This White House wouldn't have a North and South Portico but instead faced west. Architects and engineers swarmed over the site with rolled up plans under their arms. James Hoban's original plans had been lost, but the plans had been redrawn when the West Wing was added in 1901 and the men were digging the foundation according to those archived plans. There were at least sixty men digging during the daylight hours to finish the two-story basement.

Stacks of granite and marble blocks, and pallets of lumber stood off to one side, ready for use when the foundation was finished.

It was late afternoon and the sun beat down on the exhausted men. They had been digging since 8 o'clock that morning. One of their fellow workers circulated with a pail full of water and a ladle to allow the men to drink water about once an hour. At one o'clock in the afternoon they were each given a peanut butter and honey sandwich. The rest of the time, unless they needed to go to the bathroom, they worked without a break.

Using the crook of his arm, Roger was wiping the sweat from his brow, when he heard a moan, and a tall, elderly man dropped his shovel and collapsed into the deepest part of the hole.

Roger noticed that the guards all walked over to the edge of the hole to see what was going on.

Mitchum pointed his baton at two of the workers. "Get his ass out of there and take him back to the dorm. He'd better be ready to work tomorrow. I won't give him a second chance." He made a throat cutting gesture as two of the men quickly pulled him from the hole and half-carried him toward the new workers' quarters.

Roger overheard Mitchum tell a subordinate, "He needs to be back out here tomorrow. If he goes down again, take care of him." And he gestured toward the woods behind the site. "We can't waste food on someone that can't work. This job is a major priority, and I'm not taking the fall if it isn't finished on time."

They finally allowed them to finish around six o'clock in the evening. Roger had always been a hard worker, and running his own farm had been back-breaking work, but he had never before shoveled dirt for ten straight hours. He ached from the top of his head to the tip of his toes. He glanced over at Ashe, who looked as exhausted as Roger felt. They crawled up out of the deepest hole to the unexcavated portion of the basement, on the back side closest to the woods. Armed guards waved their rifles at them gesturing for them to form up in their platoon.

Their morning had started off with a four mile hike from the National Guard Armory, where they had spent the previous night, to the worksite.

"From now on, you'll be staying in one of the dormitories here at the college. First we'll go to the cafeteria for some chow and then you'll be shown to your rooms, where you'll bunk with the same person you were with at the armory."

As they marched toward the cafeteria, Mitchum turned to his aide, "Make sure they double up in the rooms. We don't want to have to use too many men to guard over them. The dorm rooms can't be locked from the outside so make sure there are at least two guards in each hallway, and that they stay awake all night."

Late that night, just as Roger was beginning to fall asleep, he heard a whisper, "Psst, Roger. Come over here."

"Why? What's going on?" As he slipped across the room in the dark, he heard Ashe sit up in bed.

"Me and some of the other guys; Cole, McKinney, and Harvand, have been talking the last couple of weeks about getting out of here. This might be our chance. You know the old guy, Smith, that fainted in the hole today? They're going to make him get back out there tomorrow. There's no way in hell he's going to be able to work all day without collapsing again. Keep an eye on him and if he looks like he's in trouble, you need to be ready."

"What do I have to do?"

"Start digging closer to the back of the foundation where it isn't as deep, and as soon as you see him go down, make a break for the woods. Six or eight of the other guys are going to make the break with us. Hang onto your shovel in case you have to use it as a weapon. Hopefully, the guards will be distracted with the old man like they were today. Whatever happens, don't hesitate to use that shovel if you need to."

He hesitated, and then added, "You realize this is a point of no return. Once we make a break for it, if we don't make it, they'll kill us as an example to the others."

"They'll be shooting at us. How are we going to get away?"

"Man, you just have to run as fast as you can, zigzagging to get to the woods. There'll be a bunch of us and, hopefully, we'll take them by surprise. Once we get through that wall of Virginia Creeper, everybody's going to scatter. But you and me, we need to stick together. I have a plan. The rest of the men are all going to try and escape to the east into the Appalachian Mountains. I'm thinking that you and I should peel off and get up to that bridge that crosses the river just north of the campus. We'll head back west through Charleston and into the hills. I once had some family that lived in Kentucky, and believe me, if we can get into the mountains of Kentucky they will never be able to find us."

"What about my family?"

"Man, you have to get out of here before you can help them. This may be your only chance."

"Why are you doing this for me?" Roger asked him. "I just met you yesterday."

"I never liked doing anything alone, and for better or worse, you're my roommate. If you have any reservations at all about this then just don't run when the rest of us do. This is our best chance, we may never get another one. Are you in?"

"I'm scared. I really want to go with you, and I'm sure I will, but I just need to think about it. I promise though, if I don't go I won't tell them a thing."

"I know you won't, Roger, you seem like a good guy. We could have been friends in the old days. Now get some sleep. We're gonna need our energy and I don't know when we'll get to sleep again."

***

The next day dawned cold and dreary. When they walked out of the dorm Ashe looked up at the sky, then over to Roger and just shook his head. Roger didn't wish the old man ill will, but their escape was contingent upon Smith passing out from the heat.

After breakfast they were marched back to the worksite. They labored all morning until their brief lunch break when the clouds finally began to burn off, and the temperature began to rise. The hole had become so deep they couldn't throw the dirt out, so a large wooden bucket had been lowered down to them. It filled up quickly, and it took three men hauling on the rope to pull it up and empty it each time.

Roger was nervous, and worried that the guards would notice. He kept his head down as he dug, but glanced up periodically to see how Smith was doing. He tried not to look at his co-conspirators so as not to alert the guards that something was up.

Beginning to think the old man was going to make it through the day, Roger became discouraged and slowed his digging to conserve his strength. He'd been thinking about the escape all day and was now so determined to make it happen he actually considered making a break for it, regardless of whether or not Smith went down. As he dug, he slowly moved toward the back of the foundation. Glancing up he saw Ashe staring at him, and as if Ashe could read his mind, he surreptitiously shook his head at Roger.

Just then the old guy collapsed, tumbling down the slope into the mud in the bottom of the hole.

"Smith! Get up," one of the workers, Hegstrom, yelled at him. "He's okay, Mitchum. We'll get him up. He'll be able to keep working." He and another man grabbed Smith under the arms and hoisted him to his feet.

"Get him out of there," Mitchum said to two of the guards. "I've had it with him."

They laid their weapons on the ground at the feet of a third guard and climbed down into the hole.

Suddenly, several men, who had all moved toward the back of the foundation, were scrambling up the slope toward the shallow end. They each carried a shovel and two of them rushed the guard. The soldier jerked up his AR-15 and was able to get off one shot, hitting one of the men square in the chest and sending him flying backward into the hole. The second escapee swung his shovel with all his strength, nearly decapitating the soldier when the edge sliced into the side of his neck. Bright, arterial blood squirted everywhere, cutting off the soldier's scream. He dropped his weapon and fell to his knees, grabbing his throat. Tumbling into the hole, he landed on the body of the man he had killed.

"Guys, over here!" The man picked up one of the weapons, and as a guard on the other side of the foundation began to fire in his direction, he returned the fire, directing it in Mitchum's direction. Cole and McKinney scooped up the other two rifles as they sprinted by, heading for the woods. Mitchum had dived to the ground when the first shots were fired.

He jumped to his feet screaming, "Shoot them! Don't let them get away."

A half dozen guards, that had been on the far side of the foundation, began firing after the fleeing prisoners. Three of the escapees had weapons, but didn't return fire as they, Roger, Ashe and the other men sprinted for the woods. They were now seventy five yards from the guards who were coming around the edges of the hole in hot pursuit. Just before he entered the woods, Roger looked over his shoulder and saw Mitchum with a radio to his lips. One of the pursuing guards stopped and fired off several rounds and Roger saw one of the escapees go down, thrown forward onto his face.

"Roger! Dammit man, come on," Ashe screamed at him.

Roger plunged through the hanging Virginia Creeper into the deciduous forest beyond, as bullets swished through the vegetation on either side of him. He was almost jerked off his feet when Ashe grabbed his arm, pulling him in a new direction.

"This way," Ashe said in a low voice. They peeled off to the north running as fast as they could through the tangled undergrowth, jumping moss covered logs, and weaving between the close tree trunks. The canopy was so dense it was almost dark, with rays of light penetrating in only a few places, and Roger could smell the damp soil and thick vegetation.

The gunfire continued and they heard return fire from deeper in the woods. Roger hoped the guards would follow the reports of the rifles and wouldn't realize that he and Ashe were heading in a different direction.

The sounds of pursuit diminished and they were able to slow their pace slightly, while trying to catch their breath. "Lucky the other guys got those guns," Ashe told Roger. "They'll be following the direction of the gunfire and hopefully won't come after us." He was panting already and Roger worried the larger man wouldn't be able to keep up the pace.

The trees began to thin, and they stumbled out of the woods onto an asphalt road. "This is the road that goes over the bridge. If they have the bridge guarded, we're in serious trouble, because it would be hard to get across the river. Can you swim?"

"If I have to. I don't know this area at all, so you lead and I'll follow." He knew he needed to let Ashe lead the way and set the pace.

The vegetation was thick on either side of the road and as they came around a slight curve they could see the bridge ahead. Hunkering down in the bushes, they checked the area out as far as they could see.

"I don't see anybody, do you?" Ashe whispered.

"I don't. They would've heard the gunfire and maybe they left to go help. I saw Mitchum radioing for reinforcements."

"Okay, stay behind me and be as quiet as you can be." They snuck through the bushes until the vegetation ran out just before the bridge. It didn't appear to be guarded. Unfortunately, their jumpsuits were very recognizable so they couldn't just stroll across the bridge, hoping nobody would realize they were escaped prisoners.

Crouching low and praying nobody was around to see them, they scurried over the bridge, breathing a sigh of relief when they reached the other side without being detected.

"In another few minutes there's going to be hundreds of guys looking for us, so we need to keep moving and get through town as fast as we can." Ashe pointed west. "The main city is behind us, Civic Center and the airport, but we need to get out of these clothes, and there're still plenty of stores on this side of the river. I don't know if it will do us any good, though. Have you seen any civilians that weren't prisoners in the work camp? I've just seen soldiers and prisoners."

The afternoon sun had drifted lower toward the horizon as they'd made their escape, and now it settled behind the distant hills in the west. Trying to catch their breath, they walked down a deserted sidewalk in West Charleston feeling like they were the only survivors left in the world. Just ahead on the left they came upon a shopping mall. Quickly crossing the parking lot, they pushed open the double doors of a Sears Department Store and entered the dark interior.

"Let's hurry up and get changed," Ashe said. "Be sure you get some sturdy boots." Ashe had a much smaller selection of clothing then Roger due to his size. After changing into civilian clothes, they left the building as the last of the light disappeared into the west.

A fat, orange, full moon had risen and stood above the horizon, allowing their dark-adjusted eyes to see the city before them. Roger felt as though he were walking through the streets of a dying world. Shadowy buildings jutted into the sky, and they heard the rustling of rodents and the plaintive cries of night birds. They walked down the sidewalk, talking in whispers, as if the dead could hear them.

The sweat had dried on their skin and the evening had cooled. Both were dressed in jeans, belts, and flannel, long-sleeved shirts, and had chosen medium-weight jackets, and baseball caps. Roger's longish, brown hair stuck out from his cap and fell beneath his ears.

Across the street, he spotted a sporting goods store and took off running, calling out to Ashe, "Come on, we can get supplies."

The glass, double doors of the sporting goods store were locked. "Damn, you'd think people would have been in and out of these stores, and would've left the door open. Maybe this means the stuff inside is untouched."

Raising his leg, he slammed his boot into the glass with all the force he could muster, but only succeeded in hurting his foot.

"Here, get out of the way," Ashe told him. He stepped forward and gave the door a mighty kick, sending spiderweb-like cracks through the pane. Kicking it again, a solid sheet of cracked glass flew from the door into the interior of the building.

"That's how it's done my little friend." They stepped into the dark interior.

"First job is to find some flashlights," Roger said. "They're usually in the glass counters at the front of the store." It took them ten minutes going from case to case until they finally located a counter full of Maglites. "Now we're in business." He flicked the switch and although the light didn't seem to be at full power, it came on, illuminating a treasure trove of camping supplies.

"We each need a backpack. Let's go."

They found the backpacks in the far corner of the store, selecting a medium for Roger and an oversized one for Ashe. Going up and down through the aisles they picked supplies they hoped would help get them through the hills and into Kentucky. They each packed an extra flashlight and some batteries, paracord, emergency blankets, and a tube tent. They found a selection of Leatherman tools and a small first aid kit.

"I'll carry the stove and a couple of pots, and you grab some of those small butane cylinders. I don't see any guns or ammo. Either this store never carried them or our friends the storm troopers got 'em all. But we need to find some knives." They split up and searched the aisles until Roger heard an exclamation from Ashe.

"Hey Roger, over here. There's a ton of them."

They each grabbed Swiss-type pocket knives, and strapped on sheaths containing wicked looking knives with six-inch blades, each sheath having a knife sharpener. They were rushed, but knew their lives depended on having the ability to survive the trip that lay before them. They added additional supplies, such as biodegradable soap, straw-type water filters, mosquito spray, and magnesium fire starters.

Then they found the greatest treasure of all… food. Roger had gone to the aisle where the Mountain House food would normally have been displayed, but it was empty. On a hunch, he got down on his hands and knees and looked in the cabinet underneath. In the very back, far corner he saw a cardboard box. He reached in and pulled it out, excitedly cutting it open with his new blade. Mountain House Beef Stew… a case of twenty four. He couldn't believe his eyes.

"I'm so damn hungry, I could eat one of these right now but we just don't have the time. We really need to get moving." The two men each strapped a stuffed sleeping bag and pad to their backpacks. On the way out they discovered display racks with various brands of beef jerky and pemmican. They stuffed as many as they could in their packs and pockets, and exited the store heading west on Highway 64, chewing on strips of the tough beef jerky.

At the edge of town they passed a bicycle shop. Roger was elated. "Oh man, we could really go a lot faster on a bike."

"I'm sorry, Roger. I used to ride a bike when I was a little kid, but there's no way I could ride one now. They don't make bikes big enough for me."

"Let's check 'em out. Maybe we can just use one to carry our stuff." They entered the bike shop and Roger felt like a little kid on Christmas morning. He didn't know too much about bikes but he'd always had an old bicycle around the farm. Ashe had gone into the repair shop at the rear of the building while Roger pulled a bicycle off the wall. It had a rack and a small basket on the back.

"Let's go Ashe. We can take turns putting our pack in the back of the bike."

Honk, honk!

Roger turned and stared in amazement, as Ashe rode out of the back of the bicycle shop on a three wheel bike, his backpack stuffed in a basket on the back. His bright, white teeth glowed out of a gigantic grin on his face as he squeezed a rubber ball on the handlebar of the tricycle.

Honk, honk.

Roger, laughing, said, "Okay, now you just look stupid."

On the bicycles, the men were able to travel much faster, and since the moon had moved higher in the sky they were able to see the terrain ahead. After a few miles the road began to climb. Ashe's trike only had three speeds and, as the road became steeper, he was huffing and puffing, spinning in low gear. They were only fifteen miles out of town when Ashe stopped in the middle of the road and said, "That's it Roger. I can't ride it anymore. I'm done." Even in the coolness he was perspiring heavily. Swinging his leg over the seat, he stood waiting for Roger to ride back to him. He put his baseball cap on the backpack and rubbed the sweat from his forehead with the sleeve of his shirt.

"Do you think you can push the bike so you don't have to carry your pack?"

"No, man, that's way too awkward. I don't mind carrying the pack. We'll just have to go slower. I can't do the bike thing anymore. I feel like I've got a red-hot poker up my ass."

"Well, I'm going to... Oh shit!" He was staring back the way they had come and Ashe swung around to see what had attracted Roger's attention.

"They're coming. We need to get off the road." Roger could see headlights in the distance that disappeared periodically as the vehicle took the curves and crested small hills. The light shone brightly in the dark night. They quickly moved to the south side of the road and pushed the bicycles into the dense foliage as far back as they could before the wheels became entangled in the creeper. By now Roger could hear the engine of the car.

He took a last look out to the road as the sound of the engine grew louder. In the bright moonlight, clearly visible, and right in the middle of the road... sat Ashe's hat.

"Oh No. We're toast."

Roger started toward the road but the sound of the engine indicated the car was too close. Ashe grabbed his arm. "Don't be crazy, Roger. It's too late. Come on let's go." They grabbed their backpacks and slung them around onto their backs and took off running through the woods. The trees weren't as dense as they were on the valley floor so they were able to make good time. Roger didn't know where Ashe was getting his energy, but he was keeping up as Roger led the way.

Suddenly they heard the sound of a baying dog.

"Crap! They've got dogs."

Their flight became a grueling test of endurance. They were already tired from working all day, and then their flight from captivity. Now, mile after mile, they ran through the forest, trying to stay ahead of the sound of the baying dogs. Roger prayed fervently that they weren't running in circles, as they plowed through the woods.

The sound of the dogs was drawing ever closer. They were using a flashlight with Roger's hand over the beam to cut it down to a sliver of light. Had they not had the flashlight they would have run straight over the bank of a small stream flowing downhill to their left.

"Ashe, we need to travel in the stream for a ways. I have an idea. Let's throw something into the water and hope the dogs follow it downstream." They quickly unhooked Ashe's sleeping bag and rubbed it on their faces and hands. They went down the bank and into the cold water, where it swirled around their calves. Roger walked downstream several yards and placed the backpack on the bank of the river. Returning to Ashe, he reached into the water and picked up several baseball-sized rocks, throwing them at the bag until he dislodged it and it began to float downstream, bouncing off of rocks. The men turned and waded upstream, staying as near to the center as possible.

It seemed like only minutes before they heard the sound of the men and dogs reaching the river. Trying not to splash too much, they struggled against the current of the creek, slipping on algae covered rocks. After a short while, it became obvious to them that the sound of the barking dogs was diminishing.

"Thank God, it worked. But we can't slack off now. Let's stay in the stream for another quarter mile or so and then we'll take a chance on heading back into the forest."

Morning found them still trudging uphill. They'd heard no further evidence of pursuit and had traveled many miles toward their destination. They were done, exhausted, and couldn't go another step. Pulling off their backpacks, they slumped to the ground. Afraid he would go to sleep, Roger stood up and pulled the stove out of his backpack and set it on a flat rock.

"I need one of those butane canisters."

Ashe could only point in the direction of his backpack, unable to move. Roger had filled the water jug from the stream and added a water purifying tablet to it just before they left the creek behind them. He boiled the water and prepared a package of beef stew and they both gobbled it down for breakfast. They fell asleep, hoping their pursuers had given up for good.

They slept most of the day and only made a few more miles before stopping for the night. A cold front had moved in, bringing dismal, cold rain. They used a plastic tarp to erect a cover and set up a tube tent under the rain fly. During the afternoon, as they had hiked southwest, Roger had pointed out a few edible plants and they'd made a soup to go with their beef stew.

"Hey, Roger. I don't suppose you know how to start a fire with one of those magnesium starter things."

"Of course I do." He gathered rocks into a circle, just under the edge of the tarp, and cleared the brush away for a few feet all the way around the campfire. He then built a little teepee of increasingly large sticks and branches, and shaved kindling off of a larger branch. Using leaves and the kindling, he took out the magnesium fire starter and glanced over at Ashe who was staring back at him, fascinated with the process.

Then he reached into his pocket, took out a Bic lighter, and grinning over at Ashe, lit the leaves and kindling on fire. He pushed the little, burning bundle into the middle of his pyramid of sticks, where they began to catch fire.

"Hey man, that's not fair. Where'd you get that lighter?"

Roger laughed. "I picked it up back in the sporting goods store. There was a whole barrel full of them. I've got a dozen in my pack." He started adding larger branches to the fire, and even though the fuel had been damp from the rain, he soon had a comfortable campfire burning.

The men sat staring out at the gentle rain, and as the fire burned down Ashe looked over at Roger and saw tears in the man's eyes. "Hey Rog, what's up?"

"This reminds me of camping with my kids." He sniffed and wiped his eyes with his shirtsleeves. "I wonder if I'll ever see them again." He turned and stretched out on the sleeping bag they had spread out on the bottom of the tube tent and Ashe could see Roger's body shaking with sobs.

The next morning they arose early, packed up their stuff , and by afternoon had reached a ridge. They scrambled up the side of the hill, slipping on the mud and pushing through the dense, wet foliage. Roger turned and looked back out over the valley.

"Come on, Roger, let's get moving. They could be coming after us any minute."

"My family's down there. I'm going to have to figure out a way to come back to get them."

"Not going to happen, my friend," Ashe told him. "You might as well get used to the idea that they're gone forever. If you go back and try to rescue them, you'll get captured, and chances are they'll kill you."

"I don't care. I can't just leave my family behind."

"Look, Roger. Your kids have been taken to a re-education camp. Your wife is in a camp for women. They use them to do their cooking, their laundry, and, well… for other things. They're surrounded by scores of soldiers. You don't even know where they took them, and you will never find them. Now get real, and let's get going. It's a whole different world, and if you want to live you have to play by the new rules."

After hiking three more days they finally climbed a hill and found themselves on a wide two-lane highway. Roger stood looking out over the hills and valleys they had traversed, and turning like a zombie, followed Ashe over the hill into Kentucky.

13

The group had stayed up much later than normal, singing and telling tales of their lives before the war. When morning arrived they decided to sleep in and get a late start. They seemed reluctant to leave the beauty of the mountains behind them, knowing they were heading out into the plains. Not wanting to lose the whole day of travel, they packed up and left around noon. As the horses became conditioned, and the people became accustomed to their routines, they were making better time. Coming out of the mountains a couple of hours later they saw a small town in the distance.

"I think you guys better stay here while me and Chang check it out," Mike told Mark.

"What's the map say it is?" Mike handed Mark the battered map.

"I think it's Costilla. It's not a real big town but maybe we can find some supplies."

"Well, don't take too long. It'll be dark in a few hours and we need a place to camp."

The guards split up, two to the left and one rider to the right. Jimbo rode his motorcycle alongside the lone man on horseback.

They were back in less than an hour.

"It's deserted. But it looks like there's a few small buildings, so maybe we can search for supplies. They've got a campground that has restrooms. They're only pit toilets but at least we don't have to set up the latrine. I think it would be a good place to camp."

Chris had walked over to the conversation. "Good. Can we get hookups?"

Costilla turned out to be less of a town than a collection of old houses and older trailers. It stretched out over a mile along the road. As they moved through town they remained vigilant, feeling like the town was haunted with the spirits of the casualties of war.

It seemed completely deserted but didn't feel like it. Low clouds had gathered and made the day dark and cold, even darker than it should have been. Mark felt a chill as they passed a food store with all the windows busted out and with the wind moaning through the gap.

"You know Mark, I have a feeling were being watched," Lori whispered. She sat on the wagon seat, her rifle across her lap. "Kevin, Ashley, you guys get down in the bottom of the wagon and stay there until I say you can get up."

She looked around nervously and thought she spotted something moving off to her right, but when she snapped her head around in that direction, it was gone.

Kevin was whimpering, curled into a ball in the back of the wagon and Ashley lay beside him, her eyes squeezed tightly shut.

Mark's head continually swung right to left as he too, felt the strangeness in the air. Lori saw something disappear behind a falling down storage shed and stared at the spot for several minutes, hoping to see what it was. But nothing moved and she felt the small hairs on the back of her neck rise up.

The horses looked around nervously.

Matthew and several of the other men had fanned out on either side of the wagon train, their weapons at the ready, as a thickening mist swirled around them. Something hit the side of the wagon and Mark jerked the reins as the horses picked up the pace. The wind shook the canvas of the wagon as Lori crawled into the back with the kids and sat by the tailgate, her rifle pointed to the rear.

She thought she could she shadows in the mist but couldn't pin down anything solid. They seemed to sway with the moans of the rising wind. The trip through town seemed unending.

Then suddenly they came out of the mist into bright sunlight. Behind them a solid wall of fog cut off the road back into town, strange shapes swirling in the mist. Lori shook her head, not sure if it was real or her imagination, caused by the tension of the past hour.

They hurried north, away from the uncanny village of Costilla.

***

A couple of miles further up the road they came to a Shamrock service station.

Jesse, Chang and Danny ran over to the service station in a crouch. They disappeared inside and were back in less than a minute empty-handed.

"Picked clean. I wonder if there's any gas in the tanks," Danny said, "I think Jimbo's gas cans are getting low." He and Jesse unscrewed the lid of the tank and Jesse dropped a small pebble into the dark hole.

"I think I heard a splash. Did you Danny?"

"Yeah let's get the pump." The tank was almost empty but they were able to get enough to fill one of Jimbo's five gallon cans.

The outriders returned to the wagon train and a discussion was held about spending the night. They made a unanimous decision to move on and camp away from the town, none of them feeling comfortable with the eerie feelings and sense of malevolence they had felt. They set up camp a few miles to the north and posted extra sentries for the night to be on the safe side. The eeriness persisted and they spent a restless night.

***

The next day they crossed into Colorado and rode over the bridge that spanned the Rio Grande. The sky was clear and no one even pitched a tent as they all decided to sleep out under the stars. Mike, Chang, Carlos and Greg had a poker game going. All these men were in their late thirties or early forties and tended to hang out together. They sat on a blanket in front of the chuck wagon and used an upside down box as a table. A lantern hanging on the side of the wagon illuminated the game as they played for waterproofed matchsticks.

Mark, Lori, Chris and Aaron sat in front of Mark's wagon in lawn chairs, all but Chris drinking a beer. The desultory conversation revolved around the kids, the strange trip through Costilla, their journey, and what they thought they might find at the end. Ash, Kevin and Skillet were all asleep in their wagons and the young adults were playing hacky sack on the far side of the campfire.

Sheri gazed over at Jesse, wondering why she hadn't noticed before how nice-looking he was. They had hung out in different circles in the shelter but were spending more time together on this trip.

"What?" Jesse asked her, startling her out of her reverie just as the hacky sack came her way. She deftly kicked it up with the side of her foot and it sailed high in the air toward Sam.

"What do you mean, *what?*" she asked him, as they both kept their eyes on the footbag.

"You were staring at me." In his best imitation of Sandra Bullock in "Miss Congeniality," he sang, "I think you like me, you think I'm pretty."

She started laughing and glanced his way just as the hacky sack hit her on the knee. "Damn, that wasn't fair. He distracted me."

"You're out." Willy said.

She walked over to the side of the wagon and, sitting in her chair, took a swig from the whiskey bottle. Jesse was the next to leave the game and Sheri suspected he missed the sack on purpose so he could join her. She started to hand him the bottle but he held up his hand. "I'm an athlete, remember?"

"Listen, dude, It'll be years before there are any more organized sporting competitions. We could die tomorrow, so let's enjoy life while we can."

Even though she was an Olympian, Sheri had always been a partier.

"So, if you're such an athlete, how come I hardly ever saw you in the gym when we were in the shelter?"

"I always went when you weren't there."

"Why the hell would you avoid me?"

He paused for a second as if embarrassed, and then told her, "I had a crush on you. Clay and Danny teased me about it so I didn't want to fan the flames. I stayed away from you."

"Well, Clay's dead, and Danny seems to be growing up, so I guess we can hang out all we want, huh?"

He looked over at her and their eyes met. He started to say something as he reached for her hand.

Then the moment was shattered as Willy kicked the hacky sack high over Danny's head and it landed smack in the middle of the fire. Coals crackled and a shower of embers soared into the sky. They all just stared into the fire as the hacky sack burst into red flames, a bright spot in the yellow coals, and was consumed in seconds.

"Well, I guess I'll go to bed," Willy said.

"You're such a dick," his brother told him, as they headed off to their sleeping bags.

Everyone else called it a night, and they were lulled to sleep by the murmuring sound of the Rio Grande.

***

As they rode westward the next morning, a dark, smoky plume was outlined against the sky. They'd been traveling for over two weeks, and were looking forward to reaching the small town of Antonito... but the smoke cast a pall over their anticipation.

Their supplies were running low, they needed new clothes and they hoped to find more beer. Hours later, as they drew closer to the town, the plume of smoke appeared wider and was being blown southward to the horizon.

Riding on the seat beside Mark, with Kevin in between, Lori looked horrified. "Oh my God, Mark. This looks bad. It looks like the whole town's gone up in smoke."

Before Mark could even suggest it, Matthew crawled up from the back of the wagon where he had been sleeping, and suggested, "Einstein and I are going to ride ahead and check out the town. I think you should make camp here and wait for us to report."

"Thanks Matthew, I was hoping you would do just that. Be careful."

"We will. Mike, Aaron and Greg have sentry duty. We should be back in a few hours." He climbed down from the wagon and whistled for Chief. Once Einstein had saddled Jasper, they rode off at a canter toward the billowing smoke in the distance.

Circling the wagons, they made camp, waiting for the men to return with news of the town. It was now midafternoon, and except for the smoke in the west, the sky was clear, the sun shining brightly. A couple of hours later it began its descent. The children, Sheri and the Yancey boys were playing tag around the wagons when dust clouds in the distance indicated Matthew and Einstein were returning.

They came galloping across the plains and pulled up the horses to a trot before entering the perimeter of the wagons. Matthew dropped Chief's reins and approached a group standing around a roaring campfire while Einstein tied his horse off to one of the wagons.

"Hi guys," Matthew greeted them. "It's bad news and good news. About half the town, mostly to the east of the main street, has burned to the ground. To the west of the road, the town is still intact. We didn't see any inhabitants. It doesn't seem very large but it's bigger than the last place. I think we'll still be able to find supplies."

Einstein walked over and stuck out his hands to warm them by the fire. The temperature had begun to drop now that the sun was close to setting. It had dipped behind the smoke on the horizon creating a spectacular display of orange and yellow colors fanning upward.

"When we get there in the morning, me and Matthew will go ahead and check it out more thoroughly to be sure it's safe. Then the rest of you can come into town."

***

Morning arrived with a stiff wind blowing out of the north. Even though Matthew and Einstein had been part of the night sentry crew, they were insistent that they check out the town again that morning before the rest of them arrived. The wagons moved out toward Antonito. Matthew and Einstein were mounted, with Jimbo on his motorcycle and Mike, Greg and Mark preceding them on foot. They split up and approached the town from different directions.

Half the town had burned and the ruins were still smoldering. A couple of hotspots could still be seen burning at the extreme north side of town. They crossed Main Street to the west, dismounted, and cleared one section. Weapons out, they moved from building to building shouting, "clear!" once they determined it was empty. Matthew left Chief back on Main Street where the others were searching, and went ahead on foot to ensure they weren't surprised by anyone.

Once they had cleared a complete block, Jimbo jumped on his motorcycle and headed back to get the wagons. They drove them into town and turned left on Main Street, riding past the yellow railroad station for the Cumbres and Toltec Narrow Gauge Train. The historical train ran between Antonito and Chama, New Mexico. There were several brown, observation cars, each with a dozen large windows, and an old fashioned steam engine. They stopped in front of the Narrow Gauge Railroad Inn.

"Man, I'm looking forward to sleeping in a bed tonight," Jimbo told them. "Mark said to leave the wagons here. Einstein's already set up some sentries and the rest of you can come into town on foot. It seems to be safe."

Aaron climbed into the wagon with Chris. "Honey, I'll stay with the baby since she's running a temp. You go on into town and see if you can find us some clothes."

"What you really need is a good bath."

"Yeah well, good luck. If you find a tub full of really hot water let me know and we can share."

Chris jumped out of the wagon and started toward town on foot, along with Lori and half a dozen others. Even though the way had been cleared, they approached the town with caution. On the right side of Main Street all that was left of the buildings was bent steel, collapsed concrete and bricks, and smoking ruins. Chris saw a sign, partially burned and leaning against a brick wall that simply said *Library*.

Weapons out, they ran across the street to the Dutch Mill Bar and Restaurant. The signs were all fading and several hung loose from one end. There was a hotel next door and they slipped into the recessed doorway.

"I wasn't looking to spend the night," Chris said. "Can you tell me where Neiman Marcus is?"

"We'll be lucky if we can find a store at all," Mike said, shaking his mop of brown hair. "I don't see any."

"Mike, you're always so negative. I'm sure there's a Saks at the end of the block."

"What I want is someplace with kitchen supplies." Skillet was already heading onto the sidewalk and moving toward the next store in line.

It soon became apparent that this small town had very little of what they needed. There was a single, main street through town, with a few east-west roads containing only houses.

Chris walked out into the middle of the road. "Come on, Lori, let's walk up to the end of town and see if we can find any stores."

"Hey, where are you girls going?" Chang said.

"It's okay, Chang," Chris said, "the town's been cleared. I think I can see a store up on the left."

Skillet ran over to them. "I'm going with you. I need some new pots and pans."

The three of them walked up the middle of the street. Smoke drifted over and around them from the small fires still burning in the buildings on the east side of the road. There were towers of some kind, maybe for water, that had paintings of Native American and pioneer families. *They must have been beautiful before the war*, Chris thought.

They spotted a Family Dollar store recessed behind the adjoining buildings with a parking lot in front. They hurried inside to see what kind of treasures it held. Although the store didn't have a very good selection, it had a few clothes, kitchen utensils, and canned goods. They rummaged through the merchandise, and piled the things they wanted to keep by the front door. Skillet had grabbed three pans and a griddle and added them to the stack.

"I guess I'll have to bring back a couple of the horses to pick this stuff up. I'll go back to the motel and get Fred and Ethel. I'll see you two later."

Chris and Lori went up and down the aisles selecting items for the pile, and Lori found several outfits for each of the kids. They spent the next twenty minutes looking for clothes for themselves.

Chris pulled a blouse off the rack, held it up in front of her, and said to Lori, "Ooh, I like the colors on this one, what do you think?" She did a pirouette… and was blown completely off her feet.

She slid across the floor and came up hard against a counter, wrenching her shoulder. Momentarily dazed, she shook her head to try and clear it. There was a crash and she covered her head as burning debris cascaded around and over her. Her heart pounded in her chest as she realized she was pinned under a beam.

Lori was further toward the rear of the store and dove to the carpet alongside a counter. Something had smashed into the roof of the store and, within a single minute, the burning object fell through the roof of the building bringing down part of the ceiling with it. The store was immediately filled with smoke as the burning debris began to burn brighter and hotter. She crawled around the end of the counter and found Chris crammed up against the other side.

"Chris, Chris, come on get up." Chris's arm was almost yanked out of the socket as Lori pulled her out from under the debris. "We need to get out of here... now!" Lori swatted burning embers from Chris's back and hair. Her ankle was bound up in some timbers and Lori burned her hands jerking the boards off Chris's leg.

The store was filled with smoke, and as Lori pulled Chris toward the back of the room, another loud crack signaled the impending collapse of the remainder of the roof.

Lori glanced up as she tugged at Chris afraid they wouldn't get out in time. Thoughts of the kids and Mark flashed through her mind. "Hurry! The roof's coming down."

"Wha... What happened?"

"I'm not sure. An explosion I think. Something heavy landed on the roof. You need to get down and crawl, stay under the burning gases,"

They began to crawl quickly around the counter and toward a hallway leading to the back of the building. Lori noticed Chris was lagging behind. "Chris, please hurry," she begged, "we need to get out."

"I hurt my shoulder. I'm going as fast as I can." She began to cough. Lori jumped to her feet in a crouch, and holding her breath ran back and bodily lifted Chris to her feet, dragging her down the hallway to the rear door. Thunderous crashes came from behind them as the entire ceiling of the building gave way.

The heat was so intense Lori could barely breathe as she slammed into the back door. Reaching down, she turned the knob, as Chris slumped to the floor. Grabbing Chris under the arms she dragged her out into the sweet air behind the building.

The wind was blowing the smoke toward the south and east but both buildings on either side of the store were fully engulfed in flames. She had no choice but to drag Chris straight back away from the buildings, although she couldn't see any way to get to the street. As they put some distance between them and the inferno, the heat lessened to a degree, and Lori gulped in deep breaths.

"Do you think you can get up? We need to get between those houses to the side street. This whole end of town is going up in flames."

"Yeah," Chris panted, holding her left shoulder with her right hand, "let's go. I'm better now. I can breathe." They made it out to the street but, with the buildings on both corners in flames, they realized they couldn't get out to Main Street. They went west and then south, cutting through the grounds of Antonito High School. The wind fed the forty-foot flames and one building after another caught on fire as it moved south, cutting them off.

They were becoming exhausted when Lori said, "I think we've outdistanced it. "Let's head back to Main Street. All the guys are gonna be looking to rescue us and I don't want anybody getting hurt, when we're okay."

They started back toward the east, and just as they came opposite a building on the left, it burst into flames, fanned by the stiff wind. The heat assailed them and Lori grabbed Chris's arm, pulling her toward the street. Chris cried out in pain.

Moving as fast as they could, with Lori helping to support her, they rounded the corner onto Main Street and found half a dozen men racing toward the north. Mark was in the lead and when he saw the women he immediately changed course and hurried to their assistance.

"Lori, thank God. Hurry! The flames are moving fast. The whole town's going up."

"Chris is hurt."

Mark threw his arm around Lori as Matthew jumped off of Chief, and he and Chang hoisted Chris into the saddle. As well trained as Chief was, his eyes were rolling in fear, and he was skittering sideways away from the burning buildings. The heat was intensifying as fire moved toward them. The smoke was blowing directly down Main Street, swirling around them and cutting their visibility to almost zero. The smoke burned their lungs as they breathed. The horse screamed and trembled, but Matthew had hold of the reins as they all hurried toward the south where the smoke had thinned.

Mark turned around and looked back toward the fire. What had looked like a few, small, hot spots on the east side of Main Street had been fanned by the wind into a raging inferno. It jumped the Highway following the explosion of a propane tank. Mark could see a half of the tank lying in the middle of the road.

The smoke thinned as they ran south, and as they came abreast of the Cumbres and Toltec Railway Station they met Skillet riding in their direction.

"Guess I'm not going to be picking up those supplies we set aside," he said ruefully.

"Supplies? Were lucky as hell we didn't lose Lori and Chris."

"Just kidding man."

They all made it back to the Railroad Inn, where Aaron hurried over to help Chris down from the horse. Her big eyes, wide enough for the whites to show, were blinking in a face covered with soot. He hugged her tight and said, "Doesn't look like you found that big tub full of hot water."

"No, I guess you're gonna have to wash every inch of my body yourself." He laughed and hugged harder but stopped when he saw her wince in pain.

"Honey, what's wrong?"

"I wrenched my shoulder, and I think I have some burns on my back. I've scorched part of my hair, and inhaled smoke and burning gases. But don't worry, I'm just fine." She passed out, her knees buckling. Aaron caught her, picked her up and carried her to their wagon.

"I don't know about you guys," Mark said, "I really don't feel like spending the night here. No telling if the flames will make it down this far, but I think we should head out on Highway 17 for a few miles before we camp."

They all agreed, and even though they had unharnessed the horses, they prepared to leave again. The animals, grazing in the weeds at the side of the parking lot were unhappy about being re-harnessed and the mustangs reared and whinnied. Finally calming them down they got the wagons moving, and as they were pulling away from the motel, Einstein looked around and said, "Hey everybody, where's Jimbo?"

"I see his bike over by the motel," Sheri said as she rode over and pounded on the door.

Jimbo came out, wearing a tee shirt, boxer shorts and his old, olive, drab cap. He squinted into the bright sunshine and scratched his whiskers.

"Hey, what's going on?" he yelled, when he noticed they were leaving.

"Did I miss something?"

14

The Horde stayed in Kingman, Arizona for six days. They started in the downtown area, on the south side of town, staying in a Motel 6 on Beale Street. Using a manual pump, they drained the underground gas tanks in the Chevron station next door, topping off the tanks in all of the vehicles, and filling several five gallon gas cans they carried in one of the pickup trucks.

"We need to get out of this town ASAP," Chase told Bing when they first arrived in town from Vegas. Memories of cruel children teasing him, and calling him Andy Devine, came unbidden to his mind. "I hate this place."

"How come, Chase? It's got a lot of railroad history. I like trains. And Andy Devine grew up here."

Chase shot him such a look of hatred that Bing said, "Sure Chase," and sped away under the freeway overpass, swinging into the parking lot of the Motel 6, the others all following behind.

Kingman turned out to be a gold mine for the gang, and Chase had to give in to let the Horde stay longer than he wanted. There were no residents living in this part of town and they found canned goods and bottled water in markets along Beale Street. It took two days to clean out the stores and fill the beds of the pickups. Sleeping in late, they mounted up and roared east on Beale until it swung around the curve and headed up to the newer section of town.

Andy Devine Boulevard. It mocked Chase as he flew north at over 100 miles per hour.

For some reason, his voice was even scratchier than usual.

Pulling into a motel parking lot just past the I-40, the cyclists climbed from their bikes and waited for Nutts to come out with keys. A restaurant stood in the corner of the lot. Most of the gang members pushed in, sitting at tables and booths, where they opened and consumed cans of Spam and Vienna Sausage. They drank bottles of warm soda.

Rod wiped grease off his beard and his leather vest with his bare arm.

"What's that big building over there? Looks like a hospital." Rod was pointing out the window. "Maybe there's some drugs. Maybe some Dilaudid or Oxy. Let's check it out."

"If you find anything, you better bring it back to Chase," Bing said. "If you don't, he's liable to blow your fucking brains out."

"Why doesn't he go with us, then?" Nutts asked.

"He's a loner, and for some reason he's in a worse mood than usual. You should be glad he's not here."

Speeding down Stockton Hill, they arrived at Kingman Regional Hospital in ten minutes. They searched through the hospital but found very little of value until they reached the pharmacy. It was locked up tight, but using their weapons, they blasted through the door and window and poured into the interior.

"Fuck, man, look at all this stuff." Johnny grabbed handfuls of packaged medications and threw them into the air. They stuffed Ambien, Restoril and other sleeping meds into white paper bags, along with a large variety of narcotics. They found Vicodin, Dilaudid, Percocet and Oxycodone. It was a druggie's dream come true. Rod had already taken three of the 2 mg Dilaudid. Others were washing pills down with bottled water.

Bing wasn't one to do drugs, but he filled bags full of the pain and sleeping meds to take to Chase. He took off his blue bandanna and wiped his face. This was bad. These guys were going to be harder to control than usual.

Some men went out to the floors and gunned down the Pyxis machines. They shot open the drawers and used knives to break into the compartments. Every man had his pockets full, and had stuffed bags to put in the saddlebags on their bikes.

It was almost dark when they returned to the motel. Chase had come out of his room and was wondering where all the bikes had gone when Bing rode up with his booty. As the others started to arrive, Chase met them with gunfire, shooting his weapon over their heads.

"You Motherfuckers have any drugs, you better hand them over. I'll be the one to hand 'em out. Otherwise you'll all be worthless."

With sullen looks they handed over the bags but most of them held back what they had in their pockets, taking a chance Chase wouldn't search them. Fortunately for them, he didn't.

***

In the morning four of the bikers were dead. Unlimited access to drugs had proved too much and they had died, not only from overdosing, but from mixing the drugs. Chase ordered the bodies thrown across the street and their bikes given to men that were riding double.

"That leaves more supplies for the rest of us," he told Bing. "They held out on me and I'm sure the others did too. Tell the men they better turn over what they squirreled away or I'll kill each one of them as I search them for drugs. And it won't be an easy death."

The bikers had taken enough drugs to kill a dozen horses. They spent the night in a stupor and most didn't wake until noon. Bodies unused to any kind of meds for almost two years reacted with massive headaches and nausea. When Bing told them to turn over the drugs they popped painkillers and sullenly handed over the others.

The third day in Kingman was spent recovering.

On the fourth day Chase roused them to action. "Now that you pussies are better, let's scavenge what we can from this dump and get out of town."

That's when they discovered the colony.

First, they came across the fairgrounds where the townspeople were raising livestock. They had cattle, goats, sheep and pigs. When the bikers rode onto the fairgrounds they were met with gunfire. Three men were hit, their choppers careening into parked cars and a fence.

"Fuck! Pull back to the street," Chase yelled.

Withdrawing to the far side of the parking area, they roared up to Chase.

"They won't fucking get away with this. I want every person taking part in that ambush, dead. Get behind those cars in the first row and lay down a barrage. Bing, choose six guys and follow me."

He swung into the street and Bing had to scramble to follow. They went down a side street to the far side of an arena, where a gate led into the dirt road that ran in front of the stables. Screaming down the central road in the fairgrounds, they came up behind the group of defenders.

The men bravely stood their ground as the motorcycles bore down on them, firing at Chase and the others, but Chase didn't care if his men died, and that gave them an advantage. Three of the four defenders went down. The fourth man threw down his weapon and put his hands in the air. Chase shot him in the forehead, and throwing open the front gate, allowed the rest of the Horde access.

The squealing and screaming of the animals could be heard as they slaughtered every one of them.

"Hey boys," Chase called out, "another fucking barbeque."

"Yeah," muttered Cutter to Bing quietly, "at least it ain't human."

They cooked the meat and gorged themselves on the first fresh meat they'd had in many months. They could have fed the entire horde for weeks had they kept some of the animals alive.

"Hey Chase? Where do you think were gonna end up?" asked Bing, as he chowed down on a leg of mutton. I was thinking it might be nice to go somewhere down south, like Arkansas or Alabama. They have lots of water down there and I don't think they would've been bombed like Denver or Colorado Springs. What do you think?"

"Shut up Bing. We'll just keep moving until I say we found the right place."

Rod had food smeared in his beard, "Hey Chase, I like Kingman. It's been really good to us, huh?"

Chase took out his .45 and shot the man through the chest.

***

Two days later they rode out of town, east on I-40. They'd found the rest of the residents and killed every man, woman and child, losing two more men and one of the women in the process. The crops in the fields were mostly grown, producing a cornucopia of produce. Chase ordered them torched. Even the most evil of the members of Satan's Horde were shocked by the wanton violence and destruction.

Chase removed his gloves almost every hour, rubbing on alcohol gel, and the others, always worried about Chase's sanity, were becoming concerned for their safety. Cutter approached Bing the morning they were to leave town. "Bing, what the hell are we going to do about Chase? He's getting guys killed and he even shot Rod for no reason."

"Look, man, we've had steak, pork chops and lamb for two days. We have an unbelievable amount of drugs, and gallons of alcohol we found in that bar. The pickups are jammed full of shit and we're getting out of this town. We'll worry about Chase later."

"We should let him take off at his insane speed and then take a different road."

Bing chuckled and agreed, "He'd come back and track us down. Probably kill us all."

The day was warm and the gang wore short sleeve t-shirts and leather vests. Bing's ever present bandanna was yellow but his long, gray hair still blew backwards in the wind. Flagstaff, Arizona was the next large town on their route as they climbed steadily out of Kingman, and the trees changed from Junipers and Pinyon pines to Ponderosas. Motoring through Williams they saw the turn-off for the Grand Canyon. *Always wanted to see the Grand Canyon,* Bing thought. They came into the beautiful, mountain town to find Chase sitting in the middle of I-40 reclining against the sissy bar waiting for them.

"Gas up and head north on the 89. We're heading for Kayenta up in the Navajo Reservation."

Bing was perplexed. "Damn, Chase, that's really out of our way. Why're we going up there?"

Chase almost looked a little embarrassed. "That's where my Mama lives." He sat up on the bike and, with a deep throaty rumble, it sped down the off ramp, Chase leaning to the inside of the turn onto the 89, his knee almost touching the ground.

"Is his mom a redskin?" Cutter asked.

"You got me. I ain't askin' him."

Arriving in Kayenta, Arizona in the late afternoon, they decided to stay in the Holiday Inn just off Highway 163. As always, Chase was waiting for them to arrive.

"You guys stay here, I've got to go someplace. If you see anyone, don't fuck with them. Got it?"

"Sure Chase. When you comin' back?"

"I don't know. Just wait here 'til I do."

He didn't return until the next afternoon. He wore dark shades and his rusty voice was scratchier than usual. Bing could swear the big man had been crying but wisely didn't say a word. The bikers were all in the parking lot, starting up the bikes and putting their belongings back into their saddlebags. The pickups and the van swung around the bikes and the driver of the van yelled out to Chase, "Where we going?"

Chase looked back the way he had come, sitting silently on the big Harley for a minute and then, as he took off, he yelled, "Durango!"

15

It took a full week for the wagon train to get through the passes between Antonito and Chama. The road was at times quite steep, and with only two horses or mules pulling each wagon, they had a rough time getting up the hills to the La Manga Pass at 10,230 feet. Mark and Mike tied ropes on either side of the lead wagon and let their horses add their strength to that of the primary pair. As the other wagons fell behind, they did the same thing for each of the other two.

The high country still had patches of snow, but the trees had leafed out and painted the hills in shades of green. The temperature, cooler at this high altitude, was still pleasant and the sun warmed them all afternoon. The narrow gauge tracks of the Cumbres and Toltec Railway crisscrossed the highway several times and ran off through flower-filled meadows. They could only make ten miles a day and, not getting all the way through the pass, ended up camping on the asphalt of a scenic overlook. The view toward the north was breathtaking, with pine covered slopes, sheer rock cliffs and a meandering river in the valley below. Fluffy clouds floated overhead.

Once through La Manga Pass, they spent the rest of the day getting to Cumbres Pass, also at over 10,000 feet, then finally began the long descent toward Chama and Highway 64. At some point they re-crossed into New Mexico. Lori had worried about the kids at these high altitudes but the only person bothered by the altitude had been Mike. He developed a throbbing headache and vomited over the side of the road. Aaron told him the only help for it was to get to a lower altitude. Fortunately he didn't develop any worse symptoms and recovered as soon as they descended into the valley.

Since the war, life had been hectic; trying to learn new skills, fighting off mutant monsters, and building a new town. Mark had been finding it hard to relax and just take one day at a time. He still had that built-in alarm clock, like the white rabbit, that said *I'm late, I'm late, for a very important date.* But on this trip he was finally letting go of the stress and was enjoying each day as it came.

They rode into the charming, mountain town of Chama at two o'clock in the afternoon, passing by the western terminus of the railroad. The scouts had cleared the way, and they pulled the wagons a quarter of a mile into the center of town. They stopped right in the middle of the street.

"I don't care what happens in this town, I'm spending the night in a bed," Jimbo whined. "I've had enough of the ground."

"There's a nice motel just down the street," Einstein pointed out. "We saw a bed and breakfast, a couple of restaurants and a bar. I'm going to go down and see if there's any booze left."

Everyone climbed down from the wagons and stretched their stiff muscles. The men who had been walking, went to the side of the street and sat down on a wrought iron bench just beyond the sidewalk. Lori, Chris and the kids headed straight for a store with clothes in the window, and found the door unlocked. It was full of merchandise, including Native Indian style clothing, colorful t-shirts and turquoise jewelry. Greg stood by the door, his rifle at the ready while the women and kids tried on clothes. With her shoulder still sore, Chris had trouble with trying on blouses, and almost cried when she looked in a mirror and saw her beautiful hair burned on the side of her head.

When the women and kids had finished, Lori covered for Greg as he selected some jewelry, putting on a beautiful turquoise necklace.

Skillet pulled his wagon forward and parked it in front of a restaurant. He would use his own equipment for cooking but the travelers would be able to eat at real tables. Two guards stayed behind the wagons and two moved forward a hundred yards down the road while a few of the men unharnessed the horses and mules. They led them between two buildings to a grassy area out back, alongside the river, and strung up a rope corral so the animals could graze.

They spent the afternoon until dinner, checking out the stores and replenishing their dwindling supplies, including batteries, rope and clothing. Skillet was thrilled to find some air-tight, five gallon containers of wheat and rice and a pantry containing baking essentials, such as baking powder and salt.

When dinner was ready, Skillet and the Yancey's carried everything into the Branding Iron Motel and Restaurant, where they pulled several tables together in the center of the room.

"Why do you think this place is so untouched?" Lori asked. "Except for a layer of dust, it looks like it might have before the war. Nobody's messed with any of it. It's just like Antonito."

"I'm thinking if there were any survivors they left town as soon as the bombs fell," Aaron said. "They must have realized there wouldn't be any more trucks bringing food and supplies. If it were me, I would have headed for the nearest big town where there would be a lot more people."

"What about the radiation?"

"Not everyone knows about that stuff. Maybe they didn't think about it. Or maybe there wasn't any this far from the blasts."

The conversation continued and they decided that regardless of why the residents left, they were grateful to have new clothes. There was even a small clinic and Aaron found another stethoscope and a handful of drug samples.

The morning dawned bright and sunny with no fog and no clouds in the sky, but only a few of them saw the dawn, as the others were all snug in real beds. Skillet didn't even fix breakfast until mid-morning. Sentries were swapped out and the night shift crawled into bed. In the spirit of Mark's new laid back lifestyle, he suggested they remain in town for another night, and there were no dissenters.

The second night in town, everyone gathered in the bar where Einstein had discovered a cache of beer and liquor. They had become used to room temperature drinks and all sat around talking and just chilling out. Ashley and Kevin were in the corner, playing with new toys and Aaron held Karen, who was asleep on his shoulder.

"This is great," Chris said. "It looks like our problems may be behind us."

"Oh no, why do people keep saying things like that?" Lori just shook her head. "Bad omen."

"Whatever."

***

One hundred miles lay between them and Bloomfield, New Mexico. It took five days, the first half through pine covered hills, that gradually gave way to juniper trees and scrub. As the highway wound between low hills and through fractured canyons, they started noticing oil and gas wells, some by the road, and many in the valleys they passed through along the way.

Chris was becoming tired of the constant traveling, especially with a baby. Unlike Mark, who was beginning to enjoy a more relaxed attitude, she found fifteen to twenty miles a day boring. She enjoyed the evenings around the campfire, the camaraderie and conversations, but she wanted to get to their destination. The thought of making this trip, turned out to be much more exciting than the trip itself.

In Willsburg, she'd had a job that was both important and interesting, trying to increase the yields on the farms, working with good friends Samuel and Rana, and feeling she was making a real contribution. She missed it.

Her spirits perked up as they neared Bloomfield, the first good sized town since Raton. The small towns had been deserted, but in Bloomfield and Farmington she hoped to meet new people and hear some news.

Aaron sat on the seat beside her, driving the mule team. "Chris, what's wrong? It's not like you to be down like this."

"I'm okay, honey. Just bored with the slow pace. We've only traveled three hundred miles or so in four weeks."

"Yeah, but it's been through some really beautiful country and I've kind of enjoyed the whole camp-out thing. Even in the pouring rain."

"Especially in the pouring rain. That's my favorite part. But we could have driven three hundred miles in a day, comfortably, before the war, and still enjoyed the scenery."

"You will drive yourself nuts if you constantly compare the old days to the current reality. Let's see what Bloomfield brings, okay?"

She was enjoying her new role as a mother, but she was still the modern woman that had traveled the world as a scientist. She wondered if she would always feel out of place in the lower-technology world they now lived in.

16

A constant drizzle fell, as Roger and Ashe gingerly walked down the animal trail they had stumbled across, trying not to slip on the slick mud. Wandering for two days, they'd made their way deeper into the Kentucky back country. The foliage was dense, curving over their heads, and they pushed the wet branches aside as they made their way down the trail. Even though they wore their plastic ponchos, now ripped from the branches, water seeped down Roger's neck.

Ashe set the pace. "Do you think we should just stop and spend the night? I'm soaked through to the bone. It's going to be dark in a few hours anyway."

"I guess so. Do we even know where we're going? You don't still have those relatives living here, do you?"

"No. They moved to Tennessee."

"We can't stop here. We need to find a clearing. I'm just concerned that our food's running low and we have no idea where we are, where we're headed or when we'll get there. Makes me almost wish I were back digging holes. At least we had three meals."

"I hope you're kidding."

"Yeah, but just partly."

It was another mile before the trees opened up into a small meadow. The game trail continued along the side of the clearing and continued into the bright green vegetation on the other side.

A few saplings grew part way into the meadow, giving them something to tie their tarp to. In fifteen minutes they had it up and the tube tent pitched, with the sleeping bag spread out in the bottom, holding the sides apart. The tarp extended beyond the tent giving them a space to build their fire. Since it was Ashe's turn to cook, Roger let him try to start a fire using only the chunk of magnesium.

"You doing okay over there?" he asked as he returned from the bushes.

"How the heck do you do it? You make it look easy. I give up."

Roger had the fire going in five minutes.

"Are we going to eat stew or save it? We're running low on the Jerky, but there's plenty of Pemmican," Ashe asked.

"Let's splurge. Maybe tomorrow we'll get another rabbit."

"That was a lucky shot."

"Skill, my man."

Ashe used a Bic to light the stove, and set a pot of water on it. "Yeah, but you broke the bow."

"I made the bow, and I can fix the bow. Call me Dan'l Boone."

"Does this miserable rain ever stop?"

"You're the one that said, 'Let's go to Kentucky.' But this time of the year it rains a lot in North Carolina too. Especially since the war."

They ate their meager rations and sat side by side staring out at the rain.

"I need to get back and find out what happened to Jess and the kids. Amanda must be so scared."

"Man, I don't know how many times I have to tell you. You won't be able to find them."

"I still need to try."

"They'll catch you and throw you back on a work crew, or if they know who you are, they will hang you. The problem is, there isn't any civilian population left in the towns for you to hide in. Any one running free is fair game."

"If I can find them, we can go west, where the government can't find us. There must be free people they haven't captured yet." He threw another branch on the fire. "You haven't said much about your family. Did any of them survive the war?"

"I don't like to think about it. I was married but we never had any kids. The divorce was bitter."

"I'm sorry, man. Did you have anyone else?"

"My sister, an aunt, and a lot of friends at the school. I went underground at a mall in Danville. Don't know what happened to the others."

Roger nodded and they fell silent, each wrapped in their own memories. When darkness fell they wrapped themselves in their Mylar blankets. "It's getting cold, Rog. I'm hitting the sack."

They crawled into the tent, and fell asleep to Roger humming Elvis' rendition of *Kentucky Rain*.

***

Gunshots brought them instantly awake as they scrambled out of the tent into a dew-soaked morning.

"That sounded close," Roger whispered. "Get the tarp and tent down. Quickly." Roger started untying the ropes that secured the tarp to the trees and Ashe was rolling up the sleeping bag.

"Knock the fire ring apart."

He folded up the bright, orange, tube tent as Ashe kicked the stones apart and scattered the wood, embers and ash over an area of several feet. Stomping on the coals, he poured water on them to snuff them out, then spread them out even farther. Grabbing some branches he scuffed up the ground and covered the area with leaves. They stuffed their belongings into their packs, and faded into the woods just as they heard voices coming along the trail, from the opposite direction they had come from the previous evening.

Roger was thinking about the movie *Deliverance*, as they heard the voices coming closer.

150

"We need to get out of here." Roger tugged on Ashe's arm and they dove deeper into the forest, trying to put as much distance between themselves and the voices as they could. Roger glanced back as the head of a column of hikers came into view.

His jaw dropped and he stood frozen for a moment in time. When he could take his eyes off the newcomers, he glanced at Ashe and saw a similarly shocked expression on his face. The men, or creatures, came into the clearing and the one in the lead raised its ugly head and sniffed. It kicked the leaves that carpeted the floor of the small meadow, turning up charcoal.

There was only a light breeze and, fortunately, they were downwind from the others. Ashe wrinkled his nose as the rancid smell reached them. The men were tall, their bodies out of proportion. Their heads seemed large for their torsos, and their arms unnaturally long. When the lead man saw the remnants of the fire, he bared fangs instead of teeth. There were seven of them, four carrying hunting rifles. Their clothes didn't seem to fit right, and they all carried huge packs that looked like they were over fifty pounds apiece.

"Psst, let's go." They very carefully continued to withdraw into the woods, careful to make no noise. When they had gone a hundred yards, they heard the sounds of pursuit behind them. They'd been discovered. Terrified, they threw caution to the wind and sprinted through the forest below a solid green canopy.

"What the hell are those things?" Ashe yelled as he leaped over fallen logs, crashing through the underbrush as though pursued by the devil himself.

"I don't know. But they must be from the same family 'cause they all look alike."

They were breathing hard but showed no inclination to slow down. Coming to a hill that descended into a valley below, they could hear water running, a river or even a waterfall. Looking back, Roger saw a splash of color and knew they were still being pursued.

"Down we go," he said as they both went over the edge. They tried to hold themselves back from falling down the incline, but Roger caught his foot in a root and, flipping in midair, crashed down on his back, bounced up to his feet, and continued in an out-of-control series of summersaults down the hill.

"Roger! Try to flatten out to break your fall," Ashe screamed, as he ran down the hill, barely in control. He crashed through some trees just in time to see Roger's pack flip into the air and Roger disappear over the edge of a cliff.

"Oh shit, oh no." Ashe skidded to a halt, just managing to keep from flying over the edge himself, and peeked over the precipice.

There, ten feet below in an aquamarine pool, treading water and searching around for his pack, was Roger. A small waterfall spilled into the pool on the left and the river continued downstream from the pool.

Ashe heard loud noises behind him, and whirling around, saw the men sliding down the embankment in their direction. One of the men raised a rifle and fired a shot in Ashe's direction. Roger's pack lay in the trees between the ugly men and him. Knowing he couldn't go back for it, he didn't hesitate, leaping off the cliff to the pool below. Hitting the water, he sunk beneath the surface, cutting his leg on a sharp rock, and waving his arms wildly, rose to the top, sputtering and coughing. Roger pulled at his arm and shoved him downriver.

"Keep your feet pointing forward."

They slid down a series of algae covered chutes and out into the rapids of the river itself.

"If this weren't so dangerous, it could be a lot of fun," Roger yelled.

"Yeah, a real Disney adventure."

Both men pointed their feet downstream and floated, bobbing along the swift current. They tried to use their feet to push off of rocks as they were swept along by the rapids, but Ashe, still wearing his pack, got turned sideways and slammed into a protruding, algae-covered rock. Dazed, he slipped below the surface and flailed about, trying to swim. He swallowed several gulps of water and was panicking, when the river

152

widened and the water slowed. He crawled out onto a low bank, aided by Roger.

"Ashe... Ashe, are you okay?"

"Where are they?" he answered, pulling off the pack and trying to stand.

"On the opposite side of the river. They're coming downstream. Go Ashe. Let's leave these bastards behind." They were exhausted, and their legs would barely carry them as they headed into the woods once more. Roger took a last look and saw the men standing at the edge of the river, pacing back and forth along the bank. They seemed afraid to cross... and that was fine with him.

When they felt safe enough to pause, they sat on a downed log and bandaged Ashe's leg. Blood soaked his pant leg below mid-calf. Ashe grimaced and sucked air through his teeth, when Roger poured iodine over the nasty, three-inch-long gash. He pulled the edges together with butterflies and wrapped gauze around the leg, taping it with paper tape.

"I don't think it's real deep. Good thing the first aid kit was in your pack. When we stop for the night we can inventory and see what we have left."

"There's no way we can go back for your pack."

"No. Let's just get out of here."

Completely soaked, cold, miserable and scared, they slunk away into the woods, to put as many miles between them and the monsters as they could, hoping to never see the likes of those things again.

17

Jesse entered the camp from a bathroom break out in the bushes.

"Well, in case anybody was wondering, the rattlesnakes survived the war." He sunk suddenly to his knees and then pitched forward onto his face.

"Shit. What's wrong with him?" The Yancey's ran over to Jesse and started to pick him up by his arms when Sam noticed blood on his jeans. Sheri, Danny and Jimbo ran over to see what was going on.

"What the hell?" Sam said. "He said something about a rattlesnake. Look at his pants." Sheri ran to the Chuck wagon and returned with a blanket. They rolled Jesse over and slid the blanket under him. Then they carefully worked his pants down until they could see the bite.

"Oh man, will you look at that? It bit him right on the ass," Sam exclaimed.

"Why didn't he use the latrine?" Sheri asked, her heart racing with anxiety.

"He was embarrassed. He always went out into the bushes. Damn! It bit him right on the ass," he repeated. "Hey bro," he said, looking up at his brother who was standing slightly behind him, "I think you need to suck the poison out of the bite."

Willy was backing away, shaking his head back and forth. "No...I... ain't no way I'm sucking the poison out of his ass."

"Relax, they say that's a myth," Sheri said. "We just need to clean up the wound and keep him warm. Somebody needs to get Aaron right now."

"Hey Danny, take Jasper and go get Aaron, he's out on guard duty," Willy told Danny. "You'll have to take his place until someone can relieve you."

"No, Dude. I just had guard duty before these guys. Somebody else needs to go," Danny whined.

"Shut up Danny," Jimbo told him. "I'll ride ol' Jenny out and bring Aaron back. You just go out and take his place or you'll answer to me."

Grumbling, Danny went to the tether and saddled up Tulip. Jimbo was already bouncing across the uneven plains to fetch the doctor. A crowd had gathered around the fallen man and several of them lifted him into the back of Chris's wagon. Mark and Lori, who had been napping in their wagon, and were awakened by the noise, climbed in with Chris and Jesse.

"Wow, it's bruising up pretty badly," Mark said. Chris handed him the first aid kit and he used several alcohol pads to clean the site, causing Jesse to groan as he tried to turn over. The wound had bled freely and Mark hoped it had washed out some of the rattlesnake venom.

"It doesn't look like a clean strike," Lori said. "It's torn open. He must have heard it and jumped just as the snake struck. The edges of the bite marks are jagged. That's probably why it bled so much. That could be a good thing."

"I don't suppose there's any anti-venin in that first aid kit, is there?"

Chris had dumped out all the first aid supplies and was rummaging through them. "No, I don't see any."

"Damn. I wish Aaron would hurry up and get here." Just then, they heard the sound of galloping horses and shouts, and a minute later Aaron climbed over the tailgate of the wagon.

"Kind of crowded in here. Lori, Chris, you ladies mind if me and Mark take over?"

"No," Chris told him, "considering the location of the bite I think you two gentlemen should definitely take over." The two women climbed out of the wagon and joined the rest of the folks at the campfire to wait until Aaron had a chance to examine Jesse.

They were almost to Bloomfield and had camped in one of the cleared off areas around a natural gas well. The hills were green, but the vegetation was scrub, with very few trees, just a few scraggly junipers. This particular well didn't have the rocking pump that characterized the oil wells. There was a large, green tank and pipes covered the well itself.

Sheri glanced back at the wagon where her friend lay hurt. Trying to keep her mind off Jesse, she asked, "Do you think those things need electricity to get the gas out of the ground?"

"Electricity is needed for some of the functions," Greg Whitehorse answered. "The gas in this area is in the San Juan Basin, a huge natural gas reservoir that extends almost to my home in Arizona."

"Is the gas under pressure? Does it just flow to the ground?"

Greg laughed. "If it were only that easy. The gas is trapped in tight shale. Have you heard of fracking?"

"Hey, yeah, I have. But I don't know what it is," she admitted.

"They inject water, containing fracking chemicals, into the well. It can be thousands of feet deep, as much as ten thousand. It's called hydro-fracturing because it fractures the rock that contains the gas, freeing it to come to the surface. There's a lot of controversy regarding fracking. There's worry over the amount of water it uses, although it gets a lot of water back that's trapped in the shale with the gas. Folks wonder if the fracking chemicals will contaminate their drinking water but the fracking is usually well below the aquifers. The fracking water is full of toxins too, and it needs to be treated or the water needs to be stored underground."

"I guess we don't have to worry about it anymore, do we?"

"No, I guess we don't."

They heard hoof beats coming from the road and Matthew and Mike rode into camp.

"We checked out the nearer edge of Bloomfield but didn't see anyone," Matthew reported.

"But we didn't get shot at," Mike added. "So that's a good sign."

"Damn, I hoped we'd find someone here. Bloomfield's like eight or ten thousand people," Sheri said.

"Yes," Matthew told her, "but it's part of the Farmington Metro area. There's about ten miles of highway between the two towns. I came here for a field trip with my geology class in Grad school. We studied their natural gas production. If there are survivors I think they may have congregated in Farmington, just like the people from the surrounding communities moved to Eagle Nest and Willsburg in the New Mexico Colony."

Greg grinned. That was the longest statement he'd ever heard Matthew make.

His smile faded as he looked over toward the wagon, as did Sheri.

"What's going on?" Matthew asked.

He saw Mark approaching the campfire from Chris's wagon, a look of concern on his face as he joined the others.

"Hi Matthew, Mike. We've had a little excitement since you guys left. Jesse's been bitten by rattler. He went into the bushes to do his business and was bitten on the rear end."

Mark shot a disapproving look at Willy who was snickering at the statement.

"Seriously Willy? It's not funny. We don't have any anti-venin so he's just gonna have to fight it off on his own. Aaron's with him now."

Matthew started off toward the wagon. "I've seen a couple of other guys with snakebites on my grandfather's ranch. Let me go take a look."

He climbed into the wagon, returning a few minutes later. "From the distance between the two puncture wounds it looks like it was a pretty big snake and Jesse's not a real big guy. That's not good. It's an ugly looking bite."

***

They took turns watching Jesse through the night. He spiked a fever, and was burning up, with sweat pouring down his face, even as he shivered violently.

"It's so cold," he told Lori.

He was covered by a mound of blankets.

"Is Sheri here?"

"She's right outside, Jesse."

Morning came creeping earlier than Lori had hoped. She'd spent half the night bathing Jesse's forehead with a cool, damp cloth and trying to keep him covered as he tossed and turned, throwing the blankets aside.

In the cool of the false dawn, Aaron climbed over the tailgate to check on his patient.

"Aaron, why is he still unconscious?"

"I think it's part of an anxiety reaction." He put the back of his hand on Jesse's forehead and held the stethoscope against his chest. "Some people, when they're afraid, get hypotensive and nauseated, and tend to faint. Like when they get their blood drawn. But this is worse and it's got me worried. Has he been drinking water?"

"On and off, when he's been conscious."

"We'll try to get him up and see if he needs to pee. I'll get a couple of the guys. Skillet and Sam are up and Matthew just rode back into camp. We'll let it warm up out there first."

The baby woke up and began to wail and Chris stirred at the front of the wagon. Lori lit the oil lantern so Chris could see to change Karen's cloth diaper.

"I'm hoping for a Costco full of Pampers in the next town."

The camp was stirring, and beginning its morning routine. People kept coming by to check on Jesse as they prepared to enter Bloomfield. Sam, Aaron, and Greg lifted Jesse over the tailgate and woke him enough to go around behind the back. When they returned they were almost carrying him as they boosted him back into the wagon.

"This isn't good Lori," Aaron told her. "There's so much blood in his urine I could see it on the ground, and he has a bloody nose. Rattlesnake venom has a hemotoxin and a neurotoxin. Different snakes have different percentages of the two. If this rattler had a high percentage of neurotoxin he'd probably be dead already. He may be bleeding internally. I'll get a volunteer to spell you so you can get some sleep, and they can ride in back with him while we go into Bloomfield."

The column got moving, as they headed toward the unknown in Bloomfield and Farmington.

Aaron was riding alongside the wagon, and they had barely begun the final couple of miles to the city limits when Sheri, who was watching over Jesse, jumped out of the back of the wagon and ran to catch up with him.

"Aaron! Jesse's breathing real funny. Like he's choking. Please hurry." She was fighting back tears and not being successful.

"Hold up everyone. Hey Mark," he called out to Mark in the lead wagon, "pull up and wait a few minutes." He handed Sheri the horse's reins and climbed into the wagon, pausing as he went over the tailgate. "Sheri, you wait out here, okay?"

He knew the symptoms immediately, the broken breathing that accompanies the final moments of life. His breathing became more ragged. Jesse took three quick, short breaths, and then no more. Lori came over the tailgate and Aaron shook his head. "He's gone Lori. Dammit!" He slammed his fist into the side of the wagon. "If we'd had some antivenin I think I could have saved him."

Chris was in the front of the wagon crying softly. Lori handed Aaron a blanket and he pulled it up over Jesse's head, smoothing back his chopped up hair, as Lori climbed out of the wagon to tell the others. Sheri knew from the tears running down Lori's face that Jesse was gone. She ran to the back of the chuck wagon, and went to her knees in the dirt, sobbing for her lost friend.

Looking up as Jimbo came around the corner, she jumped into his arms.

"There, there, little lady. I'm sorry as hell." He held her against his chest, feeling her tears soaking through his shirt. "I guess you and Jesse were getting kind of close, eh?"

"Oh Jimbo, it isn't fair. He was so young and healthy. I can't believe he's gone."

He held onto her and let her grieve until Mark came for him. "Jimbo, can you help us dig a grave?"

"Yeah, I'll be right there. You gonna be okay?"

She nodded and slid down against the wagon wheel, burying her head in her hands.

The men and Lori took turns at digging the grave. Although it was still early, the day was warming and the shovels were getting dull. When it was deep enough they brought out Jesse's body, wrapped in the blanket, and lowered it into the grave. Jimbo brought Sheri from behind the wagon and prayers were said before they covered him.

"How will we mark the grave?" Sheri asked. She broke down again, sobbing, "I can't just leave him out here without even marking the grave." She sniffed and wiped her nose on her sleeve.

Jimbo handed her a bandana. "Don't worry, I'll take care of it. He walked off around the wagon and she heard the motorcycle start up as Jimbo headed off in the direction of Bloomfield.

Not knowing what else to do, Skillet made coffee and they all awaited Jimbo's return. The children didn't want to leave the wagon and Lori stayed inside with them. They had been close to Jesse. He often played football and tag with them.

It was forty minutes later when Jimbo came back bearing a few pieces of lumber. As he went to the chuck wagon to get a hammer and nails he said to Skillet, "Found these just inside the town. Do you have that permanent marker?"

They drove the cross deep into the ground at the head of the grave. It simply said,
Jesse – Runner.

18

"Periscope depth Mister Carter."

"Aye Captain. Bring us up to seventy feet," he called out. The planes on the conning tower of the submarine changed angle and the sub rose out of the depths into shallower water. "Periscope up," Finney said. The XO scanned the surface of the water as he turned 360 degrees, gazing through the glass eye above on the surface of the ocean.

"Captain, land bearing 260 degrees."

The Captain had been concerned about not having some of their modern navigational aids, such as satellite GPS. They'd cruised at twenty knots, more than five knots below maximum speed, covering twenty five hundred miles in just under a week. The enormous submarine surfaced a mile off the coast of Hawaii, The Big Island. The XO stepped aside and the captain confirmed his observation. "Periscope down."

He turned to the XO and said, "If the President's correct, and the Chinese are making a move on the United States, then they're still beyond the Hawaiian Islands. Are we getting a reading on the radiation?"

"Yes, sir," Finney answered. "We're picking up faint traces of neutron radiation. It looks like the Chinese hit the islands with their neutron bombs instead of hydrogen bombs. I'm thinking they wanted to preserve the islands for some reason. Radiation is at a safe level, sir."

"Naval Base Pearl Harbor in Honolulu has huge amounts of high-grade fuel and docking facilities. I believe, Mister Finney, they intend to utilize that base as a refueling station. So far, though, we haven't seen any signs of them."

"No, sir, but the president seemed to feel they might be on their way. What are your orders, sir?"

Dombrowski turned to the Chief of the Boat, "Carter, maintain current depth, all ahead one-half. We're going to very carefully approach Pearl, using passive sonar only. We'll dock and search the base for supplies. The men deserve a few days of shore leave. Then we'll take up the search on the other side."

The submarine passed the big Island of Hawaii, and cruised beyond Moloka'i and Maui to the Island of Oahu. As she approached the entrance to Pearl Harbor the Captain ordered the chief petty officer to bring the sub to the surface. They slowly entered the harbor, and circled Ford Island clockwise, looking for any signs of life. They passed the Arizona Memorial and the *U.S.S. Missouri*, or "Mighty Mo," an Ohio class battleship that was docked at Ford Island and was now a ghostly Museum. Finding nothing, they sailed into Magazine Loch toward the submarine docks.

They were empty, with the exception of a single sub that was being overhauled at the time of the attack, almost two years before. The rest of the Pacific Fleet had been deployed to respond to the Chinese and Russian missile launches. The *Louisiana* docked at the largest submarine berth, and for the next several hours the officers and crew were busy with preparations to stay at the base for a few days. Even on the surface, the submarine was unable to pick up any transmissions that might indicate anyone was alive. The neutron bombs had been very efficient at killing all life in this three-hundred-mile-long chain of volcanic islands.

Since the war, this was the first time the submarine had actually been able to dock and the morale of the crew was at an all-time, post-war high. *At least*, Dombrowski thought, *they don't have any place to desert to.*

***

Phillip Canfield tapped a pencil against the desk chair's arm, keeping a beat to the music. He had appropriated a couple of AA batteries from stores and powered up the handheld, digital, music player. He had over a thousand songs recorded in the device. Leaning way back in his chair, he propped his feet on the desk, a cord running from the recorder up his chest to the ear bud in his right ear. Needing a haircut, his brown, wavy hair hung over the bud. He kept his voice low as he sang along with Adele, "Rolling in the Deep," his head bobbing, and a big grin on his face.

Since relieving Mason, Phil had been in the tower at Hickam Air Force Base for over an hour, and had closed the blinds over the western and southern windows to keep the intense sunlight from spoiling the mood generated by music he hadn't heard in years. The song ended and he pulled his feet off the desk, allowing the chair to fall to the floor. Jerking on the cord, the ear bud popped out and he flung it onto the desk as he rose to saunter over to the window. He pulled the cord to raise the blinds and squinted southwest toward the open ocean, as the late afternoon sunlight temporarily blinded him.

As his pupils shrunk and he could once again see out the window, his jaw dropped.

"Oh shit!" He ran over to the desk and grabbed his binoculars, returning to the window and raising them to his eyes. In the magnified field of view he saw dozens of ships - all types, shapes and sizes. There were obvious military vessels, fishing boats and a half a dozen enormous cruise ships. He wasn't real familiar with Chinese craft but he recognized a Type 071 Amphibious Warfare ship and a couple Type 052C Luyang II Class destroyers.

Taking into consideration the height of the tower, the horizon was approximately forty miles away. To his shock, the fleet had already closed to half that distance as he had shirked his duty, rocking out to the tunes. The military vessels had anti-ship missiles that could blow the *Louisiana* out of the water and as soon as she began to move, they would pick her up on their sonar, if they hadn't already.

Hoping he hadn't destroyed their chance to escape, Phil snatched the two-way radio off the desk, shoved his music player into his pocket and flew down the tower steps. He bounded out onto the road and sprinted toward the sub docks a few miles away. The captain had specifically chosen the tower at Hickam to give them the farthest line of sight to the horizon... and he had blown it.

Ignoring all radio protocol, he screamed breathlessly into the radio, "*Louisiana*, this is Canfield! There's a huge fleet of ships, dozens of 'em, approaching the islands from the southwest. I repeat, they're coming right now. Approximate distance is twenty nautical miles." He crossed runways, passed base housing and cut through yards to shorten the distance to the sub. Mason had probably already arrived and Phil knew if he didn't get there by the time they were ready to leave, they would have to leave him behind.

***

Hankins had been lounging in a lawn chair on the dock next to the sub. He jumped to his feet and ran down the plank to the sub and dropped through the hatch. "Mr. Finney, sir, the Chinese are coming! Canfield says they're only twenty miles away. He says there's dozens of them. A whole damn fleet." He skidded to a stop in front of the shocked XO.

Finney started bellowing orders, "Hit the klaxon and get everyone aboard. If they get to the channel entrance, we're toast." The siren went off, summoning the crew back to the boat. Captain Dombrowski hurried into the Command Center, not even wearing his signature baseball cap.

"What's the trouble, Mr. Finney?"

"The Chinese have been seen, sir. They're only twenty miles away. There are dozens of ships. If we don't get out of the harbor within 30 minutes they will box us in and we'll be a sitting duck."

"How the hell did they get so close before the watch spotted them?"

"Unknown, Captain. The call just came in."

"Well, for damn sure, they know we're here. They probably haven't sent a missile our way because they don't want to damage the facilities. They know they have us way outnumbered and I doubt if they know we have nuclear missiles left on board."

The engines had been running while tests were being performed, and other systems were quickly brought on line. Men were sliding down the ladder into the boat and hurrying to their stations. 24 year old Patrick O'Neal slid behind the wheel in his bathing trunks, dropping his towel on the floor beside the console. The lights were dim, battle station red. As the crew settled into their familiar routine, their calm voices called out the status of the engines, communications, weapons, and other systems.

"Ten minutes, Mr. Finney. Any more time than that and we won't make it."

"Sir, there are still several men that haven't returned."

The captain swung around to face him. "Don't you think I know that?" he exclaimed. "God knows I don't want to leave those boys behind, any more than you do."

Two more men dropped through the hatch. "Who's still outstanding?"

The chief called for a roll call from the departments, as preparations continued.

"Five minutes." The captain glanced over toward the chief.

"Baraza, Canfield, Perryman, Holder and Cross, sir."

As if summoned, Cross hit the deck from above.

"Where did the others go?" Dombrowski asked Cross.

He hesitated, then spurted out, "They went to find pineapples, sir. There were some warehouses a couple miles away."

"Are you aware I ordered that no one go further than a quarter mile away?"

"Yes sir. They told me they'd be right back. I waited as long as I could but I don't think they heard the klaxon, sir."

Dombrowski looked like a brewing storm. "Two minutes. Prepare to get under way."

Then, "One minute."

"Close the hatch. Reverse engines one-eighth."

Just then a thunk was heard on deck and a voice screamed out, "Don't leave me!" The hatch was flung back open and Phillip Canfield dropped through to the deck, falling and twisting his ankle as he rolled to a heap at the captain's feet.

"Welcome aboard, Canfield. Get to your station and we'll discuss your performance at your observation post later."

Phil limped toward the radio room, sweat streaming down his face, and not just from the physical exertion of sprinting three miles to the boat. Dombrowski noticed something on the deck and leaned down to pick up a small music player that had fallen from Phil's pocket. The captain slipped it into his pocket.

***

The *Louisiana* carefully stayed over the center channel of the harbor, where the depth was 45 feet. Out of the Loch, she turned left and headed straight for the harbor entrance. As soon as they passed the promontories into the open, the sonar screen lit up like a Christmas tree, indicating the fleet bearing down on them. The channel continued in shallow water, so they needed to stay on the surface. Dombrowski figured he had only a few minutes to get to the shelf break, where he would be able to dive into deeper water. He prayed the Chinese would continue to hold off firing their missiles, for fear of closing off the entrance to the harbor, but he knew the minute they thought he was clear enough, they would launch.

"Coming up on deep water, sir." Boldonado called out from the sonar console.

"Just a minute more. O'Neal be ready. Brace for impact. They're going to hit us soon."

"We're clear, sir!"

Finney's eyes were wide as he grabbed the railing around the dual periscopes. The crew braced themselves as the captain nodded at the chief. "Take us down to level 500, Chief. Emergency descent."

"Dive, dive," The chief yelled out. "500 feet, deep descent."

Diving planes rotated, and the slope of the deck altered abruptly, as the sub nosed downward at a steep angle heading for deeper water... and safety.

Suddenly the submarine was slammed to the side, and anyone not holding on was flung to the deck. Dombrowski thought of the Starship Enterprise, as she tossed around her crew when they were hit by photon bombs from Klingon or Romulan vessels.

He wished he had her shields.

The boat rolled to the left and then slowly started back to vertical when it was hit again. Sirens were ringing loudly and the lights dimmed, before slowly coming back on. The stabilizers brought the roll under control. Another concussion followed, but as the sub dove ever deeper the impact was less. Missiles continued to slam into the ocean above, but when they leveled off, they no longer felt the effects of the barrage from above.

"Damage report!" Carter shouted into the comm. He relayed the reports of damage and injury to the captain as each department reported in. There were no reports of hull damage or flooding but several men had sustained injuries.

The weapons room and the galley each reported someone had broken an arm. There were numerous reports of abrasions, bruised limbs and torsos, and a serious concussion... but the worst news came from the engine room.

"Captain Dombrowski!" the speaker blasted. "The engine room reports that Ensign Cravitz has been killed. He smashed his head into the bulkhead. His neck broke, sir."

Dombrowski barely controlled his fury as he stormed off the bridge with, "See to the damage Mr. Finney, and give me a full medical report after the men have all been attended to… and send Canfield to my quarters."

They had narrowly escaped serious damage as the sub penetrated the dark waters, heading east at top speed.

19

Discouraged and disheartened, the travelers from Willsburg approached Bloomfield, New Mexico. They passed a green sign, leaning halfway over and partially covered by a large bush, that stated, "Bloomfield, 2 miles."

"Hold up everyone," Mark called out, "let's wait for the scouts to return." It was still fairly early in the day after the tragic morning. They sat around the wagons waiting for Matthew and Chang. Kevin and Ashley were throwing around an old, filthy, Nerf football, full of holes where the foam had been torn out.

Sheri rode her bike back the way they had come, gazing eastward toward a lonely grave in the high desert. She was careful not to go too far beyond Greg, who sat astride Tulip, watching out for Sheri and making sure she came to no harm. She was still in shock, but her grief was intense, tears rolling down her cheeks as she tried to shake a feeling of unreality. She only vaguely heard voices behind her, as the scouts returned and gave the go-ahead to enter the town.

Bloomfield seemed deserted. Once again they were mystified by the absence of life, and were haunted by the notion that they may be the only beings left alive on the planet.

The clippity clop, clippity clop of the horse's hooves on the highway almost lulled Mark to sleep. His head was bobbing as the sun rose higher in the sky, coming over the top of the wagon and warming his head. He came abruptly awake as he heard a shout in the distance up ahead.

"Hey, Mark, someone wants to talk to you."

"Lori, can you come up? Take the reins? There's somebody up ahead." Lori climbed out of the wagon onto the seat and Mark handed her the reins.

"Who is it? Be careful." She hauled back on the reins and the wagon came to a halt.

"I don't know, but I'm about to find out." He climbed down off the wagon seat and strode forward to where he saw a man with a white flag, standing next to Jimbo, who sat astride his old motorcycle. The man put a hand over his eyes to block the sun and waved as Mark approached.

"Hi, are you Mark? My name's Don. I'm the forward scout for Bloomfield." He stuck out his hand and Mark shook it.

"Yeah, I'm Mark. We're very glad to finally see somebody. We've come cross-country from Raton and every town along the way has been deserted. Is there anyone in Bloomfield?"

"Not really. Almost everyone has drawn back to Farmington. We're trying to stay together because it's easier to trade and set up markets. We don't have that many vehicles and it would be hard to get around if we were spread out too far."

"How many of you are there?" Mark asked him.

He crossed his arms, a puzzled look on his face. "Gee, I don't really know but I think there are a few thousand of us."

Jimbo whistled. "Wow, that's great. How did so many survive?"

Don shrugged his shoulders, "Not sure. Some people stayed in their basements for a while. But even the people that stayed outside did pretty well. Our main problem was each other. As soon as the trucks stopped rolling into town with food, people panicked and started fighting each other. The Metropolitan area around Farmington, Bloomfield and Aztec probably had sixty thousand people but I'll bet there's not more than five or six thousand left."

"Do you guys have a central government? Someone in charge?"

"Farmington's about ten miles from here. A lot of folks live in the house they lived in before the war, but a quite a few have moved closer to the downtown area. When you come into town you'll be south of the city. There's a group of people living in the hospital, and in homes around that area. It's close to the rivers, so it's a lot easier to transport water. Just ask somebody and they'll tell you where the Civic Center is. The guy in charge is named Jeff Hunt. If it hadn't been for Jeff there might not be anybody left. He stepped in and got people to quit fighting and to start cooperating. You guys'll be safe and nobody will bother you as long as you don't go in waving your weapons around."

"They aren't gonna try and take them from us, are they?"

"Naw, everybody in town's armed. I'm just gonna hang out here at my guard post, and make sure you're not being followed by any bad guys." Don grinned and waved them by.

"Okay. Well, thanks Don, we're just passing through but we'll probably see you in town. We'll be here for a few days."

Mark jogged back to his wagon and climbed up on the seat, a big smile on his face. "We've finally found civilization," he told Lori. "Don says Farmington has thousands of people."

Mark shook the reins and the wagon train moved off to the west. Everybody's spirits lifted as they looked forward to meeting new people and replenishing their supplies.

Sam and Willy rode by the wagon. "We're gonna go on ahead and start dickering for some horseflesh. We'll see you guys in town."

Lori looked a little worried. "Do you think it's safe to separate?"

"I don't think it's a problem. Don seemed like a reasonable guy. I think it'll be okay. You guys hightail it back here at the first sign of trouble."

Lori wasn't completely convinced, having gotten used to being security conscious. Most of the ten miles between Bloomfield and Farmington were fairly built up, with stores and businesses along both sides of the road. It looked to Mark like this highway had been recently worked on, prior to the war. The weeds and shrubs were thick along the side of the road but the road itself still remained fairly clear of vegetation. The sun blazed overhead and Matthew and Einstein crawled out of the wagons as the canvas heated and the interior became too hot to sleep.

Being anxious to get to town, they pushed the horses, reaching the outer limits of the city of Farmington in only four hours. As they got closer to Farmington they began to see people. Everyone waved to them as they rode along and Lori began to feel safer when no one exhibited aggressive behavior. The river was visible to their right and fields on both sides of the road were planted in crops. Highway 64 curved northward and crossed the river, and along the river banks, Mark could see a huge field filled with tents and booths.

"Lori look, there must be five hundred people over there. It looks like a gigantic farmers market. I guess that's as good as any place to get some information about where we can park the wagons." They took an off ramp to the right and found a side street that descended down to the fields, pulling up the wagons along the side of the road. Mike, Danny and Carlos took up positions around the wagons, nonchalantly keeping an eye out for any problems, as Mark and Lori walked out onto the field after taking Ashley and Kevin to Chris's wagon, where they would be easier to protect.

They maintained their alertness as they approached the crowds in the field, who were milling about the displays and retail booths, but everyone nodded in a friendly manner. In a few minutes Mark and Lori were more at ease. A small group of three men and two women were standing in a circle talking and laughing. They were all neatly groomed, the men clean-shaven and wearing their hair short, unlike Mark, who sported a three day old beard and long hair below his ears.

Mark waited patiently for one man to finish talking and then asked about accommodations.

"Hi folks. My name's Mark and this is my wife Lori. We just came into town and were wondering where we might find a safe place to park our wagons. We need a camp, as we'll be sleeping in them for a few days."

He was careful to keep his hands in sight.

One of the men reached out a hand, giving Mark's a firm squeeze. "I'm Craig. This is Bobby, Sheila, Phyllis and Rhett. Welcome to Farmington. Where'd you come from?"

"Originally from Eagle Nest, but we swung by Raton to drop off some people that had lived there before the war. It's been a long trip, and we just want a place to rest up before we head on to California."

Phyllis shook her head, her blonde, pony tail wagging back and forth. "Why would you want to go to California? They probably got hit real hard."

"Most of us were living there when the Chinese attacked us. We're trying to find out how people are doing. You know, who survived. And we want to know if the Chinese have followed the attack by invading our shores."

"Yeah," Rhett said, "it's not unreasonable to think they had a plan. A lot of us have been wondering the same thing. If you come back this way, maybe you can fill us in."

Craig pointed past the tents on the far side of the clearing. "The best place for you to hole up is just east of the market. The Shamrock Ranch has a lot of room for your wagons. I'm sure Jack Heifert will let you camp in the big, cleared area by the river. We all keep our horses boarded over there."

Mark thanked them and waved up at the road where the wagons were parked. Mike saw them and got everyone moving. In an hour, for a reasonable fee, they had received permission to camp, and had circled up in a large meadow by a crook in the river.

Lori looked over the camp. "I feel secure for the first time since we left Willsburg."

Matthew walked up beside her and Mark. "Yes, but I'll schedule sentries anyway."

174

"You're right, Matthew." Mark looked around at the thriving town. "No matter how civilized it looks, we've learned to never let down our guard."

20

Jon stood with his back against the tree, listening carefully for the footsteps he thought he'd heard in the distance. Peeking out from around the trunk, he could see three men coming out of the alley, obviously following him. He'd always been careful when he left the hotel, to go in a direction away from his house. This morning he had skirted Fort Lewis College and entered the woods on the east side of town. He was angry and tired of playing games with this pampered group of corporate animals. He spun around, and crouching low, disappeared into the brush and trees behind him. In three minutes he had lost them.

The traps held more game than at any time in the past month, which suited Jon because it would shorten up the time he spent hunting that day. He was frantic to resume his search for a working vehicle. Stuffing the carcasses in his old satchel, he circled to the south and headed back toward town. He'd already searched the garages, and tried to start the cars, in the upscale homes along the east side of town… and had been frustrated once again.

Staying well south of the downtown area, he turned west until he came to the river and, taking the first bridge, headed into neighborhoods he hadn't yet searched. He's already stashed a new car battery in the bushes at the end of the bridge. He picked it up on his way, and checked out the first garage he came to.

All afternoon he hauled the heavy battery from garage to garage, searching the houses for keys and hooking the battery up to each car he found, praying one of them would start. His major concern was that the battery he was using was dead, but he had no way of knowing that.

His time was running out... when his prayers were answered.

In the eleventh garage he found a Ford Taurus, and after swapping out the battery, turned the key... and the engine roared to life. He was scared to death someone would hear it running, but didn't dare turn it off until it had idled for fifteen minutes. The car had just less than a quarter of a tank of gas. He would have to find more, or it was going to be a short-lived getaway. It had been almost two years since the war and he worried that the gas may have gone bad, but the engine seemed to be running smoothly. He shut it down, hid the keys, and headed back for the Parker Hotel.

***

Carelessness can undermine even the best intentioned men. A week after finding the car, and going home to tell Mary the news, Jon exited his garage through the small door in the back. He snuck across the backyard, slipped into his neighbor's yard and went over the fence. As his feet touched the ground, rough hands grabbed his arms and the barrel of a gun was jammed against the back of his head.

"Where have you been Jon boy? I could swear we heard children laughing."

"You guys are crazy. I was just checking my traps."

"We may be crazy, but were not stupid. I heard somebody and it wasn't you."

The wind swirled the dirt around the weeds that poked up through Palmer St. and caused the traffic lights in the intersection to sway wildly. Lee pulled open the rear door of the hotel and gave Jon a shove in the back, sending him stumbling into the lobby. The four men paused inside the door to allow their eyes to adjust to the dim lighting and then crossed the lobby past the registration desk to where Ben, Jessica and Vance were sitting in chairs around a beautiful, polished table.

"You were right Ben," Michael said. "We followed him and he led us to a house on the north side where he disappeared inside. We figure he went down to the basement because we looked in all the windows and we couldn't see anybody. But we heard kids laughing, so we know he has somebody stashed down there."

Ben frowned, "Oh, Jon boy, do you know how much trouble you're in? Have you been stealing food from us and taking it to someone else?"

Jon stood clasping his hands in front of him, his head lowered. He remained stubbornly silent.

Ben jumped to his feet, and putting his hands on John's chest, gave him a shove that sent him tumbling backwards onto the floor. Then he raced forward and stood over Jon, screaming at him, "You stupid fuck! I trusted you. We could have killed you the minute we found you, but I let you stay alive so you could hunt to bring back food for us, and now I find out you been holding out on me."

Jon scrambled back on his feet and elbows until his head and shoulders came up against the wall. He tried to sit up, but Ben kicked him in the hip, spinning him sideways. Falling back to the floor, he curled into a ball on his side, clasping his hands over his head to protect his face.

"I'm sorry, Ben, I had to feed my family."

"You've been here all along haven't you? You even lied about that." Ben's face was red. He shook back his hair and crossed his arms. "We're going to pick up that family of yours and so help me God if they're not half starved, I'm going to kill you all." He turned to the men and waved toward the door. "Go get them and bring 'em back here."

Jon tried to jump to his feet, but Ben slammed him back against the wall. Harris stepped forward, and he and Ben each grabbed one of Jon's arms and held him, as three guys hustled out the front door to fetch Mary and the boys. Jon struggled and tried to break free. He pulled one arm loose but two other men stepped in and helped to subdue him. He lifted his feet in the air, trying to kick Ben.

"Take him up and lock him in his room," Ben commanded.

Jon still struggled, more scared than he'd ever been in his life. They wrestled him across the room, but before they entered the hallway that led to the staircase, Ben said "Hey, listen. What the hell is that?" They all stood for a moment listening to what sounded like a swarm of bumble bees.

"Christ, it's motorcycles." Ben and Jessica hurried to the windows.

"There's a hundred of them! They're right outside and they've got Paul and the guys I sent for Jon's family. The assholes led them right to us." He and Jessica took off running for the back of the hotel and the other two men, releasing Jon, followed after them like scared jackrabbits. Jon scrambled into the solarium and hid behind a chair. The front door slammed open and, between the leaves, Jon saw a vision from hell. An enormous, wild-eyed apparition stormed through the doors, followed by a score of filthy, rough-looking characters. The giant stopped in the middle of the room and started to look around, but just before his eyes rested on Jon's hiding place, there was a commotion from the hallway and Ben, Jessica and several others were herded back into the lobby.

"Lookee what we found Chase. They were trying to sneak out the back."

"Get off me you asshole." Ben tried to jerk away from the foul smelling man that held his arm. The man delivered a tremendous kidney punch and Ben fell to his knees gasping.

"You need to have a little more respect, man."

Chase just stood and stared at Jessica. "Strip her." Jessica screamed and tried to dart back into the hallway but she was grabbed by Bing and two others. She fought back but was no match for these men and in less than a minute, stood naked before them.

"Turn her around boys." He walked up behind her and looked over his shoulder. "You guys can have them." And he gestured toward Ben and the others as he unzipped his pants and grabbed Jessica.

Ben and the other men were fighting their assailants and Jon knew he would never get a better chance to escape. He jumped to his feet and flew through the open door, past dozens of motorcycles, leather clad gang members with chains hanging from their belts, and a few women. One hundred yards to the North, he ducked between two buildings, running as fast as he could. He had gained a few moments as the surprised cyclists didn't know what was happening. Now he heard shouts, and motorcycles starting up, as the pursuit began.

Glancing back over his shoulder he saw the bikes flying around the corner, accelerating in his direction. He juked left, running through a side yard and out onto another street, only to find more motorcycles roaring up from the South, just two hundred yards away. He fled directly across street and into another side yard. This time there was a fence and he scaled it quickly, his heart in his throat.

"Dammit!" someone shouted. "Get around to the next street."

If he stopped to try and hide, he knew they would find him. Climbing over fence after fence to slow his pursuers, he made it to the river. He turned and ran north, through a small park and across a wide, wooden, pedestrian bridge. Turning right, he passed a skate park, and climbed an embankment where he jumped over a metal railing and sprinted across the street. Motorcycles had followed across the bridge but were unable to climb the steep embankment. They sped back a hundred yards to a ramp that climbed up to the street, and immediately resumed pursuit. But Jon had disappeared between houses and climbed farther up the hill into a maze of apartment complexes. The cyclists cruised up and down the street, trying to catch a glimpse of the fleeing man.

Cutter turned to Vic, "Chase is going to be pissed we lost him."

"We'll get Bing to tell him. He probably won't shoot Bing."

Gasping for air and running on adrenaline, Jon crossed into the neighborhood where he had found the car. He ran to the back of the house and crawled into a small space under the porch. Pulling himself into a ball, he lay in the dark, breathing heavily. The usual afternoon rain began, pounding a rhythm on the wooden planks above his head. Water ran into his hiding place, soaking his side that lay on the ground, until he was chilled completely through.

He could occasionally hear the deep rumble of a motorcycle as it passed down the street in front of the house.

Jon waited for hours in the cramped, damp space until the sun went down behind thick, dark clouds that blanketed the horizon. He hadn't heard the choppers for a couple of hours. Knees and shoulders aching, he slowly crept out of the dark hole and tried to stretch his burning muscles, but his anxiety about Mary and the kids got him moving again. Sneaking around to the side of the garage he slipped through the door. Jon felt under the workbench, finding the keys where he'd hidden them the day he'd located the car.

It'd been three days but he was confident the car would restart. He climbed in, shoved the key in the ignition... and she started right up. He was still worried about the sound of the engine, but he was several blocks from the river and even farther from the hotel. If the cycles were no longer in the neighborhood he would be okay.

With a sinking feeling in his stomach, he realized he didn't have the garage door opener. A quick glance told him it wasn't attached to either visor. He rummaged through the console and felt under the seats. Nothing. He searched the workbench and looked for a button on the wall. His heart leapt when he saw the button, but when he pushed it nothing happened. Going back to the garage door, he peeked behind the car and let out a sigh of relief, discovering a handle he'd missed, because the back of the car was only inches from the door.

He felt like a contortionist as he wormed his way between the car and the garage door, and grasping the handle, simultaneously pulled it and the door upward. It squealed and groaned, but he was able to raise it over his head. Giving it an extra shove for good measure, he got back in the car and popped it in reverse, backed out of the garage and, with a sudden sense of freedom, headed for the river.

Jon didn't dare turn on the headlights, and even though it was now dark, he could see by the light of the moon, and he was amazed at how quickly he covered the ground. Having traveled everywhere on foot for the past 22 months he felt like a NASCAR driver. Two blocks away from the bridge he pulled to the curb and shut off the engine. He quietly exited the car and closed the door.

Sneaking along 16th St., he said a small prayer of thanks that he'd been so cautious, as he caught sight of a light just on the other side of the bridge. As he worked his way closer he could hear voices in the dark and he knew they had closed off the bridges to town with sentries. His only chance was to go north around the River Bend and see if they had thought to close off the railroad bridge for the Durango and Silverton train.

Back on his feet, Jon felt like it took forever to get to the bridge, but it was worth it when he found it unguarded. Carefully stepping from tie to tie, to prevent a misstep that could sprain or even break an ankle, he crossed the bridge and made his way home. He was trembling… afraid of what he might find.

As he opened the door to the basement, he heard a whimper and a flashlight stabbed the dark, temporarily blinding him. Even though deaf, Mary had felt his footsteps as he descended to their hideout. He started to sign to her but she dropped the flashlight and threw her arms around him. Holding her only for a moment, he pushed her away and felt for the flashlight. Many months ago they had hung black plastic over the two windows in the basement which prevented light from being seen from the outside. Mary removed them during the day to give them meager sunlight.

Turning on the flashlight just long enough to light the oil lamp, he signed to Mary, "A huge motorcycle gang just rode into town and we have to get out of here."

"Where will we go?"

"I have no idea, but we have to get out of here now. I'll pack some stuff in our backpacks and you wake up the kids."

Suddenly, Jon heard the sound of a motorcycle. He put his finger to his lips and signed, "Keep the kids very quiet," as he shut off the lamp. Feeling his way to the hidden space between the studs, he removed his rifle and two boxes of .22 LR ammunition. He went to Mary and placed his hand on her chest, a signal to remain where she was. Then, very carefully, he climbed the stairs and went to the front window. The motorcycle moved very slowly past the house. There was no indication the driver had any suspicion that Jon's house was occupied.

When the chopper had turned the corner, Jon breathed a sigh of relief and went back to the basement. "We need to wait until closer to morning when, hopefully, they'll be asleep."

21

Although none of Mark's group was aware of it, the next day turned out to be the weekend. The farmers market took place in a huge, flat field just north of the river. It was circular and at least a quarter of a mile in diameter. A wooden stage was built right in the middle, with a four-piece band playing country music. To the east, there were three, huge, pole tents and several areas covered over by tarps. Chairs and tables were set up under the tarps and people were enjoying lunch. The marketplace was filled with customers wandering around the stalls, either purchasing, or bartering, for produce and other goods. The market was busy every day, but the difference with it being the weekend was that children were everywhere. The Farmington survivors had started schools, and during the week the children spent their days as all children for decades before them had done... griping about having to go to school.

A large ranch with two red barns, a line of horse stalls and an oval arena was adjacent to the marketplace. There were bleachers on both sides of the arena with press boxes at the top of the bleachers on the river side.

The wagon train from the New Mexico colony had received permission to camp on the grounds of the ranch, and the wagons were drawn up in their usual triangle. Unable to let go of their situational awareness, the group still posted sentries. Mike, Carlos and Chang were spread out around the wagons, but were un-mounted and lounging about in lawn chairs, each with a soda or a beer in his hand.

Skillet, just happy to have someone else cook for a day, had gone to the marketplace to get barbecued ribs. Kevin and Ashley were playing dodge ball at the ranch with a dozen other children and the sound of happy kids made Lori smile.

Mark and Lori approached Sheri. "Would you mind keeping an eye on the kids? Mark and I are going to explore a bit."

Still shocked and saddened by Jesse's death, Sheri nodded her head. "Sure, I was just gonna hang out here at the wagons anyway."

"Make sure they stay in the area around the wagons."

"Don't worry. They'll be safe," Carlos called out. "We'll help Sheri."

Mark and Lori wandered through the marketplace, but were surprised that they couldn't really find anything they wanted to buy. Mark slipped his arm through Lori's as they walked. "Funny how you get used to not having a lot of extra stuff. We can all chip in and let Skillet buy whatever we need for the coming trip."

"Yes, but I still need to get a few things for the kids. We eat a lot less than we did before the war but they're still growing like weeds."

Just outside the marketplace, on the road that led to the Civic Center, they found a comfortable bar. It was one of the things Mark missed about the old days. He was a runner, and after a long trail run on the weekends he and his buddies would always hit a little bar in the Santa Monica Mountains.

There was a line of booths along the wall on one side of the room, and the rest of the room was taken up with round tables and wooden chairs. They sat at a table, unsure if there was a waitress, but within a minute a woman walked up and asked them for their order.

"What do you have?" Mark asked.

"We still have a lot of liquor and, of course, beer. It's going fast, but Jillian, the owner, had some of the guys rig up a still. I think we're gonna be good for a long time."

"Sounds good," Mark said. "I'll just take a beer. Anything you've got."

"Same for me," Lori said.

"You know," an old man at the next table said, "whiskey's way better for you. Tastes a whole lot better, too."

Mark looked over and saw a man who looked to be in his sixties, with white hair sticking straight up, and silver stubble covering his cheeks and chin. He wore coveralls with no shirt.

"Well, sir," Mark told him, "I've just always liked my beer. But I'll buy you a whiskey if you'll tell us some things about your town. We just got here from Raton."

The old man lurched to his feet and stumbled to the table, pulling up a chair. "What do you want to know?" The waitress put a shot of whiskey in front of the old man and rolled her eyes at Mark and Lori.

"What's your name?"

"I'm Clarence. They call me Butch. Butch Errington."

"So tell us what happened in the war. How did so many of you survive here in Farmington?"

"Hell if I know," he slurred. "We heard that bombs were coming, and then the lights went out. Didn't take long and everybody was fightin' and killing each other." His eyes glazed over and he stared off into the dimness.

He spoke as if in a trance. "Gangs came through just shooting people for no reason. Neighbors turned on one another, stealing food. Whole families starved to death 'cause they didn't prepare for even short-term disasters. If it hadn't been for Jeff Hunt, everybody'd be dead." He stopped talking as though he'd gone to sleep.

Mark looked over at Lori and she shrugged her shoulders. "We heard that name once before. Who's Jeff Hunt?"

Butch threw back the jigger of whiskey in one gulp. "He was a supervisor out at the power plant. Just got a bunch of guys together and they put a stop to the gangs. There was a lot more good people than bad guys. A major skirmish took place right here in town and the bad guys lost. Hunt got folks together, started the marketplace. Got people growing crops. Made the kids go to school."

"Where can we find this Jeff Hunt?"

"You can just head north from here till you hit Civic Center. He and the rest of the government hang around up there." He looked through rheumy eyes at Lori. "You know, you're kind of a pretty thing. You wanna go with me to that backroom over there? I haven't had any sex in a long time."

Mark jumped to his feet but Lori put her hand on his arm. "Mister Errington, I think our conversation is over. Thanks for the information. I think you'd better go before my husband tears you to pieces." The old man, his head waving back and forth, looked up at Mark, and seeing the anger in his eyes, struggled to his feet.

"Okay lady, but you missed out on a really good time." He belched and turned away, stumbled and went to one knee, pulling himself back up by the chair.

As he staggered away, Lori said, "Welcome back to civilization."

Aaron and Chris came into the bar from the bright sunshine beyond the door. They stood a minute, allowing their eyes to adjust to the dimness, and then spotting Mark and Lori, came over to the table. Chris had Karen in a canvas baby carrier against her chest. She'd purchased it from a group of people that had cleaned out a Walmart.

"Hi guys," Mark greeted them. "What's up Aaron? You look worried. You want a beer?" Mark signaled to the waitress, holding up two fingers. Aaron held a chair for Chris as she unharnessed the baby. Then he took a seat beside her.

"Mark, we've got something to talk to you about. We... me and Chris, aren't going to go any further with you guys." He hurried on when he saw Mark's look of surprise. "We really just wanted to get an idea of what the world was like out here. I think we've seen that."

"But we haven't even gotten to California, and Chris, I thought that's what you wanted to see."

"I did. I just didn't think it through, how hard it would be with the baby." The waitress came over and popped the tops off of two beers putting them in front of Chris and Aaron. "I thought I was searching for home, but I found out I already know where home is. I really miss Daniel and Rana and all of our friends in Willsburg." She looked over at Aaron for support.

"Were gonna go back, Mark. Sam and Willy will be herding their horses back to Platte Valley and we're going to go with them. Carlos and Chang have decided to stay here. They've seen enough. They like the idea of a larger town."

"Well, I'm surprised of course. Chris, what will happen if we decide to stay in California? I might never see you again."

Tears sprang to Chris's eyes. "I know Mark, but I don't think that's going to happen. I think when you get to California you're going to find a radioactive wasteland. I don't even know if it'll be safe for you to try and get to the coast."

"Yeah, but that's what we were trying to find out."

Lori reached over and put her hand on Chris's. "Chris, I know how you feel. Sometimes I am so scared for the kids, so I completely understand that you don't want to go on. I don't know what we're going to find, but if California is uninhabitable, then I think we may end up coming back to the New Mexico Colony." She looked over at Mark and raised her eyebrows.

He grinned his little sideways grin and said, "You know what? I never really thought that far. I guess I just figured I would move Lori and the kids into my house in Newport Beach. Or even to Will's mansion on the bluff. But if I really think about it, you're probably right. We may not be able to get within one hundred miles of Newport Beach. You guys have to do what you think is right for you and Karen."

They looked up as the door opened and four silhouettes, that turned out to be Matthew, Einstein, Danny and Jimbo, entered the room and looked around until they spotted their friends. The newcomers grabbed another table and slid it alongside the first.

Matthew noticed the tears in Chris's eyes. "Hello. Is something going on?" Jimbo stuck four fingers into the air.

"Chris and Aaron have decided to go back to Willsburg," Lori told them.

"I think we've had enough adventure," Aaron said. "We set out to see what it was like outside of our Valley and to ensure the Holcombs got home okay, and we've done that. It's really hard with the baby, and you guys can travel a lot faster without us."

"How about the rest of you guys?" Mark asked.

"I'm still in," Matthew said.

"And me," from Einstein.

"Me and Danny are coming too," Jimbo said. "I know Sheri wants to go on. She and her parents lived in San Diego, which was probably a primary target, but she has an aunt and uncle that lived in Lompoc and she's hoping they survived. It's pretty close to Vandenberg Air Force Base, though. So I'm not too optimistic."

"We can all get together at camp one of these nights and find out what everybody wants to do." Mark drained his beer and held up a finger.

22

"I want every one of them found, do you hear me?"

Major Burr Cartwright stood at attention, sweat trickling down the side of his face. "Yes, Mister President. We have dozens of men and dogs searching for them. We rounded up eight escapees and we believe there are only two more."

"Well, you need to capture those two. I can't believe you let this happen. We can't allow an attempted escape to go unpunished. If it does, we're going to have attempts from all the other camps."

"Yes, sir. Colonel Faricy and I are aware of the seriousness. We've taken Captain Mitchum into custody."

"Have him brought to me, Major."

Cartwright motioned to a soldier standing at attention by the door and the soldier left the room. The president continued, "I want the eight escapees executed. Set up a firing squad in front of all the workers in the camp. No, wait! Lock them up and make sure they don't get away. Tell one of the construction engineers to have a gallows built in the field just north of the White House. Tell him to make it a two-holer. When it's finished, I want all eight of the escapees to be hanged two at a time. Leave the last two dangling for a couple of days to make sure the other workers know what will happen to them if they try to escape."

Major Cartwright gulped, "Yes, Mister President, right away."

The president turned to General Ladner, "This is one reason why we need to get more soldiers and more weapons."

The general, who was sitting on a leather couch against the wall said, "We've stepped up our efforts to recruit soldiers from the camps, Jeremy. We have a total of almost one hundred young men over the age of sixteen that we've found in the last thirty days."

"When will they be ready to go?"

"It'll take about ten weeks to condition them. We've already found uniforms for every one of them but, of course, we won't arm them until they've been fully trained."

There was a soft knock on the door. "Come in," Rissman yelled. The door opened and Captain Mitchum was pushed into the room. He wore filthy, rumpled, sweat-stained, uniform pants but didn't have on a shirt or shoes. Hands tied behind his back, he stood in front of the president, his head bowed. His hair was tangled and he had a three-day, scruffy beard, his face and chest damp with a sheen of sweat.

"Get down on your knees, Mitchum," Rissman said.

Mitchum hesitated, and the soldier behind him put a hand on his shoulder, pressing downward. He awkwardly lowered himself to his knees and looked up at the president, fear in his red-rimmed eyes.

"You were in charge of the men who escaped?"

"Yes, Mister President."

"Well, what the hell happened?"

"Sir, one of the workers collapsed and while the guards were distracted, the prisoners made their escape attempt. They managed to get some weapons from the guards and were firing into our midst. We almost immediately captured eight of them, but two of them separated from the others and we were unable to find them. I don't know if they've been captured yet, but I'm sure every attempt is being made."

"Well, Mitchum. I'm sure you're aware that this kind of thing can't happen."

"No, sir. I mean, yes, sir"

"Somebody has to be held accountable. And that somebody, is you. You were the ranking officer in charge of the detail."

"Yes, sir," Mitchum said in a whisper. "I take full responsibility."

Rissman looked up at the soldier standing behind Captain Mitchum.

"Kill him."

Mitchums' eyes grew round and his Adam's Apple bobbed up and down as he swallowed. The soldier pulled a large .45 caliber pistol out of his holster and shoved it against the back of Mitchum's head. Mitchum closed his eyes, his face scrunching up, waiting for the blast.

General Ladner came to his feet. "Jeremy. Might I suggest an alternative? You're already going to make your point by hanging the escapees. We just discussed the fact that we need more soldiers so it doesn't make any sense to kill the ones we have. We're having some dissension in the camps up north and I think Captain Mitchum could be used as a mole."

The president held up his hand to the soldier who was ready to pull the trigger. "Tell me what you have in mind, Charles."

"As you know, sir, our primary agricultural area is up around Parkersburg. There are two camps that supply workers to these farms. There have been two or three rebellions by the workers in these camps and I believe we could insert Captain Mitchum into one of the camps to gather information and find out who the ringleaders are for the rebels. It would be hard work. He wouldn't be getting off easy. It could take quite a few months before he was accepted and once he's identified the insurrectionists, and we put down the rebellion, he could be reinstated as a member of our military. He would have to start at the bottom, of course, and work his way back up."

Rissman thought for a minute and held up his hand to the soldier. "Sergeant, you can put your weapon away."

Mitchum's shoulders slumped as the tension left his body.

The president stared at Mitchum trying to decide whether he wanted to use him as a spy, or satisfy his own need to avenge the affront he'd experienced when the workers had escaped.

"Do you think we can trust him?"

"It's not like he can run away. He'll be one of the workers, and if he doesn't play his part well, they're likely to kill him."

The president looked over at General Ladner. "Put him on the train

23

Farmington was two different cities.

During the day there were a few thousand citizens who were learning to make their way in the new world, working in the fields, or the marketplace, and some were beginning to try and restore the refineries and power plants. Their children went to school.

But at night it was a different place. Downtown Farmington rolled up the sidewalks when the sun went down and people tucked in their children for the night. After dark, the marketplace lit up with oil lamps and lanterns and the night people came out to play. Across the street from the marketplace Jillian's bar was closed, but the old hotel next door was open for business, a lantern with a red glass hanging beside the doorway. A steady stream of men went in and out of the doorway.

"Damn fool kid," Jimbo said, scratching his beard, as he saw Danny enter the building. "He's gonna catch something and there isn't anything we can do to cure him. Especially since we're not gonna have a doctor for the rest of the trip."

"He'll be okay. Once we leave here we may not find another town like this one. Let him have a good time. I'm gonna go find out what's going on in those tents," Einstein told him. The stalls were empty for the night but a rock band was playing on the stage. There were a couple of rows of folding chairs most of the way around the band, with rough looking men and women singing along, bottles of liquor and beer in their hands. With the weather warming up, the women were scantily clad, some sitting on men's laps.

Mark, Jimbo and Matthew wandered over toward the tents where they heard shouting and cheering. The oil lamps cast an orange glow through the night and Mark felt like he'd been cast back through time to the early days of San Francisco and the Barbary Coast.

The three men ducked through the flap of the door, in time to see the final few seconds of a bareknuckle, boxing match, as one of the fighters slammed a vicious hook into the ear of the other, and sent him crashing to the ground. Loud cheers and groans were heard, and silver coins changed hands, as the winners collected their bets. The interior of the tent was lit by oil lamps hanging in the center of each of the four walls, with two others attached to the supporting poles. Flickering shadows of the patrons in the raucous crowd were thrown on the canvas walls of the tent.

Mark could see blood running from the nose and ears of the man that had lost the match, as two burly men grasped him under the arms and hauled him toward the back of the tent, the toes of his boots digging grooves in the dirt. The winner, eyes wild, had his fists in the air and was shouting, "Who's next? Who wants a piece of Maxwell?"

A young woman came up to Mark and thrust her hips at him seductively. She was dressed in a leather halter and shorts, and was wearing a belt with holsters, tooled with a piece of leather that held a bottle of tequila on either hip.

"You want a tequila shooter?" She laughed and shook her blonde, wavy hair back from her shoulders. "Or maybe you want a little something else?"

"I'll take the shooter. How much?"

She pulled out a jigger and filled it to the brim with tequila. "Just one little ol' silver dime, cutie."

Swallowing the tequila Mark almost choked. "Whew, where'd you get that tequila?"

"Bobby makes it. Says it's about 160 proof. You want another?"

"Sure, why not?" He handed her two pre-1964, silver dimes.

A small, greasy-looking man with a pockmarked face shouted out at Mark and the others, "Hey, you guys want to take on Maxwell?" The three men shook their heads vigorously, not wanting any part of Maxwell. A fit looking man pushed his way through the crowd.

"Let's get it on!" he yelled, and before Maxwell could react, the challenger swung a vicious uppercut to the giant's jaw. He screamed as he bit down on his tongue, and blood squirted from his mouth. The crowd cheered their appreciation, as Maxwell staggered backward into the ring of spectators. They grabbed him by the arms and pushed him back into the center of the ring where the newcomer aimed a double blow at Maxwell's rock-hard abdomen. Oohs from the crowd indicated that was a mistake… as Maxwell didn't even appear to feel it.

Maxwell grinned and smashed his forehead into the other's. The man stepped back, shaking his head. Stunned, he fell to his knees. A roundhouse kick to the side of the man's head, knocked him unconscious to the ground.

Again, shouts and cheers went up as money changed hands. Maxwell stood in the center of the cleared space, grinning, with blood running down his chin onto his chest.

Someone pushed Mark from behind and he tripped forward toward the fighter. When he tried to retreat, the man shoved him again.

Mark turned around and saw a knife at the man's throat.

"I think you want to leave us alone, friend." Matthew said softly.

The troublemaker hesitated and then nodded his head. Matthew stepped aside as the man, scowling at him, left the tent.

"I think we better get out of here before we're forced into a fight with the big guy," Mark said. Matthew nodded in agreement and they quickly went out into the cool, night air, Jimbo reluctantly following them.

The next tent had an even larger crowd, around a four-foot-high, wooden railing encircling the center space. Mark and the others made their way around to the far side of the tent where the crowd was thinner. Working their way forward, they saw two red roosters fighting in the center of the ring. Razor blades had been attached to the rooster's spurs and one of the cocks was bleeding profusely from his head, where his comb had been nearly sliced off. The crowd was yelling over the sound of the birds screeching, and the fluttering of wings. Feathers flew into the air above their heads

Mark glanced over at Matthew. His dark eyes were swirling pools of anger and disgust. This time Jimbo willingly followed as they circled back around to the entrance and escaped the tent.

"I'm pretty much a libertarian," Mark said, "but some things ought to be illegal."

Matthew nodded. "For now, men will do as they please. As the population grows, and governments get bigger, there will be more attempts to regulate behavior. I'm not looking forward to the day when we see a proliferation of laws like we had before the war."

They walked around the field, enjoying the cool night air. Finding seats by the stage, they sat for a while, listening to the music. It seemed strange, a rock bank singing heavy metal to the music of acoustic guitars and a set of drums.

Mark drank several more tequila shooters as the girls with the holsters circulated through the crowd. "Come on Matthew, live a little," he told the young man and tried to get him to drink a shot. Matthew had been nursing the same beer for the past hour.

"No, I think I'm good."

"I don't think I've had this much to drink in a dozen years, but I sure am having fun." Mark's crooked grin seemed to be permanently attached to his face.

Jimbo matched Mark shot for shot, and Matthew had a rough time getting the two of them back to the wagons. "Hey, wait Matthew. I'm staying at the hotel," Jimbo tried to tell him, as Matthew half carried him to their camp by the river.

"Not tonight my friend. You're just going to have to spend another night on the ground." Matthew threw a sleeping bag down on the ground and Jimbo was asleep the minute he stretched out on it.

Lori had climbed down from her wagon when she heard the men returning, and casting Mark a disapproving look, said "Boys night out, huh? I should have gone with."

Mark stood in the dark, weaving slightly. "We had a wunerful time. Jush me and the boys." He burped loudly.

"Saw a cockfight."

"Oh, that's just great. Come on then. And try not to wake the kids."

As she hoisted him into the wagon, he said, "Tomorrow night you can come with us."

"Not a chance. I doubt if you're gonna want to go out tomorrow night either."

She turned as she climbed over the tailgate. "Thanks Matthew," she called out softly.

"No problem," she heard from the darkness over by the horses, and wondered what they would have done without the quiet, young man.

24

In two days, the sub had distanced itself from the Chinese fleet by a thousand miles.

"Bring us about, Carter."

"Aye, Captain. Coming about to 260 degrees. Depth seventy five feet."

"Periscope up. Check out the surface Mr. Finney."

Looking through the eyepiece of the periscope, the XO turned 360 degrees and found nothing but endless blue water.

"All clear, Captain."

"Bring us to the surface, Carter."

"Yes Captain."

The sub surfaced hundreds of miles from the nearest land, surrounded by wide-open ocean, but no one took pleasure from the open air or the tiny waves lapping at the side of the vessel.

By the time the captain climbed onto the deck, preparations had been made for two events to take place. A shrouded body lay on the deck at the forward end of the boat, the remains sewn in canvas and weighted down for the long descent into the depths. "The Navy Hymn – Eternal Father, Strong to Save," was playing from a boom box on the deck.

Captain Dombrowski presided over the ceremony for Ensign Cravitz' burial at sea.

"Unto almighty God we commend the soul of our brother departed, and we commit his body to the deep…"

When the prayer was finished the captain nodded at the seamen who stood alongside the body, and they turned it and eased it over the side of the submarine where it slid beneath the smooth surface and disappeared from view, as it descended into the dark waters.

Dombrowski turned to Commander Morris. "Bring the prisoner on deck. And turn off the music."

Seaman Canfield's head appeared in the hatch as he was led above to face his punishment. His eyes sought out his captain's, hoping to see some sign that Dombrowski had decided to show compassion or leniency.

He saw only a cold, dark stare.

Pushed from below, he continued the climb to the deck where his hands were again secured behind his back. Captain Dombrowski personally led the frightened young man to the forward end of the sub, where the body of the man whose death he was responsible for, had lain only minutes before.

He raised his voice so the others on deck could hear him. "Seaman Canfield, you are to be executed for dereliction of duty, resulting in the deaths of Ensign Cravitz, Commander Holder, Lieutenant Baraza and Petty Officer Perryman, and endangering the lives of every man on this boat. Not to mention, had we been destroyed, potentially allowing the invasion of the United States of America."

"But Captain. We don't know Holder, Baraza, and Perryman are dead."

"No, but they've probably been captured and tortured by the Chinese. And if they're still free, they are about to be die by our own hand."

He attached a concrete block to Canfield's ankle with a small, leather strap. Taking out the music device he'd found when Phil had fallen at his feet, after jumping down the hatch, he shoved it in front of Canfield's face.

"You were listening to music and not paying attention to your duties, allowing the Chinese fleet to approach our position, and almost getting us trapped in the harbor. Seaman Canfield, turn around and face out to sea." The captain reached behind him and pulled a black, cloth hood from his back pocket and reached up to put it over Phillip's head.

"I don't need that," Canfield said, ducking his head away.

"As you wish, Seaman Canfield. Turn around."

When Canfield turned back, he wished he'd put the hood on, as he faced five men who had come on deck with rifles. Leaving him standing there alone, Dombrowski walked along the deck until he stood behind the firing squad.

"Ready!" he called out. The rifles were brought up in unison. Seaman Canfield raised his head and stuck out his chest.

"Aim!"

"Fire!" The five weapons fired simultaneously, kicking backwards, white puffs of smoke rising from the barrels, as Phillip Canfield dropped like a stone to the deck.

Captain Dombrowski had hoped Canfield would fall into the ocean, but he lay in a heap on the forward deck. He walked to the body and knelt down to check for a pulse. Finding none, the six-foot, three-inch captain, and twenty-two-year veteran of the U.S. Navy, with tears streaming down his face, shoved Phillip Canfield into the sea.

Rising to his feet, he stood looking out over the water until he had regained his composure, and then turned back to his men.

"Let's get this job done," he said as they slid through the hatch and re-entered the sub.

"I have the Conn, Mister Finney. Carter take us to firing depth."

They leveled off at 75 feet, the sub facing toward the west and the enemy they'd left behind.

"Well, gentlemen, this is it." Dombrowski stood in the red light of the combat alert status, surrounded by the officers and crew of the *U.S.S. Louisiana*. "It turns out our decision not to fire our missiles during the war, was a good one. At that time we had received launch codes, and thanks to Mister Albright and his programming skill, those codes are still operational."

He looked at the men that had followed him for two years, through a nuclear war and the aftermath, not knowing until recently if they had a reason to stay aboard the boat.

"It's obvious now that the Chinese started the war so they could invade the U.S., and probably other countries as well, once the war was over. There was intelligence that suggested they had shelters for a large number of citizens, that would allow them to survive a nuclear war. Boldonado detected twenty-four, different ship's signatures. Several are military vessels. They are using fishing boats, and even commandeered cruise ships as transports. Each of those cruise ships can carry three thousand people... more if they cram them in. I believe they held off firing missiles at us, because they needed the fueling facilities and stored food at Pearl for all those ships and people. We were lucky to get away. They couldn't possibly imagine that we still have nuclear missiles."

The captain looked troubled as he continued, "That fleet probably carries at least 20,000 individuals that are ready to invade and take over the United States. They may have other fleets heading to Southeast Asia or South America. We can't worry about them. We have to protect what's left of our own country."

"Captain, many of those people are civilians," Mr. Finney said. "We can't just kill them. We can use torpedoes to take out the military vessels, and then we can escort the civilians to California."

Dombrowski seemed to consider this. "They, the civilians included, consider themselves an invading force. I'm sure they were hand-picked by their government to survive, and would cause considerable trouble once they arrived in the United States. Our citizens don't need to fight a ground war against the Chinese, who have superior numbers and weaponry. We have orders from the President of the United States to take out that fleet."

Finney raised his voice and stepped toward the captain. "Military officers have the right, and the responsibility, to question orders. This isn't right. You can't just blow 20,000 people to pieces. That would be a war crime."

Dombrowski's face darkened. "Mr. Finney. We can discuss your philosophical objections to our mission in private. You will not question my orders in front of the crew or I will have you confined to your quarters. Am I clear?" Dombrowski was over a half-foot taller than his XO and stood glaring down at him.

Finney moved back a couple of feet and lowered his voice. "Sir, what is the worst that can happen? If they get to America, in another twenty or thirty years, they will be assimilated and the population will be homogeneous. There will be peace. We don't have to murder these people!"

"They won't be assimilated. They will conquer. A country and its people have a right to exist. They have the right to defend themselves with all possible means. And we, Mr. Finney, are those means. Your relatives lived in the South. What if they had survived and lived in Northern California or Utah? Would you be so quick to let the invaders onto our shores?"

Finney looked stubborn but didn't answer the question.

The captain glared at Finney. "Weapons room. Prepare missiles one and twenty four, for launch. You have the coordinates."

The weapons officer responded over the comm, "Preparing missiles one and twenty four, for launch."

The XO made one more objection. "What about Holder, Perryman and Baraza?"

"My orders were to get no further than a quarter mile from the dock, with the exception of the watch at Hickam. They disobeyed those orders and unfortunately will pay a dear price. They may even have been captured by the Chinese. I will take it to my grave that we had to leave them behind. That is all, Mr. Finney."

The captain stood stock still for a full minute.

"Fire missile one! Fire missile twenty four!"

***

The *Louisiana* spent the next two weeks circling the Hawaiian Islands, checking for any sign of the Chinese fleet. Captain Dombrowski had been concerned that the fleet would have left the islands before they had fired their missiles, so they had targeted the second one east of the islands.

Cruising at periscope depth to allow them protection from the radiation, they circled in a counter-clockwise direction, their instruments taking readings through the periscope mast. As they approached from the east, the radiation became detectable.

"Captain, I'm picking up a significant amount of air born radiation, however, I'm not getting any reading in the water yet."

"Don't get any closer. Change course to 350 degrees until it's clean."

Continuing in this manner they circumnavigated the island chain, staying just beyond the limit of the radiation. The captain believed the most likely directions would be west, toward their original destination, or east with the intention of returning to China. They didn't detect any vessels in either direction.

Dombrowski, Finney and Communications Officer Crane sat in the Officer's Mess, finishing dinner and discussing their next move. "Gentlemen, I'm considering heading to China, to see if we can find out if they're sending any more fleets to other countries or even to the United States."

Lieutenant Commander Crane nodded his head. "We're unable to get through to the States, so I think we need to use our judgment on this one. We've come this far, and I for one would feel a lot more secure if we knew there were no more coming."

Even Finney had to agree. "Without regular maintenance, this boat will not be operational forever. Now may be the time to ensure the safety of the country."

"We're only a third of the way across the Pacific. Do we have enough supplies to make it there and back? We won't be able to resupply at Pearl."

"Yes Captain. I'm sure the Philippines are not an option."

"Okay, let's go get this boat pointed toward China."

25

Every time Jon went out to scout, he found sentries blocking his path. There was now a guard at the railroad bridge and he had no idea how he and his family would get to their escape vehicle. The gang had spread out, and were systematically searching stores and houses in the town.

It had been a week, and with Jon unable to hunt, they had gone through their meager supply of food. They had two stuffed chairs in the basement facing each other and Jon and Mary were having a conversation, trying to decide what to do… when he heard a door slam loudly.

"Stay here." He grabbed his rifle and ran up the stairs. He quickly determined no one was in the house, so he went to the window, standing alongside it to keep from being spotted from outside. Peeking around the window jamb, he could see a man and woman enter a house across the street and two doors down. On his side of the street he saw two men cross the lawn and enter the house next door. He jumped up and ran back to Mary and the boys.

"We have to hide. Hurry, they're coming." He stuck his finger in a small hole in the wall and pulled away the drywall that covered a small, hidey hole, maybe six-feet wide and four-feet deep. He motioned the kids into the hidden space. Mary grabbed the lamp and the backpacks, pushing them into the back of the space, while Jon raced to the windows and pulled down the plastic. They threw sheets, they had set aside for that purpose, over the two chairs, in an attempt to make it look as though they were in storage. He looked around and picked up a few small items off the floor, and a small table, and thrust them into Mary's arms. She threw them into a back corner behind an old washing machine. Flipping the children's mattress onto its side, Jon leaned it against the wall. He folded Mary's cot and shoved it under the stairs. Stepping over the bottom stud, Jon pushed back into the space with Mary and the boys, pulling the drywall into place. He barely had room to hold the rifle horizontally. They held their breath and waited.

Someone was coming down the stairs. Jon held his breath and prayed the boys wouldn't cry out in the dark. He felt Mary shift her position behind him. One of the boys made a tiny whimpering sound and Jon held his breath, praying that whoever was in their basement hadn't heard the faint whine.

But no such luck.

Light flashed in Jon's eyes, as the cover of their hiding place was thrown aside. Jon couldn't see, and didn't think... he just leveled the rifle and pulled the trigger. There was a grunt and the sound of a body falling as Jon leaped forward from the cramped hole in the wall. A man lay on the floor in the middle of the basement. Jon started toward the basement stairs when he heard the sound of footsteps running across the floor upstairs. The front door slammed.

Realizing they'd been discovered he motioned for Mary to follow him. She tossed him one of the packs and grabbed Josh's hand. Jason followed them, he and Josh's eyes wide, as they stared at the body splayed out on the floor. Jon held out his hand, palm forward to have them wait, and crept to the top of the staircase. Mary and the boys waited until he returned from a quick check of the house and quickly gestured for them to come up the stairs. They went through the house and out the back door. Jon glanced over his shoulder at the little garden in the corner and wondered if he would ever see his home again.

Following Jon's well-worn path through the adjacent backyards and down to the river, they made their way to the railroad bridge. Signing to Mary, Jon gave her instructions. He left Mary and the boys in a clump of flowering bushes, one hundred yards from the bridge, as he sneaked toward the guards. He got as close to them as he dared. Two motorcycles were parked on a grassy swale next to a drop off to the Las Animas River.

Jon jumped to his feet and sprinted fifteen yards across open space to the gleaming Harley. The owners of the two bikes shouted, and leaped in his direction, trying to intercept him. He grabbed the bike by a handlebar and the seat, and heaved with all his might, watching with satisfaction as the bike rolled forward, over the edge and plummeted down the embankment to the river. Reaching out with his foot, he shoved the Honda, which was right next to the edge, and watched as it tumbled after the Harley. Without so much as a glance at the bikers charging down on him, he turned and headed south as fast as he could go, the enraged bike owners trying to catch up to him.

Now was the time. Once the bikers had passed her position, Mary grabbed the two packs, and telling the little boys to follow her, ran to the bridge. She slung one of the packs onto her back and dropped the other to the ground. Taking each boy's hand, they slowly and gingerly stepped from railroad tie to railroad tie, making their way across the bridge as fast as they could go without getting injured. Following John's instructions, she hurried away from the tracks and made her way to a line of retail stores that lined the Boulevard to the west. Being deaf, Mary had never strayed too far from home, even before the war, and she wasn't familiar with the West side of town. Jon had told her to find a hiding place and wait for him.

Within a few minutes she peeked around the corner of the building to see Jon running back toward the bridge with the two bikers in hot pursuit. He had easily outdistanced them. As Jon reached the bridge, he grabbed the backpack off the ground, and high-stepping as fast as he could, spanned the bridge.

Mary couldn't help but smile as the bikers stopped on the south side of the bridge. One of the men leaned over and puked on the ground and the other stood gulping in air. Knowing they would never catch Jon, they gave up and walked to the edge of the embankment looking down at the motorcycles. One of the men picked up rocks, flinging them at the tangled mass of steel below. She watched them flinging rocks and kicking dirt over the edge as she waited for Jon to make his way back to her.

Mary felt a hand on her shoulder and swung around to find Jon beckoning to her. He'd circled the line of stores where he approached her position from behind. Not wanting to carry the boys, they had to slowly make their way across town, heading for the car.

Nutts and Snake, were terrified to tell Chase they'd lost their bikes. They headed to the Parker Hotel and sought out Bing. "Hey Bing," Nutts told him, "we've found the guy we been lookin' for. He has a bitch and two kids with him. Can you tell Chase?"

Bing grinned, knowing the men were so afraid of Chase that they didn't even want to bring him good news. "Get the guys together. Chase is gonna to want to find that guy." He entered the hotel, finding Chase snorting a line at the registration desk.

"Chase, I have good news." He waited for Chase to respond, but only received silence. "Cutter says he saw the guy we've been looking for just across the river. His old lady and kids are with him."

Chase swung to face him, and in his rusty voice said, "Get the Horde moving. That fucker's not getting away. Send a couple guys upstairs to finish off those assholes. Wait... let me do the woman one more time and then everyone meet in the parking lot. You got ten minutes."

The gang quickly assembled in the parking lot, ready to get revenge for Jon escaping from them. Bing heard shots coming from the upper floors of the hotel.

"Damn," he told Nutts, "we could have taken the chick with us."

With Mary and the kids, and having to try and stay hidden from the bikers, it was taking them a forever to make their way to the car. They had to hide twice while choppers cruised past slowly.

"I hope it takes a while for those guys to get back to the hotel, since their bikes seem to have fallen into the river," Jon signed.

"Yes, that was very unfortunate," she chuckled. "How far is it to the car? Do you think they'll try and follow us?"

"Their leader looked insane. I think he'll pursue us to the ends of the earth. We need to get out of town and hope he doesn't know which direction we went."

It took them another half an hour to locate the car. Jon and Mary quickly buckled the boys into the back seat and Jon started it up. He made a U-turn and headed south.

As they passed one of the river crossings they were spotted. Driving with the window down, Jon heard shouts and the sound of motorcycle engines firing up. He had a sick feeling in the pit of his stomach, knowing he probably wasn't going to be able to lose the bikers. It looked like the entire gang was mounted up and ready to pursue them.

Jon slowed the car and reached for the rifle. Across the river he saw a huge rider on a Harley who was directing the other riders.

Mary tugged at his sleeve. "What are you doing?"

"If I can take down the leader, maybe they won't follow us."

"That's crazy. You'll just make them mad."

He stuck the rifle out the window, took aim and fired. The bullet hit the seat just behind the big man's butt, ripping through the leather. The giant's head jerked up and his eyes narrowed. Even from this distance Jon could see the man was infuriated.

Shit, Mary was right.

Jon stomped on the gas and sped away.

***

Blood pressure rising, and his face beginning to flush, Chase turned an evil countenance to Bing. "Let's go. I'm going after that prick and you had all better be able to keep up with me. Nobody shoots at me or hits my bike without signing his death warrant." He shoved it in gear and the rumble of the 1500 cc engine was deafening, as he shot off toward the car heading south.

Bing swung his chopper around in a tight circle. "Cutter," he shouted, "We're leaving town, NOW. Chase says we need to keep up or we're fucked." He sped off after the devil incarnate, trying to keep up as he heard the growl of sixty choppers following him.

26

The sun climbed higher into the sky, as everyone carried their breakfast dishes to the Chuck wagon. Some of the folks had chosen to spend a few nights in a Ramada Inn by the bridge that crossed over the Las Animas River. Mark and Lori had always thought their bed in the wagon was pretty comfortable, so they had chosen to stay with the wagons. Mark had a raging headache and was hung over for the first time in many years. He climbed into Chris's wagon and rummaged through the first aid kit until he found some aspirin. Stumbling down to the river, he pushed through the brush and knelt by the rocks at the river's edge, where he vomited until he trembled. Sitting back on his haunches he buried his head in his arms until his stomach settled down, and then washed his face and choked down three aspirin.

Back at the wagon, Lori took one look at him, smiled, and said cheerfully, "Hi Honey, you don't look so good."

"I'm fine, but I think you're right. I won't be doing any partying tonight."

"Let's go look up the local government. I'd love to hear what's happened in this town since the war," she said, as she hooked her arm through his.

They walked north through town, asking directions to the Civic Center.

Farmington was beginning to show signs of deterioration, despite the fact that the residents had made an effort to maintain it. It was just too big for the number of survivors. They found the Civic Center and climbed the short set of steps to the front doors.

Jeff Hunt sat on a desk in the main office, legs crossed Indian style. He was around six-feet tall, with broad shoulders and light, brown hair neatly trimmed. Three others in the room were all well-dressed and groomed. None of them had the long hair or beards that Mark's group wore.

"I'm glad to meet you," Mark told him as they shook hands. "This is my wife Lori. I hear you're the man that saved this town."

Jeff nodded over at Lori. "I don't know about that. I just got a few guys together to stop the bloodshed. There are a lot of good people in this town and they've come together to try and bring back a little civilization." Mark was pleasantly surprised. Jeff seemed like an easy going guy rather than someone with ambitions of power.

"Some of our people are passing through town, and a few have decided to go back to Willsburg. I like what you've done here and if we didn't have other places to go, I think this would be a good place to live."

Jeff unfolded his legs and swung them over the edge of the desk, leaning on his hands. "I think so. This area sits over a huge reservoir of natural gas and oil. We're hoping we can get the power plant going and start back up the wells."

"Do you know how to do it?"

"Well, a lot of the guys who knew how to run the plant were killed in the fighting, but we've found that there's enough men left with specialized knowledge that we're hoping we can get the power back on real soon. There's a refinery in Bloomfield. We've spent the last year getting guys trained."

One of the other men, who had introduced himself as Liam Jensen, said, "The plan is to use the fuel that was stored at the plant to get the power back on. When we have the power going we can get the wells and the refinery up and running. We're almost ready to give it a try."

Jeff added, "A couple of guys came through here about a month ago from up north, somewhere in Idaho, and they said there are a bunch of communities up that way. I guess Utah and Idaho were places that a lot of people moved to, in anticipation of a war or societal collapse. They're pretty self-sufficient and we're thinking we can set up trade with them when we get our refineries going. We're getting more cars repaired every day and they're all going to need gas."

"You may be able to trade with the New Mexico Colony as well." Mark said. "Have you heard anything about California? Has anybody come through here from there?"

Jeff said, "No one's come through here from California, but the guy from Idaho said they had received a message from someone in the northern part of the state. There's a group of people living in southern Oregon as well. Once we get more cars working we can send out people to make contact with others. Communications have been really bad since the war but we've received a couple of messages in the past week so were thinking that the atmosphere is finally settling down."

"We're on our way to California. I came from Newport Beach and we just want to find out what happened there. I'm also a little bit worried about the Chinese. I used to work for an aeronautics company and we had a meeting with the President of the United States just before the war."

"You knew the President? That's pretty impressive. Do you think he survived?"

"Maybe. They had special bunkers for him and the rest of the government, so I don't know. Anyway, the Secretary of Defense said the Chinese had two types of bombs, regular hydrogen bombs and a new type of bomb called a neutron bomb. The latter has a substance called Red Mercury as part of the payload, and instead of regular radiation, it creates a very intense neutron radiation that destroys life but doesn't harm infrastructure. The intent seemed to be to leave cities unharmed, but devoid of life."

Jeff understood the implications immediately. "Whoa, that sounds like they wanted to be able to use our cities after the war. Do you think they're planning to invade?"

"I think it's something we have to worry about. That's another reason I want to get to California. I need to know if my home survived, and I need to find out if there's anybody left that can fight against a Chinese attack."

"Oh man," Liam said, "we're just sitting here in our little corner of the world planning on rebuilding civilization and China might be on its way?"

"I don't think you should live in fear, but you need to be prepared."

A radio, sitting on a desk in front of Liam, came to life with a burst of static. "Civic Center, are you there?"

Liam reached out and grabbed the radio. "This is the Civic Center. This is Liam. What's up?"

"Hi, Liam. This is Zabriskie up at the Aztec post. I just had a car go through here doing about eighty like he was being chased by the devil himself. He's coming your way, so keep your eyes peeled for... Oh shit! It really is the devil himself! There must be a hundred motorcycles on this guy's tail. They're only about a quarter of a mile behind him. At the speed they're going, they're going to hit Farmington in about five minutes. You better get a bunch of armed guys out to the barrier."

Jeff and the other three men jumped to their feet and ran for the door. "Come on. I think were gonna need all the guns we can get." Mark and Lori chased after the four men as they headed out to the parking lot and jumped into an old pickup truck. They let Lori take the passenger seat with Jeff driving and the others hanging on for dear life in the bed of the truck.

As the pickup truck flew down Main Street toward the highway, Mark saw Jimbo and Danny riding the motorcycle down the street. They each had an assault rifle hung over their back and guns in holsters strapped to their waists. Mark knocked on the back window of the truck. As Lori slid it open Mark yelled to Jeff, "Slow down alongside that motorcycle." Pulling up alongside Jimbo, Mark gestured for him to follow them, and cupping his hands around his mouth yelled, "Follow us. We've got bad guys coming into town."

Jeff was blasting the horn as they went, and the men in the back of the pickup truck were calling out for everyone they saw to follow them to the north highway barrier. Liam was broadcasting on the radio for every available person with a weapon to join them. Within a few minutes they pulled up to the intersection of Main Street and the highway, and piled out of the truck to take up positions on either side of the road. There were businesses and retail stores along the four-lane road. The townspeople had positioned a barrier of hay bales, two deep, two high, and four long, in one of the northbound, and one of the southbound lanes.

Mark and Lori only had their handguns, but all of the men at the barrier and most of those just arriving, had various makes and calibers of rifles. The call to arms had been answered by dozens of men and women, most running up the streets, but quite a few arriving in cars and trucks. By the time Mark spotted the speeding vehicle in the distance, he estimated there were at least one hundred and fifty people in the stores, behind dead vehicles and hiding behind rusting dumpsters, for at least one hundred yards up the Highway.

Jimbo and Danny had taken up positions beside Mark and Lori toward the front of the defenders. Mark felt almost unarmed with just his Sig .45.

The roar from the car's engine could be heard as it came over a rise in the road and barreled down the highway toward the barrier. There was plenty of room to pass the bales of hay as the townspeople had never completely blocked the road. Until now, most travelers had arrived on horseback, wagons, or on foot. Mark reasoned that the people in the car were probably good guys, since they were being chased by a pack of motorcycles. His analysis proved to be correct when he heard the popping of gunfire coming from behind the car.

"Here they come!" yelled Jimbo. The car appeared to be about a half-mile away when it looked like it was starting to slow down.

"What the hell's he doing?" Danny asked. "Why's he stopping?"

"He's fishtailing. I think they got his tire," Mark replied.

The car continued to whip back and forth until large strips of rubber flew from a back tire. Sparks flew from the rear of the vehicle as the rim hit the pavement. Slowing further, the car pulled to the right side of the road and stopped. The doors flew open and a man ran around the front of the car to where a woman was trying to get something from the back seat. In a few seconds the man and woman, each carrying a small child were running toward them.

Mark heard Lori gasp as the motorcycles came over the hill and into view. "God, there's so many of them."

"Lori, keep your head down. We don't need to fire until they get alongside of us."

The two lids of the dumpster were open and Mark could see between them. The family slowed and the woman went to her knees, trying to hand the child she was carrying to the man. He set the other boy down and the two little guys started running toward the town, as the man grabbed the woman by the arm and tried to pull her after them. The gunfire continued, and Mark couldn't imagine how they would make it to the barrier without being hit.

"Open fire!" Someone yelled from across the street. The townspeople returned fire, a hundred and fifty weapons firing at the gang.

Suddenly, Danny jumped up, stepped around the end of the dumpster and sprinted for the family.

27

Jon almost lost control of the car as the rear tire was hit and the vehicle began to fishtail. The back of the car bounced, and the rim hit the road, sparks flying as it screeched down the road. Jon jerked the steering wheel of the car to the right and slid to a stop at the edge of the right-hand lane. Jumping out of the car, he raced around the front of the Taurus to the rear door, throwing it open. "Come on! Come on!" As Jon unfastened their seatbelts, the two little boys, bawling loudly, quickly climbed out of the car. Jon grabbed Josh and shoved him into Mary's arms. Sweeping up Jason, they began to run down the side of the road, the sounds of motorcycles in the distance behind them.

"Come on, Mary. Hurry!" he gestured to her, but Mary couldn't go any faster. She was weak from months of living in a basement with very little sunlight or fresh air. The weight of little Josh in her arms was too much and she stumbled and fell to her knees. Pain shot through her legs and it was all she could do to keep from dropping the child to the ground.

She was sucking air. "Jon, I'm sorry I just can't go on. Here take Josh. Go."

Jon could see something in the distance across the right side of the road. It looked like some kind of a barrier and he saw movement behind it. He waved his free arm at the people and tried to pull Mary to her feet. Signing one-handed, he said, "Come on Mary. There's somebody up ahead."

She sobbed, "I can't Jon. I just can't go on. Please take the boys and go!"

The menacing growl of the motorcycles grew louder and John knew they only had a few minutes. He set Jason on the ground and screamed at the boys, "Run, run to the barrier!" Grabbing Mary by the arm, he jerked her to her feet. He screamed in her ear, wishing she could hear him, "You're not gonna stay here and die! Not after everything we've done to survive. Come on Mary. Please run."

He glanced up and saw someone running toward them. In the distance he heard a shout, "Danny, get back here. What the fuck are you doing?" Then he heard the sound of a motorcycle starting up behind a dumpster. The boys had slowed to a walk and it was all Jon could do to drag Mary along at a slow clip. He looked behind him and wished he hadn't. Scores of motorcycles came over a small rise in the road, bearing down on them. In front of him, he saw a young man sprinting as hard as he could in their direction and, behind the young man, an old motorcycle swept around the dumpster, flying in their direction.

More gunfire erupted and Jon could hear rounds slapping the ground on either side and behind him. The motorcycle in front raced past the running man, as the rider fired his weapon toward the oncoming horde. Swinging around behind Jon and Mary, he headed back toward the barrier, sweeping up little Jason in his arms as he went by. Danny reached Josh, grabbed him up and yelled at Jon, "We've got the kids. Come on, hurry." The gunfire continued behind them, and on both sides, from the storefronts, answering gunfire could be heard.

With renewed effort, both Jon and Mary started running after the two men carrying their precious children. The sounds of the motorcycles behind them suddenly diminished and Jon glanced back to see the line of choppers slowing down.

Then he heard an inhumane scream. He looked back to see one motorcycle, a huge Harley, coming down the highway toward them, the rider with a maniacal look on his face. His eyes were wide, the whites showing all around even from this distance, and his teeth were bared in a horrible grimace. The front wheel lifted off the road and the bike picked up tremendous speed, traveling for twenty yards on its rear wheel alone. In one hand, the man brandished a huge revolver. As he came screaming down the highway, the front tire settled back on the road and he began firing at the fleeing people. Just before they reached the barrier, Jon saw the man carrying Josh get hit in the back. The young man stumbled a few steps forward, and dropped Josh to the ground, pitching forward onto his face as the little boy flew out of his arms.

The entire line of bikers surged forward after their leader.

The motorcycle rider was still screaming, a high-pitched wail, like a supernatural phantom, and he was emptying the revolver toward John and Mary. A piece of asphalt kicked up and hit John in the back of the head. He thought he'd been hit. Someone stepped out from behind a dumpster, firing his weapon at the biker, and grabbed him and Mary, throwing them down just as the rider flew past.

Answering gunfire cut down the motorcycle rider a few seconds before he reached the barrier. Plowing into it at over one hundred miles per hour, hay bales flew everywhere and the chopper flipped ten feet into the air, tumbling down the road in a shower of sparks, the sound of screeching metal echoing off the buildings that lined the highway. The rider was catapulted over the handlebars, coming down directly on his head. There was a loud crack and the man tumbled down the roadway, leaving smeared splotches of blood, until the body came to a halt in a tangled heap, with arms and legs and neck bent in directions never intended by God.

Jimbo rode up on the Indian motorcycle and handed Jason to Jon, another bringing him Josh, who was bleeding from both knees and scraped up hands. He swung the bike around to face the choppers roaring down the highway. Bullets zinged around them.

A biker was hit in the chest, and his bike flipped over, skidding into the dumpster and knocking it backward into Mark and Lori, slamming both to the asphalt. Jimbo brought up his rifle and shot the rider point-blank as he tried to come to his feet. Mark scrambled up, and hearing a shout of pain across the street, he saw one of the townspeople spin around and topple to the ground

The motorcycles flew by, the riders firing at the defenders on both sides of the highway. Riders and townspeople alike were hit by flying bullets, as the bikers swung into the parking areas before the shops, firing into the stores. Smoke filled the streets from weapons fire, burning wrecks of choppers, and from tires, as the bikers spun 180 degrees and sped back toward the north.

In the chaos, two choppers collided and one flew into a storefront. Mark saw men and women dodging the flying, burning vehicle as they poured lead into the rider. A man ran out of the building with his arm on fire and was tackled by two others, who threw him to the ground and swatted at the flames with their bare hands.

Then the last of the choppers were flying back toward the north.

"Get a medic over here!" Someone was trying to staunch the flow of blood from the man who had collapsed across the street. A woman with a large backpack slid down beside him and, flinging open the pack, began to administer to the bleeding man.

Jimbo did a wheelie as he followed the bikers north, skidding to a stop at the body of the young man that had saved the children.

"Aaron!" he screamed. "Someone get the doctor."

Scared to death, he pulled Danny into his lap, trying to put pressure on the wound.

***

Sporadic gunfire continued as the bikers passed the crippled car. Another hundred yards and they turned to face the town. The smoke was clearing and they could see the guns pointing in their direction.

The gunfire had ceased and Bing looked over at Cutter.

"Dude, I think we're seriously outnumbered here. It would be suicide to take these guys on anymore, and Chase is either dead or they've got him. I say we get the hell out of here." They heard another shot from the south and a lucky round struck one of the men to Bing's left. Flying backward off his bike, his motorcycle toppled to the ground.

Two men were astride a single bike behind the fallen rider.

"Duncan, get that bike and let's get out of here," Bing ordered. The man on the back jumped off and grabbed the now rider-less motorcycle. Bikers were revving their engines waiting for some sort of direction. Bing swung around and screamed out at them to get back. The bikes at the rear had room to turn around and they sped off toward the north. Like an onion being peeled, the rest of the choppers turned around line by line, until at last, Bing and Cutter swung their cycles in a circle, revving their rumbling, Harley engines. Just before taking off to the north, Bing looked over his shoulder and fired three shots toward Jimbo as a parting gesture.

"Hey Bing," Cutter yelled over the noise of the engines, "where we going now?"

"Albuquerque."

They left the fallen riders where they lay.

***

"Somebody get the doctor, get Aaron!"

"Lori, get one of those cars to go get Aaron." Mark grabbed Danny's rifle from the ground and ran to where Danny had fallen.

"Come on, kid. Please, Danny, hang in there until Aaron gets here. You're going to be all right." Jimbo sat on the ground, holding Danny. There was a pool of blood forming under him as Mark raced to their side.

Danny was conscious and looked up at Jimbo. "Hey, man. You're scaring me. Am I hit that bad? Did they make it? The kids?"

"Yeah, Danny. The whole family is okay, thanks to you, and it looks like the bikers decided we were too much for them."

A crowd was gathering around, and Mark enlisted aid in getting Danny turned over. He was bleeding from both an entrance and an exit wound, just above the scapula on his right side. They managed to get Danny's shirt off and Mark used it to apply pressure to the wound on his back.

"Here, buddy, use this." Someone behind Mark tapped him on the shoulder and handed him a mesh with a substance embedded in it.

"What is it? What do I do with it?"

"Slap it on the wound. It will stop the bleeding. Here, I've got another one for the front."

He raced off to help with the other casualties.

When Lori arrived with Aaron in the back of a pickup truck they found Jimbo holding Danny in his lap, with one hand holding the clotting mesh in place on his back, and Mark holding the other. With the help of a couple of other men, they hoisted Danny into the back of the pickup truck where Aaron, taking care not to dislodge the mesh, examined him. Danny had passed out, either from pain or shock.

"Let's get him back to camp. I think he's going to make it, thanks to whoever had the quick clot. It's a great thing because most battlefield deaths occur due to bleeding."

Mark smiled at Lori, careful not to touch her with his bloody hands. "I guess this means we can't think of Danny as a spoiled, little brat anymore."

Lori hurried over to the family sitting behind the dumpster. The boys were crying and the young parents looked shell-shocked.

"Are you guys all right?"

"Yes, I think so. I'm Jon and my wife is Mary."

Jon climbed to his feet, unable to believe it was over. Not only had they escaped with their lives from Ben's buddies, and the bikers, but there was a community of regular people here.

Mary said something, her voice slurred. The skinny young man turned to her and answered in American Sign Language. Lori realized the woman was deaf.

"Can we get one of the medics to take a look at the boys?

"Of course. As soon as they attend to the more seriously injured."

"Lori, we're ready to go." Mark called.

"Be right there." She turned back to Jon. "We're heading back to our camp and one of the doctors is a member of our group. Do you want to come with us?"

Jon signed to the woman, then turned back and nodded his head. "Yes, please."

Lori lifted one of the boys from Mary's arms, as Jon extended a hand to help her up. They climbed into the back of the pickup with Danny, covered by a blanket, and Aaron and Mark. Lori sat up front with Jason.

Ten minutes later they arrived back at the wagons and Aaron had his hands full caring for his patients and putting up with Jimbo's hovering.

28

Each day ran into another as they slogged their way through the backwoods of Kentucky. Three or four miles into another day's hike, Roger and Ashe came out onto a dirt road. It was barely recognizable as such, with knee-high grass growing up through the dirt, and puddles of muddy water hiding ruts and potholes. The rain had ceased temporarily, but the clouds were low, and mist swirled around them as they walked. The road disappeared into the fog a hundred yards down the road.

"What do you think?" Ashe asked.

"I think it might lead somewhere other than this interminable forest. Let's follow it."

"Which way?"

Roger shrugged his shoulders. "Right."

The road trended downhill, for which they were grateful. A few more miles and it widened and seemed in better repair. The fog had lifted but the day was still dreary. They stopped and Ashe removed his pack. Stuffing their ponchos into a side pocket, they sat on the wet ground, eating some jerky and washing it down with water.

"What's that over there?" Ashe was pointing across the meadow. He shouldered his pack and moved closer to the object. It turned out to be an ancient, rusting, car frame. "Looks like it was burned," Ashe commented.

"Hey, there's another one." Roger walked over to it. "It's a washing machine. I think this is a junk yard. We'd better be careful. We may be coming to civilization."

They jogged over to the tree line and snuck through the edge of the forest trying to stay hidden. The trees in the forest were too far apart and they were having trouble finding cover.

Coming out onto an intersecting road, they heard, "You boys get your hands in the air."

Roger's heart jumped into his throat and he threw his hands into the air. "Don't shoot! We don't have any guns."

"You have some mean-looking, pig-stickers strapped to your legs. You just unbuckle those belts and drop 'em on the ground."

They did as they were told and, as he dropped the belt, Roger looked at the men. There were four, large, white guys and a black man, all armed with rifles pointed directly at them.

"Smitty, get their belts," the leader said.

"Sure, Billy." The small, bald, black man handed his rifle to a hulking, young fellow with jet black hair and beard, and leaning in, grabbed the belts. He bounced back out, as if thinking Roger was going to grab and devour him.

Ashe said, "Really, we don't mean… "

"Shut up! I'll do the talking. Get down on your knees, big guy. We don't much like African-Americans around here." He stressed *African-American* and grinned at the others as if he'd made a joke. He pointed his rifle right at Ashe's face. Ashe looked at the rifle and slowly lowered to his knees in the wet grass.

Roger was done. He'd had enough. The pain of his family's loss had set him on edge. Their escape from the work camp, being chased by dogs, running from huge ugly guys, searching for help while trudging for days through the mountains, and now this, had infuriated him.

"What the hell are you talking about?" He gestured toward the small black man. "What's he? Pink?"

He grabbed Ashe's arm and lifted him to his feet, and turning to Billy screamed at him, "He hasn't done anything to you. Leave him alone. We're the good guys, you asshole. We just escaped from a FEMA camp in Charleston, from our great and magnificent President of the United States and we've had enough! We don't want to hurt anyone, so if you're going to kill us just do it. Otherwise take us to someone we can reason with."

Billy looked like a little boy who'd been chastised. "Well... we weren't gonna kill you. Not unless you jumped us."

"Billy, let's take 'em to Mama," the hulk said.

"Shut up, Bernie." He squinted over at Roger. "Did you say the President?"

"He's still alive and he's going to be coming for you."

"Huh? We didn't do anything."

"I didn't either, but they took my farm and my family. We all need to stick together if we're going to fight them."

"Bernie's right," one of the other men said. He was scary looking with a high forehead, wide, dark eyes and ears that stuck straight out. "Let's take them home."

Billy thought for a minute and nodded. He waved the rifle down the road, "Get movin' then."

The road wound in and out through the junk yard, filled with rusting appliances, farm equipment and stacks of rotting lumber. Eventually they came to valley that had surprisingly neat rows of crops, with funny-looking scarecrows standing guard. Roger realized they were department store manikins.

A large, white farmhouse stood across the field, with a faded-red, partially-collapsed barn behind it, the only color in the expanse of green surrounding the small valley. They led them to the rear door of the farmhouse.

"Go get Mama, Chuck."

The ugly man disappeared into the house and returned a few minutes later with a beautiful, petite woman. She was probably in her fifties but had smooth skin and thick, wavy, dark hair without a trace of gray and looked much younger. Roger looked at Ashe and saw the same surprise that he felt. She looked

227

Roger and Ashe over and motioned them to follow her into the house. They went through a kitchen into a living room with threadbare carpet and Norman Rockwell prints on the walls. The furniture consisted of lumpy, stuffed couches and chairs, and dark end tables covered with doilies.

She pointed to the couch. "Sit. You want tea?"

"Yes ma'am. That would be great."

"What are you doing here?" she asked in a low musical voice.

"Ah, ma'am, like we told your boys, we escaped from the President's work camp. We were building a new White House over the ridge in Charleston."

"He survived then. The rest of the government?"

"I don't know. I'd just gotten there when we made a break for it. Ashe," he nodded toward his friend, "was there longer than me."

She looked at Ashe and raised her eyebrows. "Well?"

"I worked building the railroad between Charleston and Parkersburg. I only saw Rissman once, and that was when we finished the spur that allowed them to bring the old steam locomotive from the museum. He gave a speech but we were too far away to hear. I didn't see anyone else I recognized."

A young woman around seventeen brought their tea, smiling shyly at Roger, and disappeared back into the kitchen. Mama, they found out her name was Grace, served them in china cups.

She quizzed them at length, hungry for news from West Virginia and other areas to the east. They took turns telling their own stories, what they had seen in their homes and towns and how they had been captured by the military. She wanted to know about radiation and what had been bombed in the war.

"How many soldiers do they have?"

"I'd say at least a thousand and many others down south," Ashe said. "They have working trucks and jeeps."

That jolted her. "When do you think they'll be coming for us?"

"They're moving south first. They think there's more survivors down that way. It will probably be a while."

"What did you boys do before the war?"

Roger didn't think she'd be impressed that he owned a flower shop. "I was a farmer and Ashe was a High School Principal."

Grace looked at Ashe. "Thought he sounded educated."

She called in the five men and introduced them. The quieter man whose name they hadn't heard was Pierce. Then four women came down the stairs. Grace introduced them as her son's wives.

"Ashe, I think we can use your talents if you wouldn't mind." She put her fingers between her lips and let out a shrill whistle. Roger and Ashe were both shocked, as at least fifteen children came flying down the stairs.

"Think you could teach these kids? Don't want them to lose everything they learned before the war."

"Yes ma'am, I'd love to. But I want to establish something. That we're friends, equals, and that we're free to leave whenever we want."

"Of course. There's a house you can use a quarter mile down the road. It's across the street from Smitty's. If you help work the fields and hunt, we'll share our food."

"It's a deal," Roger and Ashe said at the same time. Everyone laughed.

"Welcome brothers."

29

Two days after the fight with the biker gang, the entire group from Willsburg sat around the campfire finishing up their dinner. After the dishes were cleared away and the kids were asleep, they turned the conversation to the future.

Mark looked around the small group of travelers. "It looks like some of you have decided not to go on. I'm disappointed, of course, but you each have to do what you think is best. Let's start with Chris and go around the campfire to see what each of you wants to do."

"Aaron and I are going back to Willsburg." She reached out and took Aaron's hand. "It's just too difficult with the baby and they need us back home."

Aaron added, "I feel bad leaving you guys without a doctor, but your group will be smaller and probably travel a lot faster without us."

"Yeah," Chris said. "And I think you'll be returning to Willsburg too, after you get to California and find it's been bombed back to the Jurassic Age. Maybe sometime in the future we can all move back to the coast. After the radiation's gone. If we even want to by then."

"Okay, so Sheri, what are you thinking?" Mark tilted his beer toward her.

"I'm going on. I can't take the freezing winters in New Mexico and I'm hoping to find my aunt and uncle in Lompoc.

I'm sure San Diego was wiped out and my parents and brother are gone, but maybe Vandenburg was spared, since it's more of a spaceport than a military base. I won't slow you down."

Mark chuckled, "I'm sure of that. Chang?"

"As you all know, me and Carlos have been friends for most of our adult lives. He helped me when my wife died of cancer, and I went through his divorce with him. We kind of like a bigger town than Willsburg. We're grateful I got the box that led us to the shelter, and everything you guys have done for us, but I guess we'll stay here in Farmington. Carlos met a woman a couple of days ago and he really likes her."

Carlos ran his hand through his thick, dark hair and looked embarrassed. "I'd like to think it might lead to something. You can let us know what it's like in California."

"Okay, how about you Jimbo?"

"Oh hell, I'm going with you. I really want to see what's happening out west. I'm originally from the Bay area, before I moved to Denver. And we might find out what the Chinese are up to. I thought Danny would be coming with us but he obviously needs to go back with Chris. He doesn't want to stay here, away from most of the people he knows. He talks like he's an independent grownup, but this group and those back in Willsburg mean a lot to him."

"Hey Jimbo," Mike said, "you've never said anything about what you did before the war. Most of us figured you were a crook."

Jimbo squirmed in his chair. He seemed reluctant but finally blurted out, "I was a ballet teacher."

Everyone just stared. Mike started to laugh. "Okay, you don't have to tell us."

"No, really. I was."

"Yeah, Jimbo."

"So, Sam, how about you?" Mark asked quickly.

"Me and Willy are taking the horses back to the ranch," Sam said. "We bought a dozen mares and one fine stallion. I want to thank all of you that chipped in some gold. Anyone else going back can ride along with us. Since we don't have to go through Raton, we'll take the shorter, more direct route. We can get there in two weeks."

"It won't take that long," Mark said. "I bought the Taurus from Jon and Mary. Jimbo went out to the highway with me this afternoon and we fixed the tire. Chris, Aaron, Karen and Danny can drive back in a day, going through Taos. Anybody else going back can ride with the Yancey boys."

Chris said excitedly, "Hey Mark, that's great. I'm ready to be done with this little adventure." She squeezed Aaron's arm.

"Greg. How about you?"

"I will go with you as far as Ganado, Arizona," the geologist said. "My family would have gone to Canyon de Chelly, as the other Navajo would have. I believe they could have survived in the canyon."

"Matthew?"

"I'm in."

"Me too," Einstein added.

"Mike?"

"I'm goin' on."

"Well, we don't need three wagons. If I could talk Lori into going back with Chris we wouldn't need the wagons at all, but she almost killed me when I suggested it." He smiled over at Lori. "Skillet, you still thinking of moving on?"

"I'm going with you. You need someone to drive that wagon and without me cooking for you, you'd all starve to death. But you realize we'll be crossing the desert in the middle of July?"

Mark sipped his coffee, thinking before he replied, "We could wait until fall, but we don't want to get too comfortable here, so we need to go as soon as we're prepared. We'll take one wagon and load it up with water barrels. The kids can sleep in the back end. The rest of us will ride horses and camp in tents. We should be able to fill the barrels along the way."

"Well, if we can't, it'll be a real short trip."

"Thanks for that observation, Mike. We can travel at night and sleep during the day."

Skillet said, "I want to use the mules for the wagon. They'll be a little tougher in the heat than the horses. But, I'll miss Fred and Ethel."

"Good idea. Let's get some sleep and get ready tomorrow to leave on the day after. Okay?"

Everyone agreed and turned to their wagons and tents. When Mark and Lori were snuggled in their bed he tried once more to dissuade her. "Lori, seriously, the trip across the desert is going to be brutal. Do you think we should expose the kids to that?"

"We will never leave you, Mark. We've gone over this many times before. Now shut up and go to sleep."

He did, but it took a long time.

***

Chris clung to Mark when he hugged her goodbye. "Please be careful and don't take any chances," she told him. "I know you guys are going to come back. California had to be hit hard in the war, and you're not going to find anything worth staying for." She sniffed back tears as she backed away and looked up at him.

"You're probably right, but I have to find out."

"I know. But you know where home is. So when you satisfy your curiosity, please come back."

Mark abruptly turned away, his own emotion almost overwhelming him. Chris was like a sister to him, and he had every intention of seeing her again. She climbed into the passenger seat and Aaron handed her the baby from where he sat behind the wheel. Danny half reclined on the rear seat, his back on a pillow against the window. He was pale, his right arm supported by a sling.

The gas tank was full and the tires were good. Mark was concerned that if the car broke down they would be stranded, and there would be no way to communicate with anyone if they had trouble. Sam and Willy had agreed to follow the road, when they could, so if the car broke down they could assist them. Sleeping bags and supplies were stuffed in the trunk, in case they had to camp by the car until the Yancey's arrived.

The day was warm, the bright sun halfway from the eastern horizon to the zenith, but somehow it felt a little colder as Mark watched the car drive away toward the east. Lori came up to Mark and wrapped him in her arms.

"We need to get moving ourselves," she said.

He nodded and they walked over to the wagon, all packed and ready to go. Matthew rode Chief, and Einstein sat astride Tulip. Jimbo rode his bike, and there were two, five-gallon, gas cans strapped to the sides of the wagon, resting on wooden shelves. As Mark mounted Jasper, he realized he wasn't looking forward to riding a horse for several hours each day. He figured he could occasionally spell Skillet, or ride along on the seat beside him. Lori rode a bay gelding they had picked up for a reasonable price at the ranch, and Mike had a golden palomino. Greg had purchased a pinto and, of course, Sheri had her bike. They had two pack mules. One belonged to Greg, and the other carried supplies that wouldn't fit in the wagon.

Mark had a feeling of déjà vu as he remembered six weeks ago, leaving Willsburg. There was a crowd of people seeing them off. Carlos, his girlfriend Lisa, and Chang were there, as well as a group of townspeople including, Jeff Hunt and several others that Mark had come to know over the past week. Ashley and Kevin waved out the back of the wagon as they moved off toward the south, heading down Highway 371.

Once again, they had decided to stay on or near roads since they were usually the easiest routes through mountain passes.

***

Being a smaller group, they made better time than before. There was a greater sense of urgency since it was late June and they hoped to get through the desert while the weather was cooler. When they reached Indian Service Route 5 they turned west until they reached Highway 491, *The Trail of the Ancients,* and followed it to Gallup, New Mexico. Greg had hoped to find survivors in these Indian lands, but so far, the area had been empty. It was populated by coyotes, rabbits, a few herds of deer, and hawks flying high above.

Of necessity, they only had one sentry at night, but the trip had been uneventful. As they moved through Gallup, they once again had the feeling that they were being watched. The town was overgrown, and advertising signs had faded and had fallen to the ground. Many windows had been broken and glass littered the sidewalks and even out into the road. They kept the horses to the center of the highway to protect their hooves.

"I think maybe it's just because we expect there to be people in the towns," Lori speculated. "I just believe all these houses and stores should be occupied, so my mind imagines survivors."

Einstein rode beside her, his brand new, black, cowboy hat pulled low to block the sun. "You may be right, but I thought I saw movement back there when we pumped Jimbo's gas." He scratched his scraggly beard. "The fact that we found some food, though, makes me think it's deserted."

"Well, nothing could be spookier than Costilla," she said.

They found a water tank and filled the barrels, adding bleach to sterilize it. As they traveled west they passed red-rock cliffs and old, deteriorated teepees that had been part of a modern trading post just under two years before. Scorching sun, wind, and blowing sand had taken their toll on the manmade buildings and, in that short time, nature was already reclaiming the land. Weeds grew high along the side of the freeway and were poking up through cracks in the concrete and asphalt. The right lane was half covered over with wild grass.

When they reached Chambers, Arizona they had a sad parting with Greg Whitehorse.

"Really Greg, are you sure you want to do this?" Mark asked him. "You don't know if anyone's there. What if you get to Canyon de Chelly and it's deserted?"

"Yeah," Lori added, "you'd be all alone."

"I'm going through Ganado first to see if anyone's there. It was my home before the war. I would have stayed with my family, but I was in Flagstaff for the start of the new semester when the alarm went off. It was quicker to fly to Albuquerque than to try and get to Ganado on my Harley. When I got off the plane, the warning of the attack had already gone out and the airport was absolute chaos. I stole a car from the lot and drove to the shelter. Otherwise I would have gone to Canyon de Chelley with my people. Matthew, you are part Indian. You would be welcome if you wish to join me."

"My friend, I thank you for the offer. I don't know where I belong, but I know I haven't found it yet. Maybe someday I can visit and see if I feel that my home is with you and your people. But not today."

Greg shook hands with everyone including the children. Kevin wrapped his arms around Greg's leg. "Please don't go, Uncle Greg."

Taking his hat off his head and allowing his black hair to fall around his face, Greg gently unwrapped the boy, and went to one knee to look him in the eye. "It's been my honor to have known you all." He hugged the boy and Ashley stepped forward to hug the Indian's neck.

He stood, brushing the dirt off his pants. "If none of my family or my tribe has survived, I will return to Farmington and probably to Willsburg. Otherwise, go in peace, my friends. Maybe we'll meet again someday." He mounted his pinto and reined its head around to the north. They stayed in place, watching him, as he and his horse and the pack mule kicked up dust, until they disappeared over a ridge and were lost to sight.

With heavy hearts, they continued on. During the next two weeks, they moved beyond the Painted Desert and Petrified Forest, and passed through the small towns of Holbrook and

Winslow to begin the long climb into Flagstaff. Although it was now early July, the temperature in Flagstaff was comfortable. Mark knew that wouldn't last. They resupplied in Flag, passed Williams, and descended toward Kingman and the California desert beyond.

30

It had been a long haul from Farmington. The two hundred and sixty miles to Flagstaff had taken them almost two weeks and another five days downhill to Kingman. The freeway led through town and over a hill toward the Colorado River.

As they reached Andy Devine Blvd., Mark called out to Skillet, "Let's pull off and refill the water barrels. Matthew and Mike said they'd meet us at the hospital."

As they rode toward that prominent landmark they noticed evidence of fire. The ground was scorched for many acres of what looked like had once been crops. A few patches of corn stalks, and a trellis with climbing beans had miraculously escaped the fire.

Lori dismounted and waded into the overgrown patch of vegetables. "I'm going to pick anything that looks okay. I'll meet you at the hospital."

Mark waved Skillet onward and swung off Jasper to cover Lori as she made her way through the few unburnt rows, adding beans to a bag she had slung over her shoulder. Mark heard her gasp, and saw her back quickly away from something on the ground between the corn rows. "Mark!"

He already had his rifle out and immediately jumped forward to her side. The wind shifted and the smell of putrefying bodies assailed them.

"Whew," Mark said, as he threw his arm across his face. Lori had moved behind him. Pulling a bandanna out of his hip pocket, he held it over his nose, partially blocking the sickly, pungent odor. He went through the rows and returned to Lori, where she stood with her rifle pointed away from Mark to cover them.

"There's at least twenty people dead over there, including children. It was a massacre. Let's get out of here and meet the others at the hospital."

They mounted up, glanced around for any danger, and kicked the horses into a gallop to leave the ghastly scene as quickly as possible. When they arrived at the rendezvous point, Matthew took Mark aside. "I found a fairgrounds with several dead bodies and dozens of slaughtered and partially eaten animal carcasses. This was savage. If whoever did this is still around, we're in grave danger."

"We found a score of murdered people back at the fields. Someone came through here, killing everyone and torching the fields. We need to get out of here now."

Mike rode over. "Lori told me about the bodies. You don't suppose those bikers came through here, do you?"

Mark shrugged. "That's a real possibility. Whoever did this was vicious and maybe even insane."

"The hospital has a small reservoir. Skillet, Jimbo and Sheri are filling the barrels. Let's get out of this God-forsaken place," Mike said.

***

Once clear of the newer part of Kingman, they holed up under a freeway overpass at the southern edge of town, to try and beat the heat. They pushed hard and arrived at the Colorado River in two nights of travel. Mark was worried that the bridge would be out, but it still spanned the river south of Needles, California. The green waters of the river rushed by, but they found a small inlet and everyone jumped in with their clothes on, whooping and hollering in sheer joy, as they splashed and swam in the cool refreshing water. They camped that night at the river where there was plenty of grass for the horses, and waited until the next night to continue the journey.

As Skillet had predicted, the trek across the California desert was brutal. Matthew went ahead in the twilight and darkness, sweeping a light on the road to detect rattlers that seemed to find the freeway a comfortable place to rest. Moonlight bathed the wagon as it made its ghostly way up the long highway toward Essex. The evening and night time temperatures were still warm but it was at least twenty degrees cooler than during the day. Mark had driven this highway a few times on his way to the casinos of Laughlin, Nevada, preferring the atmosphere of the smaller, gambling oasis to that of the brilliantly lit Las Vegas Strip. He told them there was a service station at Essex, but when they arrived two days later they found that the only water tank was empty, and the water pipe was busted.

There was no water.

A horse will drink five to ten gallons per day and they had two mules and five horses. Each person needed a minimum of one gallon a day but with the heat, they were drinking more. They had eight barrels, approximately fifty gallons in each one. So one barrel minimally watered the horses for one day.

The burning orb overhead beat down on them during the day, and they did their best to find shade where they could sit out the oven-like temperature. They tried not to move around too much to conserve water by not sweating, but never-the-less, trickles of sweat ran out of their hair and down their faces. Their clothes were damp from perspiration and filthy from the dust kicked up by the horses every time they left the pavement.

Even though they had all slathered on sun screen, they were turning a golden brown after weeks of being outside in the elements.

They sat in the shade of a large pile of boulders. "So Sheri," Mike said, "how do you like this heat? You said you don't like the winter in New Mexico."

"It's funny. I can ride all day in this stuff. The heat doesn't bother me so much."

"Are you kidding? It's gotta be a hundred and ten out there."

"How far to Barstow?" she asked, turning to Mark.

"It's about a hundred miles. There's a small town, Ludlow, about midway but there's no guarantee there's any water. Just like Essex. How's the water, Skillet?"

"Six and a half barrels. If we keep it to a minimum, we should just make it. There's bound to be water somewhere in Barstow."

Even the nights were hot, as they got underway at 6:00 o'clock in the evening. It seemed like a dream to them as they rode through the darkness, holing up again as the temperature climbed at 9:00 in the morning.

As they feared, Ludlow was dry. There were a few buildings, but either the pipes were broken or the pumps had failed, and there was no gravity fed water. Lori was worried about the kids, as they both showed signs of extreme dehydration. Both were listless and Ashley was barely sweating. So far, though, their foreheads still felt cool.

"Here Kevin, put this on." She coated his lips with lip balm.

"I'm thirsty Mommy."

"I know, baby, but we don't have much water left." She gave him a small sip of her own ration.

"Mark, can we get a half cup of water for the kids?"

He glanced over at Skillet. "What do you think?"

"Tulip is having a real hard time with the heat. She's been stumbling. I don't want to lose her. When we get close to Barstow if it comes down to the horse or the people, we will obviously choose people."

"Let's leave a little later in the day to take advantage of the cooler weather," Matthew suggested.

"At least there's gas for the motorcycle. I filled the cans, too," Jimbo said, as he rode up to the wagon and hoisted the cans onto the shelf, securing them with the straps. "I'm gonna go ahead and see if I can find water. It's only fifty miles to Barstow. I can strap a five gallon, water jug on the back of my seat. It's not a lot but it will help."

Sheri sat astride her bike, one foot on the ground. "I can go too. We'll be safer that way."

"That's crazy. You'll sweat more than you can carry."

"I'll hydrate before we leave. I can carry several water bottles in my panniers. You need someone to cover you while we find water."

"She's right, Jimbo," Mark said. "You shouldn't go alone. It will take us two days to get there, and if you can find where there's water, so we don't have to search for it, it will help us a lot."

They spent the day in Ludlow, in the shade of an old restaurant that once served travelers along the Old Highway 66, a nostalgic reminder of days gone by. That night, when the wagon pulled out on the highway, Jimbo and Sheri, on their non-living mounts, pulled away and disappeared into the darkness.

Even at night, the heat was oppressive and the mules walked with heads hanging low. Lori rode on the bench beside Skillet, and Tulip was tied, rider-less, to the rear of the wagon.

By the next morning, they were twenty miles closer to Barstow and Jimbo had returned with his jug full. "Sheri got really hot, pedaling fifty miles to town, even though she usually isn't bothered by the heat. I don't think it got below ninety degrees all night. She's holed up at the Marine Corp Depot, keeping cool."

"Did you see anyone, or run into any trouble?" Lori asked him.

"Naw, and we made sure it was deserted before she decided to stay there. There're water tanks at the base. Even though we didn't run into any trouble, I was glad she had my back."

He gave the kids a cup each of the lifesaving liquid and then passed around the jug so the others could get re-hydrated. They greedily gulped the cool liquid.

The last barrel of water was one quarter full when they passed the Marine Corps Logistics Base and saw Barstow in the distance. Sheri flagged them down and led them to water tanks that still held hundreds of gallons of water. They filled the barrels and drank all they wanted, making sure the animals were re-hydrated, as well.

Two hours later they were heading up the ramp onto Main Street. They searched through stores and service stations and found a few cases of bottled water and some canned goods. They were way past their expiration dates but the cold, canned beans tasted okay.

They rested up for two days, sleeping in motel rooms with the windows thrown open to the desert night. They allowed the horses and mules to rest and graze, since they'd found very little grass or other edible plant life in the desert. There was still desert ahead of them, but their barrels were full and they would be approaching the coast with its cooler weather in a few days.

***

"Radiation level is increasing. I don't think we can keep going in this direction." Mike was looking at the readout of the scintillation device, his hand over his eyes to reduce the glare. They were going west toward Victorville but there seemed to be a radioactive barrier a few miles beyond Barstow.

Mark gazed longingly toward the west coast. Past Victorville, past San Bernardino and all the eastern parts of Los Angeles County, past Los Angeles itself, lay the coast… and Mark's home.

"It's just too hot, Mark. We can't keep going in this direction."

Lori rode up beside him. "I'm so sorry, Mark. I hoped we'd be able to get through. I know how much you wanted it."

He just sat astride Jasper, unmoving. He'd known it all along, of course. But it wasn't until he saw the reading on the meter, that he really believed the home he had shared with Will Hargraves and Chris was gone... or his own home on the hill above Newport. After a few minutes, while the others gave him his space, he sadly pulled Jasper's head around toward Barstow. "Let's go back to Barstow and head northwest. We'll try to get to the coast again from the Santa Barbara area."

Twice more, they tried to go west, but were thwarted each time by the radiation.

It became cooler as they made their way from Barstow, past Boron, and then the Spaceport at Mojave, California. Each day they traveled a little later into the day until they passed over the mountains at Tehachapi and down the long grade, alongside the rushing Kern River, to Bakersfield. When they tried to go south on the 99, the radiation levels began to increase again, forcing them back to the northeast.

"Well, Sheri, it looks like you're going to get your wish to go to Lompoc. At least we can try that direction and see what happens." Jimbo threw his arm over her shoulder.

"I'm worried that Vandenberg was hit. But for the last few years it's turned toward space as its mission. At one time the space shuttle was going to be launched from there but they scrapped those plans and converted the gantries to handle SpaceX."

Skillet looked puzzled. "What's SpaceX?"

"It's a privately owned rocket that was going to be taking supplies to the International Space Station."

"Wow, that's cool. Not government?"

"Nope."

Sheri pointed west. "After we get over the mountain range into Santa Maria, it's south to Lompoc. I've spent a lot of time with my aunt and uncle, training in the hills around there. I even ran the Lompoc Marathon one year. I have good memories of the whole area, and I absolutely love Santa Barbara."

Crossing the mountains, they reached Santa Maria in mid-August. The Geiger Counter exhibited only normal background radiation. They saw evidence of life: a garden behind a house, a boy who ran behind a building and disappeared, and even a car in the distance. But no one came to greet them or bothered them, as they approached Lompoc from the north.

"Hold up," Mark shouted as he spotted something in the distance. "Look! There's an airplane." He was so excited, Lori laughed.

"There's an airport in Lompoc," Sheri told him. "Come on, I'll show you where it's at." She shot off on her bike, rode a few hundred yards ahead and then swung back to lead the slower horses down the highway.

When they arrived at the Lompoc Airport, Mark rode across the tarmac to a row of hangers along the eastside of the taxiways. He handed Jasper's reins to Lori and threw up the hanger door, gasping as he saw what lie within.

"Oh my God! Look at that," he cried out, a huge grin on his face. "It's a '41 Stearman! It looks like it's in great condition."

He walked over and ran his hand along the lower wing. He grabbed a stepstool and checked for fuel. "It's got a full tank. I don't know how old the fuel is, though."

Glancing around he saw his friends framed in the doorway of the hangar. The wagon sat out on the taxiway and he saw Matthew beyond, his crossbow across the saddle horn and Matthew looking out across the runway.

The biplane stood facing outward toward the door, and the group of his very skeptical friends.

"Mike, let's see if it'll start."

"Geez, I don't know Mark. What if the owner shows up with a shotgun?"

"There's no one around."

"Yeah? What about that airplane you saw?"

"It actually looked like a military plane."

He climbed into the rear cockpit. "Come here. I'll show you what to do."

"Mark, do you think this is such a good idea?" Lori called out. Ignoring the question, he set the mixture to 100% to prime the carburetor, then set the throttle to 10%. He activated the magnetos and showed Mike how to stand on the brakes. Changing places with Mike, he trotted to the front of the plane and, grasping the propeller, pulled it past the compression point to the left.

Nothing happened. The prop snapped back. He tried again and again until he was exhausted. Climbing up and leaning over Mike, he adjusted the throttle, to try again. "Anyone want to give this a try?"

Everyone quickly shook their head. He grasped it again and was thrilled to get a sputter out of it. One more try and it turned over... and died. He rested for a moment and gave it another try. This time the engine caught and it started up.

"Turn it off, turn it off!" Mike yelled.

"Don't worry," Mark laughed. "It's not going anywhere. Just stay on the brakes."

Mark let it run for a few minutes and then killed the magnetos. The prop slowed and stuttered to a stop. Mike leaped out of the plane, landing heavily on the concrete.

"Don't ever ask me to do that again!"

Mark reluctantly closed the hanger door and they moved away from the airport. Now it was Sheri's turn to be excited. She impatiently led them through town.

As they neared the downtown section of Lompoc, they were confronted by a group of armed men. The men didn't threaten them, rather seemed very surprised to see them. They looked well fed and reasonably clean. They numbered five.

One man, short and stocky, with sandy colored hair, stepped forward.

The others kept rifles leveled at Mark's group. Mark wasn't worried. Matthew and Einstein were out there in the town somewhere guarding their back.

"What do you want? Are you with the military?" the man asked.

"We're not military." He gestured at Sheri. "We came to find Sheri's relatives."

"Who's that?"

Sheri eagerly pushed her bike toward the men. "Doug and Carla Williamson. Do you know them?"

"How do we know you're related to them?"

"I'm Sheri Summerland. I was in the Olympics, and Lompoc gave me a parade."

One of the guys lowered his rifle. "Hey, I remember that. That's her. Doug and Carla live in the same house they were in before the war. They'll be real happy to see you."

"Thanks, come on, I know where that is," Sheri said, gesturing for them to follow her.

She shot off toward the west and watched them over her shoulder as they hurried to keep up. Jimbo kept up as the others fell behind.

A few blocks west and two to the south, she rode up a driveway in front of a beige, stucco house. The lawn was long and full of dandelions, the driveway cracked and sprouting weeds. The roof had a patch of newly replaced shingles.

"Sheri," Jimbo called out. He noticed the front drapes in the picture window being drawn aside. "We need to remember security. Wait for the others."

Just then the front door opened and a couple flew down the sidewalk into Sheri's arms.

Jimbo pulled his weapon but it was obvious this was a joyous reunion. He grinned and scratched his whiskers, watching Sheri smothered in an embrace.

The woman, dressed in blue jeans and a denim shirt, and appearing to be in her late forties was crying. "Oh my God, Sheri." She held the younger woman at arm's length, staring at her in disbelief. "Where have you been? How did you get here?" She grabbed Sheri again as the man stood back watching them. He was tall, with a full head of brown hair, but graying at the temples. His grin split his face from ear to ear.

"I've been staying in New Mexico." She finally pulled away from her aunt and gestured toward Jimbo. "This is Jimbo, a very good friend. This is my aunt Carla and that's my Uncle Doug." Jimbo switched his Sig-Sauer to his left hand and shook Doug's hand. Before he could shake Carla's, she enfolded him in a big, bear hug.

The sound of horse's hooves on the pavement brought them all around, as the rest of Sheri's companions rounded the corner. Doug looked nervous.

"Don't worry Uncle Doug, they're my friends."

"Do you mind if the horses graze on your lawn?" Mark asked, as he swung off Jasper.

Doug laughed. "Not at all. It needs a good mowing but I don't have a manual mower so I gave up on it."

The wagon pulled up in front and the others dismounted, as Carla invited them into the house. The kids timidly followed their mother inside, while Mike and Skillet stayed outside to settle the animals.

As usual, Matthew and Einstein were nowhere to be seen.

31

The basement and foundation of the White House was finished, the hardwood floor installed, and the granite walls were rising. It was a balmy day, a few fluffy clouds floating through a light blue sky with insects buzzing lazily through the magnolias and wildflowers around the construction site. Men sweated as they mortared the blocks they were using to build the wall. In the past few weeks since the construction had begun, three men had died from exhaustion and overwork, and two more were killed when a wagon overloaded with granite blocks fell over and crushed them under a pile of rocks. The militia that ran the camp didn't care about the prisoners, only that they met the expectations of the president and kept the project on schedule.

At night, the men who shared a four-person dorm room whispered of escape and made plans that most of them knew would never be carried out. They knew what had happened to the last group that had made the attempt, but took heart in hearing the rumor that two of the men had made it and were never found.

A large gathering of men and women sauntered toward the construction site. Rob Sandford and Harris Peele cast furtive glances toward the group but were careful to keep working at a steady pace. The men had learned to expend just enough energy to keep from attracting the attention of the guards.

The president scowled at the rising structure. "I thought it would be further along. What's taking so long? At this rate it won't be finished by winter."

"Mr. President," the chief architect replied, "with so few running vehicles, we're forced to bring in the materials using horse-drawn wagons. The granite blocks weigh tons and the wagons can only carry so many."

"The wagon over there looks like it could carry more."

"Sir, if we put more on it, we run a danger of the wagon overturning and dumping the load. We lost two workers when it happened last week."

"Well then, get more wagons! And more workers," the president snapped. "General Ladner, can't we get some trucks?"

The general, dressed in his camo fatigues rather than a dress uniform, shook his head. "Jeremy, we just can't spare any of the vehicles. We're getting ready to send another platoon down south. We're beginning to encounter significant resistance in South Carolina."

"Are you telling me we haven't made it to Georgia yet? Have you taken care of that dissident yet?"

The group stopped and hung back as the president confronted General Ladner. There were seven members of congress with him that day, out of the score that survived. They had learned to keep their mouths shut, after Henry Simms had been arrested by the army when he had continued to question the president's policies. No one knew where he was being held or even if he was still alive.

"We sent the 1st Southern Elite Company as you ordered, sir. So far, they've been unable to locate him. They found his house in the Atlanta suburbs but he had moved his equipment. He's still broadcasting so they think he's relocated to the hills outside the city. They've run into local militias."

"They're supposed to be the elite. Surely they can handle a few hicks."

"Jeremy, be reasonable. They are completely outnumbered. I recommend we recall them, mop up in South Carolina and go

250

back into Georgia after we recruit more soldiers. More and more men are joining with us every day, They realize it's either enlist or be put on the work crews. They get three squares a day and a decent place to sleep."

"Who's organizing the rebels in the South?"

"We've heard there's a provisional government. We need to concentrate on consolidating our power here before we spread ourselves too thin. We may end up fighting a war down there."

The president stood staring out at the rising White House. "Damn. Recall the Elite and pull back our other men. Let's step up our recruiting in the north and west. And get this damn building finished. I want to surprise the First Lady when she moves here from the bunker."

The architect gestured at the south end of the building. "The living quarters will be finished by October, Mr. President. The offices will take longer."

Rissman just stared at him. "Get more workers," he ordered.

"Jeremy, it's almost time for the call with Colonel Packer at Vandenberg. They communicated earlier that the *Louisiana* was docking at Harvest Platform."

"Well, let's get back then. I could use some good news."

***

The *U.S.S. Louisiana* had docked at Harvest, and as the crew prepared for an extended stay, Richard Dombrowski and a dozen others took the oil rig's powerboat to shore at Vandenberg. He missed Jerrod Holder, a fine officer, that had always accompanied him to shore and to the meetings they'd had with Colonel Packer.

Pineapples, for God's sake, he thought.

Lieutenant Commander Manheim had taken over as weapons officer and Communications Officer Patrick Crane was accompanying the captain to Vandenberg. Crane was more introverted than Holder but had come to know many of the Air Force officers during their shore leaves.

The boat pulled up to the dock and a contingent of Air Force personnel were there to greet them. They had radioed ahead and informed Packer of the success of their mission.

Colonel Packer and Major Whittinghall saluted smartly, and grinning, approached Dombrowski and his crew. Sticking out his hand he shook the captain's and clapped him on the shoulder. "Congratulations, Captain. Well done. We've set up a meeting with President Rissman for this afternoon. He's anxious to hear your full report."

"Thanks, Colonel. We'd like to begin re-supply preparations as soon as possible so that if the President has another mission for us we'll be ready."

"How about some lunch and then we can begin planning. The meeting with the President is at 1500 hours, our time."

The colonel gestured at a jeep that waited alongside the platoon of soldiers, who were still standing at attention. It pulled up and Colonel Packer, Dombrowski and Commander Crane climbed in as Major Whittinghall gave orders for the master sergeant to release the men. The Navy crew accompanied the airmen as they began the march back to the barracks, two miles inland.

The jeep sped off to the Command Center the colonel had set up across the field from the barracks. There were only two-hundred and sixty men on the base, fourteen were officers and the others enlisted men. The colonel had wanted to keep them quartered together. Two lieutenants and five sergeants had quarters in the barracks with the enlisted men, and the other officers were quartered in the housing behind the Command Center.

The number of soldiers was growing, as single men drifted onto the base looking for a job that provided food and shelter. Colonel Packer remembered a man who wrote an investment newsletter before the war, that claimed there was nothing more dangerous than a young, unmarried male. These were the men

Packer was recruiting and he dreamed of the day when he would have the strength of numbers to take control of the West Coast, and claim it for the new United States of America. They had a basic training program and, at least for now, guns and ammo weren't an issue. Their numbers would soon pass three hundred.

There was still plenty of stored food on the base, but they needed to become more sustainable. Packer was considering conscripting the civilian population of Lompoc to grow and preserve food for his growing force. His plan was to wait until he had an overwhelming number of airmen, and could take the town without significant resistance.

The rest of California, not laid waste by the Chinese, would then be his for the taking. Within a couple of years he would be the Supreme Commander of the western region of the United States. In their last conversation, the president had promised to make him a general. He wouldn't be satisfied until he was at the top… General of the Air Force.

32

Mark and the others gave Sheri some time to catch up with her aunt and uncle by checking the back yard and across the street, making sure no one unwanted was approaching. Carla and Sheri went into the kitchen to prepare dinner and Mark, Jimbo and Mike sat in the living room talking to Doug. Aside from the gray at the temples, Doug looked fairly young to be Sheri's uncle.

"Carla is Sheri's mother's younger sister by almost ten years. We know her folks are gone, so I'm hoping she will stay with us."

Jimbo shrugged his shoulders. "I've grown real fond of her over these couple years but I know the reason she came with us was to try and find some family. This is her home."

Doug nodded. "What are the rest of you going to do?"

"I was hoping my wife and kids and I could move back to my home in Newport, but every attempt to go toward Southern California was met with high radiation readings on the counter. I guess we just want to find out how others are faring, and what the political situation is, and then we'll probably go back to Willsburg." Mark felt Lori squeeze his hand.

There was a knock at the door and it suddenly flew open. A man stood on the porch, the point of a crossbow arrow denting the skin on his neck and Matthew's hand gripping his arm. The man's eyes were wide with fear.

"Wait, don't shoot him!" Doug called out as they all converged on the door. "He's one of my neighbors."

"Neighbors don't usually peek in your window," Matthew said softly. "Found him in your bushes." He lowered his crossbow and shoved the man forward.

"I was just trying to find out what was happening, Doug. The Council sent me."

"Well, tell the freakin' Council to come here themselves. We can all talk."

"Sure Doug." The man threw a frightened look at Matthew and turned and ran down the street.

Matthew nodded at Mark and headed back to his post..

"Do you think this Council of yours will show up?" Mark asked Doug.

"Yeah, we've been wondering what to do about the Air Force. Let's get dinner and by then they'll probably be here."

Dinner was mostly vegetarian with only a single chicken to share, but lots of garden vegetables. Jimbo took plates out to Matthew, Einstein and Skillet. Just as Doug predicted, the doorbell rang and four men stood on the porch with their hands in plain sight. Mark recognized two of them from the group that had met them earlier in the day.

They brought chairs from the kitchen and everyone gathered around and introduced themselves. Jack Putnam was the head of the Council.

"So, did you guys see any military on your way into town?"

"None," Mark told him. "Are there very many of them?"

"There's a couple hundred, at least, over at Vandenberg. We've had some run-ins. If anyone is found alone outside of town, or even at the edge of town, they confiscate their guns. We think they may be getting ready to try and take us over."

Lori asked him, "What makes you think that? Aren't they trying to help with re-building?"

"I don't think they want us to rebuild as a civilian town. They want a military dictatorship. Some of our guys got in a fight with 'em over at a local pub. The guy was drunk, said they were going to enslave our asses. They've been recruiting all kinds of guys from around here. Not just Lompoc, but from Mission Hills and Santa Maria. Any further north than that seems to be hot, radioactive. They have tons of guns and ammo at the base."

"Maybe they can tell us what's going on," Mark said. "We came here to find out about the Chinese and if the war is truly over. If I could meet with them I can get some news and maybe find out what plans they have for you."

"Mark…"

"Lori, it's okay. They aren't going to hurt me. I have dealt with military guys my entire career."

The door opened and Matthew and Einstein entered. Matthew looked at Jimbo and he and Mike headed outside. "I would like to hear what's going on if that's okay," Matthew told them, as he was introduced around the room.

"Of course," Mark said. "And this is Einstein."

"Actually," he said, "my name's Derek. I really prefer it."

Lori smiled and said, "Have a seat Derek. So what are you folks planning on doing?"

"Well, we need to do something," Brendon said, his blue eyes full of concern. "We had forty-five thousand people before the war, but there were only a few shelters when the radiation swept through here. People thought we were okay when Vandenberg didn't get hit. They didn't take shelter and tens of thousands sickened and died. It took ten months to relocate the bodies to a dump down south. And the fires burned and smoldered for two weeks as we burned 'em. If the bodies were in their houses we just left 'em there." His look was haunted.

Kurt said, "Others took off inland, afraid we might get hit later. We outnumber the military four to one but they have way better guns."

"Yeah, and at the rate they're recruiting, they will really overpower us soon. A lot of people are talking about leaving but that would make it even worse for the rest of us. This is our home."

"Where would they go?" Lori asked Jack.

"We've heard you can't go north, hardly at all, and not below Santa Barbara to the south. Quite a few families went to Ojai. The mountains seemed to have protected it. But after the first few, the others were turned back by the people that lived there. I guess they can try and go east to Bakersfield. The Kern river goes through there."

"Okay," Mark said, "don't anyone get too worked up until I talk to them. I'll go out to the base tomorrow. Any idea where they are?"

"No. We stay away from the base. We have a couple cars and some motorcycles, so we can drop you off at the front gate."

They stayed up late, as the travelers told their stories to the townspeople and heard theirs in return. After the Council had left, Mark walked out front to find Matthew. He and Derek were going to spend the night in the wagon. Matthew had put his hat in the wagon and released his pony tail. His hair blew around in the on-shore breeze, redolent with the scent of saltwater bog.

"I don't know what's going to happen tomorrow. Hopefully this will be a real shot at getting some news and helping these people. I would hope that the military would be interested in helping the country to rebuild."

"In a survival scenario," Matthew said, "the military is more likely to take care of its own. They often turn into militias, controlling people with superior might."

"Do you think they'll detain me?"

"That's hard to say, but it's possible. They haven't bothered the townspeople except for confiscating a few guns, but they may be waiting until the time's right."

"Matthew, I have a huge favor. If I don't return within, say, four days, you'll have to assume I'm lost. Don't try to rescue me. I don't want to risk the rest of you. But can you make sure Lori and the kids get back to Willsburg?"

"Of course. You didn't even need to ask, but Lori is not going to want to go until we know for sure. And frankly, the rest of us won't want to either. Not unless we know you're dead."

"I appreciate that but I can't take a risk with my family."

257

"Know that I will care for your family as if they were my own, but we'll remain in town until we know what's happened to you. I will not delay, however, to get them out of here if there is real danger."

"Thanks, Matthew. There's no one I trust more." He shook Matthew's hand and watched as the young man climbed into the wagon. Then he headed back into the house where he expected an argument from his wife.

The kids slept in a real bed for the first time since Barstow, and Mark and Lori made a bed with sleeping bags in the corner of the room. Sheri slept in the bedroom she had always stayed in when she visited her aunt and uncle, and Mike slept on the couch. Jimbo and Skillet stood guard, and for once Matthew and Derek slept during the night, staying in the wagon.

Mark was right. His head hadn't hit the pillow when he and Lori had another argument about Mark's tendency to take on the tough or dangerous jobs.

"Why is it always you?" she whispered fiercely.

"It's my nature to take charge and be the one to handle stuff. How do you think I became the CEO of Will's company? You know me Lori. I have to do this. This is what we came out here for."

"I know. The world has become a dangerous place and we both know there are risks to be taken. We need to make a pact. It seems we're always arguing about who's doing what and who's not going to stay behind. I'll make you a deal. When you feel you need to take a risk for the greater good, I will support you and keep my fears to myself. But you can never again try to force me to do what's safe for me. We're the toughest couple on Earth. Deal?"

Mark laid there in the dark and wondered *what just happened?*

"Deal."

***

The next day dawned cool and clear but Mark knew it would warm up quick. Skillet provided some dehydrated food for breakfast and it was decided that Mark would leave just after noon.

Good to their word, Jack and Brendon showed up in a battered, old Ford. They had no idea where the military personnel were quartered so they let him off at the front gate. Lori insisted on accompanying him that far. She held him tight. "Don't take any chances and keep your hands visible."

He kissed her and turned to Jack. "Good luck, man," Jack said, as he stuck out his hand. "I hope they don't shoot first and ask questions later."

Brendon slapped him on the back as he headed for the gate.

Mark walked through the gate onto Vandenberg Air Force Base with his hands in the air. One hundred yards into the base he paused and waited.

Nothing happened.

His arms got tired, so he lowered them and continued to walk down the road. There were barracks along the inside of the wide perimeter road. What had once been well-trimmed lawns were now weed patches. An on-shore breeze ruffled his hair and cooled the sweat that lined his forehead and trickled down his back. Palm trees lined the road, separating it from the parking area in front of the barracks.

Stopping and listening, the only sounds he heard were the wind, and the sounds of gulls and cormorants calling to one another. The smell of salt was in the air. A jackrabbit bounded across the road and he started forward again, wondering where the military hung out. The sun beat down as he hoofed it another couple of miles devoid of buildings or other signs of civilization. He finally saw buildings in the distance. Up ahead he could see what appeared to be a barrier across the road. He figured the military was using the western portion of the base and had set up a secondary gate just ahead.

He stopped again, thinking this might be his last chance to turn around and head back to Lompoc, back to Lori and his friends… but it was too late. A vehicle that morphed into a jeep as it materialized out of the heat shimmer on the road, came speeding toward him. He couldn't see too well but it soon became clear that three soldiers had military assault rifles pointing in his direction.

The jeep slowed and approached cautiously. It turned sideways across the lane and one of the men in the front shouted out to him.

"Stop where you are." He didn't need to tell Mark to put his hands in the air, as he had done so when the car was still one hundred yards away. "Who are you?" he called as he jumped out and approached Mark, the airman in the back seat jumping out right behind him.

"I'm unarmed," he told them. "Name's Mark Teller. I'd like to talk to someone in charge. I've come from New Mexico and would like to report the conditions to him."

The lieutenant swept his head in Mark's direction and the airman, slinging his rifle over his back, ran forward to frisk Mark for weapons. "He's clean, sir." He quickly backed away and retrieved his weapon, again pointing it at Mark.

"It's been a long, hot journey. I could use some shade and some water. My bottle's empty."

"I'm Lieutenant Darrow. Get in the jeep." The lieutenant climbed in the front and the airman slid in beside Mark. They pushed their rifles onto their backs where Mark would have no opportunity to seize them, but Mark noticed the lieutenant held his service pistol in his lap.

There was no conversation as they sped through the makeshift gate and drove toward the coast. Pulling up in front of a large concrete and glass building, the airman jumped clear of the jeep and covered him as he followed Darrow into the building. He was searched more thoroughly this time, by a senior airman, and led into a reception area with desks and railings.

Photographs of military aircraft, fighter jets, stealth bombers and a large picture of a Saturn rocket covered the walls. A portrait of President Rissman was hung next to an American flag, flanked by photos of an Air Force General that Mark assumed was the Commander of the base. This part of the building was completely enclosed by windows, and brightened by the afternoon sunlight. It didn't feel dangerous.

The young airman brought him a cup of water as Lieutenant Darrow exited into a hallway leading toward the rear of the building. A senior airman, the one that had searched him, and a staff sergeant stood by the double glass door they had entered through. Their weapons were leveled at his gut.

The airman edged over to him. "I'm Airman Tunney," he said, keeping his voice low. "What's it like out there? Is anyone alive? I'm from Phoenix. Were you there?"

"I'm sorry. We didn't come through Phoenix but there are communities starting to come back in New Mexico."

The sound of footsteps halted their exchange as the young man stepped quickly away. The lieutenant came out of the hallway followed by four uniformed men, a Navy Captain, a Navy Lieutenant Commander, an Air Force Colonel and an Air Force Major. The colonel walked over and stuck out his hand toward Mark. "I'm Colonel Packer, the Commanding Officer of Vandenberg. This is..." but he got no further as the captain stepped around him.

"Mark Teller?" He stuck out his hand and pumped Mark's vigorously.

"Richard, I don't believe it! I never expected to meet someone I know."

Dombrowski turned to Colonel Packer. "This is Mark Teller. He and Will Hargraves were on the President's Civilian Advisory Board. I've known them both for years since before I started driving boats. Hargraves' company had numerous dealings with the Navy."

Colonel Packer waved at the guards and they put away their weapons. "Please," he motioned to the hallway, "join us in my office. We need to debrief you and find out what you know about Lompoc."

Mark was a little taken aback by the gruff attitude. He was a civilian, and didn't report to Colonel Packer.

As they entered the office, an airman came through a side door with a cart loaded with coffee and pastries. Mark's eyes lit up at the sight and aroma of the fresh, brewed coffee. He'd had a cup at Carla's but he never seemed to get enough.

When they were settled, Mark spoke up first, "So Richard, how is it that you're here on an Air Force Base?"

"As you probably know, most of the West Coast has been destroyed, or is radioactive. There are no ports left capable of handling a sub."

"A sub? You still have a submarine?" Mark was astonished.

"I do. We have to dock off shore at one of the oil rigs. We have a couple of powerboats that are still operational, that bring us up the coast to the Vandenberg docks. We are most fortunate that Vandenberg wasn't hit. Colonel Packer has taken us in and helped us to re-supply."

Colonel Packer frowned at Dombrowski, "Captain, I'm not sure it's a good idea to share too much information. We don't know this man's status after two years."

"Mark has above top secret clearance."

"Well, he doesn't have a need to know."

"Benjamin, we need all the help we can get."

Packer didn't seem convinced as he glared at Mark.

"If you don't mind my asking, Colonel, shouldn't there be a higher ranking officer over the base?"

Colonel Packer was annoyed by the comment but covered it quickly. *Who the hell does this civilian think he is?*

"The Base Commanding Officer and three of his subordinates were in the air when the first bombs hit. We had a radio transmission saying their engine had quit and their instruments had failed. They were going to try and glide down but we never heard from them again. After spending the first eight months in the base bunker, we emerged to find that I was the ranking officer. We have only just reestablished communication with the east and the president has assured me he is going to promote me to a rank commensurate with the responsibilities of the base commander."

"Wait... wait a minute. Did you say the president?"

"Yes, the president is alive and reestablishing the government."

Dombrowski added, "They're in Charleston, West Virginia. There seem to be a few members of Congress who survived as well."

"That's wonderful news," Mark said. "Eagle Nest, Raton and Farmington all have communities that are recovering from the war. There must be many such places, and that means that with the government in place we have a real chance to bring back the United States."

Colonel Packer stood. "We have a call with the president in an hour. Mr. Teller, you will remain here, under guard, until we return. We'll debrief you then and you can return to your people."

Dombrowski unfolded his lanky frame from the chair and looked down on Packer. "He's going with me, Benjamin. He's an old friend and the Navy is offering him its hospitality."

Packer was furious but bit his lip. It wouldn't do any good to antagonize the captain at this time. The president would set him straight when Teller was gone.

"Very well, let's get moving."

33

Captain Dombrowski, Colonel Packer and Mark, along with several sailors, climbed aboard a twenty foot, fiberglass skiff tied off to a dock that ran out into a small bay. The dock was guarded by navy personnel who had saluted as the officers went through the gate. Green, scummy water lapped a concrete walkway that ran perpendicular to the wooden dock at the water's edge. At low tide, the walkway was probably well above the water line. Mark saw a sunken rowboat on the left side of the dock.

Powered by two outboard motors, the boat sped through the cold, Pacific waters at sixteen knots, the spray flying up from the bow on either side, a light mist hitting Mark in the face as he reveled at being on the ocean he loved. It reminded him of earlier days before the Great War.

Many of his teen years had been spent with Chris and their friends sailing on Will Hargraves' yacht, or the much smaller skiing boat, motoring around the Pacific without a care in the world. But even though he loved the ocean and the boats, he loved aviation more. Following Will Hargraves footsteps he attended The University of Southern California, studying hard to become an aeronautical engineer and then going on to graduate school to obtain his Master's degree in business.

Hard work and dedication had led to becoming the CEO of Hargraves' multi-billion dollar, aerospace company. Life was sweet, with a great job he loved, a beautiful home, his running buddies, and a hangar filled with antique aircraft. But that life hadn't included Lori and the kids, and he knew the life he had now was more real and infinitely better.

The boat bounced over tiny whitecaps as it approached the oil rig from the northeast. Now, beyond the rig, Mark could see the deck and conning tower of a huge submarine. He was awed at the size.

My God. It's beautiful. The skiff slowed and drifted through the struts of the oil rig, pulling up to a small dock, free-floating on the surface of the water. One of the sailors jumped to the dock, tying off the boat and standing at attention, as Dombrowski, Packer and Mark followed him off the boat. They climbed up an unending series of stairs a hundred feet into the interior of the facility.

The group entered a large office that Capt. Dombrowski was using as his base of operations. "How have you been Mark? You want some coffee?"

"I'd love some. Richard, this is just incredible. I never thought I'd meet someone I'd known before the war."

"Yeah, well I couldn't believe it either when Colonel Packer's men brought you to us over on the base. So Mark, where have you been?" He poured coffee for the two men and noticed that Packer seemed very unhappy. *Can he be that upset over Mark's coming to the platform?*

"Like I said, I've actually been living in New Mexico. Over two hundred of us spent almost eight months in what everyone called 'Will's Folly.' I guess it wasn't such a Folly after all. We all made it through the war and the first winter before we had to leave the shelter."

"How is Will? What a great guy."

The look on Mark's face indicated to Richard the answer wasn't good.

"He didn't make it Richard. We were forced to leave the shelter. There were earthquakes caused by instability due to the hydrogen bombs. During our escape Will was killed in a cave in."

"I'm so sorry. I seem to remember that Will was your mentor. Do you remember the meeting in Washington where we talked about equipping the fleet with Will's new sonar device? Will and I had a long conversation and he told me your story. What about his son and daughter?"

"It's a long story Richard. After the president's call, if you've got the time and the coffee, I'll fill you in."

***

"Capt. Dombrowski, we've reestablished communication with the East Coast. Ensign Santana has the president on the radio for you sir."

"Thanks, Johnson. Come on, gentlemen." They stood and moved toward the doorway. "You know the president. Right? He's going to want to speak with you." They walked out onto a companionway and up another flight of stairs, where they entered a room crammed full of communications gear. The captain slipped into a chair in front of a microphone, flipping a switch on the console.

"Charleston?"

"I'm here, Captain Dombrowski," was heard through a burst of static.

"President Rissman, it's great to hear from you again sir."

"Yes, Captain. Good to hear from you as well. Please, tell me how the mission went."

"Yes sir. We engaged the enemy just the other side of the Hawaiian Islands. We were able to determine that they were sending a large number of vessels toward the United States. There were dozens of military vessels escorting four cruise ships, that we can only assume were carrying a large number of civilians to occupy the United States. We..."

"Did you destroy them Captain?"

"We did sir. We withdrew one thousand miles to the east to ensure we were not in proximity when we launched our missiles."

"You are sure you got them all?"

"I am certain, sir. Unfortunately, they stopped at the Hawaiian Islands to refuel. We had to hit Pearl Harbor to take them out. We returned to within a safe distance and checked thoroughly for signs that any of the Chinese fleet had survived. We spent over a week there and I can assure you, Mr. President, they have been destroyed."

He looked up at Mark, grinning with a triumphal smile. "Then, sir, we sailed to within a hundred miles of the Coast of China between the Philippines and Japan. We started to encounter high radiation at that point. We cruised both north and south of that position and did not detect any additional vessels. I sincerely believe the Chinese threat is ended for good. Or at least for many, many years."

Mark was astounded that the sub still had weapons, and was blown away that they had engaged the Chinese in a continuation of the war. He thought the president seemed agitated, requiring repeated assurances that the Chinese fleet had been destroyed. The man had undoubtedly been through a lot since the war and felt a great responsibility to continue to protect the country from her enemies.

"I will file a complete report regarding this matter, sir. Mr. President, I have some other good news. Earlier today, Mark Teller of Hargraves Aerospace Company walked onto Vandenberg Air Force Base. He's been living in New Mexico and just made his way across country to California."

"What a pleasant surprise. Put him on Captain." Dombrowski stood to allow Mark to sit at the microphone.

"Hello Mr. President. I can't tell you how glad I am that you have survived and are in control of the country. How is it going, sir?"

"Mark, Mark Teller. It's so good to hear your voice. Is Hargraves with you?"

"I'm sorry, sir, but Will was killed in an unfortunate accident. We were forced out of his shelter, where we'd stayed during the war and for several months afterward. Instability created by the bombs caused a series of earthquakes and we were forced to evacuate."

"I'm terribly sorry," the president said sincerely. "Mark, I would love it if you could come out to the East Coast and join my administration. I have several cabinet members and a number of members of Congress with me, but rebuilding the country is going to be a monumental undertaking and I could use your help. I remember that you, even though you're a young man, had a tremendous amount of responsibility with Hargraves' company and I was always impressed with your maturity."

"Thank you, sir. That's very tempting, but I have only just arrived in California and need some time to see what kind of damage there's been here. Since the war, I've gotten married and have two stepchildren, and Lori would have to be part of any decision I make about our future." Mark looked up at Dombrowski and shrugged his shoulders.

"Mark, I think if you realized how big a job we have before us, and the importance, you would be more willing to assist."

"Well, no sir, I understand the scope of the task and the importance. I would certainly be willing to discuss a position in your administration once I've had an opportunity to get settled here."

There was a long pause and Mark had begun to think they had lost the signal, when the president said, "Here's the thing, Teller. We've made our headquarters in Charleston, West Virginia. We are determined to rebuild this country and Capt. Dombrowski has just freed us of the threat from China. Until we have the situation under control, I'm afraid I've had to declare a state of Martial Law throughout the United States. My word is law. We are bringing people from all over the East Coast and the South to West Virginia so they can help us rebuild." There was another blast of static.

"Martial Law, sir? Exactly how does that work."

"As you know Mark, the government has known for some time about the effects of electromagnetic pulses. We took steps to protect a number of military vehicles and weapons. We have the ability to bring the situation under control. Under complete control," he stressed. "It's only a matter of time. There are pockets of resistance here in the east and in the south. And I'm sure we will find concentrations of insurrectionists in other parts of the country when we move west. I have reports of rebels in Idaho, Utah and Montana. We will deal with them later. Colonel Packer and I have discussed how we will handle these dissidents."

Dombrowski raised his eyebrows and glanced over at Packer, wondering just what kind of discussions these two were having.

"Mr. President, I have just spent the last three months traveling cross country to California. I have seen people beginning to rebuild. I've seen towns that have isolated themselves from others and want to go it alone, and I've seen towns that are completely open to anyone. I've seen good people, and some incredibly evil people, but communities are forming and joining together to try and reestablish some normalcy. Sir, if Americans are left to their own devices our country will come back. They have formed small, local governments and at this point just want to be left alone."

"Mark, I'm going to need the locations of these communities so we can bring them into the fold."

Suddenly Mark felt a chill up his back as he realized that Jeremy Rissman wasn't the man he had known before the war, a president with the best interests of his people at heart. He had become a ruthless dictator, and Mark was afraid he had said too much.

"Mr. President, it's been wonderful speaking with you and I will get back to you in the very near future, as soon as I can convince myself that my home in Newport is no longer a place where my family and I can survive. Believe me, sir, I want nothing more than to help my country get back on her feet."

The voice over the radio had become cold and hard. "Put Captain Dombrowski back on the radio." Mark stood and moved out of the way as Capt. Dombrowski picked up the microphone.

Mark looked over at Colonel Packer. He had a smug look on his face.

"Mr. President, I will submit my report of the action against the Chinese and we will speak again soon, sir."

"Yes Captain. Very soon. I have additional missions for you." The background noise ceased as the radio went dead. Mark looked over to the open door and took a deep breath of the salty sea air.

He was scared.

"Well, gentlemen let's get back to my office. Mark you can fill us in about the conditions between here and New Mexico. We still need your information."

As they walked along the catwalk and went down the steps leading to Dombrowski's office, Packer turned toward the boat. "I need to get back to the base, Captain. Please debrief Mr. Teller and prepare a report for me. I'll talk with you tomorrow and Mr. Teller can be sent back to town."

Mark saw a frown cross Dombrowski's face as Packer went on down the stairs toward the dock. Captain Dombrowski was of equal rank to Packer, and they weren't on the base. Why was he giving orders? They entered the office and sat facing one another across Richard's desk.

"Richard, do you think I made a mistake? What do you know of the president rounding people up and bringing them to West Virginia? Are we talking FEMA camps here?"

"I don't know Mark. We just got back from blasting thousands of military and civilians into oblivion. Some of us weren't happy about that. My XO even went so far as to suggest that we let them come. He said that in one hundred years the entire Earth would be Chinese and there would be peace at last."

Mark turned and looked at him, dumbfounded. "He may have a point, but I still believe the United States of America, governed by our Constitution, the greatest document in the history of earth for governing a people, is a great and noble experiment. The first country on earth where the people run the government and not the other way around. It created a country of entrepreneurs and innovators. A country where everyone had an opportunity to make something of themselves, free to run their own lives. It's true that over the past few decades this experiment was coming to an end, as the balance of power began to shift from the people back to a dictatorial government. The initiative of a free people was being destroyed." He sat up straighter in the chair.

"This war was a terrible thing, but I thought it was going to give us a chance to return to constitutional government, small government on a local level. Now it looks like the old administration has survived, and has equipment and personnel to enslave the population under the guise of rebuilding. Hell Richard, what are we going to do?"

"I'm still an officer of the United States Navy and I still take orders from my president."

"Yeah, and you still command what's probably the greatest concentration of power left in the world, in this submarine and its armament. That's a huge responsibility."

Dombrowski stood and came around the desk. He reached out and slapped Mark on the shoulder. "Come on, let's get some dinner and we can discuss this in my office over some Glenlivet 21, I've been saving."

They drank until sunset and before Mark reached his bunk, he paused at the railing of the platform and gazed out at the sea. The sun was just setting, throwing red streaks toward him, across the water.

The oil rigs provided habitats for all sorts of fish and other sea creatures, and they in turn attracted a multitude of birds. Gulls and Cormorants dived into the ocean, taking flight again with beaks full of struggling fish. Dark clouds on the western horizon drifted in front of the dying sun and plunged the day into early night. It was still clear overhead and as the hidden sun descended into the ocean, the stars burst out, crisp and clear. Just above the cloud layer in the west a brilliant jewel lit up... Venus, Goddess of Love.

Mark thought of Lori, and realized that after tonight he would know enough to gather his family and friends and head home. His real home, not some dream from the past, but the home where his people were. Where Will was buried, and where he and Lori and the kids had their future.

34

Lori stood in the back yard and gazed out toward the north, toward Vandenberg and the man she loved. Her best friend. He'd been gone all day but she realized he couldn't be expected to return, in the best of circumstances, for another day or two. She could feel the stress building, the darkness affecting her mood,

She heard a soft cough behind her and turned to see Matthew approaching. She never would have known he was there. The cough was intentional.

"Hi Matthew. It's been a long day."

"Yes. I slept this afternoon so I'd be rested for tonight."

"Tonight?"

"I'm going to do some reconnoitering at the base."

"Really?" she said excitedly. "What are going to do?"

"I want to find out what part of the base the military is using and get an idea of their numbers. Just in case we need to move against them. There's no moon, so I don't think it'll be difficult."

"I'm so relieved. I have no idea what Mark has walked in to."

"I'll be leaving soon. Derek is going most of the way and will bring Chief back. We'll arrange a rendezvous for tomorrow afternoon so I don't have to waste time walking back. Please don't say anything to the others."

***

Binoculars brought the buildings into focus from three hundred yards away. Matthew had spent hours around the front gate of the base, only to find the military was concentrated around the western shore. He lay prone, behind a fence at the top of a rise. A line of barracks partially blocked his view. The land was a wetland, but undulated slightly and was dry in his current position. The night was warm and he could feel the humidity.

It was 0300 and the only activity was around a large, concrete building on the north side of a parade field. There were lights, not oil lamps, and he could hear the sound of a far-away generator. He spotted two guards at the entrance to the building, which he surmised was the Command Center, and two more at the door of a barracks beyond,

There were also lights, this time appearing to be lanterns, in the barracks directly in front of him. It was too dark to see anything else which was both a blessing and a curse. He rolled over and removed a Powerbar from his pack, eating it and washing it down with water. His crossbow lay beside him. He had .45 caliber, semi-auto pistol, but preferred the crossbow for stealth.

He slipped down the backside of the embankment, and walking around, did a few stretching exercises to stay loose. So far he hadn't seen any guards along the fence line. When the sky gradually lightened in the east, he began to see some activity in the compound below. There was a changing of the guards, and a platoon of soldiers was forming on the field between the Command Center and the barracks, doing calisthenics and marching to a cadence called out by an officer.

In the distance, Matthew saw an airfield. Even as he watched, a plane took off toward the north and swung around over Lompoc to disappear into the rising sun. They had seen a plane the day before and Matthew wondered if it went out each day for recon or for mapping radiation areas.

Gazing through his binoculars, he was surprised to see a squad of men in Navy uniforms. They rode in two jeeps that approached from the direction of the ocean. The jeeps pulled up in front of the Command Center where the men joined a squad of airmen. They all jumped into a supply truck that drove off to the east, where there was a large concentration of base housing, a Base Exchange, recreation areas and warehouses. He could only assume they were going for supplies.

Making sure there were no sentries, he grabbed his crossbow, slid down the back of the hill, shouldered his pack and set off for the coastline at a slow trot. He squished through the bogs, the smell nauseating him, until he came to firmer ground a few hundred yards from the ocean. Crossing over a two lane road, he trekked through coastal bushes and made his way down to the surf.

He stared in wonder at the vast expanse of the Pacific Ocean and the waves breaking on the white sand. In the early morning light, there was a trace of phosphorescence in the curl of the breakers.

White sand ran down to an embankment that sloped six feet to darker beach where the waves ran up, frothing, before receding back to the arms of the sea. He walked down and saw holes in the sand and when he scooped a handful, he was delighted to discover small wriggling animals. He'd heard of sand crabs but had never seen one. He squatted and set the sand back on the beach and watched the tiny creatures burrow back to safety. Kelp had washed up on the beach and lay in clumps. Standing, he gazed out toward the horizon, absolutely awed by the vastness of the sea.

He had never seen an ocean before in his life.

***

Just after midnight in West Virginia, with no moon, the darkness was complete. To save gas, they didn't use the generators for lights, and the guard tower was invisible.

Sandford crawled under the fence, scraping off his skin as the sharp points of the chain link scratched down his back. *Damn, should have cut 'em shorter.* He pulled himself forward out of the trench and, quickly looking both ways, jumped to his feet and scurried fifty yards across the buffer zone and into the trees.

He had timed the guard's journey around the perimeter for days, to determine when it would be safe to make his escape. He'd found the wire cutters in the old shed where they kept the gardening tools, on the ground under one of the benches. They were rusted and dull and he could barely get them to clip the chain link. He'd hidden under the bushes that filled the drainage ditch and clipped a few wires each time it was safe, until he had a hole large enough for his broad shoulders.

Standing inside the edge of the forest, he looked back to see if any of the others had followed him. Cheney and Fillmore said they would, but Sandford knew they were too afraid. The last guys that had tried to escape Camp No-Hope, swung by their necks from a noose, on the orders of the president.

He saw the light from the guards flashlights coming down the fence line from the north. Cheney and Fillmore had a window of about thirty more seconds before the guards came around the corner of the fence and cut off their chance for freedom.

Knowing they weren't coming, he turned and melted into the woods. He could feel blood running down his back and it stung like crazy... but that was the least of his worries.

If the guards spotted the cut fence he would have a very short head start, and probably a short lifespan.

If they didn't, he might have until they missed him in the morning, more than five hours from now. There was no moon, so he hoped they wouldn't see where he had broken the window in the dorm or where he had squirmed through the rut under the chain link.

Rumor had it that the campaign in the South had run into problems, so he hoped he could get past the Carolinas into Georgia, and outdistance any pursuit. He was from D.C., but had been in Pittsburg on business when he heard the missiles were coming. He drove the rental car as far away from the city as he could and then holed up with a few others in a mall. He knew his family, his wife and son, were gone, that D.C. would have been a prime target.

Sandford was captured by the military in Parkersburg as he made his way south. They put him on a work crew in the fields, growing crops for the army, until he was transferred to this new detail. He was told they needed more men to build the president's house.

The president was insane. That was clear. The power of the presidency had gone to his head, as it had to so many before him. But Rissman had military leaders around him, and the remainder of the U.S. Congress that, at least for now, were backing him. Sandford didn't know what had happened in the rest of the country but he knew he had to try and get to a place where he could live a decent life.

Survival was all he had now.

***

"I can't believe you let another one get away!" Rissman fumed and stormed over to stand above Major Cartwright who was on his knees, his head bent forward by the pistol pressed to his neck by General Ladner. Colonel Faricy had backed as far away into the corner of the room as possible to avoid drawing any attention. He was Cartwright's superior officer and the next in line for vengeance. Two uniformed and armed guards flanked the door.

"How did he get out of the compound?"

Cartwright stammered, "He... he cut a hole in the fence, sir. He snuck out between the guards making their rounds."

"Where the hell did he get a cutter?"

"That's unknown sir. It was found on the ground outside the fence. There are tool sheds around the school property that have never been searched. He probably found it in one of them."

His neck was cramping but when he tried to raise it, it jammed into the cold, hard muzzle of the general's .360 Magnum.

"I want every building that isn't fenced off to be searched. Double up the guards… and hang the men in the guard shack. They should have seen him escaping."

"Jeremy, there was no moon and the lights don't work," Ladner told him. "We can start using a generator for the lights but we need to conserve gas until we can get a refinery going."

"I said to hang them both!" Rissman paced the length of the room. He whirled and pointed at the hapless Cartwright. "You were responsible for the guard unit." His narrowed eyes switched to Colonel Faricy. "He's your man. If we don't capture the bastard today, you will personally hang Cartwright." Faricy paled. He had owned a tire store before the war. His rank came from former military service but he had never seen combat. Hanging a man was not really in his nature, but if it came down to him or Cartwright, well… he had a wife to think of.

"All of you except the general, get out of here, now!" The president waved at the guards. "Including you two."

Once the room was cleared, Rissman sank into his chair. He squeezed and rubbed his forehead with his hand and let out a sigh. "How are we going to maintain discipline if these guys keep screwing up?"

"Jeremy, I think you're overreacting. We've been rounding up work crews for over a year and there've only been two attempts. Three guys have managed to actually get away. It's not significant." He stood at ease, his hands behind his back, facing the president across the desk. His bald head shone in the light from the wall-mounted, oil lamp.

"It IS significant. It will only encourage the others."

"Quite frankly, sir, every man, woman and child thinks of nothing else but escape. They know their chances are slim to none. Hanging the last group took the wind out of their sails. They're defeated."

"We need them to come around and realize that this is for their own good."

"This generation has been used to freedom. I don't think they will ever come around. Our hope lies with our re-education camps. Once we have the minds of the kids and they believe in our agenda, then we will have the country we want. Ten or fifteen years, sir."

The president smiled a wry grin, "I'll have to start grooming a successor. I'll be over seventy by then."

"You'll still be going strong, sir."

"You know, they're calling me a dictator. That hurts, but I know this is the best thing for them. Why can't they see that?"

"Sir, you and I both agree that a benevolent dictator is better than the mess we had before the war. This is best for everyone."

Rissman looked up at General Ladner. "You're the only one I can trust, Charles. You stay at my right hand and we will rebuild this country into a perfect nation."

"I will, sir, and with Colonel Packer taking care of things in the west we'll soon have the country reunified."

"I need to think about promoting him. He can't be too high a rank, of course. It might go to his head. Although, if we reorganize the military and make you the Chief of Staff, it won't matter what rank he is. Whatever keeps him happy. But we have to bring these rebels under control. I won't put up with it. Georgia, Utah and Idaho, and New Mexico. They must be handled."

There was a knock at the door.

"Come in," The president yelled.

Sergeant Armbruster entered the room and stood ramrod straight in front of the desk. "Mr. President. There is a radio message for you, sir. Colonel Packer would like to talk to you at 1100 hours, our time. I'm to let him know, sir."

"Of course, Sergeant. Let him know to call at that time. I haven't even eaten yet, thanks to those incompetent guards."

The sergeant pivoted on his heel and slipped out of the room.

"Come on, Mr. President, let's get some breakfast."

***

Mark leaned on the railing of the upper deck, of Platform Harvest, looking out at the sea and the massive submarine. The sea swelled in rolling waves but there were no whitecaps to disturb the tranquility.

He was still amazed that the sub existed at all, let alone that it had all but two of its nuclear-armed, Trident missiles left. Footsteps on the staircase brought him around.

"Good Morning, Mark. I thought I might find you up here, after I found your bunk empty. The ocean is so beautiful isn't it?"

"Good Morning. Yes, I could gaze at it for hours. I used to have a great view of it from my front porch in Newport. It's now the 'hotspot' of the west. Where are you from?"

The captain raised his baseball cap, smoothed his hand backward over his thinning hair and reseated the cap on his head. "Originally from Madison, Wisconsin, but we moved to the Outer Banks of North Carolina when I was a kid. It wasn't too far from the Naval Base at Norfolk and I fell in love with the Navy. My family was all there."

"I'm sorry. This damned war cost us all so much."

They stood a while looking out at the ocean. Dombrowski was the first to break the silence. "I'm worried, Mark. I haven't spoken to my officers about this, but I need to discuss it with someone."

"What's going on?"

"I think Colonel Packer may have an agenda. He was thrilled to see us when we first docked at the platform, but he's been strange lately. I'm sure he's very relieved we took care of the Chinese threat. Otherwise they would have landed squarely on his shoulders."

"Yeah, I heard the president say they'd been talking."

"He's the Commanding Officer of the base but we are equal rank, and I am top dog in my little area of the world. He has no reason to order me around. I'm concerned that there's something going on. The *Louisiana* is not on Vandenberg property."

"What can he do? You can take your submarine and leave."

"He knows I'm loyal to the president and this country. I would like to know what he has up his sleeve."

"And I'd like to know the stability of the region before I take my family back to New Mexico. It's great to know the Chinese threat has ended, but we'd be looking over our shoulder all the time if we thought the government was going to be after us."

"Don't worry. I'll speak to the president and find out what's going on. Let's get breakfast and we'll head to the base. We can talk to Colonel Packer and then set up a call."

Mark took one more look at the sea, and then followed the captain below.

35

The desert-camo, military carrier sped down the road paralleling the airport runway two miles north of the Vandenberg Command Center. The Air Force technicians had set up communications in the control tower that rivaled those of the mega-antenna at the platform. The signals were better and more stable every day. Colonel Packer and his aid, Major Whittinghall, climbed out of the carrier and mounted the steps to the tower.

They entered the glass-enclosed space at the top and crossed to the communications equipment that covered a desk on the runway side of the tower. "How's the signal, Airman? Better than yesterday, I hope. I hate it when I have to ask the president to repeat himself."

"Yessir. It seems much better." The airman looked like a teenager with sandy hair and a bad case of acne.

"Well, get him on the horn."

Packer walked over to the tower window looking out on the airfield. Their recon plane was just landing for refueling. It was worth the gas to get an idea of where survivors were living, and where the radiation made it impossible. In a few weeks, long before they ran short of fuel, he would know where to begin his campaign to conquer the state.

Lompoc would fall first.

Once the new recruits were trained and armed it was a foregone conclusion. With hundreds of farm workers, their food supply would be assured, and they could begin to recruit much larger groups of men. They should hit five hundred in two months.

The only problem he could see was this new guy, Mark Teller. Packer wasn't sure of his influence on Dombrowski. He was sure the sub captain was loyal, but he wondered what would happen if the president ordered action that the captain was uncomfortable with.

"Sir, the president is on the line."

He hurried to the microphone. "Mr. President. Good to talk to you, sir."

"And to you, Colonel Packer. First things first. I have drafted an order to promote you to Brigadier General, as befits your status of Commander of Vandenberg Air Force Base."

Packer stood a little taller. "Thank you, Mr. President."

"You deserve it Colonel... sorry... General. Once California is wrapped up, Major General will be the next step. Your aid? Major Whittington, I believe?"

"Major Whittinghall, sir."

"Yes, he is promoted to Lieutenant Colonel. We are currently designing currency and coins, and as soon as we can get airline service across the country, you will begin to be paid for your services. General Ladner is now the Armed Forces Chief of Staff and you will report directly to him, as will the commanding officers of the divisions here and in the South. Captain Dombrowski will report to you until the Navy has a larger presence."

Packer was thrilled with the revelation that Dombrowski would report to him, but worried about Richard's reaction. "Mr. President, we may have a slight problem here. I am sure of Captain Dombrowski's loyalty, but this Mark Teller who showed up here yesterday may cause some problems. He didn't seem on board with your plans for rebuilding the country. I understand that you knew him before the war?"

"Yes, he was on the Civilian Advisory Board. He's only in his thirties, but he was the CEO of a billion-dollar, aerospace company. He's extremely capable and would have been a great addition to my staff. But you may be right. His politics might not be in line with what we need. Keep an eye on him and send him back to where he crawled out from as soon as possible."

"I will do that, Mr. President."

"I have a new mission for Captain Dombrowski and will be talking to him later. I will inform him of your promotion and his place in the chain-of-command."

"Captain Dombrowski is not going to like reporting to an Air Force officer."

"He will follow my orders, and I will assure him of a re-organization when the Army, Navy and Air Force numbers are greater. We are recruiting as quickly as we can and I will expect you to increase your numbers in the west."

"Yes sir. How much leeway do I have to draft civilians?"

"You have my complete backing and, since we are in a state of Martial Law, the law clearly allows you to do so."

"Thank you, Mr. President. We will increase our efforts immediately."

"Excellent. And we will keep the details of these conversations to ourselves. Am I clear?"

"Completely, sir."

***

Neatly coiled ropes and pulleys covered the dock, with fuel barrels stacked three high, thirty feet away from where the dock connected to the concrete walkway. The boat drifted in, past the boat house built at the end, and the second boat that was tied off next to the building. A seaman jumped onto the dock and pulled the boat alongside. Another seaman swung the gate open to allow the captain, Commander Crane, Mark and two ensigns to proceed beyond the supply house to the waiting jeep. The ensigns held back as the two officers and Mark climbed into the jeep. Sand dunes covered with coastal scrub, rose north and south of the dock and created a narrow defile leading up to, and crossing, Coast Road. They headed inland toward the Command Center.

Captain Dombrowski was looking for answers.

The Command Center was two miles inland and in five minutes the vehicle pulled up in front of the two-story, concrete and glass building. The sun was almost overhead as the captain and commander returned the salutes of the airmen standing guard at the door, and entered the building.

"Hello, Captain Dombrowski. I'll tell the General you're here. Please have a seat, sir." The staff sergeant turned and disappeared into the hallway.

Mark looked over at Richard, who looked back with his eyebrows almost disappearing up into his ball cap. Walking over to the captain, he bent his head toward him and whispered, "General?" The captain just shrugged his shoulders.

They remained standing, and finally took chairs only after waiting for several minutes without the sergeant returning. Mark was getting impatient, and he could see Dombrowski was fidgeting and clearly losing his patience, as well.

Mark stood up and walked over to one of the walls of photographs, walking slowly, his hands behind his back, as he examined each picture in turn. He recognized one of the men in one photo, standing next to a large civilian rocket. Mark had met Burt Rutan on several occasions. When he and his companions had passed through Mojave and seen the spaceport, Mark had seen a sign for Rutan's company, Scaled Composites, and wondered what had happened to the aviation pioneer.

The photograph of the former Commanding Officer of the base was missing and had been replaced with one of a stern looking General Packer.

Out of the corner of his eye, he saw Dombrowski come to his feet and turn to wave Mark over. It had been almost fifteen minutes. "Let's get the hell out of here," the captain said. They started for the door when the staff sergeant entered the room and started toward them, his heels clicking on the tile floor.

"Captain Dombrowski, General Packer would like to apologize, but he's tied up at the moment. He asked me to tell you that the president would like to talk to you at your Communications Center at 1700 our time. He and Colonel Whittinghall will come out to the platform for an early dinner before the call."

"We'll expect him then," The captain said brusquely.

They left the building and climbed into the jeep. Richard was looking around the compound as if he were assessing an enemy installation, noting the number and location of the airmen. Mark glanced up and saw someone at one of the windows. The glare from the sun kept him from being able to see clearly but he thought it looked like General Packer… and he was smiling.

Crane noticed the captain's heightened awareness. "What are you thinking, sir?" Crane asked him.

"I'm thinking this place may not be as friendly as it used to be and we need to get our boys back to the boat."

"Two squads are with some of the airmen at the Base Exchange Warehouse. They're getting supplies."

"Let's get back and I'll send someone after them."

They had climbed back into the jeep with the airman driver, and were quiet the rest of the way to the docks. Once they had arrived at the dock, and were beyond the hearing of the driver, Richard issued instructions to the ensigns who had been waiting for them to return. The men jumped to attention as the captain approached, clearly not expecting them back so soon.

"Ensign Udall, once you've dropped us off at the platform, I need you to go to the sub and tell Mr. Finney to be ready to leave, in case we need to make a hasty exit. Tell him there have been some developments and I will brief him this afternoon."

They spent the next thirty minutes getting back to the platform, the sea tossing the boat about as the whitecaps began to kick up in the early afternoon. A pod of dolphins escorted them back to the platform, speeding alongside and leaping out of the water. It lifted Mark's spirits in spite of his sense of impending doom.

***

When Matthew could tear himself away from the incredible sight of the ocean, he had moved north until he hit the road that led from the docks to the compound he had watched during the night. He quietly slipped across the road and spent an hour making his way to the airfield. The plane returned to the base, landing on the runway and then taxiing to a hangar on the east side of the field, just north of the tower.

A camouflaged, troop carrier, so old it looked like a Vietnam War leftover, drove up to the tower and two men got out and entered the building. Using his binoculars he saw the men enter the room at the top. Fifteen minutes later they came down, re-entered their vehicle and sped away to the south.

Brush covered this portion of the base and Matthew was able to find plenty of cover to mask his movements as he headed west for the ocean once again. He couldn't get enough of the sight of that limitless expanse and the power of the waves crashing to the shore.

As he approached the beach he saw something to the north and recognized it as some type of rocket. Curiosity overcame him and he detoured north to the rocket, cradled in a massive gantry. He had completely misjudged the size and realized how enormous it was, only when he found it to be twice as far away as he initially thought. It stood on the pad, pointing toward the skies and the worlds beyond.

A lost hope of mankind.

Letters on the side, up toward the nose, said, "Space X." He had heard of her. A private company had developed Space X to take personnel and supplies to the International Space Station, leading to other commercial projects in the future. Private business interests would do what a bankrupt government could no longer accomplish. Now it stood on its pad, poised and ready to, but never again taking off.

Sadly, he turned and trotted down the coast, making up for the time he lost trying to imagine a return to the world that had hope, and looked to the stars.

Arriving in the area just north of the docks, he sat on a dune, munching on the sandwich he had stashed in his backpack, and staring out at the ocean. The water crashed on the jagged rocks and swirled in tide pools, and he could see kelp washing back and forth as the water receded. A small breakwater jutted into the surf, redirecting the power of the waves away from the dock area. He would regret having to leave the beach, but he knew his future lay in other areas.

As he once again approached the area where the docks were hidden behind a wall of sand dunes, he heard an engine in the distance. He quickly made his way through the scrub until he was within twenty yards of the road. A jeep approached from the left, traveling at high speed. As it came over a small bump in the road, Matthew was surprised to see Mark Teller sitting in the back seat along with an Air Force driver and two naval officers. As the car flew by, Matthew could see that Mark didn't look like he was having a great day. His eyes were narrowed and he was frowning. The jeep disappeared over the edge where the road dropped down to the dock.

A few minutes later he heard the sound of a motorboat as it pulled away, apparently heading straight out to sea. Through the early afternoon haze, Matthew saw the structures of offshore, oil platforms and knew that one of the rigs must be the boat's destination. He didn't think Mark looked like a captive, and the presence of Navy officers led him to believe there must be a ship moored out in the ocean.

He had no idea it was a fully-functioning, nuclear powered, and nuclear armed submarine.

***

Flies and gnats swarmed around Matthew's head, as he crawled prone up the dune to his previous hiding spot. It was hot and humid. He slapped at the back of his neck, as a biting insect landed there looking for a meal.

The atmosphere of the camp had changed ever so slightly. There was an additional guard at the doors leading into the larger building. Men ran across the parade field with a sense of urgency, instead of the leisurely pace of the morning, and a squad of airmen were checking their weapons and adding magazines to the pockets of their camo fatigues. Two trucks pulled into camp from the east, and a dozen Navy men climbed out and were immediately surrounded by armed Air Force personnel. They seemed to be arguing, and an Air Force Master Sergeant pointed toward the west. The Navy Seamen climbed together into one of the trucks and it left for the docks. The other truck drove to the barracks down in front of Matthew and they began to unload supplies, carrying them into the building.

Something was happening and Matthew thought it somehow had to do with Mark and, quite possibly, with the townspeople of Lompoc.

He backed down the hill and trotted south to the meeting place with Derek, where he found him, right on time, with Chief's reins held in his hand.

"Hi Matthew, How'd it go?"

"Let's get back to town and I can brief everyone. I found Mark and he seems fine."

He slid the crossbow into the special sheath he'd made for it and the two men, that had spent so much of their time riding together, swung their mounts around and galloped back to Carla and Doug's place, dismounting on the front lawn and turning the animals over to Mike.

They entered the house and Matthew sought out Doug, but Lori got to Matthew first.

"Did you find him? Is he okay?"

"I saw him in a jeep and he looked okay. He didn't look like a captive. He and the Navy guys got in a boat and headed out toward the oil rigs. I think the Navy must have a boat out there."

"Navy?" Doug said. "We've only seen Air Force personnel."

"Well, there's Navy guys too, but it looks like they may be having some kind of a disagreement. An Air Force Sergeant sent the Navy guys packing. The military compound is about two or three miles from the ocean and it looks like they have at least two hundred soldiers, maybe more. I only saw a small portion of the base."

"Do you think we're in any danger?" Doug asked him.

"I think you might want to get the Council together."

Carla walked into the room. "We'll be eating dinner in a couple hours."

"We need to talk to them before then," Matthew said.

Doug nodded. "I'll go tell Jack to get the council together and we can meet here as soon as possible."

"That's good," Matthew said. "Hopefully, Mark can find out what they're planning. I'm going to catch a nap and go back after we talk to the Council. He looked free when I saw him. I hope nothing's changed and he can come back with me."

***

Tables were loaded with food, as the Navy wanted to impress the Air Force with the fact that they had plenty of food, even if the general's men had prevented the morning delivery of supplies.

Earlier, before General Packer had arrived with Whittinghall and a dozen airmen, the two squads of Navy men that were sent to get supplies had returned and informed the captain that they had been sent back to Harvest without any of the provisions they had spent the morning procuring.

"I don't know what the hell Packer is trying pull, but we've had nothing but a cordial relationship before this." He raised his cap and reseated it on his head in a gesture Mark had gotten used to.

"I hope it isn't because I pissed off the president," Mark told him. "I wonder if he's received orders from Rissman about Lompoc. They've been worried that the military was going to try and take them over."

"What would they want from them?"

"The folks in town have well-established gardens and the Vandenberg crew has to be tired of canned and dehydrated rations. I think General Packer has delusions of grandeur about taking over California, and maybe even the entire West Coast for the president."

"Well, it's not delusional if the president is backing him."

Richard and Mark had been shocked when Packer brought an entire squad of airmen to the platform. Before, he had only been accompanied by the lieutenant colonel and maybe one or two others. There were usually around twenty or so Navy personnel aboard the platform at any one time, but since the captain had ordered the sub readied for action, they had even fewer men.

Mark had counted eleven Air Force personnel. They were outnumbered by three guys.

Packer's enlistees were eating in a room off the communications area, and the four officers and Mark were in a makeshift dining room by the former Chief Engineer's office where Dombrowski made his headquarters.

During the meal they had engaged in small talk, and Mark was frustrated that he hadn't learned anything of substance. He talked about the trip west but carefully left out any mention of specific locations.

"Thank you for your hospitality Captain Dombrowski," General Packer said, as he took his last bite of fresh Grouper. "My officers and men are grateful to have some variety in their meal. I thought that since we would be here for the president's call at 1700, it would be a perfect opportunity to have a meal together and plan for future missions."

"Yes, the president mentioned that you had been discussing the handling of dissidents. What exactly are you planning?"

"Well, of course, the president will fill you in and let you know what he has in mind for the rebuilding effort, but I am not at liberty to speak while Mr. Teller is present. If I could talk to you in private, Captain? With just our senior officers."

Dombrowski started to speak, but Mark held up his hand. "It's alright Richard. He's right, I'm a civilian and don't need to be part of your discussions. I'll be in my room until 1700. I believe the president wanted to talk with me again as well, so I'll meet you then, in the radio room."

Nodding at Commander Crane and Lieutenant Colonel Wittinghall, he left the room and went down one level to his quarters. He only had thirty minutes, and he stretched out on his bunk, thinking about making the trip back to New Mexico.

But it wasn't time to make that trip yet. He needed to know what the president and his people were up to.

***

"I'm glad you all could come." Matthew disliked talking in front of a group, but he was the one with the most information. He had slept for an hour until Doug had gathered the council together. "I spent last night and today on the base trying to get some intel. The military is using the southwestern portion of the base. I didn't see anyone around the main gate or to the north of the airfield but it's a large base and there could be others."

"That makes sense," Brenden said. "That's the old Command Center, and they have some barracks there. It's only a couple miles from the airfield one direction and the Vandenberg docks in the other."

"Yeah, they could fish for food, and they could grow crops in the fertile area around the airfield," Jack added.

Matthew shook his head. "They aren't interested in growing crops. I'm sure they don't think that's a soldier's job. I believe they want you folks to provide what they need, and they are preparing for action. Your town is in danger."

"Why don't we, the Council, have a meeting with the Commander of the base and make a deal to have them buy what they need. Our fields are producing more than we can eat. We could barter with them."

"They aren't interested in bartering, either. Throughout history, the militaries of various countries, unless constrained by a constitution or a strong government, have only been interested in power. Power over the people. You need to call a town meeting and find out what kind of firepower you possess and how much ammo you have."

"We can't fight the Air Force!" Conners said, his eyes big as saucers. "They'll slaughter us."

"You will probably not be given a choice. It's fight or be enslaved. You greatly outnumber them."

"Yeah, but with California's gun laws we don't have any weapons that match up to their firepower. Maybe it wouldn't be so bad. I mean, if they guarantee that we and our families will be safe."

Matthew couldn't believe what he was hearing. He shook his head, his black ponytail whipping back in forth in his agitation. "I guess that's up to the townspeople. If you vote to roll over and be serfs, it's your choice. Or you can fight for freedom. Now's the time to decide." He stood up. "I believe they may move before morning, so it's now or never, folks. I suggest you call a meeting for tonight and find out what your people want to do."

***

The president's call came through right on time.

"Mr. President, good evening."

"Hello, Captain Dombrowski. Who's with you?"

"We have General Packer, Lieutenant Colonel Whittinghall, Commander Crane and Mark Teller, sir."

"Very good. I see you've been informed of General Packer's and Lieutenant Colonel Whittinghall's promotions. It may seem strange to you that we're so far away, but still in control from coast to coast, but I assure you it's only a matter of time until that control is more secure. After all, back in the mid-eighteen hundreds the president presided over a country that spanned the continent. There was still representative government of all the states, including California, that became a state in 1850. We will reestablish the continental railroad. We have more vehicles working every day and have just found a cache of aircraft parts that weren't damaged by the EMPs."

"That's great news, Mr. President. It sounds like you are making great strides."

"We are. So Mark, I wanted to apologize if I sounded impatient with you. I am anxious to get the country back where it needs to be. We have thousands, maybe hundreds of thousands of people throughout the country that are starving to death and we need to reach out to them and save them. Have you given my proposal some thought?"

"I have, sir. I realize now that my home in California is uninhabitable. I need to get my family relocated and then can give serious consideration to moving back east and helping with the rebuilding. But I have some questions, sir."

"Yes?" Rissman asked coldly. It was a warning to Mark but it was too late to turn back.

"I was wondering, Mr. President, what role the Congress is going to play?"

"I told you some of the members of Congress have survived, and are here supporting me."

"Yes, sir. But will there still be three branches of government? Did any members of the Supreme Court survive? Are you going to govern using the Constitution, sir? Will we still have the balance of power?"

"Where will you be relocating your family to, Mark?" That took Mark off guard.

"Uh, well, I'm not sure, Mr. President. I've only found out I can't live here anymore so I haven't given it much thought."

"Oh come on, Mark. You said you came from New Mexico. Which part?"

"I haven't decided yet, sir."

There was dead time on the call until Mark started to sweat.

Finally Rissman said, "Captain Dombrowski, we have reorganized the military structure in Charleston. General Charles Ladner is the Chief of Staff and Supreme Commander of the Military forces. Generals Spencer, Martinez, Thatcher and Packer all report to him directly. You are all that's left of the Navy, as all the Naval Ports were along the coasts and took direct hits. We, of course, will begin rebuilding the Navy as soon as we can determine which coastal areas are safe. Until then, you will report to General Packer."

Dombrowski pulled himself up taller than his six-foot-three and, with a blank stare, said, "Yes, Mr. President. If I may, sir. I'd like to recheck the West Coast for other Navy personnel. I believe the Chinese threat has been completely eliminated, so I would also like permission to travel to the East Coast by way of the North Passage above Canada, before summer ends, to check out the Atlantic Naval bases, as well. I believe a strong Navy is vital to the interests of this country, sir. China was not the only threat. If any bases have escaped destruction, we need to know it.

"I agree with you that there may be other threats, but we haven't picked up any additional chatter from around the globe that hints at any imminent danger. The radio signals are better every day now and we feel confident we can detect any problems. I feel strongly that you need to stay on the West Coast."

"But, sir…"

"Enough Captain. You can discuss these issues with your new Commanding Officer."

"Yes… Mr. President."

"And now, Captain, I have a new mission for you. Colonel Packer, please brief the Captain on the revolution."

"Revolution?" Mark asked.

Packer stood with his hands behind his back and bounced on his toes. "We have been sending our recon plane to various points within California, along the coast and inland. We've been mapping areas of radiation and looking for signs of civilization, or even small groups of survivors. We have found that the only survivors are inland."

He paused for effect, and then continued, "Two weeks ago, the plane was overdue, and we thought we'd lost her. It returned last week. It had landed in Redding, in Northern California, and was attacked by a group of militants. They were held down by gunfire but managed to take a prisoner. She was interrogated, and broken fairly easily by the pilot, First Lieutenant Halpern. In order to escape, they sent her back across the field and taxiing past her, they took off while the opposing force was afraid to fire for fear of hitting her. They took a couple of hits but made it back."

"Tell them what he reported, General," Rissman said with relish.

Just as Mark was ready to kill him, Packer stopped bouncing. "He reported that there is a huge number of people in Northern California, eastern Oregon and Washington, and in Idaho and Utah that are banding together to form their own nation. Their motto is Molon Labe. In Greek it means, 'come and take it,' referring to their weapons. They are outright defying us and risking all-out war."

"How do they even know the government still exists?" Mark asked. "Maybe they're just trying to survive. We need to contact them and let them know. Give them a chance to join."

"They have short wave radios they are using to communicate with each other, and with people in Atlanta, who are also talking revolution. They're probably even talking to your people in New Mexico," Packer said, as he glared at Mark.

Mark thought that his folks weren't in touch with anyone, until he realized he'd been gone for almost three months. The ionosphere was only now settling down to allow radio communication. The New Mexico Colony could very well be in touch with others at this time.

"So, Captain Dombrowski, here is your next mission. In order to allow the duly elected government of the United States to rule effectively and without interference, and for the good of the American people, you are to fire a Trident missile at a point central to this rogue nation, using a MERV to strike six targets at once. The coordinates will be sent to you after this call."

Dombrowski looked stricken. "But, Mr. President, these are Americans."

"You will follow my orders Captain Dombrowski! You will hit these targets at 0600 tomorrow morning, Pacific Time. And that's not all. You will hit Atlanta with a single nuclear warhead. That's where the dissidents in the south are concentrated."

Mark yelled into the mike, "This is insane, Rissman! You can't expect him to nuke Americans. Are you completely out of your mind? You..."

"General Packer, take Mark Teller into custody this minute," the president yelled into the mike.

Packer stepped toward Mark, and Mark took a swing, connecting with the General's cheek and nose, as he danced back, trying to escape the blow. Whittinghall grabbed Mark's arms behind his back, and Packer aimed a vicious blow to Mark's abdomen. He bent over and went to his knees, as Packer wiped away blood that gushed from his nose and dripped onto his spotless uniform.

"Sergeant Abramson, bring in your men and secure this prisoner."

Three armed airmen rushed into the communications room, two of them grabbing Mark's arms and hauling him to his feet, and one was watching Captain Dombrowski. The captain was frozen in place, trying to assimilate these new developments.

"And one more target, Captain Dombrowski," Rissman continued relentlessly, "a direct hit over Eagle Nest, New Mexico. It's the location of Will Hargraves' shelter and the probable location of the dissidents associated with Mark Teller."

"Noooo. You can't... you can't do that!"

Mark struggled against the men holding his arms. Pleading with Dombrowski, he begged, "Please Richard, listen to reason! This is…"

A solid blow across his left eyebrow, opened a cut above his eye and dazed him momentarily. Blood ran into his eye. Unable to wipe it away, he looked wildly at the captain.

"Dombrowski!" He tried to shrug off his captors as he struggled forward. They held him firmly and jerked him toward the door. "Richard. You know what you have to do!" For just a second the struggle ceased and Mark shook his head to clear his vision. "You know what you have to do."

The captain turned and looked over at him. Mark's eyes met Dombrowski's and he saw something flicker there.

Then the moment was gone, as one of the airmen struck him in the ribs, knocking his breath out. The general yelled, "Get him out of here," and the men grasping Mark's arms pulled him out onto the platform. They dragged him roughly down the stairs to the dock beneath the mammoth structure, Mark struggling frantically the entire way.

They can't do this. Oh God, no. Chris!

He considered trying to jump into the ocean. He was fairly certain he could dive deep enough to avoid gunfire and to elude capture, but it was seven miles of open water to the shore. He had done a few triathlons and knew he could swim a mile or maybe two, but he'd never make it seven miles. They shoved him onto the boat, pushing him into the cabin and had two men training their assault rifles at him. They were too far away for him to jump them. An hour later he heard Packer's voice telling the crew to shove off and felt the motion of the boat as it accelerated toward shore. He would have given anything to hear the conversation Packer and Dombrowski must have had in that hour.

He sat in the dark, frantically trying to think of a way to escape, but he was almost numb with fear. The sound of the motor slowing down brought him back around, just as one of the guards yelled at him to put his hands on his head and come up out of the cabin. He came on board and they pushed him onto the dock.

"Take him to the barracks and lock him up." Packer's jaw and nose were swollen where Mark had struck him, and Mark knew Packer would have him executed as soon as the missiles flew in the morning.

Packer would make him watch as the missiles flew toward his home.

36

Lack of sleep was never a problem for Matthew. He had a knack for falling instantly to sleep whenever he wanted, and waking up refreshed and alert. He had learned to do it while living on his grandfather's ranch as a kid. He loved camping out in the wilderness, survival style, making his own shelter, catching or gathering his own food and making his own weapons. Had he not developed the ability to fall asleep and wake immediately upon hearing or feeling a danger, he would not have survived.

After dinner and a nap, he rode the Appaloosa back to the base and once again Derek took the horses back to town. He would return at 1:00 o'clock in the morning and wait for Matthew to come over the hill.

Matthew brought wire cutters with him and made short work of a section of the fence. He bent it back into place so no one could tell it had been cut, unless they were right on top of it. Fortunately, there was no top bar. The fence only ran for the length of the compound, ending east and west of there. He examined the grounds with his binoculars and was unable to locate Mark. He couldn't be sure, but it looked like there were more airmen than in the morning. They were standing around the vehicles, checking their weapons and hanging with their buddies.

Skirting the fence, he made his way the two miles to the ocean, past the bog that separated the hill behind the barracks and the dunes along the beach. He quickly turned north and found himself at the road leading down to the docks. Creeping forward, he saw there were more guards than the day before, as he carefully came up behind a stack of fuel barrels. Worming his way between the barrels, he settled in to see if he could hear any of the conversation.

Two of the guards came up the road from the dock and turned around just past the barrels. "... the morning?"

"They brought the new recruits from the training base up north. It'll be a piece of cake. They won't know what hit 'em."

"What's the deal with the Navy guys?"

"I'm not sure. We'll..."

They continued back down the road to the dock, but Matthew now knew he was right about the attack on the town. With the recruits, they probably had over three hundred, well-armed soldiers. The military offensive would soon begin.

The sun had set, and Matthew was starting to crawl out of his hiding place, when the sound of a motorboat drifted in from the west. It grew louder and then cut out, as the boat drifted to the dock. Watching the dock, he noticed a group of airmen coming toward the barrels. It was too late to escape out the back, toward the dunes on the south, so he squeezed back in amongst the center barrels.

Sounds of a commotion reached him while he was pinned down by the airmen who were filling a can from one of the barrels. He was frozen in place, almost holding his breath as the yelling grew closer.

"Please, you can't do this. Your commander's crazy. You guys can't seriously support what they're doing."

"Shut up Teller. We do what we're told. We're on the side of might, my friend. You should have kept your mouth shut."

"How can anyone keep quiet about this massacre. You can't destroy whole regions of this country. They're Americans, for Christ's sake."

"I just know I'm on the winning side."

Matthew peeked between some of the barrels and caught a glimpse of Mark, surrounded by Air Force personnel. Mark suddenly made a break, shoving two men aside as he tried to run up the incline. One of the soldiers swung the stock of his rifle, catching Mark in the side and knocking him to the ground. Matthew almost gave away his position but discipline kept him rooted in place. Being greatly outnumbered, trying to rescue Mark at this time would have been suicide. By the time the men finished filling the Jerry Can, Mark had been driven away in the jeep.

Disappointed, he slipped out of the barrels, jogged south and then turned east to run the two miles to his vantage point above the compound. He had no idea where they were holding him. All he could do was keep watching and hope for a clue.

***

Pacing back and forth in the cramped room, Mark felt like a caged panther. The one tiny window in the back wall was too small to wriggle through. He tried the door a dozen times and kicked at the wallboard on all sides of his prison.

He was trapped.

Blood had run down his face and soaked his light blue shirt, leaving dark stains down his chest. It was now dry and crusted, making the shirt stiff. He was wearing a collarless T-shirt, due to the weather, and it emphasized the biceps and triceps he'd built up by performing hard, physical labor for the past two years. He'd wiped his arm across his face, smearing the blood through his stubble. He looked like a wild man, ready to tear apart anyone who dared to enter the room.

Only five hours left to prevent a catastrophe. His friends and loved ones would all be annihilated in the blink of an eye. He paced. He pounded at the door, but his efforts were unrewarded. He patted his pockets, hoping for something he could use to escape. They had searched him and taken his knife, but left him with his magnesium fire starter. *I'll burn the place down if I have to,* he thought. He hit the striker on the bar of magnesium several times in frustration and stuck it back in his pocket.

A tiny noise behind him brought him abruptly around, but darkness was complete and he couldn't see a thing. There was a cracking and a tinkling of glass from the window. "Mark," a voice whispered.

He leapt to the window and tried to see who was out in the darkness. One of the four panes had been shattered, glass cascading to the floor. "Who's there?"

"It's Matthew."

"Jesus, Matthew. How did you find me? Can you get me outta here?"

"I saw flashes from your fire starter. The window's too small for you to fit through. I'll need to try something else."

"You have to do something. They're going to nuke New Mexico! The president is crazy, and sees conspiracies in people just trying to survive and make their own way."

"The President of the U.S.?"

"Yes. Rissman. He wants a dictatorship and the Commander of Vandenberg is his lackey. You need to try and get to Richard Dombrowski, the captain of a nuclear sub, anchored off an oil rig seven miles at sea. He's the one with the nukes. He needs to be convinced not to fire those missiles. Rissman wants him to hit Atlanta and Idaho as well. He's crazy, Matthew. We have to stop him."

Nukes? "How do I get to the rig?"

"There's a powerboat at the docks."

"If I can get you out of here, we can make the attempt together. Derek is a hundred yards away from here. We'll think of something."

"Listen, Matthew. You have to get to Lori. Take her and the kids to the aircraft hangar and hide them in back. Tell her if you can get me out of here we'll meet her there. Bring Jimbo, and all our people, even Sheri and her family, if they'll come. Packer and his troops are going to invade the town in the morning. Derek knows how to fly. He told me one day. If I don't get there, have him fly Lori and the kids to safety. Please, Matthew, do this for me."

"I'm going to get you out of here, and you can fly them away."

"First, we have to get to Dombrowski, to stop the nuke attack. Get back to town and get Lori, then come back and we'll make the attempt to get to the sub." Mark completely filled him in on the rest of the situation, including the planned attack on the town.

"Please, you need to let them know."

"I'll return, my friend."

***

Lori woke the children and hastily helped them to dress. Matthew had knocked on her door and her heart had leaped into her throat, as the only reason she could think of for a visit in the middle of the night, was that something had happened to Mark.

The household was awake, Carla putting on coffee and Doug going out into the night to alert his neighbors and the Council. Voices awoke Jimbo and he rolled off the couch onto the floor.

"What's goin' on?" he murmured.

"The military is planning to attack the town at dawn," Matthew informed them, when all were present. "Mark has been taken captive, but Derek and I are going back to try and spring him."

Lori gasped, "What happened? What did he do?"

"There's apparently a nuclear sub moored off of an oil rig out in the ocean. It still has nuclear missiles."

"You gotta be kidding me."

"Are you serious?"

"Mark knows the captain of the sub. They and the Air Force commander have been in contact with Jeremy Rissman."

"The president?"

"You gotta be kidding me."

"No, Jimbo, I'm not kidding."

"Apparently, Rissman has declared Martial Law. He's trying to get the country back together. Only problem is, he's using the military to round up people, and putting them in FEMA camps, making them work to rebuild. He's separating families."

"What happened to Mark?"

"I think he pissed off the president. He refused to go to West Virginia to join Rissman's Administration. He said he thought what Rissman was doing was wrong."

"That sucks. What are we gonna do?"

"It gets worse. He's appointed the Vandenberg Commander to be the supreme leader of the west. That's why he's attacking Lompoc, to bring the civilians under military control. There are some areas of the country that don't want to join with him. He's ordered the sub commander to nuke them."

"What? That's impossible."

"You gotta be kidding me."

"Where are they going to hit?" Lori asked.

"Three targets. Idaho and Atlanta, and…" He looked her in the eye, and she knew the answer. Mark had antagonized the president and he was going to make him pay.

"It's New Mexico, isn't it?"

Matthew nodded.

The room erupted. "We need to warn them!"

"What can we do?"

"When?"

"We're going to get Mark out of there and try to reason with the sub captain, if we can get to him. Otherwise, Mark wants Lori and the kids to get to the hangar with the old biplane. If he can get there, he'll fly them out, and the rest of us will get back across country. We'll go to Farmington. Rissman doesn't know about it. Maybe we can get them to prepare to fight back."

"What if he can't get to the hangar?"

"Derek knows how to fly a small plane. He will fly you out."

"Well, I won't go."

"Lori, be reasonable. Mark has asked us to do this. We all need to respect his wishes. This town is being hit at dawn."

"We can help them fight."

"I'm not sure they want to resist. We need to get back and alert Farmington. Skillet, get the wagon and take Lori and the kids to the airport. Mike and Jimbo, go with them for protection. Sheri, we'd like you to go back with us, and of course your aunt and uncle, as well. Otherwise you may end up as slaves."

"Thank you Matthew," Carla told him, "but I'm sure that Doug will agree. This is our home and community, and it is our fight, and we will see it through. But Sheri should go with you."

"I'm staying."

"Lori, please get ready to go. Mark will go to the airport and if you aren't there, what's going to happen?" We need to get back to the base. Good luck to all of you." He whirled and ran out front. He and Derek rode away as the others stood immobile in shock.

Lori was the first to react. "Come on everyone. Let's get moving."

***

The next two hours were the longest of Mark's life. In stygian darkness he waited for Matthew to return. He paced, and thought of all the friends he had in Willsburg. He thought of Chris and tears ran down his cheeks. He imagined her incinerated by a nuclear bomb, after being miraculously spared the first time around.

Suddenly gunfire erupted in the distance. "What the hell?" Mark ran over and put his ear against the door.

The door burst inward, almost knocking him down. "Mr. Teller. Follow me."

Mark jumped into the hallway and, from the feeble light of the oil lamp, saw an ensign and two seamen standing with their backs to the wall. They turned to the right and started to head down the hallway when airmen came around the corner at the far end behind them. A loud crack of a rifle, deafening in the long hallway, blew away the entire lantern, throwing burning oil down the wall and onto the tile. The fire crept up the wall. Mark threw himself back against the wall alongside the door.

"Come on, man. We need to get out of here." The ensign grabbed his arm and pulled him toward a door at the back end of the corridor, away from the airmen with the rifle. Muzzle flashes lit up the end of the corridor beyond the spreading fire and the two airman stepped into the middle of the hallway and fired in their direction. One of the men shouted and dropped to the floor, as bullets tore into his chest.

"Who are you guys?"

"I'm Cross. The captain sent us to free you. Come on!"

"Wait!" Mark swept up the rifle and swung around to follow the ensign out the back.

"Ensign Carter, come on!" Cross yelled.

More rounds flew all around them, tearing chips of wood and drywall from the walls. Smoke was beginning to fill the corridor and visibility was becoming limited. Just as they reached the door, it was flung open.

"Hold it. You're not going anywhere Teller."

It was Lieutenant Colonel Whittinghall, and three others, all with weapons pointed in through the doorway. The colonel raise his assault rifle and shot Cross in the face, knocking him off his feet and sending gore backwards over Ensign Carter, who was still firing back down the hallway. Whittinghall raised his weapon toward Mark's face and smiled. Then the smile disappeared as the colonel, shock upon his face, looked down at an iron arrow protruding from his chest.

Mark fired twice and two of the others went down. The third fell as shots came from the rear of the building, and Mark turned to grab Carter, pulling him out of the barracks and around the corner. Matthew and Derek ran up to them, Mark having to shove the young man's rifle up, to prevent him from shooting either of his friends.

"They're on our side, kid. Listen. We need to get to Captain Dombrowski and tell him you guys freed me and stop him from firing those missiles at American Communities. How did you get here?"

"We stole their jeep. There's two more guys guarding it. The captain could only spare the five of us. Come on, we can go around the back." There was a crashing sound and flames blasted out of the door, bathing the surrounding area, and the men, in orange light, as Mark and the others threw their arms up to protect their faces from the searing heat.

They ran around the back of the building and sprinted the length of the barracks, rounding the other corner to see a fire fight going on in the parking lot. The only light was from the headlights of the jeep and the raging fire that had fully engulfed the building. Mark could hear the screams of men that had been quartered in the barracks and now had no avenue of escape from the inferno.

The two Navy men, crouching alongside the jeep, went down in a barrage of fire. A figure came out of the darkness, jumped over a body, and leaped into the jeep.

"No... stop him!" Mark shouted. But the jeep was speeding across the parade field toward the Command Center.

"Shit! Come on. We need to get to the boat. Mark heard hoof beats and turned to see Matthew and Derek bearing down on them, riding Chief and Jasper. He hadn't even noticed them leaving, as he and Carter had run behind the barracks.

Matthew stuck out his hand and Mark swung up behind him. Only Chief was strong enough to take that kind of maneuver. Derek reined Jasper in and the seaman put his foot in the stirrup as Derek pulled him up behind him. He kicked the horse and Jasper galloped off after Chief who was rapidly drawing away toward the west.

Bullets, fired randomly in the dark, flew around them as they quickly outdistanced the enemy. It was pitch black now and they had to slow to a walk to ensure the horses didn't trip or step in a hole. Mark chaffed as their time was running out.

Moving through the darkness as fast as possible, they reached Coast Road in twenty minutes. Mark never realized how important the moon was for getting around at night. They dismounted and left Jasper tied to a bush, while Chief's reins were left to dangle if needed for a quick get-away.

They snuck over to the south dune, and then using the barrels for cover, made it most of the way to the dock.

"There's no light," Seamen Carter whispered. "The dock is always lit."

The four men, weapons ready, crossed the concrete walkway that lay perpendicular to the wooden dock. They moved out onto the wooden dock, straining to see.

"Where are the guards?" Carter asked. It was minimally lighter down by the water as the ocean gave off its phosphorescent glow, and they could see the moorings.

The boats were gone.

***

"Come on Mark, there's nothing more we can do." Matthew tugged at Mark's arm.

"There must be another way to get out there."

Seaman Carter cleared his throat. "Mr. Teller. The captain said to get you out but that he didn't think we'd be able to get back to the rig. He told me 'good luck and have a nice life'."

Mark was devastated. "What are we going to do?"

Matthew actually raised his voice, which got Mark's attention. "We need to get to the airport and get you guys out of here. The rest of us will follow by land. Get to Farmington and warn Hunt and the others. Mark, there's a storm coming and we need to be ready."

Mark nodded numbly and turned toward the horses with the others.

"I recommend we head south and then east. That keeps us away from the base." Matthew gave a soft whistle and Chief came out of the darkness. Jasper whinnied softly, unhappy at being alone. They mounted up and followed Matthew's lead.

Mist rose up from the bog and fog rolled in off the ocean. Visibility was poor and they hoped they were going in the right direction.

As they rode through the wetlands along the south edge of the base, they suddenly heard the roar of engines and three vehicles flew over the ridge a mile to the north, their headlights penetrating the fog.

"How did they find us?" Mark said in Matthew's ear.

"I don't think they know we're here. I think they're heading for Lompoc."

Mark didn't realize that the night had fled, but soon saw a rosy glow in the east. The lighting improved by the minute as they rode through the muck. One of the vehicles bogged down and had to return to the fence line to find higher ground.

Figures came out of the mist, hundreds of them.

The war was on!

They were now clearly visible to the invaders. An old, troop carrier changed its heading to try and cut them off and behind the carrier, a jeep sped directly toward them. With the improving light, they increased their speed and turned more to the south, but it was still a few miles to the town and the airport. Carrying double, the horses were tiring, and Mark knew it was only a matter of time before the jeep caught them. He swung up his rifle, ready to fire when the jeep got closer.

He heard an engine and an Indian war whoop off to their right. Jimbo's motorcycle flew by, a hundred yards in front of them, with Jimbo firing rapidly at the troop carrier. He was aiming at the tires and Mark saw mud flung up as bullets hit the ground all around them. Finally, Jimbo pulled up on the bike, slammed home a second magazine, took careful aim, and fired off ten rounds. The front right tire blew, and the vehicle almost turned over as the flattened tire sunk in the mud.

They turned the horse's heads and made a wide arc around the carrier, as troops jumped out of the vehicle and started firing at them. The jeep was closing as the horses slowed down. Mark was surprised to see General Packer in the front passenger seat pointing toward the fleeing horses.

The amount of gunfire increased tremendously and Mark realized it was coming from both the north and south. He saw airmen fall as they ran into the ambush.

"Yahoo!" he shouted, "the cavalry has arrived."

Jimbo pulled alongside Chief.

"Mark! Come on. Get on the bike. It's faster," he screamed out.

Leaning forward he shouted in Matthew's ear, "I'm going with Jimbo. Veer right and get behind the townspeople's firing line. And Matthew... see you in Farmington." He didn't wait for Matthew to respond as he slid backwards over Chief's withers and splashed down in the bog.

It hurt. He rolled over and saw Jimbo siting on a stationary bike, firing at the jeep, and holding out his hand. Bullets hit the bog all around him, encouraging him to ignore the pain and jump on the bike behind Jimbo. The motorcycle slewed around and once again headed east.

Mark saw the horses heading south, as the townspeople moved forward toward the base. The sky was brighter and the sun rose into the sky over a full-scale battle. He almost fell off as the bike jounced over the terrain, which was quickly becoming firmer.

The jeep pursued him and it became obvious that it was him that General Packer was after. Jimbo gunned the engine as they suddenly slipped and slid up an embankment and came out on pavement.

The airport was a mile away.

The bike pulled ahead as they had firm footing and the jeep was still coming through the muck. "Hit it Jimbo," he called out.

"This is all she's got, buddy."

They cut through a Home Depot parking lot and shot down the street and on to the airport frontage road. Cutting between two hangars they took the turn, passed several more hangars and skidded to a stop in front of a startled Lori.

She had the hangar door open.

He jumped off the bike as it screeched to a halt. "Jimbo, cover us! Lori, help me push it out to the taxiway." Mark grabbed the chocks and flung them aside. They ran behind the plane, placed their hands on the back of the lower wing and easily shoved the lightweight plane out of the hangar.

"Get the kids in the plane. You get in the front seat with Ashley and put Kevin in the back. Be sure you use the seat belts." As she climbed in, he leaned over her and flicked on the magnetos, set the mixture and throttle, and jumped down, running around to the front of the plane. He saw the jeep scream around the corner of the hangar.

"Stand on the brakes!"

He grabbed the prop and pulled. The engine sputtered and the prop kicked back, almost getting Mark. He grabbed and pulled again, as he heard Jimbo open fire. *That's it Jimbo, slow 'em down.*

The engine fired up as he jumped back out of the way. He climbed into the rear cockpit and taxied toward the runway. As soon as he passed Jimbo, the men in the jeep started firing at the plane. No time for a run-up, he prayed nothing would go wrong. The Stearman turned onto the runway and Mark eased the throttle to the firewall.

He yelled, "Kids! Keep your heads down," but they couldn't hear him for the wind. As the plane accelerated, he looked over and saw the jeep coming alongside. The two vehicles raced down the runway side by side. Lori had her Glock out, and started unloading the full magazine at the jeep. Her shots were all over the place. Jimbo was losing ground to the faster jeep.

"Come on , baby," Mark murmured, "just a little faster."

Packer pointed an assault rifle at Lori, just as a lucky shot from her Glock hit the driver right in the face. The jeep swerved away, flipped over, and burst in to a ball of flame, as the plane reached liftoff speed. Mark pulled back on the stick and the old, but powerful plane leaped into the air and slammed sideways as it flew through the blast from the explosion. He fought for control, and swung away from the jeep, climbing as quickly as he safely could, while avoiding stalling out.

At a thousand feet, he circled back over the field and saw Jimbo waving. The motorcycle sped away toward the battle. From this height it looked like the entire population of Lompoc had joined the fight. Although the military had better weapons, they were heavily outnumbered and it looked like they were retreating to the base.

He began to increase his altitude and was still flying toward the sea when he saw it.

0600.

A squiggly streak in the sky. Being from California, he'd seen many similar vapor trials like this in the past. It usually meant a missile had been fired from Vandenberg Air Force Base.

But not this time.

It came from further out at sea. Several miles out.

He held his breath and waited for additional contrails.

And waited…

Turning the stick, he pressed the rudder, smoothly pulling a one-eighty, and heading southeast toward Farmington… or maybe toward Eagle Nest.

There was only one missile.

A two in three chance that Eagle Nest had been spared.

37

"Hey Ashe, breakfast is ready." Roger stood at the kitchen counter taking a pan of scrambled eggs off the propane stove. He spooned half of the eggs onto each of two plates and added some fried potatoes.

Ashe walked into the kitchen from the hallway. "I'm coming." He stopped and stared at the plates. "We don't have any of those sausages left? I saw Mariah wrapping some up two days ago, right after Chuck slaughtered that old sow."

"We'll get some today. This'll have to do."

Ashe loved to eat, and he'd already gained back a few pounds, spending his days sitting around teaching school. Roger, on the other hand, split his time between working in the fields and hunting. He started out thin, and was maintaining his weight with all the hard labor. Two glasses of water and eating utensils completed the table setting and they pulled up chairs. They used cloth napkins that could be washed.

"You can cook 'em tomorrow when it's your turn to fix breakfast."

They dug in. "So I hear you're getting some kids from town today. Your reputation as a professor extraordinaire has spread."

"Yeah, With Mama's grandkids, Smitty's kids, and the new ones, I'll have twenty seven. Good thing Geralyn was a teacher's aide. She's really been helping me."

"Ashe, listen. I really like these people, but at some point I need to go back to Charleston to see if I can find my family."

"Give it a rest, man. How many times do we need to go over this same terrain. You can't go back. You'd just end up back in a camp and not help your family at all."

"I can't stay here and not try. How could I live with myself?"

"That guy who came through here last week said the government is growing. They have hundreds of new recruits and twice as many vehicles since we got away. He said they even have a plane. The guy snuck through town and saw bodies hanging on a gallows. They'd probably hang you too if they recognize you. Come on, let's go to work."

The house they lived in was a 50's era, single-story, wood frame house. As they crossed the porch they waved at Essie Smith, Smitty's wife. Arlen and Essie Smith had two children, Ginny, six and Mason, eight. The kids ran across the street to walk to the farm with the two men.

"Hi Mr. Compton." Ginny took Ashe's hand and skipped to keep up with his long strides.

It was 8:20 on a beautiful summer day. August 22nd.

"Oh my God, Roger. I just realized it's the anniversary of the war. Two interminable years. Seems more like ten."

Roger didn't answer. The revelation just brought him more pain.

***

He'd only been working thirty minutes, and the sun was still low in the sky, but sweat already beaded on Roger's brow and trickled down his neck, as he hoed weeds between the rows of carrots and radishes. It was a never-ending battle. He laid down the hoe, wiping the sweat away with his left arm and stooped down to pick up the severed weeds, tossing them into the bucket that lay behind him.

Just visible under the drooping branches of a weeping willow, he could see a portion of the kids that made up Ashe's elementary class. They sat on makeshift benches and chairs. Ashe was further under the tree, lecturing them on some subject, as if he were Socrates imparting his great wisdom in an idyllic setting. The older kids were in the farmhouse working on assignments Ashe had given them, and were watched over by Geralyn, Chuck's wife.

Lynn brought him a bottle of water and took the bucket away to add the weeds to the compost pile. She was twelve years old, the same age as his daughter. She flipped her blonde hair to the side in a gesture that almost brought tears to his eyes, as he remembered that Amanda used to make the same gesture.

"Thanks, Lynn," he called to her retreating back. He saw a lightning flash appear out of the clear blue sky.

"You're welcome, Roger." She giggled, and turning to wave at him, she froze, staring toward the northeast.

Roger glanced over his shoulder and a chill ran down his spine, as he saw what he prayed he would never see again. Behind the mountain range, a malignant, mushroom cloud was rising, churning and roiling, as it climbed higher into the sky.

"Ashe!" he screamed. "Get everyone under cover. It's another attack." Pushing Lynn ahead of him, he waved at the other men and women working in the field. "Come on, hurry." He was pointing at the explosion when he heard the deep rumble, diminished by the distance. The others were heading for the willow, grabbing up the little ones as they ran.

Hitting the back door at full tilt, Roger was almost crushed as he managed to get the door open, and the workers and children spilled into the kitchen. As they all tumbled past him, Roger hesitated and looked outside for signs of additional bombs.

There didn't seem to be any.

The family crowded down into the basement and waited for three days. Smitty and Essie showed up only minutes after the bomb had hit, wanting to be with their children. The basement had been kept stocked for this possibility and Roger couldn't imagine how so many had stayed down here during the Great War.

Roger crept over to sit against the wall, next to Ashe. "What do you think is happening?"

"It's Charleston, Roger. I'm real sorry. Somebody took out the government."

"No. It can't be." He started to cry. "Maybe they took Jenn and the kids somewhere else. Maybe they weren't in Charleston." He looked at Ashe, hoping for confirmation.

"Maybe. If they are far enough from the blast and are west of Charleston, they could survive. A lot of folks were taken to Parkersburg. It's like eighty miles north. They could be okay."

Roger wiped away his tears and hung onto that possibility. It was the only thing that kept him going.

"Yeah, they could be."

They exited three days later, on another beautiful day. The wind was blowing east as the family walked out into the fields.

"This is what happened last time," Mama told him. "We didn't have to stay down for too long. The wind doesn't blow the other way. We never got sick."

She gazed toward the northeast. The cloud was gone.

"Well, I don't think Rissman will be coming for us," she told Ashe.

"No, someone's given us another chance at a new beginning."

EPILOGUE

The big, buckskin gelding tirelessly covered the two hundred and sixty miles between Amarillo, Texas and Eagle Nest, New Mexico in a couple of weeks. The horse stood sixteen hands high, big enough to carry the large man sitting astride him. Two weeks in the saddle and the stranger was glad to reach his destination. 6'2", with broad shoulders, lengthy, wavy, brown hair down to his shoulders, and a goatee, he looked every inch a burly, mountain man.

Except for his coat.

It was made from a patchwork of fabric in every color and design.

Riding through Eagle Nest he saw many signs of a thriving town. There were a few families, and several individuals, walking or bicycling down the center of Therma Way. Others rode horses, and there were two horse-drawn carriages next to a car parked in front of a restaurant. Everyone waved to him. All of them appeared armed, with the exception of very small children.

Continuing through town, he was passed by an ATV as he reached an intersection of Therma Way and a road going north. He pulled up the horse and stared at the runway of a small airport. It was a blocked off section of asphalt road, that used to be Willow Creek Rd. before the war. The numerals 37 had been painted on the road in white paint indicating the direction the runway faced. There were two metal, storage buildings on the west side of the road, the larger one serving as a hangar and a smaller one that looked like an office for the Fixed Base Operator. At the south end, two children played in a sandy area, fenced on the back and side.

A brilliant sun was directly overhead and the day was lazy, warm, with insects buzzing about in the yellow flowers that lined the building along its foundation. The sky was clear but clouds were forming on the horizon, gathering to bring the almost daily afternoon rain.

He rode forward to within sixty feet of the office building and sat and stared across the asphalt waiting for someone to show themselves. In most towns, people didn't appreciate it if you came barging into town without giving them time to check you out.

He could feel eyes on him.

Sure enough, the front door of the office opened and a handsome man, looking to be in his late thirties, stepped through and paused to check him over. The man had a rag and was wiping grease off his hands. He wasn't armed, but the stranger on the horse saw a woman behind the front window carrying an AR15 style rifle. The two children playing in the sand next to the building both drew handguns and nonchalantly stepped behind a large stack of rubber tires. The kids kept the guns pointed at the ground.

A smile played around his lips. *Good Security*, he thought. He knew there was someone else he couldn't see, that also had him covered.

He raised a large mitt of a hand, "How you doing? Mind if we talk?"

"Come on in, you're welcome here, stranger." The man had long, black hair below his ears and it waved about as he gestured toward the inside with his head. The stranger dismounted. It wasn't polite to ride up to the building above the folks on foot. It would give him an advantage.

"Can I help you with your horse?" the young girl asked him. "I like horses." She had tucked the gun back into her holster. "I'll tie him to the post over there."

She looked to be about nine or ten and the boy a couple years younger. He still had his gun, a baby Glock, pointed at the ground. His eyes swept the land in the direction the stranger had come from.

"Yes, young lady, that would be fine."

"I'm Ashley and he's Kevin." She took the reins. "What's your name?"

"They call me what your dad called me… Stranger."

She led the horse away, and giggled. "That's a funny name."

Mark had waited at the door. Stranger raised his arms and didn't make any sudden moves as Mark patted him down.

"Left my piece in my saddlebag."

"Sorry but we've learned you can't be too careful until we know you."

They walked into the office and Mark pointed at an old, reddish, leather chair angled in front of a metal desk. Stranger gratefully sank back into the chair. After weeks in the saddle it felt like heaven. The woman smiled and swooped up a baby that was crawling around on the unevenly cut piece of carpet, that covered the concrete floor in a ten by ten area beyond the desk.

"Can I get you some coffee?"

Stranger's eyes lit up as though Mark had offered him the keys to Las Vegas. "That would be most appreciated." It was polite to offer coffee or a drink, and it was okay to accept it. But it was also polite to turn down a second.

Mark handed Stranger a cup and then sat on the edge of the desk. "I'm Mark Teller and this is my wife Lori. The little guy is our son, Will." Stranger nodded at Lori and she moved to the far end of the room, where she propped the rifle in the corner. It was within easy reach.

"What brings you to Eagle Nest?"

"I'm looking for you." He chuckled at the look of surprise on Mark's face. "A guy named Matthew Pennington heard I was coming this way and told me to look you up."

"Matthew? How's he doing?" Lori left the rifle and walked over to sit on a couch under the window. If Matthew had sent this man, he was no danger.

"I saw him north of what's left of Dallas. He and I spent some time together and he told me the story of what happened to y'all from his point of view. He's a fine young man. Quiet and reserved with a touch of sadness to him."

"The war dealt him a vicious blow," Lori said.

"Yeah, he's still trying to find his way," Mark added.

"I was hoping to hear the rest of your story. You know, fill in the blanks from what Matthew told me. After all, I'm a Stranger."

Mark looked up at Lori and shrugged. "I'm not sure what you mean. Is that a title?"

"There's a score of us. Actually twenty three and growing. We love traveling and hearing the tales of what folks have been through. We put the stories to music."

Lori clapped her hands delightedly. "You're a Bard! Like in medieval days."

He nodded in a bow. "Yes ma'am. You will know us by our coats. All of us are called Stranger and we mean to be the news-bearers. We meet every other year in Kansas City to swap tales and learn what's happening throughout the country, so we can ride out and spread the word. We had the first Gathering just two months ago at the beginning of summer. I would be much obliged to hear your story and would love to perform for your community."

"Are you kidding? Everyone would love to hear you. Could you come to the town center in Willsburg? It's only a few miles from here and the only place that can hold us all. We can put you up in a cabin and you won't go hungry while you're here."

"We don't sing for pay, but I would appreciate a few provisions to get me to the next town. I'll be heading for Farmington."

Mark stood and moved to the chair behind the desk. "That will be no problem at all. Hey Derek!" he called out. "You can put down the bow and come on in here."

A scruffy looking man entered the room carrying a crossbow. His curly, brown hair hung limply and his beard was uneven. "Hi, I'm Derek." He stuck out his hand and it almost disappeared in the Stranger's large grasp.

"Mark, I finished tuning up the engine on the Cessna. I'm going to go up to Willsburg and let them know this gentleman's coming. Tomorrow night?"

"Yes, that's perfect. Thanks."

Einstein, or Derek as he preferred, waved and went out the door.

"I'm going to put the baby down for a nap," Lori said, "I'll be right back. I want to make sure Mark gets the story right." She went into the next room.

"We live in a house across the street but we spend so much time here at the airport that Lori has a crib here. Will is eleven months old and we're expecting him to take his first step any day."

After a few minutes Lori returned and pulled up a chair next to Mark's.

"Where do we begin?"

***

The coffee pot sat empty and three glasses were on the desk, each half filled with whiskey.

"So, what ever happened to the motorcycle gang?" The Stranger asked.

Mark chuckled. "They never went through Taos, and Terry Holcomb says they never saw them in Raton, so about the only way they could go is south to Albuquerque. Probably went down the 64 and 84. We've checked the radiation levels and the highway past Angel Fire is still pretty hot. Albuquerque was hit hard, so they would have had to get supplies in smaller towns. If they actually went that far, by the time they started to get sick, it would've been too late to get out. They were already dead."

"Serves them right," Lori said. "Jon, up in Farmington, told us some horror stories about when they came to Durango."

"Did you ever find out what happened in Lompoc?"

"Yeah, Jimbo and the other guys stayed behind and helped the residents drive back the military. They all got back here just in time for winter. That was a year and a half ago. Sheri stayed with Carla and Doug."

"And the sub?"

"Nobody knows for sure but Jeff Hunt says a group of guys came through Farmington, and he heard one of the men call a tall guy 'Dombrowski'. There can't be too many men with that name. I suspect there's a nuclear sub at the bottom of the ocean somewhere off the California Coast."

Lori added, "Or they could have just left it moored off the oil rig. It's not like anyone can use it."

The Stranger nodded and took a swig of his whiskey. "How many planes do you have here?"

"I have three. The old biplane we used to escape from California, a Cessna 172, and a little Cherokee 140. I fly the biplane for fun, and we use the other two for transportation. There isn't much gas so I don't get to fly the biplane very often. Einstein and I take up the Cessna and we're mapping the hot zones using a Geiger Counter." He turned and pointed to the large map on the wall behind his desk. It was a map of the United States with lines drawn with a red marker.

"The red lines show safe limits around the hot zones. I hope to get the entire Southwest map before the gas runs out."

"I thought they had a refinery going in Gallup, New Mexico and I know I saw oil wells operational in Texas. Why do you say the gas will run out?"

Mark paused, took a swig of his whiskey, and said, "Well, Doctor Laskey has a theory. He thinks we're in a honeymoon phase. He says things will get better for a while, until parts begin to fail in the generating plants and refineries. You see, every town and city has a certain number of working automobiles, trucks and other machinery. Here, in the New Mexico colony, we have generators and gasoline and even computers. Doctor Laskey thinks we may have ten years."

Lori took up the explanation, "There's a blacksmith in Willsburg that can make small metal parts for Mark's engines but he doesn't have the ability, at least at this time, to make larger parts like car engines. Doctor Laskey says we don't have enough people to staff all the factories that are needed to make parts for the refineries and generating plants. The trucks will wear out, and won't be able to transport the oil. Only a few pipelines are in use and they are getting old. The old, pre-war government shut down the last lead processing plant in the United States, believing we could get all the lead we needed from, of all places, China."

"Yeah, that was real smart," Mark said, sarcastically.

"So we have no way to make batteries for our solar power systems and flashlights, or any lead for ammo. Once we run out of ammo we'll have to revert to old style muskets or use swords and crossbows. There is just so much more we have to learn. They shut down the last factory that made incandescent light bulbs and now nobody seems to know how to make florescent ones. Once the supply chain breaks down, everything we have now that's still working will eventually fail."

"It's not that we won't come back," Mark told him, "it's just that there's going to be a period of time when everything that works now will quit working. We'll return to the technology of the 1800s. In 1870, according to Doctor Laskey, the population of the United States was three million. In only one hundred and forty years we went from having no electricity or other technology, to the highly civilized world we lived in before we blew it all apart."

He took a swig of the whiskey. "We can do that again. Keep in mind that during those one hundred and forty years everything had to be invented... but we already know the technology exists: airplanes, communications, television, computers, appliances, cell phones, and rockets. We know where were going and we have books and people with the expertise to preserve that knowledge. We have no way of knowing how many people in the United States survived, but in another one hundred and forty years the population will probably be back to the three hundred and thirty million people we had before the war. We're just really glad that the people in the New Mexico colony are learning to live without technology, because it's going to get worse before it gets better."

"Wow, I hadn't thought about all of that, but it makes perfect sense. I just assumed we were on our way back." He stood up. "You folks have given me a lot of things to think about. If you'll show me where I can stay and where I can get something to eat, I'll prepare for tomorrow night's performance."

***

The evening was warm and the town center in Willsburg was packed with people wearing light, summer clothing. When the news of the minstrel spread through the town they made a festive occasion of it. People came from Angel Fire and Eagle Nest and they prepared a huge barbecue for all to share.

Mark and Lori still had their small log cabin in Willsburg where they would spend the night, and the children were there with a babysitter. Mark looked around at the crowd and thought about all the friends that were missing. Friends who found their homes in other parts of the country, and friends who had died along the way.

Chris and Aaron were there, with Karen and the new baby, James. The Yancey brothers brought their wives. All the Thompsons, Doctor Jim and Carmen, Jimbo and dozens of others that Mark and Lori called friends were there to listen to the Stranger's songs.

He sang of unbelievable courage as people fought to survive, forming communities and pulling together to rebuild their lives. He sang of other colonies he had encountered during his travels, of their struggles and their triumphs. Of dead cities scattered throughout the country.

He told the tale of a mushroom cloud two years after the war, that ended the threat of tyranny that had slowed the rebuilding of the country and he sang the praises of a submarine commander who disobeyed orders, securing for the fledgling population of the United States, the opportunity to flourish in an environment of freedom and self-sufficiency.

He sang of evil.

Of evil creatures who were changed, transformed by radiation, and of evil humans who tried to take what they wanted by force. Evil men who undoubtedly still existed in the world outside their colony, and would need to be dealt with.

And finally, he sang about the man of vision who had provided for this group, and had provided the tools to begin their new life.

He sang of William Hargraves.

Read about the *Humanity Abides* Series

Shelter - Book One
Emergence - Book Two
The Search for Home - Book Three

at:

www.carolannbird.com

Facebook.com/humanityabides

If you enjoyed the Post - Apocalyptic Series *Humanity Abides*,
you may also enjoy:
Apocalypse Aurora by Drake Dow

And if you like Murder Mysteries and Thriller you might try:
Dying Vengeance by L.A. Bird

About the Author

Carol has had a life-long interest in all things relating to survival. Joining the Army at the age of eighteen, she was the first woman to attend the U.S. Army Chemical School, and was trained in CBR, or Chemical, Biological and Radiological laboratory techniques. Carol has participated in two 10 day backpacking/survival trips and is a certified scuba diver. She has a private pilot's license and has completed three 50k races, several marathons and many, many races at shorter distances. She graduated from California State University Northridge with a Bachelor of Science in Biology/biotechnology and has worked as a Clinical Laboratory Scientist for most of her adult life. Carol has three daughters and a son, and lives in Colorado Springs with one of her daughters, and a grandson.

Made in the USA
San Bernardino, CA
10 September 2014